ANNIE'S

NEW LIFE

Maureen Martella was brought up in Co. Dublin with five sisters and a brother. After moving to England in the sixties, falling in love with an Italian and returning home to Ireland five months pregnant, she continued to travel after having her children, ending up in Bel Air where she worked as assistant to a mortician. She now lives in rural Ireland.

£1

Also by Maureen Martella

Maddy Goes to Hollywood

MAUREEN MARTELLA

ANNIE'S
NEW LIFE

ARROW

Published in the United Kingdom in 2000 by
Arrow Books

3 5 7 9 10 8 6 4 2

First published in the United Kingdom in 2000 by William Heinemann

Arrow Books Limited
The Random House Group Limited
20 Vauxhall Bridge Road, London, SW1V 2SA

Random House Australia (Pty) Limited
20 Alfred Street, Milsons Point, Sydney,
New South Wales 2061, Australia

Random House New Zealand Limited
18 Poland Road, Glenfield
Auckland 10, New Zealand

Random House (Pty) Limited
Endulini, 5a Jubilee Road, Parktown 2193, South Africa

Random House UK Limited Reg. No. 954009
www.randomhouse.co.uk

A CIP catalogue record for this book is available
from the British Library

Papers used by Random House are natural, recyclable products made
from wood grown in sustainable forests. The manufacturing processes
conform to the environmental regulations of the country of origin

Typeset by SX Composing DTP, Rayleigh, Essex
Printed and bound in Denmark by
Norhaven A/S, Viborg

ISBN 0 09 928058 2

To my family

Acknowledgements

With heartfelt gratitude to Lynne Drew, Kate Elton and Darley Anderson.
They know why.

1

Young free and single.
Or then again . . . ?

I stepped out of the big law building and on to windswept Fitzwilliam Square, just in time to catch the cloudburst that had been threatening all day. It poured out of the heavens, lashing against my head like hilty nails. Turning my best suit into a sopping wet mess in two minutes flat.

So what? It had taken my family solicitor less time than that to destroy my whole life.

Two giggling girls pushed past me, making for the shelter of a doorway. They almost knocked me to the pavement in their eagerness to escape the downpour.

'Sorry, Missus,' one of them called over her shoulder, in the sort of tones usually reserved for the seriously elderly. Or the genuinely infirm. Bloody cheek! They couldn't have been more than a couple of years younger than me. Both of them were well into their twenties, if I was any judge. I wasn't yet thirty. Well, I was, but only barely.

Young, free and single was how I had described myself in a marketing survey my friend Fiona and I had filled in only last Christmas. I had almost added the word swinger. Just for the craic. But for once it was Fiona who urged caution.

'You could be leaving yourself open to all kinds of

propositions with a claim like that. Even if it is only a joke,' she had warned, tossing back her long, platinum-streaked hair. My hair is short and mid-brown. The kind that stops growing as soon as it hits your shoulders no matter how many high-protein conditioners you invest in.

'Anyway, having an affair with your married boss hardly constitutes swinging, you thicko,' she had dismissed me with her usual blunt affection.

I wished she were here now. Insulting me. This was one of those times when I really missed Fiona. She always cut straight to the chase. Didn't believe in mincing words. Ever. She would have known exactly how to deal with a smug-faced solicitor. She'd have had him reeling back against his flock wallpaper before he had finished breaking the news that not only was I a bastard, but I was also on the brink of being homeless.

'I am sorry to be the one who had to tell you this,' he had lisped through his gap teeth as I sat frozen with shock, 'but I'm afraid I had no choice.'

Of course you had a choice you po-faced old git, I said. But not out loud.

Out loud, I said meekly, 'I understand.'

He seemed surprised by my docile reaction. What had he expected? That I would leap across his desk and crack him on the skull with his Connemara marble penholder? The thought never entered my head. Much.

He leaned forward, his mean little forehead crinkling like a freshly ploughed field. 'I'm afraid there is no doubt. It is beyond question. You do accept that?'

I nodded, not trusting myself to speak.

His forehead went smooth with relief. 'Then let me reiterate. The matter of the authenticity of your birth certificate arose because Deedy, Dumphy and Biggs have always believed in attention to detail. The moment we were alerted to the possibility of an illegality, we began to investigate. Left no stone unturned in our efforts to discover the truth.' Translation: his lickspittle of a secretary rang the head registrar's office in Joyce House to check the validity of a birth certificate that had lain undisturbed, among my father's papers, for almost thirty years. Only to be told that it was a forgery.

'We were as shocked as you are, to discover that the original certificate had an altogether different name in place of your . . . em . . . mother's. And no name at all in the section reserved for father. I am afraid it left no room for doubt. Bernie and Frank McHugh were *not* your parents.'

He waited for my response. But what was I supposed to say to that? He had now told me at least three times, *and* in as many ways, that my gentle parents who wouldn't use a pedestrian crossing against a red light, who wouldn't keep a dog without a valid licence, had callously forged my birth certificate.

My parents? It had to be a joke. My parents had been the most law-abiding people on the planet. Always first to obey any rule, no matter how petty or pernickety it might appear to the rest of us. My God, they paid their television licence by direct debit.

'But they weren't the sort of people who would . . .'

'The evidence speaks for itself,' he interrupted sharply.

I took a deep breath, mustering as much dignity as

I could, given that I knew my skin probably had a pallor not normally associated with the living. 'Go on, Mr Diddy.' I swallowed.

'Deedy!' he corrected me sharply, for the second time that afternoon.

'*Dee . . . dy.*' I pronounced his name with great care.

'I have no idea why your parents did such a thing, Ms McHugh. No idea. But it behoves me to say that it was an extremely reprehensible act, the repercussions of which may very well affect many areas of your life.'

I chewed my lip until it felt like rubber.

'For a start you will have to vacate 59 Fernhill Crescent. The rental agreement only held as long as your . . . em . . . parents were living. Given your . . . em . . . present circumstances you will now be required to hand back the key.'

'No. You're wrong!' At last I had him on something. 'I have already been told that as the *daughter* of long-term tenants I am fully entitled to continue with the tenancy . . .' The look on his face was enough to silence me.

Determined not to cry, I raised my chin defiantly. 'Is there no possibility that it could all be a . . . a clerical error?'

He shook his head, his face expressionless.

'Why not?' I burst out. 'Are the people in the registrar's office infallible? Everything is computerised nowadays; all it would take is—'

'Your birth was *not* registered to the McHughs,' he interrupted calmly.

'But I have a birth certificate with both their names on it!' I gave it one last shot.

'You have a copy of a forged document. I think you

4

realise that by now, Ms McHugh.'

'Oh I can still use the name McHugh?' I snapped, but being a solicitor, Mr Deedy wasn't programmed for sarcasm.

'Of course. We can find no trace of a legal adoption having taken place, nonetheless you are still perfectly entitled to use the name you have always been known as.' He made it sound as if McHugh was some kind of shady alias I had been using to dupe law-abiding citizens like himself.

My eyes kept turning to a silver letter opener lying by his hand. Glistening under the desk lamp, it looked sharp enough to pierce flesh.

Something in my expression caused him to shift uneasily. He moved the letter opener to one side, sliding it out of sight beneath a bulky manila envelope, then quickly buzzed for the secretary he shares with Dumphy and Biggs.

She arrived with a beaming smile and a thick yellow notepad, to complement her thick yellow make-up. He raised a finger in the air, like one of those impatient types you sometimes encounter in the slow queue at McDonald's. 'Two coffees, please.'

I half expected Miss Yellow Pad to ask jauntily, 'Regular or Large, sir?' She didn't. Instead, she produced two coffees with such quiet efficiency and smiling goodwill that I felt sorry for wishing her dead earlier on, when she had escorted me to the bathroom, after Mr Deedy first broke the terrible news.

'Thank you,' I said to her now, with good grace. Well, with as much good grace as I could spare, given that it was apparently her curiosity that had uncovered the truth about my birth certificate in the first place.

5

A bored secretary in a small law firm had noticed a tiny discrepancy on a legal document and decided, whether out of Monday morning ennui or burgeoning ambition, to investigate further. A flurry of phone calls and faxes and, I have to admit, some astute paperwork led to the discovery that I was not who I thought I was.

My birth had been registered to a Mrs Clare Beecham. Mrs Clare Beecham? I had never even heard that name before. It meant absolutely nothing to me. And yet the mere fact of its existence on a piece of paper could apparently prove that the parents I had buried, not four months ago, were not my parents after all. The loving couple, whom I was still mourning after a tragic car crash took them to their heavenly reward, hadn't even been my legal guardians.

They had forged my birth certificate like two petty criminals on the make. Filled in their own names in direct defiance of all the rules. And I had suddenly gone from being a beloved bereaved daughter to a nameless bastard with no identity and no home in a city where a one-bedroom flat can cost upwards of the national debt of Paraguay.

The coffee served by Miss Yellow Pad was far too strong. And stomach-churningly sweet. Still I forced it down my throat. It was either that or the letter opener.

I couldn't get past the idea of my parents lying to me. And for all those years. Never once giving even the smallest hint of our true relationship. Whatever that was. Everything I had known and believed in had been a lie. Every benchmark in my life was fraudulent.

I had always been pretty secure. Well, close

enough. I had certainly known who I was. *And* where I came from.

'You're so feckin' grounded, you make me sick, Annie!' was a favourite accusation of Fiona's. 'It's probably because you're an only child. You never had to fight for your parents' attention, or share a skip of a bedroom with three slutty sisters. Or a smelly bathroom with a poncey brother who was twenty-two before he could aim properly.'

But *was* I an only child? Even that was now open to question.

If I wasn't Annie McHugh, daughter of Bernie and Frank, then who was I? I could be anyone's child. Any man's seed. A bishop? A baker? A candlestick maker? I could be the result of a grubby one-night stand. Date rape? Carnal incest? Jesus, Mary and Joseph, the possibilities were endless.

'Annie, Annie, Annie.' My father used to shake his head gently in protest when I did something unexpectedly creative as a child. Like cutting a massive hole in the expensive new sitting-room curtains, because I wanted my Wonder Woman doll to have a cloak that matched the décor. 'Where did we get you from, Annie?'

Didn't *he* know?

Why hadn't they told me I wasn't their natural child? Why go to such crazy lengths to hide the truth? Whom would it have hurt? Not them. I wouldn't have loved them any less. They were always worth loving, my decent, hard-working parents. And they were, without a doubt, as loving as any parents could possibly be. For a pair of unmitigated liars.

*

I was attempting to cross the street when a car horn blared a warning, forcing me back on to the rain-drenched pavement. Then, as if for spite, every traffic light in sight turned green, encouraging the traffic into even more desperate speeds. Now I'd have to stand here in the rain, waiting for God only knows how long, before I could cross to catch my bus.

Last time I'd been trapped at this corner was after a shopping trip with Fiona. But, being Fiona, she had ignored the signals, grabbing my hand to pull me behind her as she zigzagged her way through the rush-hour madness. 'Ah, feck them! What do they think they have brakes for?' She laughed at my protests, as we ran the gauntlet of furious drivers.

But Fiona was a long way from Dublin now. She was in Cuba. Sunning herself on Varadero beach. It was thirty-two degrees centigrade in Varadero, according to her last postcard. In Dublin it was a freezing six degrees. And the rain was running down my face, plastering my fringe to my forehead. I raced into the nearest pub.

This was totally out of character for me. When you've been raised in a nearly teetotal home, pubs are not places you normally frequent during daylight hours. A bit of a Nosferatu in that respect, I tended to wait until the sun was well and truly below the yardarm before venturing into a drinking establishment.

Besides, pubs were places where you went to meet people and have the craic. A good laugh. Not for slipping into in the middle of the afternoon because you felt like shit. But maybe there was something in my dark, unknown genes leading me to seek solace in drink? I *had* always liked the taste. Maybe I came from a long line of drinkers? Alcoholics even? Dipsos?

I had always considered myself to be a pretty sober person. But that was when I was Annie McHugh. Maybe Annie the no-name bastard was a drunk waiting to happen.

I ordered a straight whiskey instead of my usual wine spritzer. 'May as well start as you mean to go on,' my father, who wasn't really my father, used to say.

There was a blazing fire in the corner of the wood-panelled lounge bar. I got as close to the heat as I could, without actually straddling one of the flaming logs, and kicked off my dripping-wet shoes.

The lone barman threw me a filthy look. What did I care? Annie McHugh might have been embarrassed into putting her shoes back on. Annie the bastard glared back at him. When he brought my drink I feigned sophisticated nonchalance, ignoring the way he kept staring at my big toe, which had burst through the foot of my new tights.

'Keep the change and bring me another,' I said coolly.

He shot me a withering look from beneath his heavy Oasis eyebrows and we duelled a bit with our eyes. But he finally pocketed the ten pence and marched off.

By the time I had finished my second whiskey I could appreciate its appeal. I might still be homeless. And a bastard. But my suit was beginning to dry out and there was a warm, comforting glow coming to life somewhere in the vicinity of my protruding toe.

Maybe my world wasn't completely shot to bits after all. Perhaps I could deal with the terrible blows I had just been dealt without falling to pieces.

Possibility all it required was some kind of positive thinking on my part.

Fiona was a firm believer in positive thinking. She was forever extolling its merits to anyone who would listen. All right for her, lying on Varadero beach with the sun turning her an enviable shade of walnut. The mildest exposure to ultraviolet and I metamorphosed into scarlet woman, my skin taking on a startling shade of beetroot, instead of a gloriously sexy tan.

Besides having skin that tanned without a glitch, Fiona also had the perfect husband. Right now he was probably basting her with Factor 4. Or maybe he was ordering up Cuba Libres by the crate.

Not that I was jealous. The last thing I wanted in my life was a man. I had sworn off all that kind of stuff after Noel, who turned out to be the lover from hell. I had spent most of this winter cosying up to the fire with only Jane Austen for company.

Or some nights when I was feeling particularly low, I'd rent a couple of Merchant Ivory videos and allow them to transport me to another, gentler world. A world where swollen ankles could be hidden under long sweeping skirts, and cellulite hadn't yet been invented. I would turn down the lights and comfort myself with a Chinese takeaway.

Then Mr Deedy contacted me and even the hottest Ming Wah special curry lost its ability to comfort.

I sipped my whiskey and tried not to feel too sorry for myself. Think positive, Annie, I commanded myself firmly. And to my absolute astonishment it started to work. The warm glow at my feet began to spread slowly upwards, approaching my calves and getting hotter by the second.

It wasn't until the barman shouted a warning that I

realised a burning log had rolled off the fire and my tights were melting.

'Can I get you something, Miss? On the house,' he said quickly, when I came creeping back from the ladies, the remains of my Pretty Pollys hanging from my bag.

'Another whiskey. Make it a double,' I snapped.

He started to say something, but one look at my face and he reconsidered, choosing instead to go back behind the bar and face the slop tray.

Some time later he was back again, reluctantly placing yet another whiskey in front of me. 'We serve coffee, you know,' he said.

'Coffee?' I laughed. 'What kind of joint are you running here?' I asked, doing my best Mae West imitation. He stared blankly at me, then disappeared behind the bar again, leaving me alone in the corner, to contemplate the ruins of my life.

'We're closing, love.' The barman was shaking my shoulder.

'What?'

He pointed to the big clock behind the now packed bar. 'It's eleven o'clock. Closing time. Come on now, ladies and gentlemen. Have yiz no homes to go to?' he quoted from the barman's manual of wry and witty sayings.

A few feet away a big bearded man slapped his neighbour on the back, almost propelling him through the mock-Georgian window. 'You're a gas man, Mick!'

The little man steadied himself with some difficulty, his face glowing either with sweat or a surfeit of alcohol. 'I'm Seamus!' he protested.

'Ah, you're a gas man, Mick.' Big beard enveloped him in a sweaty embrace.

This was the one thing I always hated about pubs. Not the sweaty embraces – I was never the recipient of too many of those – but the fact that by closing time everyone was your best friend. It was something I was never comfortable with, all this drunken bonding between total strangers. Being expected to spill out your most personal details to someone whose name you probably wouldn't even recall the next morning. It was a trap I had never allowed myself to fall into.

'Good luck, Annie! Hope you find your real parents, love!' a voice shouted above the din.

''Night, Annie, keep the heart up!' another drinker called, before dashing out into the rain.

'Time to go home, Annie. You're flat-hunting tomorrow, remember?' The barman was back, his white apron a mock world atlas of beer stains. 'Come on. I'll call you a cab,' he insisted.

'OK.' I heard myself giggling. 'But what should I call you?' I said, slapping South Africa.

When the cab arrived he practically lifted me into it. 'See she doesn't come to any harm, Tommy,' he ordered the bored cabby. 'She's had a bad day.'

'She's goin' to have a worse one tomorrow, by the look of her,' the cabby prophesied gloomily.

I heard someone laugh in derision. It might have been me.

I was woken by a dull, persistent pounding. It took me two full minutes to realise that it was coming from inside my skull. *And* that this was Saturday. My designated day to go flat-hunting.

I managed to get one whole leg into my jeans before the room began to spin. Clutching the bedpost for support, I swore that if I got through this hellish day I would never again allow alcohol to pass my lips. Or at least I'd drink occasionally, like my father had done.

Only he *wasn't* my father.

It had all been a lie.

I turned my face into the pillow and cried until I had no tears left.

2

Life goes on. Doesn't it?

The lease on 59 Fernhill Crescent now had less than two weeks to run and I still hadn't found another place to live. It wasn't for want of trying. I had combed Dublin in search of a suitable flat. Out of the dozen or so I had viewed I had come across two that wouldn't reduce me to absolute penury and seemed *almost* fit for human habitation.

When I went back to the first one to have another look, I remembered why I *hadn't* left a deposit, despite the rooms being a decent enough size and four buses stopping directly outside the front door. The same nauseating smell that had greeted me the first time I'd viewed it was still pretty much in evidence.

'What's the problem?' The landlord seemed puzzled by my reluctance to commit.

'The . . . that smell. It's slightly overpowering,' I said lamely, not wanting to antagonise a prospective landlord this early in the game.

'I've had no complaints from me other tenants.' His foot tapped impatiently at the open door, his twelve-hole Doc Martens making little indentations in the softwood.

'You haven't?' I tried not to sound as if I disbelieved him because apart from the smell the place *was* pretty much OK. Better than a lot of the others I had seen. Certainly roomier.

He slammed the door closed, locking it firmly behind us. 'It's up to you. I'll have a queue of people fighting over it by Thursday when the ad goes in the paper. You were steeped to hear about it through a mate.'

I didn't tell him it wasn't exactly a mate. I had found the address scribbled on a piece of paper in my pocket the day after my boozy night in the pub. I couldn't for the life of me remember whether it was the cab driver who gave it to me or the barman. I didn't want even to contemplate the possibility that someone else might have had access to my pockets.

'That's just the drains you can smell. They block up once a year or so. Something to do with the weather.'

He made me feel churlish for mentioning such a tiny flaw in such a great flat, but even so, I was wary of parting with money for a place where I might have to sleep in a gas mask.

After viewing two more flats on the other side of the Liffey I hurried back to the smelly one, my tail between my legs. This time the smell met me at the end of the street, so on impulse I called on the upstairs tenant.

It was two thirty in the afternoon. She opened the door wearing a see-through black negligee and peered suspiciously out at me. 'What do *you* want?'

'I'm thinking of taking the flat downstairs. I hope you don't mind me asking but that smell. Is it in any way constant?'

'Ye wha'?'

'The . . . the smell of the drains. I find it a bit off-putting. Do they back up a lot?'

'The drains?' She opened the door wide enough to give me a full frontal that I could have done without. 'What drains?'

'The smell. Isn't that the drains? I just wondered if . . .'

'Aw. The stink, you mean. Ah, you get used to that. We hardly notice it any more. Even the clients don't mention it now. It's the old glue factory out the back there. See?' She pointed helpfully to a grimy window through which you could indeed see the outline of a big grey building, which looked as if it might belong to medieval Dublin.

'The *clients*?' I asked.

'Never say a word. 'Course they do have other things on their minds, don't they? Ha ha ha.'

The only other flat in my price range had a strange, psychedelic-looking fungus growing on all four of the kitchen walls, but I was almost out of time. It was far too late in the day for me to be getting picky. And fungus on a kitchen wall was probably marginally better than living with the fumes from a glue factory. Or passing *clients* on the stairs, I consoled myself as I hurried to the bank link to get the agreed deposit. On the way back I stopped to pick up the late edition of the *Evening Herald* and flicked through the small ads again.

Nothing.

I got back to the psychedelic house to find I had been gazumped, if that's the word. A girl with rampant acne and a young baby had already moved in, her big shiny pram blocking the narrow hallway. She refused to negotiate with me, no matter how I tried to reason with her over the door chain. Her final words pretty much summed up her whole attitude to the debate. 'Fuck off!' she drawled.

'It's nothin' to do with me, love.' The woman who had shown me the mildewed rooms shrugged. 'First come first served. I made no promises to you.' She snapped a filthy elastic band around a bundle of brand-new twenty-pound notes. 'I'm only obliging the landlord. I don't get paid for doin' this, you know. You can always leave your number, love,' she called after me. 'If the Corpo houses her' – she nodded at the big pram – 'I'll give you a ring.'

It wasn't all bad news. I got home to find a message on my machine from Mr Deedy's secretary, she of the yellow face. Would I call in to his office at my earliest convenience? Would I? My heart began to race. Had he found my birth mother?

I was there practically before sun-up the following morning.

He shook my hand, po-faced as ever. 'We have managed to trace the person whose name corresponds with the one on your birth certificate, Ms McHugh. The unadulterated certificate,' he emphasised.

But this morning nothing could upset me. All I could think about was meeting my natural mother. My palms were already moist with excitement as I waited for him to tell me when it would take place. I could hardly believe that I was about to meet the woman who had brought me into the world. The woman who had given me life. Conceived me. Carried me in her body for nine months, nurturing me with her blood. And then handed me over to strangers.

I hadn't yet decided whether to love or hate her. But I definitely wanted to meet her.

'We were most discreet.' Mr Deedy's expression was guarded. 'I used my best judgement in deciding against approaching the lady directly. Instead we made enquiries of her well-known legal representatives. Without disclosing your name, I might add.'

'Thank you, Mr Deedy. When do we meet?' I couldn't disguise my impatience.

He paused. 'I'm afraid she denies all knowledge of you.'

'What do you mean?' I blinked.

'Her representatives claim that she wasn't even *in* Ireland when you were born. She was in France. On the Côte d'Azur to be precise.'

'The Côte d'Azur?' I echoed stupidly.

'The very place. Consequently they refuse to enter into any further correspondence on the matter. Not even with Deedy, Dumphy and Biggs, I regret to say.' He looked hurt.

'I . . . so where does that leave me?'

'At the end of the road, I'm afraid. This matter is now closed. As the lady wishes to have no contact – indeed, denies any connection to you – we have no choice but to respect her wishes.'

'What about my wishes?'

'Ms McHugh, Deedy, Dumphy and Biggs have done their utmost for you,' he reprimanded. 'My advice to you is to get on with your life. Put this little episode behind you.'

'But I thought we were going to meet?' I almost screamed.

'That is not going to happen.'

I may, at various times in my life, have hated other people almost as much as I did Mr Deedy at that precise moment. If I did, I have no recollection of it.

I had come here convinced that I was about to discover who I was. Who my natural parents were. And now this little prig was telling me to go away and forget about it. *This little episode?* It was his secretary who had started this whole thing. I was happy enough to be a daughter in mourning when she took to playing Shirley bloody Holmes.

I gritted my teeth. 'If you don't want to take this any further, Mr Deedy, at least give me her address?'

'I'm afraid that is out of the question.'

I wasn't above grovelling. 'Please? I'll bet if I speak directly to her she'll admit to being my mother. Let me at least try. Just give me her phone number. Please. Please, Mr Deedy?'

I didn't want my lips to quiver. I certainly didn't want to cry. But we are not always in full control of these things. The big tears bounced down my face and slid into my quivering mouth.

Mr Deedy watched, expressionless. He might have been a man of many gifts, but compassion was not one of them. 'My secretary will see you out, Ms McHugh. If there are any other matters we can be of any assistance with do not hesitate to contact us. Deedy, Dumphy and Biggs are always at your service.'

I went straight from Mr Deedy's office to the nearest call box. Directory Enquiries got me the number I needed. 'Could I speak to Gerry, please?'

Gerry Dunning was a friend of Sam's, had been for years, ever since he gave Sam a job during a long college vacation. Gerry had a small detective agency in inner city Dublin. To hear Sam talk you'd think he was a cross between Sherlock Holmes and Shaft. I used to imagine him carrying a big Magnum .45, or maybe wearing a tweed deerstalker. He did neither.

'He earns his living following menopausal shop-lifters. And adulterous husbands.' Fiona had laughed. 'Although he is a bit tasty.'

He certainly was. When I first spotted him arriving late at Fiona's and Sam's engagement party I thought she had hired George Clooney to make a personal appearance. 'This is Gerry,' she shrilled above the loud salsa music that Sam loved. 'And this one here, with her mouth hanging open like a right gobshite, is Annie. My best friend.'

Then we were dancing, and I was wondering how someone so awesome and above the age of consent could still be on the loose. Because not only was he gorgeous, with smiling blue eyes to die for and a mouth made for kissing, but he had the wittiest turn of phrase, which had me laughing non-stop, even when the salsa music drowned out what he was actually saying.

I could have kissed Fiona for introducing us, even if she did call me a gobshite. I hoped he knew this was Fiona's idea of a joke. Judging by the way he was looking at me, he did.

We were just finishing our third dance and I was already wondering how far I should let him go when he took me home when I spotted the wedding ring and legged it to the ladies room.

'Why didn't you tell me he was married?' I cornered Fiona in the busy scrum.

'I thought I did. Anyway, he's not any more. They're separated.' She hurried back to Sam, leaving me fighting for space in front of the mirror with a dozen other girls, every one of whom had better hair than mine. I couldn't believe Fiona had been so lax. She knew how I felt about married men since that nightmare with Noel.

Outside, in the now jam-packed room, Gerry asked me to dance again but I pleaded a headache and slipped away. But by the time I got home my mythical headache was all too real.

After that first meeting we bumped into each other every now and again around the popular watering holes of south Dublin, usually when I was out for a drink with Sam and Fiona, and of course we met at their wedding. Sat next to each other at the reception, in fact.

He was as drily entertaining as ever and lots of other women at the table thought so too. Particularly the one whose nipples were showing through her fishnet top that looked as if it was set to trap sharks.

But as his wedding ring was still firmly *in situ* I kept a tight reign on my hormones.

It was Sam who, when he saw the way my eyes constantly wandered in Gerry's direction, eventually told me it was Gerry's wife who had broken up the marriage. 'But don't mention it, whatever you do. It's a touchy subject,' he added.

I tried asking Fiona about Gerry's exact marital status, but what with cutting the cake and throwing the bridal bouquet, and playing with Sam's fly buttons in full view of the assembled wedding guests, Fiona had enough to do without being quizzed about handsome married detectives whose wives had left them.

Gerry seemed surprised to hear from me now.

'Why?' I asked.

'I always got the feeling you didn't like me.'

Fortunately he couldn't see me blush. 'I don't know what gave you that idea.' I gave an Oscar-winning laugh.

'Well, it might be the way you walked off soon after we first met. Or maybe the way you tend to keep your eyes averted whenever you're in my company.'

'My parents died,' I said, hoping this would cover it.

'I heard about that. Sorry, Annie.'

I told him the full story of my dealings with Mr Deedy. The shock it had been to hear that my parents were not, in fact, my parents. That they had forged my birth certificate. Anyone else would have begun to spout trite platitudes, but Gerry just listened.

'Could you trace my birth mother for me?' I finally got to the point. 'I think I'd like to meet her.'

'You're not sure?'

'Well, I . . . yes I would like to meet her.'

'You leave it with me, then. I'll find out what I can about this Mrs Clare Beecham and get back to you.'

'I'd be so grateful.'

'Have you heard from the lovebirds?'

This time my laugh was genuine. 'Oh, yes, Fiona writes regularly. Well, she sends cards. Sam is involved in some kind of project for kids in a little town south of Varadero.'

'What's Fiona doing?'

'Keeping as far away from the kids as she possibly can, I should imagine. You know her feelings on that subject. Kids are very nice. Preferably parboiled.'

'That's Fiona.' He laughed.

'She is busy, though. Sunbathing takes up a lot of her time. Then there's the swimming. Oh, and drinking vast quantities of the local rum. Apparently that's a must.'

'So let me get this straight. Sam is working hard. Developing some project for needy kids while still involved in designing the new hotel? And Fiona is having a good time? Day and night?'

'That's about it.'

'No change there, then. They might as well have stayed in Ireland.' He laughed again and rang off.

3

Gerry rides to the rescue

Gerry was as good as his word. Less than a week later he met me in the plush Wesbury Hotel. His choice of venue, as it happened to be the place where he was keeping an eye on a client's wandering husband.

He was still dangerously attractive – Gerry, not the wandering husband – but for the first time I began to realise why Fiona tagged him a workaholic.

'No, don't sit there, Annie. A little further to the left. I need a clear view of the bar.'

I moved a couple of inches, unable to conceal my impatience. 'What have you found out?'

'It appears that your Mrs Beecham . . .' he paused to glance over at the crowded bar, before continuing, '. . . and it has to be her because not only is the name Beecham unusual in these parts, but her Christian name is spelled the same way as the one on your birth certificate: C-l-a-r-e. No "I".' He forgot about his surveillance for a second, to concentrate on my worried face. 'I think there's a fair chance that she's your mother all right. Everything tallies. She was in a private nursing home in Blackrock the week you were born. A woman who worked there remembers her. She was supposed to be having a large fibroid removed from her womb.' He grinned at me. 'Some fibroid!'

I had to fight to hold back the tears that were

always a bit too close for comfort these days.

If Gerry noticed, he gave no indication.

'I couldn't get a look at her chart, but I found out that as soon as she was discharged she went straight to the South of France. To recuperate after her surgery, my contact said.'

'So her solicitors *were* lying when they claimed she was abroad when I was born?'

'Yep. But she *did* go to France afterwards, Antibes to be precise.'

I nodded. 'Mr Deedy said the Côte d'Azur.'

'I can give you the name of the hotel where she registered, but the important thing is that she didn't leave Ireland until you were three days old. And something interesting happened that same day. You were baptised that morning, according to the date on your baptismal certificate. Pretty unusual to have a kid baptised at three days old, I would have thought. Unless she were poorly, or something. By all accounts you were a nine-pound bruiser.'

I smiled. 'My parents used to boast about that.'

He paused for a moment, looking a bit awkward. 'Did they never give you any indication that you weren't their natural daughter?'

'None.'

'What about when you got older? Were you never suspicious? Didn't you ever wonder why you were christened so quickly?'

'It never entered my head to question anything.'

'Well, maybe it should have. My guess is that they were planning on using your baptismal cert in lieu of a birth cert. They knew from the start that they were going to claim you as their natural child. Possibly to avoid the adoption process for whatever reason.

Although that doesn't have to indicate anything sinister. It may simply be that they were above the recommended age for adopting.'

I nodded.

'But then, for some reason, your folks decided to forge a birth certificate.' The sharp blue eyes held mine. 'Do you want my advice, Annie?'

'Of course. That's why I'm here.'

'Let it go. It's not worth the grief.'

'Are you serious?'

'You said you had great parents. Warm, loving people. Forging a birth certificate was completely out of character for them. So why did they do it? Why claim you as their own?'

'Why do *you* think they did it?'

'I'd guess they wanted to protect you from something. Make it difficult for anyone to rock the boat later on. Maybe you should trust their judgement, Annie. Let sleeping dogs lie. Why rake over the ashes after all this time? You have a good life. Why complicate it with all this business?'

'I want to know who I am.'

'You're Annie McHugh, that's who you are. A friend of Fiona's. A friend of mine, I hope.'

'I want to know whose child I am.'

'For God's sake, Annie, you're the same person you always were. Just because some sharp-eyed clerk going through your father's papers spotted a discrepancy and . . .'

'Secretary.'

'What?'

'She's a secretary. The woman who became suspicious.'

'OK, she's a secretary. But if she hadn't spotted the

mistake you would have spent the rest of your life happy to be Annie McHugh.' He frowned. 'Nothing about *you* has changed.'

'Yes it has. I know now.'

'Know what?'

'That I'm not Annie McHugh. What I don't know is who I am.'

'Jesus, we're going round in circles here. You *do* know who you are. You're the same person you were a month ago. *You* haven't changed.'

'For a smart detective you're not very well versed in human nature, are you?'

'Look, Annie, you can insult me all you want, it still doesn't change the fact that for all intents and purposes Bernie and Frank McHugh were your parents. If you insist on chasing your biological roots that's your choice. Personally I wouldn't give it another second of my time.'

I went cold. 'You don't want to help me, is that it?'

'That's not it. I don't want to see you get hurt.'

'It's the not knowing that hurts. And there's still a little voice in my head whispering that maybe it *is* all a mistake, some stupid clerical error. Perhaps they were my natural parents after all. Maybe the records *are* wrong.'

'They're not wrong, Annie.'

'How can you be so positive?'

He sighed. 'Christ, I'm going to hate myself for telling you this.' He exhaled loudly. 'I . . . er . . . I read the post-mortem reports on your parents.'

'No! I don't want to hear this.'

'Yes you do.'

I covered my face with my hands.

'It's OK,' he said gently. 'The report said that . . .

27

Bernie McHugh could not have given birth to you.'

I lowered my hands. 'How could they know that?'

'Her womb wasn't developed. It was like a five-year-old kid's,' he said sadly. 'I'm sorry, Annie, but she would have known that all her life. You know what I mean?'

No, I didn't know what he meant. I didn't know what anything meant any more.

'She would never have menstruated. Ever. She always knew she couldn't have a child. I'm sorry.'

Most people flush with embarrassment. Gerry paled. He even forgot to watch the bar. And for some reason I found myself consoling him. This was role reversal gone mad. 'It's not your fault, Gerry. Thank you for telling me.'

He caught my hand but I jerked it away abruptly.

He looked at me, puzzled.

I rummaged through my bag until I found an ancient hankie that I had put there some time in the stone age. I began playing with it, torn between blowing my nose or dabbing at my eyes, before I ended up looking like a panda. I never used waterproof mascara and I had put on far too much Superlash that morning. It was a trick I frequently used to build up my confidence. Along with my sparse lashes. It never did much for either.

There was a long silence. Gerry sipped at his beer. I wound the hankie around my fingers, twisting it so hard it began to interfere with the blood supply to the tips. I knew if I didn't stop I'd probably end up with gangrene. That was the way my luck was running.

Gerry reached over and gently unwound the hankie. He put it to one side. We both watched in morbid fascination as the blood slowly returned to my fingertips, colouring them their normal healthy pink.

'Your folks moved into the house on Fernhill Crescent soon after you were born. The neighbours all assumed you were their natural child. They were never told any different. In fact, your folks deliberately misled them over the years. Saying things like, "She has her grandmother's temper. Oh, you should have seen her when she was born, she had such a beautiful head of dark hair." Your mother even told one neighbour that she had a difficult time during her pregnancy and labour.'

I took a deep breath. 'What about my birth mother?'

'Her labour?'

'Why did she give me away?'

'That's the real puzzle. Why would a happily married woman give away a perfectly healthy baby? It certainly wasn't for lack of funds. The Beechams are loaded. Very toffee-nosed. Silver spoons and all that. Why would she give her baby away? But keep this in mind, Annie: the Beechams are not like us. They live in a different stratum. People like them think they don't have to answer to anybody. They have a lot of clout. I wouldn't fancy taking them on. Where would you get the money to fight them through the courts?'

'Who's talking about going to court? I just want to know why she gave me away.'

'That's what you say now. But once you start delving into the past, attitudes can change. You might change.'

'Don't be daft.'

'I'm telling you, Annie, this kind of thing can gather a momentum all its own. You can never be sure how it will end.'

'I just want to know who I am. That's all.'

Gerry was watching the bar again.

'What about her husband? Could we try approaching him?'

'I suppose we could.' He grinned slyly. 'But we'd have to bring a shovel. He died ten months ago. A major heart attack took the good judge to meet his maker.'

'He was a judge?' I couldn't help being impressed.

'High Court. Much lauded.'

'You think he was my father?' I sat up straight.

'No idea, Annie. But then I couldn't even swear that I'm the father of my own two nippers.'

I sat back, shocked.

'There's my target.'

I looked over towards the bar. A tall, white-haired man had just arrived. Two fashionably dressed girls were greeting him with huge enthusiasm. They might have been his daughters the way they were gazing adoringly into his well-lined face. But if they were, he should have been arrested for the way he was fondling their bare thighs.

'Two of them?' I asked Gerry.

'And they say the male libido decreases with age.' He was clicking away with what looked like a fancy cigarette lighter. 'Smile, you're on *Candid Camera*.' He grinned wickedly. 'You horny old bastard.'

I couldn't resist checking out the address Gerry had given me. Just a quick look, I promised myself as I caught the bus that would take me to the end of Haney Road where Mrs Beecham lived.

It wasn't all that far from the sprawling suburbs where I had just spent another futile morning searching for an affordable flat. But the moment you approached the plush, tree-lined enclave of Foxrock you knew you were entering a different world. The houses here were enormous. Big, spacious establishments with endless private gardens and high walls sheltering them from curious eyes. It was exactly the sort of place you'd expect a High Court judge to live. Or his widow.

I had to keep reminding myself that she might *not* be my mother. After all, what proof did I have? OK, a birth certificate with her name in the column reserved for 'Mother', but for thirty years I had accepted the validity of a similar document, with another name in that very column.

What I needed now was to hear confirmation of my identity from the horse's mouth. I wanted Mrs Clare Beecham to acknowledge me. I didn't expect her to clasp me to her bosom and declare undying love for me. But I did want her to acknowledge me as her daughter – at least privately. I needed to hear it from her own lips.

Only she could tell me who I was. Who my father was. She might well be the only person living who could give me that information. And one other thing: *she* had to know why my parents had gone to the trouble of forging a birth certificate for me. Why two such law-abiding people had taken to forgery in what was practically their middle age.

But if I'm to be totally honest what I mostly needed from her was to know why she had given me away. Called me a fibroid.

I had looked up fibroid in a medical dictionary, just to be sure I had my facts straight. It said that a fibroid was 'a benign tumour of muscular and fibrous tissues, typically developing in the wall of the womb'. Reading that was enough to put a dent in anyone's self-confidence, no matter how loving their upbringing.

I didn't feel half as much resentment of my other parents after reading that. They may have forged my birth certificate and lied about being my natural parents, but they clearly did it out of love. If anything they had always thought of me as being much more special than I actually was. Especially my mother. She had been the one to back me up no matter what I did. She really believed I could take on the world and win.

Bernie McHugh was a woman who had never forgiven herself for being born and reared in the roughest part of inner city Dublin, *before* it became a fashionable place to live. She had spent the rest of her life trying to rectify this early mistake, mostly by adopting a genteel, refined manner that anyone with a titter of wit could spot as phoney a mile off. She had actually confessed to me that she put her eye on my father because she knew he was a member of an exclusive tennis club. By the time she learned that he was only given complimentary membership because his late father used to be the groundsman there it was too late. They had already bought the bedroom suite.

Her faith in me never faltered. She was full of endless praise and encouragement. Especially for my shining intellect, as she called it. No matter how consistently poor my school reports were. I was always the shining star of the maths class, but pretty dismal at everything else and she needed no convincing about where to place the blame for my disappointingly low marks in every other subject: 'Those teachers! You're far too good for them, Annie.'

Without a word to my worrywart father, or me, she took it on herself to enrol me in another school that was way beyond our reach, both financially and geographically. 'It's a bit of a journey all right, but she'll get to mix with a better class of student there. And the teachers are all nuns!' she announced, dismissing my father's very real fears.

'Right so, Bernie.' He gave his standard reply to every unilateral decision she had ever taken. He was an extremely agreeable man, my father, who wasn't.

Standing outside the big iron gates looking in at the sedate Beecham residence, all my brave intentions drained away. Fear was too mild a word for what I was experiencing. Sheer terror covered it better. What if they set the dog on me? Dogs, even? A couple of Rottweilers and a bloodthirsty Alsatian? People who lived in houses like this were known to guard their property with a vigilance that bordered on the psychotic. At least, if you believed the tales that floated around Dublin nowadays.

Would the Beechams see me as part of the riff-raff? Probably. Gerry, who had a lot of experience in these matters, had recommended using caution in my approach: 'Don't just plunge in, Annie, that would be a mistake. Take your time. Make haste slowly, that's my advice.' But he would say that, wouldn't he? After all, he charged by the hour. That could well explain his devotion to the *make-haste-slowly* school of thought.

To me, a hasty approach made the best sense. Looking up at the big house, I reasoned that sometimes your only hope *was* to rush in. If you hesitated for too long, the moment might pass. You could find yourself waiting another thirty years before you got up the nerve again. And by then it could be too late. For all concerned.

I made up my mind. I would face Mrs Beecham *now*. Walk right up to her and ask her straight out.

Are you my mother? I would ask, head held high. And no matter how she reacted I would stand my ground. Demand answers. I had a right to some answers.

I pushed open the big gate.

4

Mother?

The closer I got to it, the more imposing the house began to look. It was one of those great big double-fronted efforts with pompous-looking shrubbery masking it from prying eyes. And a line of tall birches on either side, shielding it from its nearest neighbours.

I looked up at the windows and wondered if anyone was watching. Maybe I should have gone home to change. I had deliberately worn my shabbiest outfit this morning, in case I was forced to haggle over rent.

The woman who answered my knock on the heavy oak-panelled door was a crushing disappointment. I'm not altogether sure what I'd been expecting, but she wasn't it. She was small, bandy-legged and nondescript. About as plain as a person can get, without being categorically ugly.

'Mrs Beecham?' I hardly dared ask.

Before she could reply there was an angry screech from the hallway behind her: 'No! I said no! And I mean it!'

There was a loud crash like glass breaking. 'Now see what you've made me do! That vase is irreplaceable! Just you wait until Mummy hears about this!'

The little woman turned, undecided.

I stepped back. 'I'll come back another time.'

'No. Don't go. Wait here.'

35

'I mean, where do they come from?' The voice in the hallway became even louder. 'And how could you even consider allowing them to set foot in our home? Let alone inflict them on Mummy? I'd prefer her to be alone for the rest of her days rather than inflict such, such . . . illiterate morons on her.'

'Don't exaggerate, Francesca,' a slower, calmer voice said. 'It's not easy finding someone suitable. Someone who will stay.'

'I won't be part of it,' the imperious voice interrupted. 'Why can't you simply hire an agency nurse and be done with it?'

'She won't have a nurse, you know that.'

'So the only alternative is some halfwit who'll be out the door in a week? That last one was simply beyond the pale.'

'Excuse me a second, love.' The little woman closed the door, but not quite fully, so I could hear the furious whispering that now started up behind it. I couldn't make out the actual words, but there was no doubt that a serious argument was taking place.

Then the loud voice burst out again: 'No! Not another one! I tell you, Penelope, I wash my hands of this whole idea. If you continue with it I shall never speak to you again.'

There was the sudden clatter of footsteps and the door flew open. A strikingly attractive woman came rushing out, her tanned face rigid with anger. She was extremely tall and wore a cream polo neck above pale jodhpurs and dark-brown riding boots. And she was flicking a dangerous-looking whip in the air.

I stepped out of her way.

She looked me up and down, her big green eyes raking me like lasers. 'My God, Penelope,' she bellowed over her shoulder. 'This one does actually look half normal. What's your name?' She jabbed me with the whip.

I moved further back, almost coming a cropper on the loose gravel.

'Oh, forget it. She's as witless as the rest. Or are you drunk?' She sniffed the air in front of me. 'Do all of us a favour, dear. Next time wear a name tag. And leave the bottle alone.'

She brushed past me, striding to a mud-splattered Land Rover whose front wheels were embedded in a laurel bush.

'Francesca? Please? We have to decide.' A slightly shorter version of the tall blonde came out the door, a lilac-veiled hat drooping over one well-plucked eyebrow.

'Your idea! You decide!' Francesca shouted. 'I refuse to sit through another interview. Take this one if you must.' She waved the whip in my direction. 'She can't be as witless as she looks.'

The vehicle roared into life and sped down the driveway, spewing back a cloud of smoke and fine gravel. It swung into the busy road without warning, to be greeted by a cacophony of angry toots.

Francesca tooted back.

The lilac veil turned in my direction, its owner still looking vaguely distracted.

I felt like a peeping Tom. An eavesdropper. Which I was. 'I . . . I was hoping to see Mrs Beecham,' I said.

'Oh . . . yes. Come on in. I'm Penelope, her eldest daughter. Penelope Beecham Powers. That was Francesca. My sister.' She glanced towards the gate. 'Don't worry, we won't be disturbed,' she added when she saw my nervous look. 'She won't be back.'

The little woman joined her in the doorway, gesturing for me to come in.

'Rosie?' Penelope blocked her way when she followed us. 'Could you get that broken vase by the stairs, please? And some fresh coffee, if you wouldn't mind?'

Rosie pouted. 'Are you another coffee drinker?' She looked at me.

I gave a nervous little grin. 'Actually, I prefer tea.' I don't know why I said it. I love coffee.

'Good!' She scuttled away happily.

Penelope sighed and ushered me into what looked like a big library. 'Rosie insists on judging everyone by their choice of beverage,' she said. 'It can be quite irritating. She has no time for coffee drinkers. Except for Mummy, of course. Mummy can do no wrong in her eyes. The rest of us caffeine aficionados she barely tolerates.' She gestured towards a comfortable-looking chair. 'Take a pew . . . er . . .'

'Annie,' I said.

She sat opposite, her back to the tall uncurtained window. 'The last girl I interviewed drank only water. There was a conundrum, I can tell you.'

This was the moment when I should have explained that I wasn't here to be interviewed. Instead, I sat there like a rabbit frozen in headlights, thinking it was very possible that this autocratic-looking woman was my sister.

'Tell me about yourself, Annie.' She settled back in her chair.

And my mind went completely blank. All I could do was stare at the beautifully furnished room. At the portrait of Stalin above the mantelpiece. Well, I couldn't be sure it was Stalin but it certainly looked like him. I glanced at the huge collection of books lining the walls.

'You're fond of books?' Penelope seemed pleased.

'Books? Oh, yes. I love books.'

What else could I say? I could hardly say, Is that Joseph Stalin? Or, How come you have more hardbacks per square inch than the Public Library in Walkinstown?

Penelope was speaking again. 'The last girl didn't care for books. She was a strange creature. Wouldn't have tea *or* coffee. Said she was opposed to any type of stimulant.' She frowned. 'Fancy classing Earl Grey as a stimulant. Francesca was convinced that she belonged to one of those peculiar Eastern sects. Although she said she was born in County Louth.'

'Really?' I said politely.

'You must excuse Francesca, she's a little out of sorts this morning. Things haven't been going her way lately.'

They hadn't exactly been going my way either, but I hadn't resorted to shouting insults at total strangers.

'Did she embarrass you? Did you find it off-putting, walking in on a family disagreement?'

She seemed to be inferring that this might indicate a flaw in *my* character. 'No,' I lied.

'Jolly good. It's refreshing to meet someone who's not frightened of a little outspokenness.'

Outspokenness?

'Francesca can be the most charming person when she chooses. And intensely loyal.'

Charming? Intensely loyal? The woman was a nutcase, flicking that whip in people's faces.

'I can only hope our little drama hasn't put you off. I have a strong feeling that you could fit in very well here. You may be the very person we have been searching for.' I went into petrified-rabbit mode again.

'Don't look so alarmed.' She laughed. 'I appreciate how nerve-racking interviews can be, but this is not an interview per se. All we need to ascertain is that you'll get along with Mummy. Be adaptable. Jolly her along. Keep her company. I'm a shrewd judge of character and I feel that you would be perfect for this position. You have an attractive air of calmness about you.'

My blouse was practically welded to my back with nervous perspiration.

'And you've already passed the Rosie test. That was a perceptive move, saying you preferred tea. Rosie can be a little bolshie if you don't measure up to her standards.'

'Em . . . about Mrs Beecham? Would it be possible for me to see her?'

'Oh, didn't they tell you? She's still in hospital. They had to reset the wrist.'

'The wrist?' What was this?

'Yes. Dreadful business all that resetting. But she never complained. Not even when she fell. And it was quite a serious tumble. That's why we must have someone here full time. As a companion, mind, she doesn't need a nurse. Rosie takes care of her medication.'

'Is she ill?'

'Certainly not!' She was insulted at the suggestion. 'We don't like her being alone in this big house, that's all. Rosie disappears as soon as her work is done.' She sniffed. 'We need someone living in. Someone sensible. Like you, Annie. Not some little flibbertigibbet whose only interest is the latest fashion fads and taking calls from her male admirers.' She spoke with the confident air of someone convinced that I wouldn't be troubled by either. 'Is there anything you'd like to ask me, Annie?'

'Er . . . when could I see Mrs Beecham?'

'Now that's exactly why I'm certain that you are the best person for this position. Not one other applicant asked that question. All they were anxious about was the salary and their days off. You're the only one who asked to meet her.'

I decided to come clean. 'Yes, but that's because . . .'

Rosie scuttled in with a loaded tray. 'Milk? Sugar?' she asked, pouring tea into a large china cup.

Then I was stirring my tea and being offered a fresh cream cake, and I remembered that I hadn't eaten since early morning. And fresh cream cakes have always been my downfall. What harm could it do to hold off on telling Penelope that I wasn't a job candidate? Besides, the more time we spent together the more chance there was that she might drop a few precious nuggets of information about Mrs Beecham.

The cakes were tempting: mouth-wateringly fresh and bursting with cream. And a thick coating of icing sugar. Some of them even had a glazed fudge topping. Before I knew it I was sinking my teeth into one of them. And then I was hooked.

Penelope showed little interest in the cakes, but I was reaching for my third when I realised what a greedy impression I must be making on the first blood relative I had ever met. Fortunately Penelope was so intent on filling me in on all the details of the job that she didn't seem to notice. Just the same, I rerouted my hand to the milk jug. Bad manners to eat *all* the cakes. But with the milk jug now in my hand I had no choice but to pour even more milk into my already creamy white tea. 'I love milk,' I answered her puzzled look.

'Good for your bones.' She nodded approvingly.

'And teeth,' I said.

'And nails.'

'Skin as well.' It was becoming a competition.

'And hair, of course.'

'And . . . er . . .' My knowledge of the health benefits of milk completely exhausted, I sipped the now cold tea.

It was vile.

Having dispatched most of the cream cakes and finished off my cold tea, I now had to find a way to leave without causing offence. I couldn't just walk out without an explanation. If I did that what hope would I have of returning when Mrs Beecham was here? I would be tagged as the woman who ate her way through a plateful of cakes and then legged it, without as much as a by-your-leave.

Penelope was still talking. Practically down to PRSI numbers now. 'Let me show you the room that goes with the job.' She suddenly sprang to her feet.

And then somehow we were halfway up the stairs and, short of making a break for the door, I couldn't think of a polite way out of the situation.

The thing was, despite Penelope's jolly-hockey-sticks manner and slightly overbearing way of speaking, there was a certain warmth to her. I quite liked her. At least she didn't display Francesca's sheer arrogance towards me. And what harm could it do to look at a room she seemed so anxious to show me? I was in no hurry to get back to work. It was one of Noel's days to be in the office until six. I hated those days.

Besides, I rationalised, the more I saw of the house the more I could learn about the Beechams. The longer I spent here the more inspiration I could get as to how to approach Mrs Beecham next time. That was the one thing I was in no doubt about. There *would* be a next time. Now that I had come this far there was no turning back.

I studied Penelope as closely as I dared, while we climbed yet another flight of stairs, doing my best to spot any genetic characteristics we might share. There wasn't a single one that I could see. I had more in common with Fiona than I had with Penelope.

She was somewhere in her mid-thirties, I guessed. Almost Nordic in her colouring, she didn't appear to have a single mousy brown gene in her make-up. Plus she held herself beautifully. Walked like a trained model. Here was a woman content in her skin.

What worried me was that it was Francesca and I who appeared to share a couple of attributes that might identify us as sisters. Our height, for one thing.

'*And* it's fully self-contained. Practically an apartment.' Penelope threw open a door and stood back, to allow me to enter the room first.

And it was love at first sight.

No other word for it. I had stepped into every flat seeker's dream. It was only sheer self-discipline that prevented me from dropping to my knees and kissing the gleaming hardwood floor. Or tearing around the room sniffing the vases of fresh flowers that stood on all available surfaces. Throwing myself on the big brass bed in unbridled ecstasy.

43

I had spent weeks viewing every rancid dump in the city. I'd actually wept after losing out on one of them, despite seeing the mouse droppings on the draining board. And I was being offered this?

'Well?' Penelope looked anxious. I have no idea why.

This was paradise. Twice the size of anything I had previously viewed, it ran from the full-length windows at the back of the house to the jutting bays at the front. Sixty feet at least. And the day outside might be grey but in here it was all warmth and sunshine. Even the stippled walls had a Mediterranean look to them and the lush green plants climbing to the exposed beams on the ceiling made it even more glorious.

Keeping my excitement in check, I crossed to the iron-railed terrace that overlooked the back garden. The terrace alone was bigger than the last two apartments I had viewed.

The terracotta bathroom did seem small, but that was only because it had a shower and a bath that could seat six.

There were even real oil paintings on the walls. Not prints. Genuine oil paintings. And OK, they were all of extremely fat women, one of whom had three breasts, but you can't have everything.

'Have you seen the walk-in closet?' Penelope asked.

Correction. You can.

There was even a teas-maid by the bed. A bloody teas-maid? I looked around for the flaw. There had to be a flaw.

Penelope saw my worried frown and her face fell. 'You don't like it?'

'I love it!' I tried not to screech. I was so blinded by

lust, I actually forgot it went with the job. 'I'll take it!' I heard myself shout.

'Oh, you won't be sorry.' Penelope practically applauded. 'Look here, it has piped television. Sky news. All the stations. And Mummy is a most lenient employer.'

That's when the penny dropped. I hadn't just taken a room. I had taken a job.

So what? I hated my present job. Having to face Noel three times a week was cruel punishment for what had been nothing more than a stupid affair, after all, and I desperately needed a place to live. I looked around the room again. How could anyone refuse this?

And what an excellent way for me to meet Mrs Beecham. I could become her devoted companion. Make myself indispensable to her. Give her the opportunity to get to know and love me, before I broke the happy news that I was her long-lost daughter. She'd probably beg me to stay for ever. She'd certainly never rebuff someone she was already enthralled with. Someone who was her loyal companion.

I got an adrenalin rush that practically raised me off the polished floorboards. This had to be destiny. Well, it had to be something more than pure chance that brought me to the Beechams' door on this particular morning. I couldn't wait to tell Gerry.

'You what? Tell me you're kidding,' he spluttered down the line.

'What's the problem?' I asked. 'The more I think about it the more brilliant an opportunity I realise it is.'

'Brilliant? Have you gone crazy? I told you to tread warily and you're moving in with them?'

'I'm going to work for them.'

'Even worse! For a start you'd be impersonating a health worker.'

'No, I wouldn't. She doesn't need a trained nurse.'

'That's not the point. They obviously took you to be some kind of practical nurse. You'd be there under false pretences. You can be charged with that.'

'With what? Penelope said the one thing she doesn't want is a nurse. All she wants is a companion. Any thicko can be a companion. All you have to do is read out loud and make soothing noises and be dead boring. I can be boring. Anyone who knows me will vouch for that.'

'Jesus Christ, Annie, what planet are you living on?'

'Oh, don't be such a killjoy! I'm really excited about moving in with them.' I laughed. 'To be honest they are all a bit peculiar, at least the ones I've met. Completely eccentric.'

'Then you'll fit in perfectly, won't you?'

'Don't be mean, Gerry.'

'Annie, you can't get away with impersonating a nurse.'

'I told you they don't want a nurse. And Penelope insisted. She said I'm perfect for the job.'

'Why? Because nobody else is stupid enough to take it? What are they paying? Three fifty an hour?'

'The room is fabulous!'

'I knew it. Three fifty an hour. Below the minimum wage. Do you know how much they'd have to pay a registered nurse?'

'They don't want a nurse.'

'Typical. Loaded with money but they won't pay for a proper nurse. What if she has some kind of . . . turn?'

A little dart of fear nudged me in the chest. My excitement began to fade as the enormity of what I had done started to seep in. 'What do you mean, a turn?'

'A cardiac arrest or something? It's not all that improbable at her age. What is she? Nearly seventy? There must be some reason why they want someone to keep an eye on her full time. Suppose she goes into heart failure? Or has a stroke? Or collapses? What will you do then? Read to her? You'd have four minutes to revive her before she suffers irreparable brain damage. I can't believe you're even considering this.'

'Well, I can't believe you've just downgraded a perfectly healthy woman in her sixties into an ailing geriatric who's going to collapse with heart failure the minute I set foot in her house. Were you always this maudlin?'

'I'm being realistic. Trying to talk some sense into you. Jaysus, Annie, this is like something Fiona might come up with.'

'Do you really think so?' I felt a sudden surge of confidence.

'That wasn't a compliment! If I'd thought you were going to pull a trick like this I never would have helped you to find her.'

'Well, I'm sorry you don't approve, but I'm going ahead with it anyway.' I paused. 'Don't tell me you wouldn't want to know why your mother gave you away?'

'Unfortunately for me, my mother *kept* me. I spent half my life wishing she hadn't.'

'See, that's the level most people think at. Until it happens to you, you can't even imagine how rotten it makes you feel to learn that your own flesh and blood didn't want you. Your own mother? Think about it!

47

It has to say something about what you are. How crap you must be. I need to know why she rejected me. I know a bit about her now and I know she's never going to unburden herself to someone who approaches her out of the blue. This is a perfect way for me to gain her trust.'

He sighed. 'This whole conversation is pretty irrelevant anyway. The minute she susses your name you'll be out on your arse.'

'Well, actually that's why I'm calling you. I need a driving licence and some other stuff in the name of Annie Mackem.'

'Mackem? Where did that come from?'

'I'm not going to tell you, you'll only start shouting again. The thing is, Penelope misunderstood me. She thinks it's my name.'

'Sweet living Jaysus! Have we just entered the twilight zone?'

'Well, I was nervous. Then I heard her on the phone to her brother. "Her name is Annie Mackem and she's perfect," she said.'

'Oh, Annie.'

'Look, can you get me some papers in the name of Mackem or not?'

'Forget it. You'll land the two of us in Mountjoy.' There was a note of finality in his voice.

'Well, thanks a lot, Gerry. Remember that time you were investigating the phoney warehouse deal? And Sam got you pet food labels and big empty tins so you could hide the video camera? Well, where do you think Sam got them? And who do you think asked her boss for the loan of a truck? Checked that the firm's insurance covered you and Barney? Third party, fire and theft.'

'That was you?' He was shocked. 'Sam never said.'

'I asked him not to.' I didn't say that I asked Sam to keep quiet because I was scared that if Gerry knew he might ask me out to dinner as a thank you, which could have put us in a desperately embarrassing situation. Imagine sitting in a warm, candlelit restaurant, with a lot of wine inside you and suddenly a long leg begins to rub gently against yours, making unmistakably lecherous overtures. I mean, Gerry might have been compelled to respond.

'OK, so I owe you a favour,' he said. 'But you didn't have to do anything illegal.'

'And I'm not asking you to. I won't be doing anything essentially wrong here. I have a full driving licence so it's not as if I'd be breaking the law. I just want a kind of mock one to leave lying around the house, in case . . . in case anyone gets . . . curious. I'll keep my real one in my bag when I'm driving.'

'Jesus, Annie, I don't know. This is all a bit . . .'

I changed tack. 'So you'd see me out on the street, then?'

'What? Oh, the flat business? It won't come to that.'

'It already has. I'm not only rootless, I'm homeless as well, remember? And here I have a chance to kill two birds with the one stone and . . .' I began to sniff '. . . you won't help out.'

He swallowed hard. 'Don't cry, Annie. Give me time to think.'

'Gerry?'

'What?'

'While you're thinking about it, will you get me a few references? I need some saying that I'm the most capable companion to dear old ladies, since . . . since

Whistler painted his granny.'

'His mother, Annie. He painted his mother.'

'See! Everyone wants to immortalise their mother. And you'd deny me the right to meet mine?'

He actually laughed. 'Jesus, Annie, you have some neck. I never would have thought.'

'I want to know why she gave me away.'

'Her loss.'

'I *need* to know.'

'Then what?'

'Then I'll leave. Why would I stay with a woman who threw me out as a baby? And the job is hardly a major step up the career ladder, is it?'

'Exactly my point. Now you listen to me, Annie McHugh, I know their kind, they'll treat you like a skivvy. Like some kind of indentured servant.'

'Oh, don't be such a pessimist. No wonder your wife ran off. Oh God, I didn't mean that, Gerry,' I said quickly. 'It's just . . . what happened to your sense of adventure? Isn't that why you opened the detective agency?'

'I opened it because I couldn't think of anything else to do.'

'Same difference. Will you help me or not?'

He hesitated. 'What happened to the real applicant?'

'What?'

'The woman they were obviously expecting to interview. What happened to her?'

'Oh, her. I met her on my way out. She wouldn't have suited them. Far too prim and proper. I told her the job was gone.'

'And she believed you?'

'Why not? I told her I was a Beecham.'

5

Never look back when you're forging ahead. Well, perhaps just occasionally

I expected to meet with some opposition when I gave in my notice, but I was wrong. Noel hardly raised an eyebrow when it was brought to his attention. Maybe he was relieved. Glad to be seeing the back of me. There was a time when he was glad to see any part of me, but that was well in the past.

I remember the first time I saw him. He came striding through the main office like a born-again Pied Piper, his adoring little entourage in hot pursuit. I had, of course, seen pictures of him in the papers long before I got the position as PA and general factotum to his office manager. Noel was, after all, semi-famous. Renowned for being the simple country boy who took control of a small pet food company and turned it into a multimillion-pound business overnight. Well, over seventeen years.

It was thanks to Noel's razor-sharp business acumen that Pussy Grub was now quoted on the Stock Exchange.

The media adored him. 'A Cinderfella for our

times' a Sunday supplement called him.

I have to say that I had been quite underwhelmed when I first saw his picture in the press. There was nothing remarkable about him that I could see. It wasn't that he was unattractive. He was after all tall . . . ish. Handsome . . . ish. Going slightly grey . . . ish. But he was old. He had to be hitting forty. I was twenty-five, then.

There was nothing in the photos to warn you that when you met face to face, Noel had a way of looking at you that made you feel like a star. Made your skin go all tingly.

I had been working in the Pussy Grub office for a week when he arrived back from a successful marketing trip to America. The whole office was buzzing with his great achievements over there. There were even rumours that in Washington he had been asked to stand in as a special adviser to the Irish ambassador. Quite an accomplishment for a man who had begun his working career sticking labels on tins of pet food at fourteen and a half. And married the boss's daughter at twenty-two.

I would never in a million years have considered myself to be one of those sad women who fall for their married boss until Noel swept into the Pussy Grub office.

'Close your gob, Annie, you'll catch flies,' one of the filing clerks whispered when she saw my expression.

'Oh my God, Fiona, you won't believe it.' I lay back on her bed. 'Your hand actually tingles when he touches it.'

'Jaysus!' Fiona wasn't impressed.

'I'm telling you, Fiona, your hand actually tingles.'

'Is that a fact?' She continued painting her toenails dark blue, focusing on not disturbing the cotton wool balls that separated her narrow white toes. 'Just make sure he doesn't get to tingle any other part of you. I'd say he's a right cute hoor. I've seen pictures of him, smiling into his wife's face.'

'What's wrong with that?'

'Nothing. Once *you're* not stupid enough to get the hots for him.'

She was right, of course. Noel was a married man. No question about that even if he did spend all week in Dublin, only going home to the Midlands at the weekends. And even then, only three weekends out of four, people said.

Still, that tingle had been real. I hadn't imagined it. And it wasn't as if I was on the lookout for a man or anything. Quite the contrary: I could take them or leave them. An attitude no doubt formed by my first sexual encounters, which had taken place in the back of a Ford Cortina owned by a young student accountant who worked with my father.

We would go to the pictures, then leave before the end and drive up to Bushy Park to make out. I was nineteen, then, the only remaining virgin of a class of twenty-eight Loreto Convent girls who came from some of the staunchest Catholic families of post-Vatican Two Ireland.

One night we went to see a French film that was the talk of the town for its explicit sex scenes. It was a huge disappointment. Even with the help of subtitles I couldn't make head nor tail of the story, which was set in a French port and had a lot of swarthy-looking men alternating between shooting each other and trying to goose women who only took the cigarette out of their mouths for a close-up. The only scenes worth watching were those where a heroic young Algerian made passionate love to a luminous young Frenchwoman, who was either a schoolgirl or a prostitute. Or maybe both.

The student accountant's deep breathing began to reverberate as far down as the front stalls. When I turned to say something to him he silenced me by ramming a hot tongue halfway down my throat.

I was frozen to my seat with shock. It wasn't that I objected, on principle, it was just that I would have preferred some little forewarning of intent.

I lost my virginity that night. I'm convinced that the student accountant did as well, although he did his utmost to give the impression that he was well-versed in sexual matters. But he was as awkward as I was when it came to the actual deed. Afterwards I sometimes wondered how we had managed it at all, what with both of us being so clumsy and passing car lights interrupting us every second, and my sweat-drenched body sliding off the back seat of the Cortina with every thrust of his.

He never asked me out again.

He did still call to 59 Fernhill Crescent with great regularity. But this was because he shared an office car pool with my father. I soon got over the embarrassment of spotting the scene of the crime pulling up at our gate at seven fifty each morning. I even took to opening our front door when Father wasn't ready. But the most the student accountant ever said to me was, 'Looks like rain.'

Once he actually slipped into the hallway and stood whey-faced by our big mahogany coat rack. He looked directly at me, staring so hard that my heart began to pound in expectation. And dread. I guessed that he was getting ready to ask me something. And he was. 'Did your father take home my umbrella, by any chance?' he asked in his singsong Cork accent. 'I wouldn't trouble you, but it did cost a fair few bob.'

He eventually married a fellow accountant and had three children. I heard later that one of them attended a school for the mentally impaired.

Noel wasn't a wet day back from New York when he called me into his office. 'Close the door, Annie.' He had adopted the American policy of only using first names. 'I believe you're the best organiser in the whole firm.' He smiled.

I blushed scarlet. To have him notice me was flattering enough. To have him pay me such a compliment was beyond bliss.

'I have a few rough ideas here, a few proposals I threw together. Maybe you could put some order on them? Would you do that for me, Annie?'

'Oh, yes.'

'Good. Here we are, then.' He handed me a massive folder. It was at least five inches thick and bursting at the seams with loose foolscap pages. 'All right, Annie?' He leaned towards me, his slate-grey eyes smiling into mine.

My knees almost gave way and it had little to do with the weight of the two-ton folder. 'Yes, sir.'

'Call me Noel. Please?'

And it might have been that word please. Or maybe the way he said it.

Whatever it was, I knew that nothing Fiona or anyone else might say could stop my heart pounding at the mere thought of this man in his underpants.

'Annie?' he called as I was pushing open the door to the main office.

I turned. 'Yes, Noel?'

'I'll need twenty copies of each proposal before Friday. Readable copies, please. And have them properly bound, nothing slipshod. Thank you, Annie.' He picked up the phone. 'Get me Washington.'

That was Monday morning.

By Thursday morning not only had I retyped and double-spaced every single page in the cluttered folder but also taken the liberty of tightening up Noel's slightly erratic paragraphs. I highlighted all noteworthy financial figures in coloured print for easy access, and here and there rectified his minor accounting errors.

I was rushing to catch my bus when my mother stopped me. 'Are you sure about that blouse, Annie? Isn't it a bit too eye-catching for the office, love?'

It certainly caught Noel's eye. He gave a sharp intake of breath when I leaned over his desk to place the pile of folders in front of him. The way he was staring made me wish I had left the second button of the red silk blouse open as well, as I had first planned.

That Friday evening he stopped by my desk to thank me for what he called my *superior* work. The whole office hushed to listen. 'You're a gem, Annie. I hope we're paying you enough.'

'Oh, yes,' I drooled, ignoring the frantic signals from my co-workers. And that was the start of it.

Within a month I was the office star. Nobody else was allowed to handle Noel's important proposals. Of course, this meant that we had sometimes to work late together. Which meant that I frequently missed my bus.

He began giving me a lift home in his Merc. And one snowy night he kissed me.

The following night it was still snowing so the heat in the building was turned up as we worked late on his most recent proposal.

We ended up on the carpet under his desk, forgetting all about the Chicken Korma and fried rice that we had specially ordered from the nearby Chinese to keep our energy levels up.

And carpet burns and the odd stubbed toe aside, it was the best sex I ever had.

'The best sex? Compared with what? A bit of pumping in the back of a Ford Cortina?' Fiona dismissed my claim out of hand.

'You don't understand,' I said.

'You're right. I don't,' she admitted. 'His wife gets a big house in the country, two horses, a silver BMW and winter holidays in Florida. And what do you get? Carpet burns on your arse?' It wasn't that Fiona objected to clandestine affairs on moral grounds. She just thought that wives got a better deal.

I didn't even attempt to convince her of how thrilling it was to spend two whole days with Noel on the Dingle peninsula. And of course I knew that he had hired the thatched cottage to impress visiting Americans. *And* that they had taken a rain check, because they had to fly to Brussels unexpectedly. But that didn't detract from my pleasure.

We lazed around in front of a big turf fire. Cooked freshly caught salmon on a charcoal barbecue, in the rain. And walked for miles along the moonlit beach, only stopping when the wine we'd had at dinner made us so heated we had to search out a private spot behind the sand dunes.

'You need your head tested,' was Fiona's reaction. 'A quick ride behind the rocks? Is that all you're worth?'

'Don't be disgusting!' I slammed down the phone.

It was roughly two weeks after that magical trip to Dingle that my period went astray. At first I put it down to stress and I was almost four weeks late when I finally gave in and bought a pregnancy testing kit. I used it in the middle of the night, terrified that I might be disturbed. I had never even seen one before so when the two distinct red lines came up I tried to convince myself that it was a trick of the light. That was at four thirty in the morning. By eight o'clock I was forced to accept the truth.

I was pregnant.

Noel was in America.

When he phoned the office to ask if there was any outstanding business that needed his attention, I somehow got up the nerve to tell him that yes, there was.

'Don't tell me, it's that little arsehole of a bureaucrat in Industry and Enterprise. What's his problem this time?'

'It's not him. This is something altogether different. This is personal.'

'What do you mean *personal*?' As if he had never heard the word before.

'It's to do with . . . us. You and me.'

'You and me? What are you talking about?'

I nearly hung up.

'Annie, come on, what is it?' He was seething with impatience.

'It's . . . it's about . . .' I took a deep breath. 'You remember that missing item I mentioned to you a few weeks back? And you told me not to worry, that it was bound to turn up. You said it was just my nerves. Well, it wasn't. And it hasn't.'

I was being as discreet as possible – after all, we were on a business line.

There was a long silence. 'Now you listen to me, Annie.' His voice was even when he finally spoke. 'I don't want to hear another word about this. Do you hear me? Not another word. You're a grown woman, you know what's what. I shouldn't have to remind you that you went into this business with your eyes wide open. So don't you start behaving like some misguided office junior. You know what has to be done. You get on with it and I'll see that you are fully reimbursed for any expenses incurred. I'll see that you are not out of pocket in any way. Deal with it, Annie. Without delay. Do you understand me?'

I understood him. Only too well.

I rang the only person I could confide in. 'Fiona? I'm in trouble.'

It was Fiona who got the number of the clinic for me. Fiona who took days off work to travel with me. Fiona who held my hand when I began to shake so much that I couldn't write my name on the consent form. And it was Fiona who kept my secret, never telling a soul.

6

Gerry drives to Haney Road. By the scenic route

Moving my personal possessions from the snug little semi on Fernhill Crescent to the big house on Haney Road should have taken, roughly, half an hour. Tops.

With Gerry's help it took a whole afternoon. First because he had to collect the van from outside Barney's flat. Barney is the younger of Gerry's two detectives. He had borrowed the van the night before to ferry a crowd of his friends to a rock concert. And then forgot to put petrol in it. But the main delay was because Gerry kept stopping the van every five minutes to interrogate me. To ask over and over if I was sure I was doing the right thing.

'Why did you agree to drive me if you think it's such a bad idea?' I fumed after our third unscheduled stop.

'Who else do you know with a van?'

Gerry always answered a question with a question. It was one of his most annoying traits. The result, no doubt, of his Garda training. Although he was always quick to deny this. But then he tended to deny most things at first. Garda training again, I suppose. After all he had been a serving Garda for eight years. And a very good one, by all accounts, until a gunshot wound to his left knee cut short his promising career in that proud force.

He never corrected people when they assumed that he had been heroically wounded in the line of duty. That he took a bullet in the ligament while protecting life and property, in the busy metropolis that Dublin was fast becoming.

In fact, he had shot himself in the knee while in hot pursuit of a cheeky urban fox that had been successfully raiding his neighbour's pigeon loft for weeks.

His picture was in all the papers afterwards. There he was, sitting up in bed in St James's Hospital. Posing like a film star with a pretty ward nurse checking his pulse, a big bottle of Lucozade growing out of his left shoulder. At least that's how it appeared in the yellowing press cutting Sam had proudly showed us in the pub one night. *Garda hero foils raid on pensioner's home*, the caption said. Apparently nobody had informed the press that the only pensioners in danger that night were the elderly homing pigeons. Or that the Lucozade bottle contained single malt whiskey, Gerry's particular favourite.

He had consequently opened his private detective agency and sometimes even remembered to limp in public. Although the more observant among us occasionally noted that he wasn't above limping with the wrong leg.

When we pulled up outside the house on Haney Road I realised why he had insisted on driving me. He was out of the van in a flash, ringing the doorbell before I had my seat belt unbuckled. He was determined to give the Beecham family the once-over before I crossed their threshold. In fact, he was so wound up he was limping on the right leg, which was always a bad sign with Gerry.

But the only Beecham in the house that day was Penelope. We learned later that Francesca was at her own place in Kildare, exercising her horses, or plaiting their tails, or whatever it is they do with horses in Kildare on a dull, wet Sunday. And Mrs Beecham wasn't due home from the hospital until the following day. Penelope had asked me to move in on Sunday so I would be well settled and ready to greet her mother when she arrived home on Monday morning.

She seemed distracted, now, as she opened the door, inviting me in while throwing Gerry a curious look, before excusing herself to answer the phone that was ringing off the hook in the kitchen.

'Did you see that?' Gerry asked as we carried my cases in. 'See the way she ran off when she saw me? Do you not find that a bit suspicious?'

'The phone was ringing. What did you expect her to do?'

I was already nervous enough without having him making me worse. I had finally admitted to myself that moving into the Beecham house might prove a little traumatic. There might be a bit more to it than the pleasure of getting a great flat so close to the city centre. I had also begun to worry that inching my way into the affections of a woman who had once rejected me might not be as simple as I had thought.

It didn't help that the big house looked even more scary than when I had first seen it. The wide staircase put me in mind of those horror films where a decapitated head is almost guaranteed to come rolling down the steps, to land in a pool of blood at the heroine's feet.

I hesitated at the first step.

'Jesus. What a creepy staircase,' Gerry said from behind me.

'Right. That's it.' I turned. 'You go home. I'll carry my own cases,' I snapped.

'What's wrong? All I said was it's . . .'

'Shut up!' I practically bellowed.

'What has you so touchy all of a sudden?' He had been lugging my heaviest case across the hall, but dropped it now with a dull thud. 'Look, if you're having second thoughts, Annie, we can just put your stuff back in the van. If you're not happy . . .'

'For Christ's sake I'm not here to be happy! I'm here because she threw me aside like a soiled rag. Called me a fibroid. I'm not leaving this house until I get some answers.'

Gerry seemed shocked by my vehemence. In fact, it even shocked me. I stood there panting. Looking around the big hallway. Ready for a fight.

'Is there a problem?' Penelope's voice came from the kitchen doorway.

I said nothing.

Gerry scowled at her, then turned to me. 'Have you decided what you're going to do, Annie?'

'I'm moving my things upstairs, of course.' I gave Penelope a tight little smile.

'Bring the cases up,' I hissed at Gerry.

'Bloody superior West Brits,' he was muttering as he half dragged, half carried the big case behind me. 'Did you see the way she looked at me?'

She was still looking at him. Standing in the hallway, now, a worried frown replacing her smile. It might have been his blatant antagonism that worried her. Or maybe she was just thinking of the family silver. Gerry looked a bit rough today. He had spent the previous eight hours on surveillance outside a massage parlour in Rathmines and he hadn't bothered to shave or shower before picking me up. He was still wearing his old tracksuit and black polo neck that had seen better days. Probably some time in the nineteen eighties.

Whenever he moved his head the big polo neck threatened to spring up over his chin and turn him into one of those scowling identikits from *Crime Line*. No wonder Penelope was uneasy.

'I don't like the look of her.' He threw my case on the bed. 'There's something not right about that woman. She's hiding something. I can tell.'

'Jesus, are you determined to upset me? All she did was open the door to us. How can you see some kind of criminal behaviour in that?'

'Experience.' He limped to the window. 'I mean what's with that hat? What normal person would wear something like that indoors?'

Or even outdoors, I thought. It was a strange-looking creation, a cross between a flat cap and a titfer. But then strange hats appeared to be a bit of a fetish with her.

'So she likes hats. Big deal.'

Gerry wasn't listening. He was checking the lock on the door, then moving on to the burglar-proof latches on the windows even though we were so high up that only spiderman could gain entrance. When he started checking the bathroom door I lost patience. 'For God's sake, Gerry, will you stop prowling! You'd think we were in Castle Dracula the way you're carrying on.'

'I knew she put me in mind of someone. It's those eye-teeth of hers. Never trust anyone with prominent eye-teeth, my old sergeant used to say.'

'Is he the one who got turned down twice by the technical bureau? And you wondered why?'

'You may laugh. But sometimes gut instinct serves you better than a whole team of forensic experts.'

'Please, Gerry, go home.'

'I'm going. But just remember, the first sign of any bother and you call me. OK? I can be here like that.' He snapped his fingers, conveniently forgetting that it had taken us all of two hours to get here this afternoon.

'I won't forget,' l said. 'You'd better go. Barney might need the van again,' I added to change the subject.

It worked. 'Can you believe he let it run dry? Some detective, huh? He didn't even see the warning light. It's that girl of his, she has him driven to distraction. But I'm concerned about you, not Barney.'

'Why would you be concerned? Look around you. How many people do you know who live in a place like this?'

'It's the people you'll be living with that worry me.'

'Mrs Beecham? She's hardly Cruella De Ville.'

'We don't know that.'

'Are you trying to scare me?' I asked.

'No! And you're right. You'll be comfortable here.' He looked around the beautiful room. 'I could be here in minutes.'

Maybe in a helicopter, I thought.

'OK, I'm off,' he said, but still didn't move.

'Go,' I commanded.

'I'll see ya, Annie.' He was gone.

Two seconds later his head appeared around the door again. 'Just a phone call, OK?'

'Get out of here.' I threw a clothes hanger at him.

I was arranging my clothes in the big walk-in wardrobe when there was a knock on the bedroom door.

'Has your friend left?' Penelope glanced around. As if she hadn't heard the rumble of the big Hiace, thundering down the drive.

'He's an ex-Garda.' I don't know why I said it. Maybe to reassure her. Or myself.

'Oh, good.' She couldn't hide the relief in her voice.

She held out a massive key ring. 'The house keys. Front door, back door. Conservatory. Cellar. Side garage.'

She pronounced it gar*age*. How my mother would have loved that.

Gar*age*.

'There's lots of food in the freezer. Feel free to use whatever takes your fancy. And there's some rather decent hock in the kitchen rack if you're partial.' She was smiling now. 'Mummy won't be back until late morning, but Jamie may call in advance. You don't mind being alone here tonight, do you?'

'No.' I was becoming a fluent liar.

'Must go,' she said. 'Jim likes me to be well on the road before dark.'

I had a sudden flash of frightened villagers hurrying indoors to board up their windows before the sun went down.

She gave a little uneasy laugh. 'And he's the one who's had his licence endorsed. Men!'

This was more like it. Slagging off men was familiar ground to me. I could match her story for story on that subject. Talk about it all night, if she wanted. But she didn't. She was in a hurry to get back to Wicklow. 'So that's it, then. You should be comfortable here, but if you have any problems, any concerns whatsoever, give me a ring.' She handed me a card. 'This is my home number. And this here, the 086, is my mobile,' she pointed out helpfully, as if I couldn't possibly have guessed that all by myself.

Maybe she was as nervous as I was. Despite the glowing references I had supplied her with, handing over the keys of this house to someone she had only met twice couldn't be easy. Then again, she had practically twisted my arm to take the job.

'Is there anything you'd like to ask me, before I go?'

'No,' I said, a little too quickly.

'Nothing at all?' She seemed surprised.

'Nothing at all,' I echoed.

'I'll be off, then. Sleep well.'

I waited until I heard the crunch of tyres on the gravel below, before hurrying down to have a quick look around the house. She had left the landing and hall lights on but the rest of the place was in darkness, even though it wasn't yet teatime. I couldn't recall it ever getting dark this early on Fernhill Crescent. Maybe the big trees blocked out the light. I turned on a few lamps. People as wealthy as the Beechams surely wouldn't quibble about electricity bills.

The big trees creaked in the wind and sent me hurrying back to my room. Tomorrow would be time enough to have a look around. When *she* was here. My mother with the broken wrist. She'd probably want to show me around the house herself. Tell me what was expected of me. Find out the sort of things I was interested in. Tell me what interested her.

I wondered if she would look more like Francesca or Penelope. Maybe nothing like either of them. Maybe she would look like me? I had to sit down to cope with this idea. How weird it would be to meet a complete stranger who turned out to have your exact features. Your exact expression.

I ran a bath and lay in it for ages, thinking about this. Conjuring up all sorts of images in my head.

When the phone rang I didn't know if I should answer it or not. After all, it wouldn't be for me. And if the Beechams had been expecting an important call surely they'd have a machine on.

When it rang non-stop for nearly three minutes I went to answer it. 'Hello?' I was breathless after running down the stairs.

'Annie? What the hell took you so long?'

'How did you get this number?'

'I'm a detective, remember?' He laughed. 'Are you OK?'

'I was until the bloody phone rang and I had to jump out of the bath and run down three flights of stairs to answer it.'

'Sorry. Just thought I'd check.'

'It's OK. I'm glad you rang.' I looked around the silent hallway.

'I'll give you a shout during the week, then.'

'Thanks, Gerry.'

'For what?'

For ringing me when I'm trying not to think about tomorrow. For caring how I am. For not telling me how stupid I am wanting to be here and wanting to run away at the same time. For being a friend.

'Just thanks.'

''Night, Annie.'

I raced upstairs and dived into bed, leaving all the lights on. I knew it was infantile and childish, but it was extremely comforting. Besides, who would know? I would switch them off in the morning before anyone got here.

7

Meet the family

I was woken by loud excited voices calling out to each other. And children's laughter. And car doors slamming. I looked at the clock. It was almost nine.

I was throwing my clothes on when I heard the dogs barking.

Dogs? Plural?

Nobody had mentioned dogs to me. Dogs had always been a thorny subject in my life. My parents had fought a running battle with our neighbourhood dogs for as long as I could remember.

I hesitated, waiting for the sound of enthusiastic barking to fade before venturing, cautiously, down the stairs.

'Well, well, who have we here?' a deep male voice said.

I jumped. But there was no one in sight. The hall was empty.

'Hello?' I called nervously.

'Hello.' He stepped out of the shadows, startling me, so that I lost my footing.

If it hadn't been for his lightning-fast reflexes, my face might have become embedded in the floor tiles.

And when I got a proper look at him I almost wished it had. It might have proved less embarrassing than my silly gawking.

'Annie? It is Annie?' he asked as I stared into his face.

All I could think was, thank God I wasn't easily attracted to men. If I were I might have been in deep trouble here. Because this one was devastatingly handsome. I noticed this quite dispassionately. Standing back to note his tall slim body, his perfect profile and his glossy black hair, which curled almost to his broad shoulders, I looked at him without a single lustful thought entering my head. Much.

'Yes. I'm Annie,' I squeaked.

Penelope appeared from the kitchen, her head encased in a silk turban.

'Ah, you've met?' She sounded disappointed. 'I wanted to be the first to introduce you. Oh, never mind.' She laughed. 'This is Annie who is going to make all our lives a lot easier. And this handsome creature, Annie, is Jamie. My darling brother.'

Brother? My insides went hollow.

'Jamie paints.' Penelope linked her arm through his as I continued to gawk.

From the look of sisterly pride on her face I guessed she didn't mean doors and windows.

'He's had several exhibitions. In Paris, of all places. One French critic said he put him in mind of a young Rembrandt.'

'Rubens,' Jamie said drily. 'And that was only because I was going through a male crisis at the time. I was painting extremely large women,' he explained to me.

Large women. So he was the one.

'Oh, don't be so modest.' Penelope gave him a playful push, which almost propelled him across the polished tiles. 'You know you have an amazing gift.'

'Penelope!' he hushed her.

Was it possible that this was my brother? This superb man dismissing Penelope's compliments in such a charming way that you just knew he couldn't get enough of them.

'Sisters.' He laughed, throwing back his beautiful head so you could see that he didn't have a single filling in his well-chiselled mouth. 'What can you do with them?'

My near hysterical laugh made him frown uneasily, but I couldn't stop myself. I had never before seen such perfection close up. He was extraordinarily handsome. I would defy anyone male or female to look at such a creature and not have their pulse quicken. And he might be my brother? Living here was going to be much more complicated than I had thought.

They were still waiting, the beautiful Beecham siblings, for an explanation for my inane laughter.

I racked my brains for a reason that wouldn't make me sound completely certifiable. Jamie's dark eyes were intent on my face, making any clear thought impossible. And the thing was I think he knew the effect he was having on me, which made it even worse.

'Here comes trouble.' Penelope turned suddenly.

Two tots came racing along the hall towards us. One of them was a little Penelope clone, down to the quick, bossy smile. The other was a fat, serious little boy with white-blond hair and scorching-red cheeks. He looked to be about a year younger than his sister who might have been five, or maybe six.

'Mummy, Rags is trying to mount Peppa. He's

'Oh, I don't know.' I blushed furiously. 'Maybe some time in the future but that's a very big question. A huge life choice.'

'I meant, would you not have preferred to work with them,' he said kindly, not even allowing himself the smallest grin, although he must have been dying to laugh.

I watched enviously when he kissed the children goodbye, picking them up so they could throw their arms around his neck. Then he gave Penelope a warm hug. I stood there, hope rising.

'I'll see you tomorrow, Annie,' he called out to me. 'I should have Mother home by mid-morning at the latest. Don't forget to put out the red carpet.'

Watching his long back disappear out the door I told myself that I was only attracted to him in a benign, sisterly way. And surely this was good. Healthy, even. Having a brother would be a completely new experience for me. Well, not *having* him exactly, but being a sister. Lots of brothers and sisters have warm, close relationships. Fiona used to share a bath with her brother, although, of course, they gave that up when they were four. Having a sisterly relationship with Jamie could prove quite difficult.

I would have to stop staring at him for a start. Train myself not to gaze into his eyes like someone simple in the head. Even the children had noticed the way I behaved when he was around. 'Why is your face all red, Annie?' Amy had asked when Jamie said, 'I'll look forward to seeing more of you, Annie.'

He turned, now, as he drove away, to give us another big wave.

''Bye darling,' Penelope called and closed the door.

'Well, children here we are. Let's show Annie around the house, shall we?'

They led me upstairs.

'This is Mummy's room,' Penelope announced, throwing open the door of a big double bedroom, which had almost as many crowded bookshelves as the library below.

It also had a small balcony similar to the one that led off my bedroom, except that this one was jam packed with potted plants.

'Mummy has green fingers,' she explained, when she saw me admiring the little bonsai beeches.

The children raced ahead of us we made our way around the house, leading us from one tastefully decorated room to the next. And the dogs followed them, leaping on to beds and expensive-looking damask chairs that didn't take kindly to heavy Labrador paws.

'In the old days these were the servants' quarters,' Penelope said grandly, when we came to the landing where my room was situated.

Was this a hint that I shouldn't forget my place? Had she noticed my self-conscious behaviour when Jamie was close? Was she reminding me that I was only the paid help around here?

'Oh, forgive me if that sounded patronising, Annie. I didn't intend it to be. This room used to be mine, after all. When the servants slept here this whole floor was divided into four separate compartments. Now there is just your room and the second bathroom. You'll live like family here.'

I got such a sudden rush of emotion that I had to turn away in case she saw how moved I was.

'I like your room.' Amy sidled up to me.

'Me too,' I said, opening the door wide.

The dogs took this as an invitation to rush in and race each other across the polished floor, barking loudly with excitement.

'Peppa! Rags!' Penelope called them to heel and they skidded to a halt like the well-trained working dogs she had claimed them to be when she first introduced us.

Then the children hugged and kissed them, telling them they were 'Naughty dogs!' between kisses. Little Simon took my hand as we went downstairs.

Rosie was busy in the big, sunlit kitchen, whipping up all sorts of interesting-looking concoctions. She gave me a welcoming smile, then returned to her beating and whipping, shouting at Peppa whenever she attempted to investigate the source of the mouth-watering smells. 'Dogs in kitchens,' she muttered. 'Shouldn't be allowed.'

Rags showed no interest in the food. He was far too preoccupied with his tireless pursuit of Peppa.

We sat around the big table in the glass conservatory that ran along the rear of the kitchen. It might have been high summer it was so warm and sunny.

'I'll open another window,' Rosie said to nobody in particular. 'All this glass only attracts the heat. And how anyone is expected to keep it clean is beyond me. Far too much glass for a kitchen.' Rosie seemed happiest when she had something to grumble about. But when it came to cooking no one could fault her.

She served a delicious brunch, filling my plate with generous helpings of scrambled eggs and the lightest bacon quiche I had ever tasted. She had special pigs in a blanket and fluffy, cheesy potatoes for the children. They begged for second helpings.

From across the table Penelope caught my eye. *Told you so*, her look said.

It was my first meal with the Beechams and it was all so relaxed and pleasant and normal, in no way the high-tension ordeal I had been expecting. And this was despite the air being constantly punctuated with cries of 'Mummy, Rags is mounting Peppa *again*'.

Rags was finally exiled to the garden, where he had to resign himself to *mounting* anything that couldn't run. Rosie tut-tutted in disapproval.

Nobody else paid the slightest heed. Certainly not Peppa, who stretched out by the stove ignoring Rosie's muttered threats. I was beginning to like Peppa, whose real name turned out to be Pepper. It was the over-refined Beecham vowels that had misled me.

I don't know why it surprised me to find Penelope such an affectionate mother. Even at the table the children always seemed to be on the receiving end of a kiss or a hug. But then so were the dogs. Nothing in the Beecham house was turning out to be what I had expected.

Living here was going to be a truly enjoyable experience, I decided. It was only my first day and I already felt like one of the family. I couldn't wait to report back to Gerry.

Amy opened the conservatory door and Rags was in like a bullet. '*Mummy*, Rags is mounting . . .'

'Time to go, I think.' Penelope got to her feet and began gathering up the children's belongings.

Little Simon jigged up and down as Amy helped him on with his jacket. 'Beep, beep, Mummy. Beep, beeeeep.'

Rosie huffed and puffed as if all this activity were too much for her but I noticed that she packed a box of home-made cakes, which she handed to Simon with a little approving pat on the head.

They were all ready to go when Penelope turned to Pepper. 'Bye-bye, darling. Be a good girl for Annie, now.' That was the first hint I'd had that Pepper was being left in *my* charge.

The rest of the gang trooped out to the big Padjero, Rags under extreme protest. Unperturbed, Penelope gave a swift demonstration of why choke chains are so called. He was settled in the jeep within seconds.

Rosie left soon afterwards. She had been offered a lift in the Padjero, but declined. 'Death traps, them yokes,' she dismissed them, pulling on a pink plastic mac. 'I wouldn't sit in one if you paid me. See them bull horns on the front? They're killers.'

Only minutes before she had said to Penelope, 'They're grand cars all the same, them jeeps. Fine and strong. Wouldn't crumple up in an accident like some of the other yokes you see on the road.'

After the excitement of the morning, the house seemed strangely quiet.

I rang Gerry.

'How are things at Castle Dracula?' he drawled.

'I'll have you know that I've just finished the most fun brunch I've ever had.'

'A fun brunch? There's posh. Don't tell me. They brought the jesters up from the dungeons to entertain you.'

'Close enough.' I laughed. 'I've met the son. And the grandchildren. *And* the dogs.'

'Dogs? They have you dog-sitting?'

'They have not,' I said quickly. 'They . . . took them with them.' I winked at Pepper who was lying at my feet.

'Well, thank Christ for that. That would be par for the course with the likes of the Beechams. Having you mind their pampered pooches while they swan around opening garden fêtes and smashing bottles of champagne against the hull of the *Titanic*.'

'You need to get out more, Gerry. Check the newspapers.' I laughed.

'Have you met the lady of the house?' he asked.

'No. Tomorrow is the big day.'

'So this is your last chance to leg it?'

'Don't be stupid. I'm not going to run away.'

'I wouldn't call it running away, I'd call it coming to your senses.'

'Get a grip, Gerry. It's not as if I'm going to stay here for ever. It's just a temporary arrangement while I . . . find out what I can.'

Pepper gave me a supportive little bark.

'What the hell was that?'

'Nothing. I'd better go.'

'You're dog-sitting, aren't you? I bloody knew it. They have you minding their feckin' dogs?'

'It's not like that.'

'You'd better start practising, Annie.'

'Practising?'

'Touching your forelock. You're going to find yourself doing a lot of that if you stay in that house.'

'Oh, leave me alone, Gerry.' I hung up.

Touching my forelock? I'd show him. I was going to do a better job finding out about my natural parentage than any trained detective. I was going to find out everything about Clare Beecham's secret history and push it into his smart investigator's face. Him and Mr Po-faced Deedy. I'd show them how it should be done.

I hurried upstairs and paused outside Mrs Beecham's door.

I took a deep breath and reached for the door handle. Then turned it, firmly and decisively.

Nothing happened. The door was locked.

8

Mrs Beecham, I presume?

I knew it had to be Mrs Beecham arriving home when I caught sight of Pepper's antics in the hallway below. The dog was practically dancing on her hind legs. A dangerous trick when you're as seriously overweight as she is. And as if this weren't risky enough, she began throwing herself bodily at the door, howling like a wolf.

Then the door was open and Mrs Clare Beecham was standing in the hallway. And my heart gave such a violent lurch that I thought it would leave my body. I stood at the top of the stairs, undecided whether to laugh or cry, or run back to the bathroom and throw up.

The woman below me was a vision. Standing perfectly still and framed by morning sunlight, she was flawless. Like one of those glossy airbrushed pictures you find yourself staring at in *Hello!* magazine, wondering how anyone could possibly look that good after the age of sixteen.

She was roughly my height, but without the awkwardness. Her unusual height suited her and didn't she know it. She used it to great effect, allowing her cream, ankle-length coat cloak to hang from her shoulders. She had one of those smooth, unlined faces that defy ageing. She could have been anything from forty to sixty. Seventy even. It was impossible to tell. Her hair was ash-blond. Whether naturally or with the help of a bottle you also couldn't tell. It was pulled back severely from her high forehead, caught in a tight knot at the nape of her long slim neck. It was the type of hairdo that had you automatically smoothing your own unruly mane. Wishing you had taken the hairdresser's advice when she recommended a straightener, saying, 'Other than that, there isn't a lot you can do with it.' Bitch!

Not Mrs Beecham. She was every inch a lady. She looked as if she wouldn't know what the word bitch meant, except maybe at a Royal Dublin Society dog show.

Even her eye make-up was classy: understated and subtle; not a smudge in sight. It toned perfectly with her lipstick, which probably cost fifty pounds a wipe because it somehow managed to look glossy without being at all shiny.

And I stood at the top of the stairs looking like an escaped madwoman, the result of a night spent tossing and turning in anticipation of this moment, completely overwhelmed by this first sighting of my natural mother.

I'm not sure what I had been expecting. Maybe a wealthier version of my own mother. Someone who wore three strings of real pearls instead of a rolled-gold cross and chain. Someone who wore a cashmere jumper instead of a Dunne's Stores blouse that you always had to buy in a bigger size than you normally wear, because they're a bit scabby with the fabric, on account of their affordable prices.

I might have expected someone like Fiona's mother.

An extremely good-looking woman, but past it.

Mrs Beecham didn't look like anybody's mother. She reminded me of one of those ever virginal prima ballerinas you read about in the gossip columns. The ones who take up teaching only *after* they have broken the heart of every dancer in the company. Male and female.

Was this person really my mother?

I half dreaded the moment of recognition, when she would look up at me and gasp in shock.

'Hello, Peppa. Did you miss me darling?' A white-gloved hand reached out to stroke the slavering Pepper.

Then Jamie was beside her, dropping a crocodile skin case by her feet. 'Annie?' He beckoned to me.

I took a deep breath and practically fell down the stairs.

'This is Annie, Mother, she'll be staying with you.'

The ash-blond head turned a fraction of a centimetre. No more. 'How do you do, Annie? Take my coat, will you?' She threw a smile in my general direction and slipped the soft cashmere coat off her shoulders.

Jamie grabbed it before it hit the floor.

She swept into the library, Pepper trotting adoringly at her heels.

This was my mother?

'Annie? Annie?' Jamie shook my arm. 'Would you mind taking this?' He held out the coat.

'Jamie? Come along!' It was a royal command.

Then she was gone. He was gone. The library door closed behind them.

And my heart left my mouth and plummeted down into the depths.

The plan had been that she would have a little nap in her room before coming down to have lunch with me, so we could become acquainted over a leisurely meal. Penelope thought this would ensure a good start to our relationship, in fact, she had mapped out the whole day with a meticulous eye for detail.

And I had been more than happy to fall in with her arrangements.

Mrs Beecham had other ideas. And Mrs Beecham was a law unto herself. That became apparent pretty quickly.

She remained closeted with Jamie and Pepper in the big library, while I hung around outside, waiting to be invited in. When the door finally did open it was Rosie who was called. To discuss the available choices for lunch.

I didn't appear to be included.

Mrs Beecham requested a light lunch, on a tray, for herself and Jamie. Maybe even Pepper, for all I knew.

I ate in the kitchen with Rosie, who chatted away happily, seeing nothing amiss with this arrangement. Her only concern was for Mrs Beecham's health: 'She'll have to watch herself, I say. Broken bones don't heal all that quickly at her age. Different for a youngster. She'll have to be extra careful. Especially now that they have her on the new tablets for the blood pressure. A cousin of mine wasn't on them for a month when he dropped dead.'

'You mean the pills killed him?' I was alarmed.

'No! He forgot to take them! That's what I'm saying. She'll want to watch herself now that she's on so many. With the angina and all that. That's how people get mixed up. Having to take all them different pills. You look terrible, Annie.' She leaned close. 'Have you got your period, love?'

'No,' I said crossly.

'I can usually tell, you know. It's a gift. My mother had it as well.'

'Her period?' I asked peevishly.

'Oh, Annie. Would you stop it.' She giggled. Then she was serious again. 'She doesn't look that well to me.'

'Who?' It was difficult keeping up with Rosie's train of thought.

'Mrs Beecham.'

'Oh.'

'Something about the way she's holding that arm. All stiff and awkward.'

'It's in a sling, Rosie. Although she has it covered so beautifully with that silk scarf I didn't even notice it when she came in.'

'I'm talking about her other arm.'

'Please, Rosie, I have a bit of a headache.' I touched my temple.

'See, I knew. You *are* getting your period. I'll get you some aspirin, love.'

'Thank you.'

She counted them out into my hand. 'Take three. Two never work. You wouldn't want to mind what they say on these boxes.' She handed me a glass of water.

'Where was I? Oh, yes. Her doctor is a devil for the drugs. Pills for this, pills for that, pills for everything. And she never complains. The woman is a walking saint. Don't talk to me about Mother Teresa, Lord have mercy on her. Mrs Beecham is streets ahead of any nun. And of course, she always had great taste in clothes. See this dress, she gave me this. And my best coat. You know the one I was wearing this morning on account of her coming home? The woman is a saint. Now I'm not saying that his Lordship didn't deserve her, him being a High Court judge and all that, I'm not saying that, but the woman should be canonised.'

'Don't you have to be dead to be canonised?' My head was really hurting now.

'What? Oh, I know that, I'm just saying . . . The woman is a saint.'

And she continued saying it, right through the beef casserole and the chocolate gateau she had made in honour of Mrs Beecham's return. The gateau which had not been chosen as part of the library lunch.

The three aspirin didn't even make a dent in my headache.

And just when I thought I'd be forced to ram the salt cellar into Rosie's still happily chattering little mouth, Jamie came into the kitchen. 'Annie?' He draped an arm casually along the back of my chair, unaware that this simple gesture caused every hair on the back of my neck to stand to attention. 'Keep an eye on Mother, will you. Dr Moran flew home from London this morning to check her out. He says she's fine or he wouldn't risk discharging her, but she's still a little shaken from the fall. Although being Mother she won't complain.'

'She won't complain,' Rosie echoed. 'I've never known that woman to complain. She's a saint, that's what she is. A walking saint. We were just saying, weren't we, Annie, your mother should be canonised.'

Jamie looked at me in surprise.

I got to my feet, anxious to forestall any further quotes that might be attributed to me.

'No, don't get up.' The hand on my shoulder was gently pushing me back into the cushioned chair. 'Finish your lunch. She's sleeping now. You stay here and chat to Rosie. Our Rosie loves a chat, don't you, Rosie?' He sounded almost flirtatious.

'Oh, go way out of that with you,' Rosie blustered as coyly as if he had asked her to slip behind the rhododendrons for a quickie.

'I'll call back in a day or so, see how she's doing.' His smile encompassed both of us this time.

But he didn't call back in a day or so. A day or so means two days at the most, by my reckoning and it was Saturday morning before he appeared again. That was four whole days. And during that time I had a permanent tension headache and only saw Mrs Beecham eight or nine times – and two of those were when she had absolutely no choice because she wanted to put her hair up and needed another pair of hands, and Rosie wasn't around.

The woman clearly didn't want a companion. Or need one. I had obviously been foisted on her by her children. Which was a bit ironic. She was a solitary woman who wasn't prepared to share her time with anyone, least of all me.

I saw more of Rosie than I did of her. I saw more of Pepper. But then both of them seemed to like me a lot more than Mrs Beecham did. Three times on that first day she dismissed my offer of help, despite having a wrist in plaster. I hung around not knowing what to do, drinking endless cups of tea with Rosie, who was kind to me but she guarded her duties jealously. When I tried to take an afternoon tea tray up to Mrs Beecham's room we almost came to blows.

'That's my job!' Rosie pouted, leaving me standing in the kitchen without even Pepper for company, because she was also upstairs at her mistress's feet.

I was called, once, out of sheer necessity, when Mrs Beecham had difficulty closing an extra long zip that got caught in the back of her Paul Costello dress.

That's when I offered to pin up her hair. 'I could do that for you,' I said when I saw how she was struggling.

She sat without speaking, as I pinned one long strand after another into a tighter French pleat than she could have managed, independent as she was.

'That's fine, you can go now, Annie.' She dismissed me the moment the hairpins were in place. 'No, leave that. Don't fuss,' she added, when I began tidying away her face creams and the collection of make-up brushes that cluttered her dressing table.

I left without a word. Mrs Beecham wasn't someone you argued with. She certainly wasn't a woman you could ever think of as your mother. I felt no connection to her whatsoever. Apart from that first surge of emotion when I saw her standing in the doorway there was nothing. She was just an employer. And a pretty stand-offish one at that. Maybe Gerry was right and it had been a mistake coming here? Maybe you can't resurrect the past.

By day three I was prepared to do anything, as much to relieve the boredom as to forge a relationship with her.

When she passed me on the landing as if I were invisible and stopped to greet Pepper with a warm pat I knew I was on a loser.

I had come here with a head full of fanciful notions. Dreams of how things would work out. I had pictured myself sitting reading to her, in her book-filled room, while the moving strains of a Mahler composition washed over us, causing her to have a sudden warm motherly intuition: *I know who you are! You're my child! Flesh of my flesh. Come to me.*

As if.

Well, she did play Mahler. And Beethoven. And Mozart. But woe betide anyone who dared interrupt her while she listened to her favourite composers.

I found myself resorting to childish pretexts to try to initiate a conversation with her: 'Did you call me, Mrs Beecham? I could have sworn I heard you call.'

Most of the time she didn't even reply, just froze me with a look. And I would creep back down the stairs to the kitchen. Back to Rosie and her happy chatter.

When Rosie left for the day I went to my room to watch TV, and sometimes I even fell asleep watching it, while some smiling weatherman told me that there was a cold sharp front due in from the Atlantic.

9

Unhappy families

On the morning of day four Penelope arrived with the happy gang. Only today they didn't look very happy. 'How are things, Annie? Is she getting out at all?' Penelope looked worried.

I shook my head gloomily.

The children gathered round the kitchen table waiting to be fed. They were distinctly out of sorts, bickering, picking on each other, and even Rosie was a bit down in the dumps.

The only happy member of the troupe was Rags, who took up where he had left off with Pepper.

It wasn't remotely like the happy brunch scene the Monday before Mrs Beecham arrived home.

'She hardly leaves her room.' Rosie emptied the dishwasher. 'All her meals have to be carried up to her. Two flights of stairs? It's no laughing matter, I can tell you.'

I was a bit on edge, probably because I had a headache. 'Don't exaggerate, Rosie. It's only one and a half flights.'

'Is that all?' She slammed the dishwasher closed although she had only half emptied it. 'Well, it seems like a lot more when you're carrying that heavy tray, believe you me.'

'I've offered to carry it for you. You won't let me.'

She sniffed. 'It's my job to see to her meals.'

'Yes, but not necessarily to carry them up to her.'

'Oh, for goodness' sake, you two are not going to fall out over who carries a silly tray, are you?'

'It's not just the tray,' Rosie said. 'I'm making a point here. She should be eating her meals downstairs. In the dining room. I mean why do we call it a dining room at all, if nobody is going to eat in it? May as well call it a dust trap and be done with it.' She climbed on to a chair to put the dishes in the high press, ignoring my offer of help. 'And another thing, she's not getting any fresh air. It's not healthy, all that sitting around, with her head stuck in a book. Reading. Reading. That's all she ever does.'

'She listens to music.' I found myself defending Mrs Beecham, I don't know why. She hadn't shown me the slightest courtesy. 'And she does her jigsaws.'

'That's another thing,' Rosie said. 'Mrs Regan threatened to walk out yesterday. She said if another one of those shaggin' jigsaw bits gets sucked up her Hoover she won't be responsible.'

'Could I speak to you in the library, Annie?' Penelope sighed.

'How is the woman supposed to keep the place clean with a blocked-up Hoover, that's what I'd like to know? She's been cleaning this house for ten years and now she has to put up with shaggin' jigsaws,' Rosie called after us.

'Thank you, Rosie.' Penelope dismissed her. 'You stay there, children,' she ordered Simon and Amy who were about to follow us.

'I want to see the shaggin' jigsaws,' little Simon pleaded.

The big library felt chilly after the steamy warmth of the kitchen. Penelope turned worried eyes towards me. 'I was the one who suggested the jigsaws,' she confessed, a little embarassed. 'I thought they might be a good idea.'

'They are.' I smiled. 'She enjoys them.'

'How do you think she's doing, Annie?'

'I . . . wouldn't worry. She is a bit solitary. But she's an intelligent woman.' Again I found myself defending her. 'She uses her balcony a lot,' I added quickly. 'So she's not going short of fresh air.'

'So you don't see any cause for concern?'

'Er . . . Well, I've only been here a few days. I don't know what she was like before.'

Penelope's chin shot upwards. 'The question I'm asking is should we be insisting that she get out and about more? Take some exercise?'

I almost laughed in her face. The idea of anyone forcing Mrs Beecham to do something was the funniest thing I had ever heard. Nobody could force Mrs Beecham to do anything. You were lucky to get a word out before she froze you with a look.

Penelope called the children, now, and ushered them upstairs. 'Say hello to Nana, children,' I heard her say.

Little Simon held back at the door. 'Want to go home,' he cried.

'Now, Simon, behave. Where are your manners?'

'Want to play with the shaggin' jigsaw,' he said tearfully.

The door closed, then, so I don't know if he ever got to play with the shaggin' jigsaw, but ten minutes later, when Penelope herded them downstairs again, his face was stained with tears. 'We are off home, Annie. I'll leave Mummy in your capable hands.' Penelope's expression gave nothing away. 'You have a good head on your shoulders. I know I can trust your judgement.'

She disappeared off to her twenty-acre haven in County Wicklow, leaving me reaching for the bottle of aspirin. Mrs Beecham, in the meantime, was locked in her room again. Listening to Beethoven. Or maybe it was Mozart this time. Hard to tell when you were all the way down in the kitchen.

It was astute little Rosie who became concerned about all the analgesics I was taking. 'You know what you need, Annie?'

I was afraid to ask.

'Exercise. You should start walking Pepper. That dog is getting fat as a pig.'

So every morning, after breakfast, Pepper and I took to walking the tree-lined roads of Foxrock, while the woman I'd been hoping to bond with remained closeted in her room, a book in one hand, the remote control of her hi-fi system in the other.

My life was not on track.

I nearly missed Jamie the next time he called. Fortunately, it was raining hard that morning so I had decided against taking Pepper for her walk, because there was no let-up in the heavy downpour.

I was still checking the sky hopefully when Jamie arrived and in the time it took him to walk from his car to the front door he got drenched.

In my experience walking in the rain tends not to improve most men. Neither their temperament, nor their looks. They end up crotchety and out of sorts, with red noses or shiny pink faces and lank hair that looks as if it could do with a good conditioning rinse.

Jamie proved to be the exception to all this. In his

long Sherwood-green mac and dark hair that some-how managed to curl without a trace of frizz, he was practically Byronic.

Whenever I had thought about him during the previous few days I had told myself that he couldn't possibly be as handsome as I recalled. Nobody could. I convinced myself that because I had met him at a particularly vulnerable time in my life I had exag-gerated his attractiveness. In fact, nervous as I was about meeting the Beechams, I would probably have considered Quasimodo to be borderline shaggable, if he had shown me as much attention as Jamie had.

But one look at Jamie as he stood dripping in the hallway put paid to that silly notion. Here was a man who would have glittered in any circumstances. He was a prince among men.

'Let me take your wet mac,' I offered, for want of something more inspired to say.

'Hey. You're not the butler around here.' He laughed.

My heart did a little hop and a skip. 'Please?' Handling his wet mac was as intimate as we were ever likely to get, given our shared genes. Unless we moved to the Appalachian Mountains.

'You're too nice for your own good, Annie.' He held out the dripping coat, his eyes promising things they could never deliver. Not legally, anyway.

Uncomfortably aware of his watching eyes, I carried it to the kitchen to dry out, not once giving in to the temptation to bury my head in its rain-soaked warmth.

A languid little wave and Jamie disappeared up the stairs, his long legs making short work of the wide steps as he hurried, all too quickly, out of sight.

I waited a full sixteen minutes and twenty-one seconds before following him. I knew the exact number of seconds, because I counted them on the big wall clock in the kitchen, which had a bright-orange second hand to help Rosie with her timing, when she baked pies, broiled steaks and parboiled four different types of vegetables all at once. Which was exactly what she was doing now. Which meant that she couldn't possibly have found time to collect Mrs Beecham's breakfast tray.

Mrs Beecham didn't like me to appear in her room for no reason. She could be quite shirty about it. But she could hardly object to me going in to collect a tray. I tapped lightly on the door and went in without waiting for permission.

'You could have left that for Rosie.' She frowned when I went straight for the tray.

'Mother's right, Annie.' Jamie smiled his slow, sweet smile. 'That's not your job.'

'Rosie's busy. And I have nothing else to do.' I took my time stacking the little china plates, one on top of the other. Tidying up the fruit dish. Sweeping crumbs on to the tray. I was so adept I might have been a trained waitress and not many office managers can say that.

'I don't think Annie is very happy here.' Mrs Beecham spoke without looking at me. 'I suspect she would prefer to be busy. I'm far too idle for her liking.'

'Oh, no, that's not true. I mean, I'm very happy. Very, very happy.' I startled myself with my insistence.

'Oh.' She sounded surprised. 'That's good, then.'

Pathetically grateful for even this tiny hint of

96

approval, I became wildly hyper and started to tidy everything in sight, including some of her books, which were scattered about the room. She may have been a voracious reader but she showed little respect for books, throwing them aside for either Rosie or Mrs Regan to pick up.

Jamie had been standing by the window when I walked in. Frowning out at the weather, as if he wasn't at all pleased with it, although it hadn't seemed to bother him when he first arrived. Now he looked as if the bad weather was just one burden too many for his perfect shoulders to bear.

He picked up a book and brought it to where I was meticulously arranging its peers in alphabetical order, even to the extent of taking down a whole shelf-full and starting again from scratch. I reckoned this would get me at least another five minutes.

He handed me the book. I checked the author's initials before making space for it.

'P' for Proust. Mrs Beecham wasn't into John Grisham, then?

Jamie watched me arrange Proust next to Orwell, his eyes sad. 'Order seems to elude me for some reason,' he said. 'Maybe I should steal you away, Annie, have you straighten out my life. Do you suppose Annie could do that for me, Mother? Would that make *you* happy?'

'Don't be facile, Jamie.' Mrs Beecham's tone was icy.

'It was just a thought.' He turned to give me a mischievous little grin.

My face went scarlet.

Were we bonding, Jamie and I? Flirting? I was so out of practice it was hard to distinguish between the two. Except that when his fingers brushed against mine as he handed me the next book I felt a decidedly un-sisterly tingle. And it didn't stop at my fingers. My flush deepened.

Mrs Beecham shot me a glacial look. 'Take my tray please, Annie. I presume that's what you came in for?'

She didn't spare Jamie either. 'Have you nothing better to do than mope around here all day disrupting the staff?'

If anything, she was even more annoyed with him. She clearly didn't approve of her son fraternising with the hired help.

I could fantasise all I wanted. Pretend as much as I liked. The truth was Mrs Clare Beecham was an out-and-out frozen-faced snob. She probably considered Proust a lowbrow. If she were to see the romantic fiction in my room she'd have palpitations. Although maybe not. I think you have to be a warm-blooded creature to have palpitations.

I picked up the breakfast tray and legged it before she could really upset me. Humiliate me even further in front of Jamie.

He gave me a conspiratorial wink as he closed the door behind me.

10

Gerry's office

Gerry's cramped office was even more shambolic than I recalled from my one and only previous visit. That was the day before Sam and Fiona left for Cuba. Sam had been quite emotional that day, having to constantly clear his throat as he said goodbye to Gerry and his staff.

'It's all this damn dust,' he had grinned, pointing to the grimy filing cabinets.

I found myself staring at them now as I lied blatantly to Gerry.

'All in all, things are going quite well in Haney Road,' I smiled, avoiding his eyes.

'*Quite* well? What does that mean?' He pushed a pile of papers to one side to make room for a couple of styrofoam cups.

I took a long slow sip of the grey coffee. I didn't actually want the atrocious stuff but sipping it gave me a chance to think. Gerry was always so damn sharp. Hard to pull the wool over his eyes. 'I could almost say I'm on the verge of a breakthrough,' I boasted.

I could say it, of course, but I'd be lying. But what the hell. If I told Gerry the truth he'd only be rushing over to Haney Road on a big white charger. 'Any day now I should know my full history.'

'Are you serious?'

'Any day now,' I was becoming an accomplished liar.

Gerry's office assistant interrupted us. 'I have to go home for an hour, Gerry. It's my da again, but I put the answering machine on. I'll sort out the calls when I get back. Hiya, Annie.' She tilted her bright-purple head to look at me. Well, her actual head wasn't purple but her hair was. Last time we met it was green.

'Hello, Sandra. How are the wedding plans going?' I had only met her once before but the whole country knew Sandra was preparing for her wedding. It was probably on the Internet.

'Great! Things are . . .'

'We'll see you later, Sandra,' Gerry cut in.

She tossed her head and left, her high-heeled sandals tapping a loud rhythm on the worn linoleum.

I turned to look after her. White sling-back sandals? In February?

'So what have you found out?' Gerry sat on his desk squashing the pile of papers.

'Sandra will get chilblains if she doesn't wear tights in this weather. Does she really think a fake tan can keep your legs warm?'

'Never mind Sandra's fake tan. What's happening with the Beechams?' Gerry wouldn't be sidetracked.

But how could I tell him that after spending nearly ten days as Mrs Beecham's companion I still hadn't managed to breach the wall she surrounded herself with. I hadn't once had a proper conversation with her. Or even an improper one.

It wasn't for want of trying. Despite being totally intimidated, I still made enthusiastic efforts to get close to her. One morning, before Rosie could beat me to it, I went into her room, handed her her morning cup of lemon tea, plumped up her pillows and asked her what she'd like for breakfast. Without once letting my smile slip below sixty watts.

She told me to get out and not to dare barge into her room again. Until I was sent for.

'She'll soften up. Don't worry,' Rosie comforted me with fresh croissants and a mountain of oatmeal cookies.

'How come you can walk into her room every morning, Rosie?'

'Ah, but that's my job, love.'

So what was my job, then? What had Penelope said that first day? *Keep an eye on her?* Jolly her along? Pretty vague job descriptions.

Especially to someone used to chasing the clock in the busy Pussy Grub office. A place where you were expected to remain sharply focused. Where one wrongly filed letter could mean the sack. Where a single misplaced figure could result in the loss of orders worth hundreds of thousands of pounds.

'So how does she treat you?' Gerry persisted, his eyes suspicious.

'Fine.' I squirmed. Then I chuckled. 'Penelope's children have started calling me Auntie Annie.'

'Auntie Annie? Where the hell did that come from?'

'It's just something kids do when they like you. They call you auntie. It's a compliment.'

'Is that a fact?' He didn't sound convinced. 'And you're happy with that, are you?'

'Of course. Don't you think it's a step forward, the kids calling me auntie?'

'Oh, sure. Better than an affidavit, that.' He shook his head. 'Have you made any real progress?' He caught my hurt expression. 'Apart from being called auntie, I mean?'

'Give us a chance.' I was starting to get really cheesed off now. 'I haven't been there a wet weekend yet. Did you expect me to have a complete family history by now? A potted biography of Clare Beecham?'

'No. But I thought the idea was to move in, find out what you could and then bail out.'

'Yes, but not all in a matter of hours,' I snapped. 'I'm not the bloody SAS, you know.'

He didn't laugh. 'Just don't get too cosy, that's all I'm saying.'

Cosy? In Haney Road? Chance would be a fine thing. The only warmth in that house came from the Stanley stove in the kitchen. And maybe Rosie, when she was in the mood.

'I'm not one of your detectives, Gerry, working under orders. I don't have to send you a written report every five minutes. I'm there on personal business. To find out what I can about my parentage. But it's not easy. I may be blood related to these people but they're hard to get close to. I can't just blurt out who I am.'

'Why not?'

'Because! Because she obviously kept me secret for some reason. I can't just humiliate her by making a sudden announcement, can I? Anyway, it's probably better that we are getting to know each other a little before I break the news.'

'Maybe. Just don't lose sight of why you're there. Don't get so involved with the family that you forget why you moved in, in the first place.'

'Oh, you mean the great room? Well, that certainly lived up to expectations.' I gave a little grin. It didn't fool Gerry.

'I see. So why do I get the feeling that nothing else has? What's going on over there?'

'There's nothing *going on*. Except that you're making me neurotic, asking all these stupid questions.' My head was starting to pound. 'So you can just feck off, Gerry Dunning. I'm not coming here again if all you're going to do is grill me.'

'Sorry, Annie. I didn't mean to *grill* you. Drink your coffee.'

'I *love* Haney Road!' I hissed through clenched teeth and then almost choked on the vile coffee.

'OK. OK. Calm down. I'm just concerned about you. Can't a friend be concerned?'

'No!'

'Christ, Annie, you're a very difficult woman.'

The outside door slammed and Barney's tall, gangly figure came hurtling into the office.

'Barney, how many times have I told you to knock? I could have been in the middle of a confidential discussion here.'

I thought we were.

Barney leaned back to knock on the open door. He was wearing a navy donkey jacket, which was splattered with dry cement. 'Knock, knock.' He grinned cheekily. 'How are you doin', Annie? Giving the boss a hard time, are you?'

'I'll be giving you a hard time if you don't get that Dillion report done by tomorrow morning,' Gerry said.

'That effin' Dillion.' Barney made a face. 'If you want my opinion he's nothing more than a double-dealing old shite.'

'I don't want your opinion, Barney, I want an impartial report on the safety aspects of that building site.'

'Well, I can tell you now that they're non-existent. He's breaking every safety regulation in the book.'

'Save it for your report.'

'See what I have to put up with here, Annie? Think yourself lucky you don't have to work with Attila the Hun here.'

The fax in the front office suddenly rumbled into life. Gerry hurried out to it.

'Is he really that tough?' I asked Barney.

'On himself, he is. But he's the best fucking detective I've ever worked with. And don't quote me on that, or I'll have to kill you,' he warned.

We both started to giggle.

Gerry came back waving a fax. 'From Declan. He can't get back before Friday. Some problem with the bloody ferry. So that's the end of our court evidence.'

'Can't he fax the evidence to you?' I asked.

'He'd have a bit of trouble putting a thousand gross of smuggled cigarettes through a fax machine.' Barney laughed. 'Besides, they're not smuggled until they actually try to get them past Customs. We had a big debate over that once. Is it illegal to . . . ?'

'You get that bloody report written, Barney. And will you stop encouraging him, Annie. I'm running a detective agency here, not a debating society.'

Barney moved to let him get back to his desk. But he turned awkwardly so the heavily cemented donkey jacket swung against the styrofoam cup on the desk. It knocked it flying, spilling dark coffee all over the already squashed papers. Barney made a grab at the cup but only managed to knock the phone to the floor. It hit the lino with a bang that split the handset in two.

Barney and I watched in horrified fascination as the

back of the handset slid across the floor and disappeared under a heavy filing cabinet.

Gerry threw the fax on to the desk in exasperation. It dropped straight into the widening pool of coffee.

'Sweet living Jesus! Give me strength! I'm surrounded by fools and incompetents.' I thought Gerry would explode.

Barney and I had to cover our mouths to stifle our uncontrollable laughter.

11

Up the garden path

After even a few short hours in the detective agency I dreaded going back to Haney Road. Despite Gerry doing a fair imitation of a frustrated pit bull there had at least been a bit of life in his office. A bit of craic. In fact, Barney and I had laughed so much that Gerry threatened to make us pay for the broken phone. 'I'm not running a glee club here!' he stormed.

That was enough to set us off again. And despite himself Gerry joined in, even though he was still shaking his head in disbelief at the havoc Barney could inflict on a small, cramped office.

Back in Haney Road nothing had changed. Mrs Beecham sat, frozen-faced as ever, every line of her body going rigid when I spilled the tiniest drop of tea on her skirt as I handed her a brimming cup. Even passing her the biscuits was an ordeal. And smiling was a complete waste of time. I told myself that it would take a flaming blowtorch to get through the wall of ice she surrounded herself with.

And still, like a fool, I persevered. When I caught her irately searching for a piece of jigsaw to complete the cloudless horizon in a sunny seascape, I reached over her shoulder to hand her what appeared to be the missing piece of sky. It was already in her grasp when I realised that it was more likely a piece of blue sea. I was on the brink of snatching it back when she slotted it neatly into place. Into the blue sky.

Luckily I wasn't expecting to be thanked. But at least she didn't tell me to get out. Flushed with success I daringly handed her another difficult piece of the puzzle and pointed. She fitted it into place without comment.

And before we knew it we were filling in the seascape together. In quiet harmony. Without exchanging a single word.

Then I made my fatal mistake. 'Isn't this fun?' I said gleefully.

Pepper and I were both chucked out. We walked down the stairs together both completely despondent.

Pepper ran off into the kitchen where Rosie was having a marathon baking session, and I was about to follow her when I heard Francesca's noisy Land Rover chugging up the driveway. It says a lot for my frame of mind that the sound actually cheered me up a bit. Francesca could at least be guaranteed to bring some excitement into the house, even if she did persist in treating me like some lower life form.

I opened the front door, a welcoming smile at the ready. After Mrs Beecham's studied coldness even Francesca's thoughtless arrogance could provide light relief. 'Good afternoon, Francesca.'

She swept past me like a whirlwind, barely pausing to throw a smelly waxed coat at me. 'She's in her room, I assume?'

It was what's known as a rhetorical question. From anyone else that might simply mean that it didn't require an answer. Coming from Francesca it meant that it didn't require an answer from anyone with a lower social standing than the queen.

I was tempted to ask mischievously, 'Do you mean *our* mother?' But I didn't.

'Fetch me some coffee. Black,' she called over her shoulder.

'Yes, Ma'am. Certainly, Ma'am.' I made a mock curtsy and threw the coat at the hall stand. It fell short, landing in a heap on the floor. I left it there. I wasn't her skivvy. I was no one's skivvy. Although anyone seeing the way I behaved around here, with my pathetic attempts at ingratiating myself with Mrs Beecham, might say different.

Had I lost all pride?

My temper rising, I picked up the wax coat, and impulsively draped it around my shoulders, then strode out the door. Francesca's Land Rover was in its usual parking space, the front of it half hidden in the shrubbery, the keys still in the ignition. For one mad moment I considered jumping into it and driving away. Mooning the local constabulary. *Stolen, officer? What do you mean? It's my sister's vehicle.*

I walked around the side of the house, deliberately leaving the metal gate swinging open. It was a small rebellion, but better than nothing.

The back garden was damp and chilly, yet still more inviting than the house. Possibly because it was a Beecham-free zone right now. I hugged the coat around me and followed the flagged pathway to the most sheltered spot in the garden. My version of running away. There was a low stone bench here, covered in a thin cloak of moss after the long winter. This wouldn't please Mrs Beecham. Nothing was allowed to grow here without her permission.

'Francesca?' a voice called from behind me. Jamie was coming down the pathway. His eyes widened in surprise when I turned. 'Annie? I could have sworn you were . . .'

Francesca? It wasn't that dark. Not even proper twilight yet.

'I thought you were Francesca. Isn't that her coat? Do you know you walk exactly like her? Long strides, head in the air.' He laughed.

He must have been drinking. Or doing drugs. If I seriously thought I walked that arrogantly I'd kill myself.

'I saw her Land Rover out front. Lacerating the hedge, as usual.' His eyes twinkled.

'She's upstairs. With your mother.' I was deliberately offhand.

He didn't even notice. 'Perfect,' he said, flashing his most charming smile. 'I was hoping I might get some time alone with you.'

I was immediately contrite. Jamie was a very popular man and he wanted to spend time alone with me? There had to be hundreds of more interesting people he could choose to be with. Well, dozens. Certainly there'd be no shortage of women. Especially if he took their hand and looked at them the way he was now looking at me. I was so flattered I didn't even care that he thought I walked like Francesca.

I didn't even try to shorten my steps as he led me over to the stone bench. It was as damp as I expected, but the moss was soft and anyway I had never believed all those old wives' tales about damp stone giving you piles.

'Annie?' His face was pale in the fading twilight, making him appear even more Byronic than ever.

'Jamie?' I tried not to sound pathetic.

He leaned closer, his expression becoming intense. 'I'm going away, Annie. I'm going to live abroad.'

As he moved towards me my heart had taken a sudden skyward leap. It fell back to earth now with a dull disappointing splat. Like birdshit on your shoulder. 'Abroad?' I repeated like a moron.

'Paris.'

'Oh. France?' I said as if there was some danger that he might be referring to Paris, Turkey.

He was holding my hand between both of his now. 'A friend of mine is hoping to arrange another exhibition of my work there. My paintings enjoy a certain popularity in Paris.'

'They do?' I tried not to sound surprised. After all, French people are reputed to be a law unto themselves, why shouldn't they like paintings of obese women with three breasts?

'Can I ask you to do something for me, Annie.'

His eyes were dark pools of temptation as he pressed my hand against his warm thigh. I could hardly breathe. 'Ask me.'

'I want you to take care of Mother for me. Will you do that for me, Annie? I know she has my sisters but they are too taken up with their own busy lives. You're different. I know I can trust you to stay with her. Not go gadding about, forgetting your responsibilities to your employer. Will you promise me, Annie?'

I was too shocked to speak. I just sat there draped in Francesca's wax coat feeling the damp from the stone bench seeping into my bones, possibly laying the foundations for painful piles for many years to come.

Whenever I had allowed myself to think about Jamie I had been concerned that our growing bond might draw us into a whirling vortex of incestuous lust, from which there would be no escape. And all he had wanted was a companion. For his mother.

I pulled my hand free and ran down the long garden, Francesca's coat billowing out behind me. I ran until I couldn't go any further. Unless if I climbed into the garden next door. And it wasn't as if I didn't consider it, even though the wall had to be seven foot high and was probably alive with creepy-crawlies under its cloak of variegated ivy.

'Annie?' He was behind me. 'Have I upset you?'

No, I'm completely ecstatic, I wanted to say. So happy that you think of me as another Rosie. Only taller. And thirty years younger. Well, twenty.

'If you are upset about Mother, don't be. She isn't ill. I just want to go away, knowing that she's in capable hands.'

Capable? How dare he? I didn't want to be capable. I wanted to be sensuous. Sexy. Irresistible. 'How dare you call me capable!' I said.

He stared at me for a second, then burst into laughter. 'Oh, Annie, you're priceless! So funny!'

I didn't want to be funny. Woody Allen is funny. I wanted to be seriously irresistible.

'You're so unfailingly cheerful.' He smiled.

I burst into tears. That wiped the smile off his face.

And I wept buckets, and wondered for the umpteenth time why, if there had to be an opposite sex, did they have to be men? Surely with all the resources at his disposal God could have come up with a better plan than that?

I buried my face in the cool, damp ivy, hardly giving a thought to the creepy-crawlies.

And then Jamie did something completely despicable. He turned me round, his hands gentle as a woman's, and kissed me. Like a brother.

I was so full of rage I grabbed him and kissed him full on the mouth. I opened my lips and waited for the hot surge of passion that I knew would carry us both away on a rising tide of lust and desire. But nothing happened. Well, the kiss was pleasant enough. Even though Jamie did appear to be a little shocked by my ardour. But there were no fireworks. No rockets springing to life. No sudden rush of blood to the groin. His nor mine.

I opened my eyes to make sure it was Jamie I was kissing. It was all right. And he was gorgeous as ever, even with his eyes screwed up and his mouth all puckered. But the kiss was a complete damp squib. In fact, it had roughly the same erotic appeal as his paintings of triple-breasted women.

He stepped back to look at me. A tiny victorious glow in his eyes, I thought. 'So.' He gave me a little teasing smile.

'I'll be getting your mother's tea now, Jamie,' I said. 'Rosie has a lot on today.'

I decided that it was time to approach Mrs Beecham with my story. Apart from the disappointing episode in the garden, which made me anxious to move on, she was always fractionally less icy after a visit from Jamie. And Rosie had served the three of them late afternoon tea in the library in front of a blazing fire.

If one of Rosie's fires couldn't thaw her I don't know what could. Either way, I was going to confront her and have done with it. Only then could I get on with my life.

I heard Jamie leave first. Then Francesca hurried

away, impatient as ever to return to the waiting fetlocks or warlock or whatever it was that kept her so entranced with rural Kildare that she couldn't tear herself away from it for more than an hour a week.

I paced the hallway for a couple of minutes, working out the best way to bring up the matter of my parentage. Maybe a little harmless question first. About the late lamented judge. Leading into a carefully worded enquiry about her children when they were first born. Were they good babies? Did they sleep well? How many did she have? I could then gently announce who I was. It was foolproof.

It wasn't as if I was going to burst in and shout, 'Surprise, surprise, here's something you'd never guess. I'm the daughter you gave away thirty years ago.'

Even Gerry had warned me to be careful about the actual words I used. 'I'm not telling you to interrogate the woman,' he said. 'Take a sensitive approach. That guarantees best results with women.' This from the man whose wife had run off? 'Say something complimentary about her late husband,' he advised.

I walked into the library without knocking and stood in front of the fire.

Mrs Beecham looked up in surprise. But she didn't seem too cross. Obviously the brandy had been opened this afternoon.

I gestured at the big oil painting that practically covered the chimney breast. 'I'm forever admiring this,' I lied. 'He was a very handsome man.'

'Do you think so?' She lowered her book, a little frown distorting her smooth brow.

'Oh, yes. Very handsome indeed. Extremely so.'

The man was the spitting image of Stalin, on a bad-hair day. Or maybe after sending millions to the gulags.

She tilted her head to peer up at the severe face. 'He *was* admired for his fine posture.'

'I can see why.' He looked like a martinet. 'I bet he spoiled the children every chance he got? A man with a face like that.'

'Actually, he was quite strict with them. Couldn't wait for them to grow up. He didn't like small children very much. Or babies, for that matter.'

The bastard.

I watched her closely, prepared to back off at the first sign of irritation. There was none. I got a swift surge of self-confidence. It was like being drunk. Or high on something. 'He didn't like children? And yet you had *three*? *Three* children? It must have been difficult having *three* children.'

Her frown deepened. Oh God, I'd overstepped the mark. 'I had help.'

Careful, Annie. One wrong word now and she'll order you out. 'Would you have liked to have more?' I said gently.

'More help?'

'More children.' I gave a nervous little laugh.

'Do you have a particular interest in children?' Her face was now developing its familiar frosty coating.

'No. None whatsoever! I just . . . I only came in for the tray.' I picked up the tea tray and darted out the door and back to the kitchen, my blouse stuck to my spineless back with perspiration.

'You're white as a sheet.' Rosie took her head out of the oven. 'Sit down, love. I'll make you a nice cup of tea.' She pulled off her pink Marigolds.

A nice cup of tea was Rosie's cure-all. From hypertension to herpes, to a woman clearly on the brink of a panic attack, a nice cup of tea was your man. 'I've just had coffee, thanks,' I managed to say.

'No wonder you look pale. Coffee rots the liver. Plays havoc with the nerves. *And* raises the blood pressure.' She lowered her voice. 'That's why *she* shouldn't be drinking it. But will she listen? Oh, no, she knows best.' She pursed her lips in disapproval. 'It was probably all that coffee that killed the judge. He was forever at it. First thing in the morning until last thing at night. And look what happened to him!' The tone was ominous.

'What did happen, Rosie?'

'Cancer. Of the liver.'

'I thought he died of a heart attack?'

'He did in the end but it was the cancer that had him on the way out, at the time. Riddled with it, he was. Yellow in the face. Like a Turk. Even the palms of his hands changed colour. Like Sunlight soap, they were. He reminded me of a woman I knew who got a terrible dose of yellow jaundice in the war.'

'Were they devastated when he died?'

'Well, I shouldn't say, but it was probably a relief more than anything,' she whispered.

'From the pain.' I nodded.

'From him.'

She said it so softly that I wasn't altogether sure I heard her correctly.

'Led them a dog's life, he did. You can't do this and you can't do that. And remember who you are. Remember who your father is. Especially poor Jamie. He never gave that lad a minute's peace. Always on his back, he was. The law. The law. His son had to be the best barrister going. Jamie hated the law. No wonder he went funny.'

She saw my puzzled look. 'You know. And

throwing away all that education to paint fat women!' She shivered. 'The judge was barely cold when he was out buying paint and canvas. But everyone to their own, I say. Not that he's any great shakes at it. But he's happy. And isn't that the main thing. Not having to go to all them psychiatrists any more.'

Her voice became even lower. 'Imagine having two of your children under a psychiatrist at the one time?'

'Which two?'

'Rosie?' Mrs Beecham was calling. 'Rosie? Could you see to this fire, please?'

'Her ladyship calls.' Rosie winked. 'Wait here. I'll be back.' She giggled happily. 'I always wanted to say that. Did you ever see Arnold Schwarzenegger in that film, what was it called again? *I'll be back*,' she said in deep macho tones, then hurried into the library, smirking happily to herself.

12

The snapshot

'Jesus, they sound like a right pack of nutcases to me.'
Gerry leaned back in his office chair.

'They are not. Mildly eccentric, maybe, but hardly
nutcases.'

'Annie, Fiona is mildly eccentric. My ex-wife is
mildly eccentric, choosing to run off with that Army
bugger. These people are feckin' nutcases.'

'They aren't!'

'Why do you insist on defending them? What have
they ever done for you?'

'Why do you keep attacking them?' It came out so
loud that Sandra stopped talking in the other office,
which was only divided from Gerry's by sheets of
timberboard.

'I knew this whole business would end in tears. I
could see it coming. The minute I gave you that
address I knew we were heading for a slippery slope.'

'What are you talking about? Everything is going
perfectly. Exactly as planned.'

'Oh, give over, Annie. If things were going to plan
you'd already be out of there. You'd have all the
answers you need. You'd know why she gave you
away. Why you ended up living in Fernhill Crescent
with the McHughs, instead of playing happy families
with the Beechams in that great big mausoleum on
Haney Road.'

I sulked. 'We can't all be trained detectives. Getting instant answers. Some of us have to feel our way into a situation first. That takes time.'

'OK. OK. I don't want a row. I just hate to see you being used.'

'Mrs Beecham isn't using me. I do nothing in that house. If anything she's . . .'

'A right nutcase?'

Despite myself I had to laugh. Still, it didn't seem right to hear someone else bad-mouthing her. That was my prerogative. 'Don't judge her, Gerry. She can't help being what she is.'

'And what's that?'

'Well, I suppose, a bit . . . a bit stand-offish. But always in a refined way.'

'She gave you away, Annie. That wasn't very *refined* of her.'

I wanted to agree with him. Tell him he was right. Tell him I would leave Haney Road straight away. That living there was more than I could stand. That it was so bloody stressful I was waking up every morning with nervous halitosis. *And* a killer headache.

He must have read my mind. 'Just leave, Annie. Cut your losses. It's obviously stressing you out, having to cope with those people. And to what end? You don't have to confront her if you don't want to. A few weeks ago you didn't even know the woman existed. You don't need her in your life.' He leaned across the desk. 'Do you trust me?'

He looked so serious, so strong and manly. I knew he'd never ask me to mind his mother. Well, she was dead, but if she were alive.

'*Do* you trust me, Annie?'

'You know I do.' He really had the most

unbelievably sexy eyes. Much nicer than Jamie's. *And* he had longer lashes. And the kind of mouth that turns up at the corners as if a smile is never far away. Jamie's mouth had a sort of downward tilt to it. A bit on the sulky side, now I came to think of it. And I know some women find that attractive but only if being a good kisser comes with it. Jamie was useless at . . .

'Are you listening, Annie?' Gerry asked.

'Yes. What did you say?'

'I said get away from the Beechams, they're bad news. Make some excuse and leave.' His hand was on mine now. You might even say caressing it. Well, patting it where it lay on the desk.

'I will. Soon.'

I was tempted to run around the desk to put my head on his shoulder. Instead, I had to be satisfied with admiring his long slim fingers. I was trying to figure why they looked different today when I realised that his wedding ring was missing. It was gone! He must have thrown it in the bin at last. That's where his marriage had belonged for the past four years according to Barney, when I had cautiously questioned him about it.

'Do I have your word on that, Annie?'

'What? Well, I . . . OK.'

I was looking at his face now. At the high cheek-bones that were almost Slavic in their pronounced sharpness. Just slanted enough to be sexy without looking overtly Mongolian.

'Are you listening to me, Annie?'

His eyes were only inches from mine. 'Gerry?'

'What?

'Do you have you any Slav blood?'

'What do you mean . . . like in a phial?' He laughed.

I shook my head impatiently. 'Oh, never mind.'

Sandra came bustling in. 'You've got an hour and twenty minutes to get to Rosslare, Gerry,' she said, indicating her pink watch.

He got to his feet. 'Come on, Annie, I'll give you a lift.'

'You can't! You haven't time,' Sandra warned.

'Of course I have time. Come on, Annie, I'll show you a few short cuts.' He hurried out.

Sandra stood, hands on hips, looking me up and down as I grabbed my bag and followed him. It wasn't a friendly look.

It was only when we got into the car that I realised he was still wearing his wedding ring. I saw it the minute he put his hands on the wheel. In the office I must have been checking out the wrong hand.

'It's your boyfriend, Annie.' Rosie held out the receiver.

'Annie?' Gerry's voice sounded distant. 'Can you meet me for a jar tomorrow?'

It was nearly a week since we'd spoken. He was supposed to ring me the next day, but hadn't. I had spent the week thinking about him. 'Why didn't you ring?' I said testily.

'Isn't that what I'm doing now?'

'Yeah. Five days later.'

'You've been counting?' He sounded surprised. 'I didn't ring because I didn't have any new information for you.'

That put me in my place. Silly Annie thinking he might ring for a more personal reason.

'I run a busy detective agency, you know.'

'What's this information you have for me?' I asked snottily.

'Meet me in the Happy Shamrock tomorrow, I'll tell you then.'

'I'll have to ask Mrs Beecham for time off.'

'Tomorrow is Sunday!'

'Yes, but I've already had one full day off this week.' I wasn't going to make things easy for him. 'I don't know if I can arrange . . .'

'You've had one whole day off?' he interrupted sarcastically. 'Well, stone me. Time off for good behaviour, was it? Christ, they're really doing a number on you. Have they started strip-searching you yet?'

'Feck off, Gerry!' I hung up. Mainly because I was feeling so miserable.

I was thirty years old and living like a decrepit old spinster. I couldn't remember when I had last been to a disco or a club, or been seriously groped. Not that I wanted to be groped, but I wouldn't mind being given the opportunity to rebuff a pair of wandering hands. Wasn't that a woman's privilege? Instead, I was spending my time with two old women. The highlight of my day was an outing with an overweight dog. It was hardly the stuff of dreams.

Gerry was my one contact with the outside world. And now he thought I was a complete eejit.

Francesca treated me like a coat rack. Penelope was nice enough but even she was starting to use me as an unpaid babysitter. Auntie Annie my arse. Mrs Beecham clearly couldn't stand the sight of me. All she wanted to do was sit around looking elegant, like an ice carving at a wedding. Look but don't touch. And Jamie was off to France, presumably to paint more naked women with weird anatomies. I didn't even want to think where he got his models from.

And Mrs Beecham wouldn't even let me read to her. In every film I'd ever seen the companion had spent her time reading to the companionee. She wouldn't even let me check the plaster on her wrist.

And now I had chased Gerry away. He'd probably never speak to me again. My life was shit.

The phone suddenly shrilled.

'You're lucky I like you, Annie McHugh,' Gerry said. 'I'll be in the Happy Shamrock from six to seven tomorrow night. Make a rope with your bed sheets if you have to but be there.'

He rang off before I could tell him how much I appreciated his patience and understanding. His loyalty and friendship. The fact that he had never once called me capable.

He must have been pretty sure I'd turn up because he had a drink all waiting for me in the crowded bar. A spritzer? I hadn't touched one of those since I left Fernhill Crescent.

He watched me take off my coat, his expression thoughtful. 'I'll take that, Annie.'

I picked up the spritzer and took a sip.

Gerry didn't beat around the bush. 'Mrs Beecham was apparently a bit of a hippie,' he said.

I almost choked on my drink. Then I laughed so hard the barman looked worried. 'You are most definitely insane, Gerry Dunning.' I went off into peals of laughter again.

He sat there without a flicker of a grin on his face.

'A hippie?' I finally managed to speak without laughing. 'That's the best I've ever heard. Sorry for laughing, Gerry, but whoever gave you that information must have been tripping. Have you ever seen Mrs Beecham? Spoken to her?'

He took a small snapshot from his breast pocket. 'Recognise anyone?'

There were three people in the snap. Three very happy-looking people. Two girls and a man. Although it was a bit hard to tell because all three had a distinctly unisex look about them. They all had mounds of wild curls tumbling down to their shoulders. And they were all wearing practically identical kaftans and enough beads to open a trading post. They could have been triplets. Stoned triplets, by the look of them.

'Sorry.' I shook my head. 'I don't know these people.'

'Look harder, Annie. At the girl in the middle.'

There *was* something familiar about the laughing girl with the wild head of hair and the huge earrings. Something about the way she held her head. The provocative yet slightly superior look she was throwing at the camera. Or was it at the cameraman?

It took me a second to realise why that particular look was so familiar. 'Is it Francesca? The daughter who lives in Kildare?'

Gerry looked smug. 'It's Mrs Clare Beecham.'

'Don't be stupid, it's Francesca.'

He turned the snap over.

There was a blurred scribble on the back. Difficult to read until you peered closely at it. It said, *Marrakesh 1970.*

'It's not her.' I was immediately on the defensive. 'Mrs Beecham doesn't look remotely like that!'

'Maybe not now. But this *was* taken over thirty years ago.'

I knew what he was inferring. 'That hair . . . it's not her. Besides, Mrs Beecham must have been well over thirty then. This is a girl. A teenager.' I squinted at the blurred face.

'You said yourself it looks like her daughter, what's her name . . . ?'

'Francesca. But that doesn't prove anything. It probably looks like a thousand other girls with long fair hair. That semi-wild look is all in again.' I pointed out. 'Mrs Beecham's hair is straight as a die. I should know, I helped her to pin it up in a French pleat only this morning.'

'Why are you getting so angry?'

'Because you brought me here on the pretext of having some exciting news and all you do is show me a snap of some bloody hippies. And then you try to convince me that one of them is a woman *you've* never met, but I spend every day with.'

'I thought you only worked five days a week?'

'Don't be smart, Gerry. Mrs Beecham is nothing like the person in this snap. She's a tall, slim woman. This girl is . . . round. And . . . she can't even bear to sit *beside* a smoker. It's practically the first thing they asked me when I went to the house: "Do you smoke?" She can't abide smokers. She thinks it's a filthy habit. Thinks it should be outlawed.'

'Not then, she didn't.' He pointed to the rocket-sized cigarette in the smiling girl's hand. Even in the battered photo you could see the smoke curling up from its loosely packed edges.

'You expect me to believe that she flounced around the world getting stoned and wearing those ridiculous clothes?'

'I never said anything about her being stoned.'

'Well, just look at the photo! You'd have to be out of your head to dress like that.'

'Not in 1970. That was high fashion, then.'

'It's not her!'

'What difference would it make if it were? Why are you getting so heated about it?'

'Because . . . because I know her and I know what you're trying to infer here. You're saying that she was some kind of drugged-up hippie, who slept around and had a kid that she was ashamed of. That's why she gave it away. Well, she wouldn't do something like that. Not . . . vo . . . voluntarily.' I began to stammer, something I hadn't done since I was in high babies. 'Sh . . . she's not that kind of woman.'

'To what? Sleep around? Or give up a kid?'

I took a deep breath. 'I wouldn't expect you to understand. Whatever else she may be she is most definitely a lady. Totally refined. Unbelievably well bred. And she's . . . she's devoted to her children.'

'The ones she hasn't given away, you mean?'

'Why are you trying to hurt me?'

'I'm not trying to hurt you. I'm trying to protect you from these people. I know their kind. They play at being liberal when it suits them. Dress in the fashion fads of the day. Pretend to be ultra cool, even. But you try crossing them and you'll soon see what they're made of. And you won't like it, I promise you.'

If only he knew. Mrs Beecham wouldn't have to pretend to be cool. She was a permanent ten degrees below zero. The original iceberg woman.

'Do me a favour, Gerry, drop all this investigating business,' I snapped.

'Drop it? You were the one who wanted her investigated. You came to me, remember?'

'Well, now I'm asking you to drop it. How was I to know you'd become obsessed?'

'Obsessed? Me?'

'Well, what else would you call it? You're on the phone to me day and night. "What progress have you made? Any new information, Annie?"'

'Jesus Christ! I think you'd better go.' He picked up his whiskey.

'I'm sorry, Gerry. It's just that all this . . . snooping into her life is . . . is beginning to leave a nasty taste in my mouth. I don't like it.'

'I warned you at the outset that you might not like what I uncovered. But don't make me the bad guy. Don't attack me.'

'I'm not attacking you. It's just that I've had enough. I'm grateful to you for tracing her and everything. But enough is enough. I've had a tension headache every single day for the past three weeks and I'm sick of it. Sick of all this pretending.'

'So put an end to it. Tell her who you are!'

'I'm going to.'

'When? What are you waiting for?'

'A hippie?' I began to laugh. 'I never heard such crap.'

'You want to believe that she's some kind of well-bred saint?'

'Do you have a problem with that?'

'Look, if my business has taught me anything it's that there *are* no saints.'

'There are so! You just mix with the wrong kind of people.'

'You look as if that's what you've been doing for the past few weeks.'

I stared blankly at him.

'You look terrible, Annie. Nothing at all like the sparkling girl I met at Fiona's engagement party.'

'Oh, forgive me for not being Miss World. Are you sure you're not mixing me up with Fiona? She was the beautiful, vivacious blonde, remember? I was the quiet one with mousy brown hair. The one nobody took any notice of.'

'I noticed you.' His eyes were direct.

I fumbled around for my bag.

'You've lost all your vim and vigour, Annie.'

Vim? What the hell was that? And how dare he compliment me? And then shoot me down. 'Thanks, Gerry. That's just what every girl likes to hear. That she's dull as ditchwater.'

'That's not what I said. Don't keep twisting my words.'

'All the sparkle has gone out of you? That doesn't need much twisting.'

'I'm saying that living in Haney Road isn't doing you any good. Is that clear enough for you?'

He was right, of course. Only I was in no mood to admit it. I picked up a damp beer mat and began to pick holes in it, braving the wrath of the overweight barman who clearly wasn't aware that Zapata moustaches went out in the sixties.

'Are you angry with me, Annie?'

I dug out a big piece of cork with my thumbnail and placed it on the bar, daring the barman to say something. 'I'm angry with myself.'

'Don't be. You're the innocent party in all this.'

'What's that supposed to mean?'

'Well, apparently the good judge was as nasty as it gets.'

I slapped the mutilated mat back on the bar. 'You

told me he was revered.'

He nodded. 'By his fellow judges, maybe. The Gardai had another take on him.'

'I don't want to hear this. Don't start telling me he was involved in some kind of filth?'

'Not filth, exactly. But the Gardai couldn't stand him.'

I laughed with relief. 'That doesn't surprise me. Rosie told me he was an old grump.'

'He was a power freak.'

'A High Court judge? What would you expect?'

'Exactly. But she chose to marry him. Stuck with him to the end. A man who was a known power freak. What does that say about her?'

I'd heard enough. 'I have to go. Mrs Beecham has tickets for a charity show in the Abbey Theatre. I'm going with her.' I tried not to sound boastful.

I had forgotten whom I was talking to. 'Oh, poor Annie. You have my sympathy. But I did warn you. I said it wouldn't be all beer and skittles at the Beechams'.' He grinned. Then he was serious again, his eyes troubled.

'What? There's something else isn't there?' I began to quake.

'I thought you didn't want to hear any more.'

'What is it? You're making me nervous.'

'Clare Beecham was the judge's second wife. He was married before. And Clare may have been pregnant when they married, so my informant said before she clammed up. But Francesca, the girl the Beechams claim to be the only child of the second marriage, wasn't born until nearly two years later. Isn't that interesting? Even elephants don't carry their young for that long.'

I sat there shocked into silence.

'Annie?'

'Pe . . . Penelope and Jamie? She . . . she's not their mother?'

'No. Their mother died when they were young.'

So lusting after Jamie wouldn't have been illegal after all. Except, of course, if the judge was my father. That would still make us half-brother and -sister. Francesca, on the other hand, was certainly a blood relative. Snotty-faced, head-in-the-air Francesca was definitely my sister. 'Do you think the judge was my father?'

Gerry didn't answer.

'You think she was pregnant with me when they married. Right?'

He nodded.

'So the likelihood is that he wasn't the father. Why else would someone in her circumstances give her baby away? Or are you going to insist that the rich have an off-season for whelping. Mustn't have a baby during the theatre festival, my dear, it's so dreadfully common.' I tried to laugh.

'Who knows what motivates people like the Beechams?' Gerry said quietly.

I gave him a look.

'Well, do you know what makes them tick? I don't. I have enough trouble trying to figure out ordinary mortals. Like you, for instance.'

'Me?'

'Yeah you! Wanting to stay in that house? And don't tell me it's because you can't find an affordable flat. They may be scarce as hens' teeth right now, but other people manage. And there's a spare room in my house any time you want it.'

'I have to go, Gerry. They'll be wondering where I am.'

'Haven't you heard a word I've said?'

'I have to find out who I am.'

'I think you like being with them, Annie. Maybe you're as much of a snob as they are.'

'Drop dead, Gerry Dunning,' I hissed and walked out. How dare he call me a snob? The Beechams were the snobs, not me. I was just going to the theatre because they had a spare ticket. I didn't even want to go.

I began to run, worried about keeping Mrs Beecham waiting. No matter how dismissive she was of me, no matter how cold, I had to keep going back. She was like a drug I couldn't keep away from.

13

A letter from Cuba

Mrs Beecham was already in her seat when I got to the theatre. And so was Francesca. But they weren't in the same row.

Penelope was in the foyer, waving my ticket impatiently. 'Where were you, Annie?' She was the headmistress questioning a tardy pupil. Fortunately we were ushered in straight away, so I didn't have to produce a note from my mother.

Our seats were in the same row as Francesca's. Mrs Beecham sat directly in front of us, fawning committee member on either side of her. Everyone seemed to be in awe of her. And yet she hardly deigned to speak to anyone.

Penelope and Francesca sat to one side of me, bickering under their breaths all through the show. If one said black the other said white and if I said anything at all they both glared at me.

The fact was, none of the Beechams noticed me. I could have thrown myself bare-arsed into the front stalls and they wouldn't have cared. I was the invisible woman.

But if the sisters were dismissive of me, they were venomous to each other. No wonder Mrs Beecham declined to join us for a drink at the interval, preferring to remain in her seat like a reigning queen while toadies of all descriptions fussed around her, some of the more ancient ones bowing to kiss her hand.

I, in the meantime, had to stand listening to the sisters bickering over who had ordered what drink in advance.

'That's my port and lemon,' Francesca insisted.

'You asked for a gin and tonic. I distinctly heard you.' Penelope grabbed the port.

'Bitch.' Francesca consoled herself with the gin. 'I hate gin, always have.'

'Well, that's most peculiar. Margery Martin claims that on the night of her thirty-fifth you and her new apprentice jockey got through a year's supply between you. That's the only reason she excused your inexcusable behaviour.'

Francesca almost choked on her gin.

'Thought it went unnoticed, did you? Walking out like that in the middle of dessert. It was the talk of the horse trials the next day. I believe you practically frightened her new brood mare to death with your gymnastics. The pair of you.'

'We slipped out to the stables to check on the new mare,' Francesca snarled. '*And* because I was in dire need of some fresh air. If I'd had to sit there any longer, listening to Margery Martin discussing the emotional needs of three-year-olds, I might have thrown up in front of the whole company.'

She greeted a passing couple. 'Hello, Jacqueline, Neil. How are the yearlings doing? Good. Good.' She turned back to Penelope. 'Now listen to me, you malevolent bitch. If you spread any more filthy gossip about me and Margery's jockey you'll be sorry.'

'I should think *you* already are. Margery says he's not exactly blessed in the area that's your particular interest.'

Francesca's face fell. 'Margery said that?'

'She did. And I think we both know she wasn't referring to the Novices Handicap!'

Penelope laughed heartily at her own wit.

'You smug toad. Just because you and Jim never tire of eating from the same nose bag and never get the urge for pastures new, don't think you can stand in judgement on me.'

Penelope was still laughing. 'The Novices Handicap?' She giggled. 'Oh dear, oh dear.'

Just when I thought Francesca might run to get her whip the bell rang to indicate the end of the interval.

This time the sisters sat on either side of me.

There was one positive outcome from the snarling exchange during the interval. Neither of them spoke a word to each other for the rest of the night, which left me free to watch the back of Mrs Beecham's elegant head and wonder how she could remain in her seat for over three hours without recourse to the toilets. Was the woman even human?

In the taxi home she glared at me as if she was annoyed to see me sitting beside her instead of running behind the car where I belonged. And this was the woman Gerry expected me to believe had once been a laughing hippie?

The man was insane.

Coming down to breakfast next morning, I could hear Rosie singing happily in the kitchen. 'There's a letter for you, Annie,' she called out as soon as she heard me crossing the hall. 'Such fancy stamps.' She held up the airmail envelope. 'My nephew collects foreign stamps,' she said pointedly. 'He'd get a thrill out of these.'

'Ah. How old is he?'

'He'll be forty in June.'

'I'll give them to you later, Rosie.' I propped the letter against the toast rack while I poured my coffee. I had bigger things on my mind, this morning, than foreign stamps. Even though these particular ones were Cuban. No prize for guessing who this letter was from.

'Do you know I could never put a letter down without opening it,' Rosie hinted broadly. 'I'd be afraid there would be something urgent in it. You know, important news that wouldn't keep.'

'I don't get important news.' I sugared my coffee, then began buttering my toast.

Rosie wouldn't be put off. 'There's always a first time. You never know, there might be an invitation in there.' She pointed to the envelope. 'I knew a woman who let a letter fall behind her sideboard once. Didn't even know it was there. And what do you think was in it?'

'A winning lottery ticket?' Rosie liked you to play the game.

'An invitation to her own sister's wedding. And she never knew a thing about it.'

I looked at her in disbelief. It was seven fifty-five in the morning, far too early for one of Rosie's horror stories.

'She didn't! She told me herself.'

'If she never knew about it, how could she tell you?'

'Well, she knew eventually. But by then it was too late. Her sister had already died. Of pulmonary tuberculosis! Both lungs raddled with it. Like black leather, they said.'

'Who?'

'The neighbours.'

She offered me a choice of apricot or marmalade.

'Marmalade.'

She stood there holding the pot of marmalade against her apron.

I gave in. 'OK. When did all this happen? During the Crimean War, was it?'

'No, it wasn't during the war.' She gave me the marmalade. 'Although I could tell you a terrible sad story about . . .'

'Someone being killed in the war by an unopened letter?'

'Now that's just being stupid. How could an unopened letter kill anyone?'

Unabashed, she went on to tell me an excruciatingly long story about a war tragedy that had no connection whatsoever with unopened letters. And even less with her life, or mine. But was still burning to be told.

I liked Rosie. I liked her cooking even better. But this morning I was far too dispirited to sit through another lengthy tale of woe. 'Something's burning, Rosie.' I took advantage of a thin grey spiral of smoke that was rising from the grill. 'I'll see you later.'

Then I felt a bit mean. Tricking her like that, when she made the best cream cakes in Ireland. 'I'll save you the stamps, they're in excellent condition,' I called over my shoulder. Then ran like hell before she could call me back.

Fiona's letter was little more than a note. Her usual impatient scribble, the opening lines as complimentary as ever:

Dear Annie,

What a sly puss you've turned out to be. Living in Haney Road, no less.

If you have moved in with some rich bastard and not told me I'll make you suffer when I get back. What's going on over there and why did you have to wait 'til I was out of the country before starting all this scandalous behaviour, you selfish wagon? I'm bored out of my tree here. Even lying in the sun can lose its charm after a while, you'll be glad to hear. Plus I had the worst diarrhoea ever, yesterday.

Write back immediately and cheer me up. Dish all the dirt or you're a dead woman.

Your loving, if frustrated friend

Fiona.

PS My frustration has nothing to do with Sam. He's still tops. He's now working on some kind of serious project for the under-twelves. Him and some bulky half-Russian woman. Talk about fat! I asked Sam if she was the butter mountain he used to rabbit on about. He didn't even laugh.

PPS Wait 'til you see my tan. You'll be green with envy.

I wrote back telling her what had happened. Explaining that Mrs Beecham was my birth mother and that I had come here to trace my roots.

I really miss you, Fiona. I could have done with someone strong and decisive to help me out when everything seemed to be falling apart. But Gerry has been great. Although we still row a lot. He's such a damn pragmatist. Anyway, by the time you get this I'll probably have left Haney Road because, to be honest, coming here was not one of my better ideas. The whole family are spoiled and selfish. And Mrs Beecham behaves as if I don't exist. I can't see that telling her who I am would make much difference to her attitude. She's a cold, unfeeling woman. Gerry thinks I'm just using that as an excuse not to confront her. So you see I haven't changed, I'd still run a mile to avoid a confrontation.

Sorry to be so glum. And brief. I'll write again when I'm feeling a bit more cheerful. Hopefully when things are looking a little brighter for me. Tell Sam I said hello.

Love

Annie

Before taking my letter to the post I knocked on Mrs Beecham's door to ask if she needed anything. I stood there expecting the usual rebuff. Instead she surprised me by calling me in.

I stood by her dressing table as she put the finishing touches to her make-up. She put on full make-up even when she wasn't going anywhere and if her skin was anything to go by it had certainly paid off. She was still a beautiful woman with skin that a forty-year-old would kill for. No wonder heads had turned at the theatre when she stood up to leave the night before. And yet viewed close up like this, she didn't appear anything like as robust as her family kept insisting she was.

She caught me scrutinising her in the mirror. Our eyes met and for a split-second, I could swear I saw a flicker of warmth in her eyes. Then it was gone. 'Don't you know it's rude to stare?' she said and handed me the money for a book of stamps.

14

A girl is entitled to a good night out now and then. Isn't she?

'Order anything you want!' Gerry grinned broadly as he waved the impressive-looking menu under my nose.

'Anything?' I didn't mean to sound surprised, but this new, magnanimous Gerry was a bit of a shock. Not that he hadn't been generous to me before. But that was with his time. Money was a different matter altogether. He might own a detective agency but I had never seen much evidence of its financial bounty.

'Anything you want,' he repeated. 'Tonight, money is no object.'

Coming from Gerry Dunning this was fighting talk.

We were sitting in one of the newest, trendiest restaurants in Temple Bar, an area that celebrates itself as the arty Left Bank of Dublin.

As if.

He had phoned to ask if I would help him celebrate the successful winding up of a long and difficult case. One he had lost many a night's sleep over, he said. But he had stuck with it and proved, yet again, that with hard work, dogged determination and a loose-tongued snitch, any case can be brought to a satisfactory conclusion.

'Thanks for coming Annie.' He seemed genuinely pleased.

I lowered my eyes. I had been so desperate to get out I would have accepted a dinner invitation from Hannibal Lecter.

Three and a half weeks' incarceration in Haney Road was more than anyone could tolerate. Even with the odd day release to break the monotony.

And the most beautiful room can lose its charm when you spend night after night sitting alone watching TV.

Jamie's brief visits had provided the only real excitement and now they had come to an end. He was ensconced in Paris with his French friend Paschal. Probably on the real Left Bank.

Francesca couldn't, or wouldn't, leave her precious Arab mares long enough to visit her mother any more. Or maybe it was the two oil-rich Arab brothers who kept her tied up on the stud farm in Kildare.

And Penelope was now completely taken up with a new Steiner school, which was opening near her estate in County Wicklow. I think she was hoping it would clean up little Simon's vocabulary.

'Hard to believe he could keep two women happy at the one time.' Gerry tucked his napkin into his collar.

'Who?'

'The husband. My client's husband. Turned out to be a bigamist, he did. A very successful one, it has to be said, until I caught him. God only knows where he got the stamina.' He shook his head in awe and crumpled a bread roll into his minestrone. 'Forty-eight years of age and able to keep two families going at the one time? That's where he was disappearing to every second week. Off to his other family. And his wife suspected him of being up to no good.'

'Well, wasn't he?'

'I suppose. If keeping two families happy can be classed as no good. Just picture it. Six kids, two wives and neither family had a clue about the other.'

He began spooning his minestrone with dazzling speed.

Gerry might be awed by the notion of a happy bigamist but it didn't blunt his appetite. He finished his soup before I started mine, then set to work with a bread roll, wiping it carefully around his plate to mop up any droplets he might have overlooked first time around. Gerry was a very attractive man. No denying that. But he wasn't exactly house trained.

Lots of girls fancied him, Fiona had told me that. Then they discovered that he was already spoken for. Because Gerry was in love. With his work. Even his wife hadn't been able to come between them.

I watched him as he practically cleared the pattern off his soup plate.

He had remarkably nice hair. It would have looked a lot nicer if he allowed it to grow more than an inch beyond his scalp, but unfortunately he wasn't remotely interested in his appearance. If he were he would hardly be sitting opposite me with his table napkin tucked into his collar. Or chewing savagely on the last crusty bread roll.

It has to be said that the Beechams, for all their faults, always displayed exquisite table manners. They invariably left enough soup to cloud the bottom of their plate, a sign of great breeding, according to my mother. And you wouldn't catch one of them with a napkin tucked into his or her collar.

Gerry caught me staring. 'What?'

'I . . . er . . . I was just wondering if either of the bigamist's wives was happy?'

'Oh, yeah. Both of them. That's the most amazing thing about the whole business.'

'But if they were both happy, then who hired you?'

'Ah, that was only because wife number one began to worry about his health. He'd started cutting back on her conjugal rights, which wasn't at all like him.' He wiped his mouth with the napkin.

'Conjugal rights?'

'Sex.'

'I know what it means, I just don't understand . . .'

'He'd cut it back to three times a week, instead of their normal five.'

'I don't believe you.'

He was offended. 'I swear to God. Anyway, it's all sorted. Thanks to yours truly. He's made his choice.' He grinned happily. 'Where's that waiter?'

'Tell me! Which one is he staying with?'

His grin widened. 'Both. They've agreed to share him. Alternate months. That way he can take things a little easier. He said it was all that driving backwards and forwards across town that was taking its toll. Not running two families, that was the easy part. And that's something else they all agreed on. City traffic is murder on the libido.' The grin became a laugh.

'Are they all mad?' I was shocked.

'Don't ask me. I only collect the evidence.'

The waiter whipped our soup bowls away, replacing them with two plates of steaming cannelloni served al dente and dripping with a rich, creamy sauce.

'Um.' Gerry held his fork at the ready.

'Black pepper?' The ubiquitous wooden pepper mill was produced with a flourish.

'Thank you,' I said.

We had to wait patiently, our mouths watering, as both pasta dishes were cheesed and black-peppered with infinite care and devotion. Only then did the waiter leave us, bowing happily before he disappeared behind a conveniently placed wicker screen.

'Christ, yer man missed his calling. He should be looking for an equity card.'

And then the race was on, but it was no contest. Gerry was already halfway through his cannelloni before I got the fork into mine.

I was still burning with curiosity about a man who could keep two women and six children happy without a single note of discord. I couldn't help wondering what his secret was.

'I haven't a clue.' Gerry shrugged.

'Well, apart from the women, were the kids at all traumatised? At least when the story came out?'

'No. They were fine. You couldn't meet six better-adjusted kids.' Gerry was growing tired of the subject. When he was finished with a case, that was that. It was over. Filed away. On to the next one. Pronto.

But I couldn't let it go without knowing more. How could two women happily share the same man? What was so special about him that could evoke such loyalty that they'd be prepared to share him? And two very different women by the sound of it. They were more than fifteen years apart in age and experience, according to Gerry. 'What is there about him that's so special?'

'Nothing. He is just your ordinary Joe Soap. Well,

ordinary sales rep.' Gerry lashed more salt on to the food he had just declared to be perfect.

'I mean, look at you,' I ventured. 'You're a nice guy, you're intelligent, you work hard. And you couldn't keep *one* woman happy.'

He threw down his fork. 'Thanks, Annie. I really needed to be reminded of that.'

'You know what I mean. It must be difficult enough to keep one family, let alone . . .'

'Not my fault if my wife decided she'd be happier living with a pouf. And you haven't heard the latest on that front yet.'

I couldn't wait. It wasn't often that Gerry volunteered information about his private life.

'He's only gone and booked a sunshine holiday for the four of them,' he snorted. 'On the bloody Costa del Sol, would you believe? Full board. In a five-star hotel. What an evil bastard!' He picked up his fork and stabbed it viciously into his cannelloni.

'Evil? But the boys will love Spain.'

'Exactly! That's why I wanted to be the first to take them there. But no, he had to beat me to it. He *has* to be the first.'

This wasn't the time to remind Gerry that *he* had never taken a holiday in his life. And had no intentions of ever doing so, if I was any judge. When it came to his sons you had to tread warily. Reason and logic tended to fly out the door where they were concerned. It would be a pretty brave soul who would remind Gerry Dunning that he'd had eight long years to take them on a sun holiday and had never once availed himself of the opportunity. It was no excuse that he thought he couldn't be away from his job for more than a couple of hours at a time. No excuse that he was convinced that if he turned his back on Dublin for any longer than a few hours the whole city would be overrun by master criminals. Or maybe bigamous husbands.

'I was going to take them next year. I had it all arranged,' he said firmly.

'You had it booked?'

'No! But I was going to.'

'Why don't you book somewhere now, then? Get Sandra to do it for you if you haven't the time.'

Loyal Sandra who worked with him every day and still considered him to be flawless.

'Where do you suggest I take them? *He's* booked the Costa del Sol? So that's that. The bastard.'

Again it probably wasn't the time, or the place, to remind him that there were actually other holiday destinations besides the ever popular Costa del Sol. When Gerry got an idea in his head it was folly to try to shift it.

The Italian waiter was hovering around the table again, but clearly afraid to interrupt what he perceived to be a lovers' tiff.

Gerry leaned back in his chair and sighed loudly, pulling the napkin from his collar.

I looked down at my lap.

The waiter leaped into the breach. 'Everything all right, sir? No problems?'

Gerry shot him a vicious look.

The waiter paled.

'Gerry!' I hissed. 'Everything is perfect, thank you.' I smiled.

'*Buono.*' He bowed with relief. And gratitude. Then he glided away, but not before taking the chance to flirt with his reflection in a nearby mirror.

'What did you think I was going to do to him? Garrotte him with my napkin?' Gerry laughed as we walked arm in arm to a nearby pub.

'It's what *he* thought you might do to him that mattered. You can be very aggressive sometimes. Well, that's not strictly true. I know you're not aggressive, but you can give that impression to people.'

He halted mid-stride. 'Aw, Annie. You know that underneath I'm just a poor misunderstood pussycat, don't you?' He grinned wickedly, his eyes crinkled up at the corners in that sexy way they sometimes did.

I moved closer.

I got the faint whiff of aftershave and that indiscernible male scent that has no name but can make your nipples go rigid. He bent towards me.

'Get off her, ya dirty bugger,' one of a gang of kids who were hanging around the pub doorway shouted, as the others chortled in delight.

'You lot should be in bed,' Gerry growled at them.

'Jaysus, it's the DS! Run lads!' The kids scattered in all directions.

We fell into the pub laughing.

'Drug squad? The cheeky little bastards. I don't look anything like that lot, do I?'

'It's your hair. They think you're trying to have street cred.'

'Street cred? Me?' He laughed.

And it was laughable. Gerry couldn't care less what he looked like. Anyone who knew him could vouch for that. He didn't give a damn who cut his hair, as long as they did it quickly. And short enough for him not to have to bother about it for another couple of weeks.

'Why don't you let your hair grow a bit?' I asked. 'It could look really well.'

'And have to comb it? Forget that.'

'Well, God forbid you'd have to comb your hair. All that time wasted, when you could be out chasing missing dogs and errant husbands. And of course, if you did begin to comb your hair there's no knowing where it could all end. You might find yourself wearing a suit when you take a friend out to dinner. Wouldn't that be a real turn-up for the books?' I teased.

'Know something, Annie? It's having friends like you that keeps a man's self-esteem brimming over.'

By closing time he was on flying form. 'Let's go to a club.'

'A club?'

'Yeah, you remember those places? Where people go to dance and have a good time? A bit of late-night craic? Are you on for it?'

And what could I say? Gerry never relaxed. Never took a night off. And his children *were* going to Spain. With the pouf. Who probably combed his hair three times a day, and put on a suit and tie, just to do his number twos.

If Gerry hadn't known one of the bouncers we wouldn't have got past the door of the trendy club, which had a number instead of a name, that's how cool it was.

Both of us being anything but, we must have stood out like day trippers in the long queue. Neither of us had a single body piercing worth mentioning and we both looked old enough to be on the electoral roll.

'Are you sure about this place?' I hesitated as the bouncer waved us in.

'It's the hottest club in town. You normally need a special key card to get into this joint. Or a girlfriend in RTE. Of either sex.' Gerry laughed.

'Which one do you have?'

'Me? I have files on half the bouncers,' he said slyly.

'Is that how you know your man?'

'I busted him once.'

'He's a criminal?' I turned to look back at the big Goliath in the evening suit. He had the overdeveloped body of someone who took weight training far too seriously. And yet bobbing above his tree trunk neck were the chubby face and overblown cheeks of a well-fed Glaxo baby.

'He's an idiot.' Gerry gave him a big wave and a wink.

We were ordering our drinks when the Glaxo baby joined us. 'I'm on a break.'

'Get away.' Gerry caught my eye.

The crowd was becoming a bit lively, forcing us to hold our drinks extra close, as we stood on the edge of the dance floor, watching the frantically gyrating punters.

'Just looking at them makes me want to go home for a lie-down.' Gerry, who was no shirker in the energy stakes, laughed.

'Ah, it takes all kinds. They're not bad kids. Most of them.' The bouncer's face was wreathed in happy smiles as he shifted his great bulk in time to the throbbing beat. 'Any work going, Ger?' he suddenly asked.

'Ah, things are pretty quiet right now,' Gerry

shouted to make himself heard over the blasting techno music. 'Not much happening in my line.'

Not much happening? He had spent the past hour bending my ear about the problems of coping with the rising demand for private detectives. He said he and his two investigators, Barney and Declan, were run off their feet. Couldn't keep up with the need for their services. That the Celtic Tiger was a boon for the private detective business. How he might even have to take on another full-time assistant, whether he liked it or not.

'Yer man's a right chancer,' he explained, when our new friend was called away to break a skull or two. 'I wouldn't give him a job if *he* paid me,' he bellowed.

'Do you want to dance?' I bellowed back.

'Do you?'

'We're here, aren't we? Might as well enjoy it.'

Then we were in the thick of it. Gyrating as good as the rest. Or maybe as badly. But I have to say that the sweating hordes who looked pretty unappetising from a distance proved to be nimble and lithe, not to mention extremely friendly, when you got close up to them. They made room for us on the crowded dance floor without comment, making us feel welcome with their wide smiles and shining eyes. Happy, happy people. And what with the rhythmic music and being surrounded by such zest for life, you couldn't help but begin to loosen up and have a great time.

Then someone else recognised Gerry and wanted to have a word with him.

'You're a popular man,' I shouted in his ear.

'Back in a sec,' he yelled.

I stayed with my new-found friends, shaking it with

the best of them. I had almost forgotten how much I enjoyed dancing.

After what seemed like no time at all Gerry was back, tugging at my sleeve. 'Let's get out of here, Annie. Come on.'

'I don't want to leave,' I protested. 'I'm just getting into this.' I smiled at the boy in front of me. And he smiled back. His smile was radiant, his eyes shining like brightly polished diamonds.

Gerry's face was like thunder. 'This place is crap. I don't know why we came here.'

The bouncer was back, miming energetically to us across the crowd. Offering us a drink.

I shook my head. I was in a club, for God's sake. I wanted to dance. I wanted to be one of the *happy people*.

Gerry disappeared into the crowd and I turned back to the dancers.

Only when I was completely exhausted, with my legs threatening to fold under me, did I go looking for him.

He was sitting by the bar, his expression glum.

'Do you still want to leave?' I asked.

He nodded. 'I don't know why we came here in the first place.'

'It might be because you insisted.'

He wasn't listening. 'See the tall guy in the grey suit, over by the end of the bar?'

'Don't tell me, you busted him once, as well.'

'No, but I should have. He's Sally's brother.'

'Your ex-brother-in-law?' I began to giggle. 'So what? Who cares?'

'I do. He says Sally's expecting.'

'It's not yours, is it?' The laughter got stuck in my throat.

'Don't be crazy! We haven't . . . It must be two years, now.'

He was actually embarrassed? Gerry Dunning looked as if he wanted to crawl under the bar with embarrassment? Or at least crawl out of the club unseen.

The ex-brother-in-law raised his glass in a mocking salute.

Gerry saluted him back. With a single finger.

15

A good night out is not always the answer to a maiden's prayer

The big bouncer volunteered to get us a taxi. 'I know all the lads,' he boasted. Then he was hassling Gerry about a job again. 'Even a couple of days' work. I could do surveillance. I'd be good at that,' he said, towering over us like a big scary baby.

But Gerry had used up his quota of tolerance for the night. He elbowed him aside and made for the door.

'Give us a chance, Ger.' The bouncer was pleading with him now. 'I think I'd make a fuckin' great detective.'

'A great detective?' Gerry laughed. 'You can't even find us a fuckin' taxi.' He hurried me out the door.

We ended up hailing a cab in the next street.

He opened the door for me.

'You didn't have to be so rude to him,' I complained. 'All he wants is a job.'

'He has a job. Breaking people's heads and worse. Didn't you see the way they intimidate some of the young punters, queuing up outside?'

'No, I didn't. And if it's such a terrible place, why did you bring me there?'

'I didn't notice you wanting to leave!'

'Well, that's rich.'

'I'd need to be, wouldn't I? Spending the night ferrying you around the city in taxis.'

'Oh, you bastard! Let me out of this cab, I'll find my own way home.'

'I'm sorry, Annie. Sorry. I'm just so bloody . . .'

'Bloody minded! Or are you jealous? Is that it? You're jealous because your ex is pregnant? You're being divorced, Gerry. Your marriage is over. Even though you persist in hanging on to that stupid ring.'

I couldn't resist.

He looked down at the ring as if he was surprised to see it, still there on his finger. As if he thought the ring fairy would have slipped into his room one night and removed it. 'You don't think I want to get back with her, do you? I don't want her back in my life. That's the last thing I want. All I care about are my kids.'

'Then why are you so upset to hear that she might be pregnant?'

'Don't you see how that would change things for the kids? It would make them a family. With the pouf!'

'What's wrong with that? Kids need families around them. It's good for them. Gives them a sense of security. Of belonging.'

'They're *my* kids,' he said stubbornly.

'I don't understand you. Don't you want them to be happy?'

'I want them to remember who their father is.'

'Well, that's up to you, Gerry. You should ring them more often. Make your Sundays together memorable. They're hardly going to look back on getting the Garda Review as the highlight of their young lives.'

'What would you suggest? Giving them a puppy?' he asked sarcastically.

'Well, I bet two little boys would be more interested in that than a baby.'

'Sally would kill me.' He started to laugh.

'I thought you didn't care what she thought?'

'The pouf hates animals.'

'Perfect.'

We were still laughing when the cab swung into the driveway at Haney Road. The sudden motion threw us together, so our faces were only inches apart.

Gerry moved closer, his arms reaching out for me.

My sudden scream startled the driver so much he almost drove into the shrubbery, á la Francesca. 'Stop! Stop! Let me out!'

'Jesus, Annie. A simple no would suffice. I was only going to give you a peck.' Gerry leaned back.

But that wasn't why I'd screamed. It was the sight of the place that had thrown me into a panic. 'Let me out. Now!'

The taxi jerked to a stop.

I peered up at the house, my stomach doing back flips. 'Something is wrong!'

Gerry blinked stupidly at me, looking really drunk for the first time.

I jumped out of the cab.

'Annie?'

The big front door was open. Swinging wide. And yet there wasn't a chink of light showing anywhere. The whole place was in darkness.

Even the two lamps that burned on either side of the door all night were off. They worked on an automatic timer, which switched them off at dawn. There was no way you could turn them off manually without dismantling the complicated wiring. Or interrupting the power supply to the whole road.

But that hadn't happened because the street lights were still on. And I could see a light burning in a nearby house.

I ran into the hall with Gerry's worried shouts ringing in my ears.

'Annie? Wait up, Annie?'

I hit the nearest light switch. Nothing happened.

I had to feel my way up the stairs, in pitch darkness, instinctively heading for Mrs Beecham's room. I ran my hands along the wall to guide me, while feeling for each step with my foot.

Her door was wide open. The room black as night. And coming from somewhere inside it were the most awful little gasping sounds.

In a complete panic, now, I stumbled around feeling for the emergency torch that was kept in the landing cupboard. I had to steel myself to shine it into the big bedroom.

'Oh, Jesus!'

It looked as if a tornado had struck. The furniture was overturned, bedding strewn across the floor, the contents of drawers scattered everywhere.

And in the middle of it all sat Mrs Beecham. Only she wasn't just sitting on the only upright chair in the room. She was tied to it. Her wrists and ankles firmly bound with rope.

'Oh, sweet Jesus.'

'I'm all right,' she kept saying as I tried to untie the knots that were cutting into her thin wrists. 'I'm perfectly all right.'

She was not all right. Even in the jumpy torchlight I could see that. Her face was chalk-white, her eyes sunken almost hollow. The bottom part of her nightdress was dripping wet and there was a small pool spreading beneath her chair, getting bigger even as I struggled with the grimy rope.

'Gerry! Gerry!' I screeched like a banshee. 'Up here. Hurry. Oh, please hurry.'

I had never been so glad to have Gerry for a friend. He was sober before he reached the top step, taking charge immediately where someone else might have panicked. Especially as we had only the one torch between us and I was in no hurry to relinquish it.

He gave up trying to wrestle it from my hand. 'Shine it here, Annie.'

He had Mrs Beecham untied and off the chair in seconds. We were both helping her to the bed when he noticed the dripping-wet nightdress. He hesitated, unsure for the first time. 'Annie?'

'The fuse box is under the stairs. Will you check it out?' I gave him the torch. 'We'll be OK.'

My eyes were getting used to the darkness. Even so, it seemed to take me for ever, fumbling around, before I managed to get her a clean nightdress.

'Thank you, Annie.' It might have been heartfelt, but her tones were clipped as ever.

I was pulling the nightie down over her raised arms when the lights suddenly flashed on, making me blink. She instinctively covered herself.

Gerry was back with us in seconds. He got a warm quilt from the wardrobe and put it round her. All the time assuring her that *yes*, she was all right. And *yes*, everything was OK now. 'Stay with her,' he whispered to me.

I tried to appear as confident as he was, while he went to ring for an ambulance.

The cabby had already been on to the Gardai.

I tucked the quilt even tighter around her shoulders, mumbling stupid, inept platitudes. My voice trailing off whenever I looked around at the trashed room. 'Everything will be grand,' I kept saying, not believing a word of it.

I was worse than useless. Completely embarrassed at being thrown into such intimate proximity to the woman who had always managed to keep me at arm's length, even when I was pinning up her hair.

Gerry might have been born to deal with the situation. He seemed to know exactly what to say. And do. He was unbelievably great. Unbelievably considerate and gentle. She might have been his own mother, the way he was handling things. Well, maybe not his own mother. He couldn't stand her. But someone like that.

And despite having to concentrate on comforting poor quivering Mrs Beecham, he never forgot to be the professional detective. 'Don't touch anything, Annie,' he warned me. 'Bound to be fingerprints,' he explained. 'Mustn't smudge fingerprints. Lots of evidence.' He smiled at Mrs Beecham.

I actually felt her relax against my rigid shoulder.

Gerry was in his element. I could have kissed him. It was thanks to him that the colour was returning to her cheeks, the look of terror fading from her eyes.

'Did they . . . hurt you?' he asked.

I turned away, too frightened of what I might hear. Then, always a glutton for punishment, I darted a quick look back at her, just in time to see her shaking her head.

Gerry's relief was unmistakable. He straightened up and cheerfully suggested I make a pot of strong sweet tea.

I would personally have opted for the whiskey bottle, but Gerry was adamant. 'She's not hurt,' he whispered. 'But just the same, I think tea is as much as she should have before the doctor gets here. Make it strong and sweet.

'Let's get you properly warmed up, now. Can't have you catching cold.' He was rubbing her blood-less hands and wrists, getting her circulation going again.

'Oh, thank you. But the heating is on. You don't have to worry about me catching cold when the heating is on.' She was already back to her superior way of speaking.

It didn't intimidate Gerry. 'I know the heat is on, love.' He nodded, 'It's just that after you've had a bad fright your body temperature can drop. Not good for you at all.' Despite her protests he continued to massage her wrists.

I had never seen this side of Gerry before. Even with his young sons, whom he adored, his manner tended to be a bit offhand. Brusque even. That was his way.

With Mrs Beecham he was completely different. So gentle, I was amazed.

I hurried downstairs to make the tea.

The Garda car and ambulance arrived within seconds of each other.

All of a sudden the whole place seemed to be

overrun by competent people in navy uniforms. And in a peculiar way their presence, which should have been reassuring, had completely the opposite effect on me. They made everything appear even more chaotic and nightmarish. Frightening. And the drinks cabinet downstairs seemed to be such a long way off, now that I was back in the bedroom.

The ambulance crew were trying to persuade Mrs Beecham to be stretchered out, when her own doctor arrived in a cloud of cigar smoke.

'Who called him?' a resentful voice asked.

I said nothing.

It wasn't that I liked Dr Moran. Nobody could like Dr Moran. But he was Mrs Beecham's personal physician. The one who knew her best. He glanced around the room like the lead actor in a bad melodrama. 'Everybody out! Thank you!'

The two Gardai ignored him.

But the ambulance crew gave way. Dr Moran was, after all, a consultant.

He opened his bag with such a dramatic flourish that you kept expecting overexcited cameramen to leap out of the wardrobe and commence major filming.

He leaned over Mrs Beecham, his expression that of a man about to perform pioneering cardiovascular surgery right there on the rumpled bed. 'How are you, Clare?' he boomed, then stuck a thermometer in her mouth so she couldn't answer. 'Clear the room, please!'

The detective in charge was examining a lacquered Chinese bureau that used to hold Mrs Beecham's jewellery and other personal treasures. At least, it had been a lacquered bureau. Now it was more like a collection of badly splintered wood, albeit beautifully lacquered wood.

The detective sighed loudly and held up a piece of the door, with the lock still intact. 'Tsk, tsk, tsk.' He shook his head.

'Clear the room,' Dr Moran said again.

The detective straightened up, raising a questioning eyebrow at the doctor. He was a huge giant of a man whose size alone would have intimidated most people.

Dr Moran was not most people. 'You already have descriptions of the three culprits, I believe? Anything else can wait until morning,' he barked.

The big detective and Gerry exchanged long, pained glances.

'My patient and I require privacy. Any pain, Clare?' he boomed.

As he was medically trained he couldn't possibly have been unaware of the improbability of her giving a lucid reply, while the thermometer was still stuck in her mouth. But Dr Moran played to his own rules.

Gerry headed for the door. He was limping on his right leg, I noticed. I could sense a major row brewing.

'I'll be outside if you need me.' I ducked out behind him.

Then I had to go back in again. 'Excuse me, Dr Moran.' I addressed the back of his head. 'But if they're taking Mrs Beecham to the hospital, shouldn't I pack an overnight bag for her? All her things are in here.' I gestured at the rifled presses.

He didn't even bother to turn. 'Get on with it, then, girl,' he intoned.

I pulled a face behind his back.

The big detective seemed hugely amused by this little display of anarchy.

Even Mrs Beecham, locked in her enforced silence, attempted a weak smile.

'Don't try to speak,' the doctor barked, as he saw her mouth twitch.

Then, practically in the same breath, he was asking, 'No pain at all? None? None,' he answered his own question. Which was probably just as well, as his was apparently the only voice he ever listened to.

I packed a change of underwear and fresh night-clothes in a small valise, then, braving Dr Moran's wrath, went about the room collecting Mrs Beecham's favourite hairbrushes and face creams. And anything else I thought she might consider essential for an overnight stay in hospital. Like loo roll that couldn't double as sandpaper.

Then I went downstairs to join Gerry and the big Garda detective, leaving Mrs Beecham to the tender mercies of Dr Moran, who was checking her blood pressure and loudly humming 'Nessun Dorma' at the same time.

I had hesitated before leaving the room. 'All right?' I didn't actually say the words, just mouthed them to her from the doorway.

She gave a little inclination of the head. Other people nod their heads, Mrs Beecham inclined hers like a reigning monarch.

'Are you still here?' Dr Moran turned.

Gerry and I stood watching as they lifted her into the ambulance.

Covered up to the chin in rough Eastern Health Board blankets, she looked frail and old, with little sign of the autocratic bearing that had turned heads that night in the theatre. I wondered if I should have offered to go in the ambulance with her. 'I'll come and see you in the morning,' I called out, surprised to find that a gigantic lump was starting to form in my throat. I might have made my way into the ambulance then, except that it would have taken a stun gun to get past the posturing Dr Moran.

They were closing the doors behind her when I heard her call my name. 'Annie?'

'Wait. Wait,' I shouted at the ambulance driver.

'What is it?' I hurried over, my heart pounding with expectation, my foot already on the bottom step. Was she going to ask me to go with her?

'Did you put my bristle hairbrush in the bag? Those plastic brushes are useless. And did you pack my Clarins face cream?'

Dr Moran elbowed me aside and the doors were slammed shut.

'Don't look so worried, Annie. She's all right.' Gerry grinned at me.

'You seem pretty confident.'

'Demanding bristles instead of plastic? And her favourite face cream? Trust me, she's not going on the critical list.'

I had no choice but to trust him. Dr Moran wouldn't lower himself to fill me in on the details of her health. I was only the paid help. No consultant worth his salt would discuss his patient with the paid help.

'She'll be all right, Annie,' Gerry repeated, taking my arm to lead me back into the house.

We watched from the doorway as Dr Moran spat the remains of his fat cigar on to the gravel and stepped into his Jaguar. He swept past us and down the drive, almost sideswiping the ambulance, which was pulling away at the same time.

'Now there goes a true pillar of the community,' Gerry said solemnly.

I wasn't sure if he meant Mrs Beecham or the doctor.

And I didn't dare ask.

16

God bless all professional counsellors

The Gardai appeared to share Rosie's belief in the curative properties of tea. It was offered around like snuff at a wake the night of the burglary. A steaming-hot cup materialised out of nowhere at every break in the conversation. All I had to do was hesitate or falter in my story of what I had seen for another cup to be pressed into my hand. Before I got to finish what little evidence I had, I was awash with the stuff.

The big Garda detective snapped his notebook closed and sighed with disappointment. 'So you didn't see anything of the intruders? Not even their car?'

'Sorry.'

'Not your fault.' Gerry came over with the teapot. 'Top up, Annie?'

I shook my head. 'At least you have descriptions of the men from Mrs Beecham. Isn't that good?'

They exchanged glances. 'Didn't she give you a full description? You can trust her. She's very sharp. She wouldn't get the details wrong,' I insisted.

'Three men in black? All wearing balaclavas?' the Garda said drily. 'Ah, they'll have those lads in custody before morning.'

'You mean . . . ?'

'Not a hope in hell.' Gerry was pouring more tea.

'What about fingerprints? Won't they help you to trace them?'

'Oh, the fingerprints? Right. How could I have forgotten about the fingerprints?'

I had a feeling they were laughing at me. 'You said there would be fingerprints.' I turned to Gerry. 'You told me not to touch anything, in case I disturbed them.'

He flashed his familiar lopsided grin. 'That was for Mrs Beecham's benefit. She was in shock. I would have said anything to lessen her stress. Help her relax. She needed to believe that the men who violated her privacy wouldn't get away with it. That they'd be caught and brought to justice.' His voice hardened.

'You mean they won't?'

The Garda gave another resigned sigh. 'We'll do our best. But with no fingerprints and no descriptions to speak of.' He shrugged. 'They broke a window to gain access. Hardly an original modus operandi. This isn't *NYPD Blue*, you know.' His grin was ironic. 'We don't have scriptwriters to help us out when we come up against a brick wall.' He sounded depressed. 'Shame the dog was in the vet's.' Now I was depressed.

But Gerry was hell bent on keeping me cheerful. 'The main thing is nobody got hurt. That's always good news.'

'So they'll get away with it? They can break in and terrify the life out of Mrs Beecham; tie her up in her own home; leave her there to die, for all they knew. Then disappear with her jewellery and anything else they take a fancy to. And they'll get away scot-free?'

'We could get lucky with the paintings. That's the only mistake they made, taking those two oil paintings. At least we know we're not dealing with art experts here.'

They both had a good laugh at that.

'Detective Inspector Brogan says they weren't worth lifting off the wall.' Gerry answered my enquiring look.

'But they *are* oil paintings. They must be worth something.'

'Maybe to the artist.' He smirked knowingly. 'But they wouldn't exactly set hearts aflame in the National Gallery, if you know what I mean.'

'The son of the house is the culprit there, I believe.' The Garda's shoulders began to shake again.

I was starting to dislike this man. 'I suppose your Detective Inspector Brogan fancies himself as an art expert, does he? Some flat-footed redneck, just out of the bog and he thinks he knows everything about art?'

His colour heightened. 'He has a Fine Arts degree.'

'So has the night watchman in Pussy Grub!'

That stopped him in his tracks. And it wasn't strictly a lie because he will have one, in two years' time when he graduates. If he stays away from the drugs.

I stormed off, leaving the two of them with their mouths hanging open.

How dare they insult Jamie's paintings?

Jamie had once been compared with Rembrant. Or was it Rubens? Anyway, it was one of those great visionaries of the art world, whose names will never be forgotten.

Not worth taking down off the wall? Who did they think they were? I mean I didn't *like* Jamie's paintings, but I didn't go around sneering at them.

After I locked myself in my room and refused to answer any knock on the door, the Garda decided that he could wait until morning for a complete list of the stolen items.

I had already conferred with Gerry on the best way to tell the family: 'Should I phone the girls now, or what?'

Well, how was I supposed to know what to do, in such a situation? I had no previous experience of this kind of thing. Was I to waken people in the middle of the night and scare the wits out of them? Was that absolutely necessary? And if it weren't, wouldn't it make more sense to wait until morning?

'Get real, Annie.' Gerry was back to his usual tactful self. 'I assumed you had already contacted them. The family has to be informed straight away. Especially the next of kin.'

I stared belligerently at him.

'You're not the next of kin, Annie. No matter what you might like to think. Legally you don't count. You don't even exist.'

'Says who?'

'Look, this is not something I want to debate with you right now. All I'm telling you is that it's basic policy to inform the next of kin.' He paused. 'Just in case.'

My heard began to pound. 'In case of what?'

He shrugged.

'You said she's perfectly all right. Even the doctor said she's all right.' A little knot of black fear began to form somewhere in the pit of my stomach.

'She is. It's just important to follow procedure. Even in situations like this, where the victim appears to be in no danger whatsoever.' He might have been quoting from a manual, he was so cool. So bloody detached. So capable of standing back and taking stock no matter how traumatic the situation.

Once a Garda, always a Garda. Or was that the Jesuits?

My brain was beginning to go into meltdown with the stress of the whole thing. And I hadn't yet spoken to the family.

I rang Penelope, taking care to assure her, straight off, that her mother wasn't hurt. 'In fact, she'll be fast asleep by now. No sense in you driving all this way just to sit in hospital reception. Wait until morning. Dr Moran says she's fine. They didn't harm her. He gave her something to make her sleep. No, I promise you she was so relaxed her eyes were already closing before they got her into the ambulance. No! It's just policy. It was here so they used it. It doesn't mean that she actually needed one.'

'Are you sure, Annie?'

'Positive. I'll give you the number of the hospital. You can ring them, set your mind at rest.'

'Thank you, Annie. I'll do it straight away. Before I contact the others.'

'Goodnight, then.'

'Annie?'

'Yes?'

'Thank you. Thank you for being there for her.'

But I hadn't been. I had been out clubbing. Dancing like a dervish until the small hours with a bunch of sweaty, drugged-up strangers, who wouldn't know their own names if you tattooed them on the inside of their eyelids. And I would have stayed there even longer, enjoying myself, if some big gob hadn't upset Gerry by telling him his wife was expecting.

I was the one who made it easy for three vicious

thugs to break in and rob Mrs Beecham. If I'd been here with her, like a proper companion, I could have raised the alarm. Or at least done something to prevent her being manhandled and terrified out of her wits. And Penelope was thanking me? What for? For being a complete and utter fraud?

I hung around my room until I couldn't stand being alone in it any longer. Twice I had slipped into bed and tried to sleep. I had even changed into my nightdress, thinking it might help. It didn't.

I threw a warm cardigan over it now and went downstairs.

At first I thought everyone had left. The place seemed deserted. Then I heard the deep rumble of male voices coming from the kitchen. Gerry and the bulky detective were sitting next to the stove, holding a post-mortem on the robbery. And from what I could hear they found it more interesting than upsetting. They certainly didn't sound as if they would lose any sleep over it.

'It was some job, all the same. They didn't put a foot wrong. Didn't take anything that couldn't be easily fenced. Apart from the bad artwork.' The Garda gave a little snort of amusement.

'Lucky they *were* professionals,' Gerry was saying. 'Put a gang of strung-out druggies in the same situation and we might have been looking at a very serious outcome.'

'What's the matter with you people?' I burst in on them. 'You don't think there was a serious outcome here? Are you nuts? Mrs Beecham is in hospital. Her jewellery is gone. They took the paintings off her wall.' I searched my brain for something that might shock them out of their complacency. 'And . . . and there's a bloody big hole in the conservatory window!' Even while I was saying it I realised how stupid it sounded.

'Take it easy, Annie.' Gerry was on his feet. 'All we're saying is that nobody got hurt here. That's the most important thing, isn't it?'

I pushed past him and stormed off into the garden down to my favourite spot.

He came after me. 'Why are you getting yourself in such a state, Annie? What's going on here?'

'We've been burgled! Haven't you noticed?' I said sarcastically.

'You know what I mean. Stop playing stupid games with me. And give over being so ratty to the investigating Garda. The man is only doing his job. He's a professional.'

'A professional what?' I turned. 'A professional feckin' tea drinker?'

'He's entitled to a break.'

'Big bogger!'

'Annie! Will you calm down, for God's sake? Why are you getting yourself so worked up? It's all over. And look at you. Walking around the garden half naked at this hour of the morning. Where are your clothes?'

'None of your business. And I'll walk around half naked if I want to.'

The truth is I nearly died when I looked down and realised that you could see right through my nightie. I tried pulling my cardigan down past my thighs, but it kept springing back up again like elastic.

Gerry took off his jacket and draped it round my shoulders.

I held it closed, covering as much exposed flesh as

I could. 'I suppose you expect me to thank you for that,' I said sulkily.

'No.' He frowned.

'Good, because you'd be a long time waiting.'

'Annie?' He looked even more puzzled.

'You and your Gardai friends. All lads together, aren't you?'

'What's the matter with you?'

'Nothing serious!' I mimicked the big Garda's Kerry accent.

'I don't know what's got into you, Annie, but I think you should watch your manners.'

Something about the way he said it, the tone of his voice, triggered warning bells in my head. He was going to walk away. I knew it. The thought terrified me. Frightened me even more than the big black cloud that had been hovering over me all night since I first saw Mrs Beecham slumped in the chair. 'Don't go, Gerry.' I grabbed the front of his shirt.

And without warning the tears started. Big, wet splodges that bounced down my face and off my chin, some of them detouring into my mouth so I could taste the salt and bits of lash-thickening mascara they carried with them.

This was what I had been dreading all night: that I might start to blubber and give myself away for the terrible person I was. A person no one could love.

Gerry reached out and drew me close, which only made me cry all the harder. 'What is it, Annie? You can tell me.' He held me even tighter. Lucky he didn't have as much as a biro in his pocket or both of us would have been stabbed. But all there was between us was the warm scent of musky aftershave and sandalwood soap, and I wished we could stay like this for ever.

'Tell me what's really bothering you, Annie?' His hands were gentle as he brushed my hair from my face.

'I can't. You'd only hate me.'

'I'd never hate you. Don't be stupid.' He wiped away my tears with a big grey hankie. At least I hoped it was grey. Gerry wasn't too fond of washing machines.

It might have been because he called me stupid. Or maybe it was the tender look in his eyes when he said it. Whatever, it made me confess something that had been on my mind all night. 'I kept thinking, what if they'd killed her?' I said. 'And the thought was more than I could bear. Not because I have any special feelings for her. Although I do feel pity. How could you look at her and not feel pity? But all I kept thinking was that if they'd killed her, or if she died, I'd never find out why she rejected me. Now do you see how selfish I am? The poor woman was robbed, terrified, tied up for God only knows how long. And all I could think about was myself. How despicable does that make me, Gerry?'

17

Leopards and their spots, and all that kind of stuff

By mid-morning next day the house was practically back to normal. I had showered and dressed, the place was reasonably tidy and the glazier had almost finished replacing the broken glass. And Rosie was back in the kitchen.

She had come in the back door at ten to eight, her face chalk-white. 'Annie? What's happening? Why is there a police car out front? Oh, my God, look at the window. Is . . . is Mrs Beecham . . . ?' She blessed herself.

'It's all right, Rosie. We've had a break-in but everything is fine now. It's all sorted.'

Poor little Rosie. If she was shocked by the break-in, wait until she heard what was coming tomorrow. I had given Gerry my word that the moment Mrs Beecham came home I would tell her who I was.

The good news had come earlier that morning. Two other houses in the area had also been burgled in exactly the same fashion. 'So your house wasn't specially targeted.' The voice on the phone was cheerful. 'The gang were just Bank Holiday opportunists. That's when they break in. Assuming everyone is away. Minor criminals, that's all.'

'Oh, very good,' I said.

I knew I would find it much more difficult to hide my feelings when I finally confronted Mrs Beecham, although Gerry had come up trumps again by getting a professional counsellor to ring me and bolster my confidence.

'I can practically guarantee that your birth mother will be cautious, but warmly receptive, to what you have to say,' was the final thing she said before rushing off to her next appointment.

'How dare you! How dare you approach me with such a vile fabrication?' Mrs Beecham shot out of her chair, her fine-boned face turning purple with fury.

I drew back in dismay.

This wasn't right. It wasn't supposed to go like this. Gerry's counsellor friend had promised me. And she was a trained professional.

So why was Mrs Beecham reacting like this? Why wasn't she cautious but warmly receptive? Why was she standing there looking at me as if I were something she had accidentally carried in on the sole of her Gucci loafer?

She must have misunderstood me. 'I don't think you understood, Mrs Beecham. What I said was that I'm your . . .'

'Don't you dare repeat that awful calumny! If you have a single shred of common decency you will leave this room before I'm forced to call for help.'

For help? Against whom?

Her breathing was becoming funny. She seemed to be having trouble drawing air into her lungs and a little rim of sweat was starting to form on her upper lip, which was still quite purple.

Oh, my God. Was she having some kind of attack?

'Please, Mrs Beecham, I didn't mean to upset you.'

'Upset me?' She put a hand to her chest. 'What did you think would happen? Did you think I would welcome this vile fabrication?'

She dabbed at her lip with a hankie. The rim of sweat disappeared and her breathing began to slow down, becoming even again. She was almost calm now. If still not warmly receptive. 'My daughter?' She spat the word. Looking at me as if I were one of the fox turds Pepper once brought into the house and put by the fire.

Was this the same woman who had almost smiled at me, when I helped her after the burglary? Who had said, 'Thank you, Annie,' when I helped her into a clean nightdress? 'I want you out of my house right now.' A big blue vein was pulsating furiously in her neck, threatening to break through the fragile white skin.

'No, you don't understand. It's not a fabrication. I had to tell you. I couldn't keep it to myself any longer. I thought you had a right to know. I *am* your daughter. I can prove it. I have my birth certificate in my room. I was born on the twenty-eighth of November nineteen seventy in the Stella Maris nursing home near Blackrock. I weighed nine pounds four ounces and it was exactly midday. The angelus bells were ringing out.'

I was speaking at warp speed because I didn't want her to embarrass herself by making further denials, which she'd have to retract, when she realised I was telling the truth. 'You probably remember the angelus bells ringing out from the church down the road. Lots of patients apparently complained about the noise they made. Said they found them irritating

174

when they were in labour. Well, maybe not the Catholics, but certainly the other denominations. Not that there would have been all that many other denominations in the Stella Maris then, because it was run by nuns.'

I knew I was babbling, but I couldn't stop. As long as I kept talking she wouldn't be able to deny me.

She reached out to grasp the wide mantelpiece, her knuckles whitening as she held on to it.

I was convinced she was going to faint, fall against the big brass fender and split her head open. Collapse at my feet and die, under the stern gaze of the judge.

I wanted to put my arms out and support her. Tell her not to worry, I didn't want to cause her any embarrassment. I certainly didn't want to kill her. I didn't even want to upset her. If she wanted me to I would go straight to my room now and keep quiet. For ever. Never tell another living soul what I had just told her.

She didn't faint. Or die. She pulled herself together with an effort that belied her fragile appearance and sat down in the big wing chair, her colour quickly returning to normal. Even in her distress, she moved with such regal grace you'd swear she was completely at ease. If you didn't spot the look of fear in her eyes.

But I hadn't meant to hurt her. She had to know that. 'I didn't mean to upset you, Mrs Beecham. I just need to know about my roots.'

'Your roots?' she said scornfully. 'What should I know about *your* roots? You're a servant in my home. Nothing more.'

She might as well have stabbed me in the chest with the big brass poker. It would have hurt less. 'Mrs Beecham, please . . . Couldn't we at least . . .'

'Is this about money? Is that what you're after? Did you charm your way into my home so you could blackmail me?'

Charm? Me?

'Did you plan all this?'

'No! Well maybe I did . . . but not in the way you might think . . . I never wanted to . . . I didn't mean . . .' It kept coming out wrong. And the harder I tried, the worse it sounded.

I began again. 'No. Let me explain. I . . .'

'You *are* a cunning little madam, aren't you? Coming here, biding your time. Waiting patiently until you caught me at my most vulnerable?' Her eyes were hard. Wearing their familiar icy glaze. 'How clever you were. Hiding your true colours all this time. Living in my home.'

'No, you've got it wrong. I didn't plan to . . . well, it wasn't exactly a plan. Well, maybe it was, but I don't want anything from you, except the truth. And I think I have a right to that.'

She was on her feet again.

I stepped back. But I needn't have worried. She had no intention of coming near me. She crossed to the big window, her spine ramrod straight. I recognised this move. I had seen it often enough in this very room. She was dismissing me. Waiting for me to leave.

To hell with that. 'Did you really tell people that you were having a fibroid removed?'

'What are you talking about?' She didn't turn.

'You said you were in the Stella Maris having a fibroid removed. When I was born.'

'And you came here to punish me for that?'

'I . . . no. I wanted to know why you . . . gave me

176

away. Taking the job here was a complete accident. I just happened to be here on that particular morning and Penelope mistook me for one of the applicants for the post.'

'You just *happened* to be passing? Passing *my* door en route to whatever little slum you inhabit?' Her chin was practically pointing at the ceiling.

And that's when I knew she was never going to acknowledge me. Not if I stayed here until doomsday arguing my case, trying to prove who I was. Not if I pushed my birth certificate under her nose. Up her nose. Not if I had a blood test *and* a skin scrape to validate my DNA. There was nothing I could do to make this woman acknowledge me.

I had approached her so gently. So discreetly. Intent on not hurting or embarrassing her. But I knew now that I was wasting my time. Maybe I had known all along and that's why I kept postponing this moment. Maybe I instinctively knew that if I approached her with the truth she would reject me out of hand. Again.

Bernie McHugh, the mother who had brought me up, had come from the toughest, poorest part of the inner city and she wouldn't treat a dog the way this woman treated me.

I tapped her on the shoulder. 'You snobby old bitch. You look at me when you insult me. I haven't done anything to embarrass you. I haven't told a living soul about our true relationship.' Except for Gerry. 'And believe me I won't be boasting about it. It's no pleasure for me to find out that instead of being the lady I took her to be, my birth mother is a twenty-four-carat bitch.'

She moved away. 'Don't you dare manhandle me.'

Manhandle? A tap on the shoulder? She'd never know how close she came to being smacked across her elegant, well-bred face.

'I want *you* out of my house. Now,' she said, her voice icily calm.

'Don't worry, you couldn't keep me here if you nailed my feet to the floor.'

She didn't react.

'I'm sorry I ever came here. Sorry I ever set eyes on you. And . . . and . . .' I racked my brain for something to wound her with, anything to shake that icy composure. 'I hope your jewellery and your crap paintings are at the bottom of the Liffey where they belong. Do you know what the Garda expert called the paintings? Mediocre. Not worth the canvas they were painted on. A bit like you, Mrs Beecham: all style and no substance.'

'I want you out of my house.' The calmness in her voice only fuelled my rising hysteria.

'You won't believe this,' I said, 'but I actually thought that underneath your cold, frigid exterior there might have been a little chink of feeling for me. How's that for a joke?' I opened the door. 'Oh, and I want to thank you for giving me away. It gave me the opportunity to be brought up by a warm, loving mother, instead of a cruel, heartless bitch.'

Rosie followed me up the stairs. 'What's going on? What was all that shouting about?'

'You'd better ask your Mrs Beecham.'

'My . . . ? Ah, now, give her a chance. She's still in shock from the robbery.'

'Is that what ails her? So shock makes you cold, selfish, and intolerant, does it? That's a new one on me.'

18

Three months' salary in lieu of notice

Gerry came hurrying out of his office to meet me. When he saw the suitcase he practically levitated with glee. 'Well done, Annie!'

Sandra sat at her desk pouting. Eyeing me suspiciously as I passed. From the look on her face, I might have been the grim reaper coming to wreak havoc on her happy little world.

'Poor Sandra,' I said, when Gerry and I were safely ensconced in his office. 'She thinks I'm after her job.'

'No harm. Keep her on her toes.' Gerry wasn't a man to indulge in sentiment.

That could explain why he didn't want to hear the details of my conversation with Mrs Beecham.

'All I care about is that you're out of that damn house.' I had never seen him so pleased. 'And no more talk about you looking for a flat. My house has two bedrooms gathering dust. Three, when I'm on night surveillance. You can take your pick.'

'Thanks. But only temporarily, mind. Until I get my head straight, then I'll have to . . .'

'Sure. Sure. But in the meantime why let all that space go to waste?'

'Once I know I'm not in your way. Or likely to start

tripping over your smalls in the bathroom.'

'Smalls?' He grinned. 'I don't know who you've been talking to. Where I'm concerned no woman has ever used that word.'

'Oh, please, enough about the legally blind,' I said waspishly.

But there was no denting Gerry's good humour. He laughed off every insult I threw at him. And kept the quips coming back, thick and fast.

It was exactly the kind of banter I needed to help put Mrs Beecham's bitter face out of my mind.

When Gerry announced that he was taking me out for a slap-up lunch in a nearby hotel, Sandra almost threw a fit. 'You haven't got time, Gerry.' She followed us to the door, wobbling precariously on her six-inch wedges, her skintight Capri pants showing off her long twenty-year-old legs, as only tight Capris can. She looked as if she never allowed a morsel of solid food to get past her oesophagus. As if she existed on a regular diet of MTV and spring water.

'Mr Walsh is going to ring you.' She was becoming agitated. 'He wants to run over the details of the new security plans for his factory.'

'Give him the mobile number.' Gerry held the door open for me.

'You said I'm not to give that out except in an emergency.'

'I changed my mind.'

'Mr Walsh won't be happy,' she said gloomily.

'Who is, Sandra? Who is? And are we meant to be happy? That's the question I ask myself every day of my life.' We left her looking completely perplexed as he caught my elbow and led me out through the honking traffic and across the road.

We ate in the silver service restaurant of the almost new hotel. Almost new because it was in fact a well-established hostelry, which had been taken over and refurbished by an American company said to have the Midas touch. But the atmosphere was undoubtedly European. The background music was undiluted Mozart and there were four glasses at every place setting. I could only imagine what a lunch might cost here.

Despite my gloom, which I was doing my best to disguise, my heart still did a little flip at the sight of the comprehensive menu. Good food could always restore my faith in life. 'Great menu,' I remarked.

Gerry frowned darkly at it.

I took another look. Had I missed something? And sure enough, there it was, way down at the very bottom. Gerry's *bête noire*. It was in very small print, but unmistakable. It said fifteen per cent service charge. I waited for the explosion.

There was none. He put the menu aside and began chatting happily, pointing out various well-known faces around us. And not only did he smile his way through lunch, ordering a very expensive bottle of Châteauneuf-du-Pape, something or other, but he also paid the bill without demur. *And* tipped the waiter, something I had always thought was against his religion.

Then he drove me to his house and carried my case up to the biggest bedroom.

Later on that evening, still in a jovial mood, he sent Declan and the Hiace to Haney Road to collect the rest of my belongings.

I'm not altogether sure but I think he chose Declan

over Barney because of his physical appearance. I have to say that I know for a fact that Declan had once dived into a swollen river to rescue a litter of drowning pups, but you'd never think that to look at him. He has the thin, emaciated face and narrow, lashless eyes of a cold-blooded killer. And he's the only person I know who can speak without moving his lips.

Mrs Beecham was either not at home, or too appalled by the sight of Declan stepping out of the old Hiace to show her face.

It was Rosie who handed him a sealed envelope with my name on it. *Annie.* That's all it said.

I opened it warily, convinced that it had to contain, at the very least, an abusive missive. If not a nail bomb.

In fact, it was a cheque. For three months' salary in lieu of notice. Mrs Beecham might be a cold, heartless bitch, but she wasn't a cheap one.

It was the only consolation I could garner from the whole sorry episode. Because no matter how often I told myself that it was her loss, her misfortune to refuse to recognise her own flesh and blood, the rejection still hurt like hell. I tried to convince myself that I was as well off not knowing why she gave me away.

What you don't know can't hurt you, the old adage said. What idiot thought up that piece of crap?

I could only compare the pain I was feeling to having a blind boil festering somewhere deep beneath your skin. You couldn't see it, smell or touch it but you knew it was there because whenever you thought you had finally succeeded in ignoring it, it suddenly hit you with a vicious dart of pain, just to remind you of its presence.

I told myself that a mother who rejected her own child, twice, wasn't worth fretting over, but I can't honestly say it helped.

What did help tremendously was the opportunity Gerry gave me: he allowed me to work like a Trojan in his office. And overworked as his tightly knit staff were, instead of being resentful of this newcomer suddenly appearing on the scene and meddling in what had previously been their domain, they were on the whole more than happy to accept my offer of a helping hand.

Every morning Gerry and I drove into town together. He would open the office, collect his post and then disappear off to whatever assignment he had accorded himself.

I'd get stuck into the shambles he called his ledgers, determined to impose some kind of working order on files that didn't appear to have been sorted since the great flood.

Checking through these left no doubt that Gerry and the other two investigators were good detectives. Why else would they be in such demand with the canny citizens of Dublin? But their typed reports were for the birds. And their bookkeeping system bore little relation to reality.

'Who's in charge of the bookkeeping? Mulder from the *X Files*?' I asked Sandra who was still in the throes of a major sulk.

'Nobody's in charge of anything,' she said snottily. 'We're a team here. We all muck in.'

'I'd never have guessed.' I sighed, looking at the ledgers.

I had a word with Gerry when we were alone in what was laughingly called *his* office. 'How can you run a business like this?' I pointed out the mess the books were in. 'I'm surprised you haven't gone bankrupt.'

'Er . . . now that you mention it, the chartered accountant has been making all sorts of funny noises lately.'

'And you thought he was doing animal impressions, did you?'

He sat back and laughed.

'I'm not kidding, Gerry. There's a bill here for a Mr Weaver that should have been sent out in May . . .'

'That's Sandra's job. She's probably a bit behind. It happens.'

'. . . in May 1997,' I finished.

'Oh, she wasn't even here then, she only started in ninety-eight.' He smiled proudly. 'Straight out of school. And a two-week FAS course.'

'This whole place is a shambles. I don't know how anyone can work in it.'

'We're a bit pressed for space all right. But there's nothing we can do about it. I tried renting next door to give us a bit more elbow room, but as you've no doubt seen somebody snapped it up for a Cyber Café.'

'I don't even mean the cramped conditions. I know how difficult it is to get suitable premises in town. I'm talking about the whole set-up. Nobody makes proper use of your computers. You constantly refer to back files and yet you don't even have a database.'

'Hold on, Annie. I think you've got the wrong end of the stick here. We're not office clerks, we're detectives. Our job is done out there.' He pointed to the street. 'We don't sit at desks all day, playing with computers. We're out there working.'

'I appreciate that. But you still have to keep some kind of order. How can you find anything in this mess?' I pointed to the mounds of paper on the desk.

'It's not easy, I'll tell you that.' He laughed.

'It's not a joke, Gerry. What the hell does Sandra do all day?'

He drew me to the door to point into the even smaller office at the front of the building.

Sandra was sitting with the phone wedged between her shoulder and her ring-covered ear. She was mumbling words of sympathy to an obviously distraught caller, as she scribbled quick notes in a desk diary. With her free hand she reached over to switch off the steaming kettle. 'I'm really sorry, Missus, but I'll have to put you on hold for a sec. I have someone on the other line.' She hit a button 'Yeah? The Dunning Investigative Agency. Can I help you?'

She threw four tea bags into a pot and lashed boiling water over them, while switching back to the first caller, to tell her not to worry, her problem could be sorted. If she kept calm. It was a miracle that she didn't scald herself as she reached over the teapot to jot down further notes with her free hand.

19

We all have hidden talents. Don't we?

A week after Mrs Beecham threw me out and I began my therapeutic blitz on his office, Gerry offered me a bona fide job. 'It is not *charity*,' he blustered. 'I don't give people jobs out of pity. We've needed someone like you for a long time. Although we didn't always know it. Besides, I have a feeling that if I don't put you on the payroll pretty quick, someone else is going to come along and snap you up. I never knew you were such an organisational genius. How did I miss that?'

I blushed. 'Maybe you never looked hard enough?'

But of course, except for when I asked him to trace Mrs Beecham, Gerry had only ever known me socially. And socially I was a walking disaster.

How could he have known that in an office environment I came into my own? That even the most obstinate figures leaped to my bidding. That with a press of a button I could get the most obtuse computer to cough up documents that had long been given up for dead.

Sometimes I even astounded myself with all this effortless efficiency. And yet when I was in Haney Road I couldn't hand Mrs Beecham a cup of tea without spilling half of it and tripping over my feet.

'Do you have any other hidden talents I should be aware of?' Gerry leaned across his desk, his eyes flirtatious.

And all because of a neatly rearranged file or two? And maybe a couple of columns of figures that I had made sit up and behave. Amazing the things that turn men on.

'You've transformed this place,' he said.

This was true. I had. You could now walk through either office without breaking your neck falling over piles of discarded printouts. Or the greasy remainder of a takeaway.

'I can't believe what you've achieved here in a single week. The last time I saw my actual desktop was some time in ninety-eight. I swear to God I thought I was in the wrong office when I came in this morning. I never knew I had an in and out tray.'

'You didn't. I bought that yesterday.'

'Jaysus. I hope you got the money from petty cash?'

'That's not a subject I want to discuss right now.' I grimaced.

'The in and out tray?'

'Your petty cash. I'm almost sure your present system is illegal.'

He clapped his hands in glee. 'Oh, Annie. Welcome to the Dunning Investigative Agency.'

'Madhouse, more like.' I wasn't going to get emotional. Therein lay danger. Gerry was really a bit too attractive when he smiled. Fortunately, that wasn't too frequent an occurrence even though his mouth gave the impression that there was always one lurking just behind it. But despite his dry wit he tended to be quite morose a lot of the time. At least that's how I saw him. But he was smiling now. And in the cramped office we were a bit too close for comfort.

I had to keep reminding myself that he still had that ring on his third finger, left hand.

Gerry's staff greeted the news of my legitimate employment with open enthusiasm. At least the two investigators did.

Sandra's reaction was a little different. She gave in her notice.

'You can't accept it,' I told Gerry. 'Apart from the fact that she really does work hard, I couldn't have it on my conscience. Talk to her. She admires you. Thinks you're great, for some reason.'

He raised a questioning eyebrow, but he did speak to her. Did his utmost to explain that my position with the agency wouldn't in any way infringe on hers.

The outcome of this little talk was that she threatened to walk out that very afternoon.

I took her to lunch. 'Sandra,' I addressed her sulky profile. 'I've seen the way you are with people. You have a terrific rapport with them. You bring out the best in them. You have a fiancé who adores you and Gerry thinks the world of you. And the clients have been known to send you thank you cards. I've seen them,' I added quickly, when she looked surprised. Although how anyone could miss seeing the cards was beyond me. They were pinned to the aeroboard behind her desk. Near the damp patch that resembled a defecating poodle.

'The only thing *I've* ever been good at is organising an office. I'm a complete failure at everything else. Every boyfriend I've ever had has walked out on me. My parents died on a holiday I persuaded them to take. My friends can't leave the country fast enough.'

I deliberately left out the business about Mrs Beecham. That was still too raw.

'Are you serious?' There was a little flicker of interest in her heavily made-up eyes.

'What I'm trying to tell you is that I'm no good with people. Or with anything living, if it comes to that. Give me a plant and it withers within the hour. And my father once bought me the cutest little hamster imaginable. Big mistake!'

'Ah.' I had her total attention now.

'Yeah. It was all shiny brown eyes and soft, warm fur. Really cute. I put his cage right next to my bed, because it was midwinter and I didn't want him to catch cold. I even threw a blanket over it. When I woke up next morning he was stiff. Dead. A few hours in my keeping and he gave up the ghost. For no reason that anyone could fathom. Not even the vet. Not even the vet's wife, who was a complete know-all. So, do you see what I'm telling you, Sandra?'

'Yeah.' She nodded understandingly. 'You're the kiss of death.'

'Well, I wouldn't put it quite like that. Although you could be right. But what I'm saying to you is that we all have our own special talents. Yours is with people and the agency needs that.'

She started to laugh. 'Did your father kill you when he found out about the hamster? Mine would have. He'd have beaten the shite out of me.'

'Er . . . no. My father wasn't the kind of man who would beat the . . . out of anyone. He hugged me until I stopped crying. Then we went fishing.'

'He took you fishing?' She was completely amazed. 'Instead of hitting you?'

I had to smile at the idea of my gentle father hitting

anyone, let alone me. He was so protective of me he wouldn't let a fly alight near me. At the first sign of sickness, or a fractionally raised temperature, he broke out in a cold sweat, but it wasn't only illness that brought out this fearful anxiety in my father. He was a man who couldn't close his eyes at night until he had removed every electric plug from its socket. This was *after* he had double-checked all doors and windows. He would have had a brace of Rottweilers patrolling the garden if he didn't suffer from a morbid fear of dogs.

'Better safe than sorry' was his motto.

That's why it seemed all the more cruel that he should have died in such a senseless accident. The Gardai said he was driving perfectly when it happened. Cautious as ever. Well within the speed limit. Road conditions couldn't have been better. The traffic wasn't heavy. And visibility was A1 because it was such a clear night.

But all this meant very little when the other car was driving on the wrong side of the road. And came tearing round a bend at seventy-five miles an hour. Joyriders, the papers called them.

The occupants of both cars were killed instantly. Didn't know what hit them, according to the investigating Garda. 'Your father was the innocent party,' he said gently.

It wasn't much of a consolation.

I went to bed that night feeling like an abandoned child. Four months later Mr Deedy called me into his office to tell me I had been precisely that all my life.

'My da drinks,' Sandra confided. 'That's his problem. When he's sober he's a different man. He wouldn't be anything like your father now. He never took me out, or anything. But he's OK. Except when he has the drink on him. That's why I like Jimmy. He knows when to stop.'

Jimmy was her fiancé. He worked in a garden centre. 'He knows everything about plants. After we get married we're going to have a huge garden.' She smiled. 'But we'll probably have a baby first.'

'Before you have a garden?' I was surprised.

'Before we get married. We've been saving for ages for our wedding but it takes years. Do you know how much a white wedding costs?'

'No idea,' I confessed.

'Well, every time we think we have enough, the price of everything goes up. Jimmy says we should just go to a register office. Just the two of us. Tell nobody. But I want a big white wedding. With a striped marquee and a band and everything. And me da giving me away. In tails. I don't care if I have to save for another *ten* years. 'Course, Jimmy mightn't want me then because I'll be full of wrinkles.' She laughed heartily.

In ten years she would be the exact age I was now.

'I'll send you an invitation, Annie. If we ever make it to the altar.'

'Thank you, Sandra. You won't mind me bringing my Zimmer then, will you?'

'Bring who you like. As long as you have a good time.'

'You're a magician, Annie,' Gerry said when Sandra withdrew her notice. 'I believe you're even invited to the famous wedding!' He tactfully avoided mentioning that I had been the cause of Sandra threatening to leave in the first place. 'Her only worry now is this database you keep going on about. She's terrified that if you go ahead with it she might have to learn how to use the computer properly. She likes to think of it as a typewriter with pictures.'

'Your whole office is way behind the rest of the world,' I said. 'All your files should be on your hard drive. And backup disks.'

'Ah, don't get too carried away here, Annie. I'm not sure I want to start dealing with floppy disks and databases. Last time I tried to put the files on the computer the whole thing crashed.'

'That won't happen, I promise you. I've already checked them for viruses.'

'There you go again, trying to blind me with computer jargon.'

'Stop acting the fool. You probably know as much about computers as I do. Didn't you use them when you were in the Gardai?'

''Course not. We were still using stone tablets then.'

'Very funny. OK, you stick to the detective work. Leave the office management to me.'

'Know something, Annie, you have the look of a woman with a mission. Why do I feel you'll have the lot of us at the mercy of IT before the year is out?'

I could only hope.

It wouldn't have taken a detective to notice that I was in my element here. It was exactly what I needed after my rejection by Mrs Beecham. I loved putting order on chaos. When everyone else lost the head over missing files or dud feedback I could sort it out with a flick of the wrist. Once it didn't involve personal problems.

194

When Sandra found the date stamper on her desk she was practically orgasmic. 'Did you see this, Gerry? Isn't it brilliant?' She stamped everything in sight.

'Paid for it out of petty cash, did you?' Gerry grinned at me. 'Oops, mustn't mention petty cash.'

I could hear him laughing all the way out to his car.

20

A visit from curly head

Hard as it was, I absolutely refused to let myself think about Mrs Beecham. She had hurt me enough. Caused me too much pain. I wasn't going to let her have any more power over my life. Besides, I had a whole new life now. I was the office manager of the Dunning Investigative Agency. No easy job, that.

Not that Gerry and his team weren't skilled detectives. Worthy defenders of law and order. They were, but the way they ran their office was criminal.

And Sandra was incorrigible. Depending on which TV show she had been watching she could arrive as Madonna, Britney Spears or even Miss Whiplash.

The only person she consistently admired was Gerry, so I put this little weakness of hers to good use.

I treated her to coffee and chocolate doughnuts in the nearby hotel. Then took the opportunity to point out the smartly suited receptionists. 'Don't they look really attractive?' I smiled, offering her another doughnut. Chocolate was Sandra's Achilles' heel. Although you'd be hard put to believe it, as she had a figure that wouldn't be out of place on a Parisian catwalk.

'Stuck-up cows,' she said, looking at the receptionists.

'They're not really,' I said. 'Tailored suits do give them an air of formality all right. But that's good for business. It makes people respect them.'

'Huh!' Sandra bit into another doughnut, sending a shower of chocolate particles down the front of her red bustier.

I played my ace. 'Gerry really admires these receptionists.'

She snapped to attention. 'Did he tell you that?'

'Never stops.'

The chocolate doughnuts forgotten, Sandra was now studying every move of the three well-groomed women behind the reception desk.

I suppose what I did might be classed as manipulative. But I only did it for the agency. And Gerry. I owed him so much. He had been my saviour. Without his support I don't know how I would have survived being rejected for the second time by Mrs Beecham.

Besides, Sandra was big into self-improvement anyway. That was her third favourite topic. After the wedding and cellulite.

Within a week it was like having a new receptionist in the front office. The tight Capri pants disappeared, to be replaced by smart business suits. Her heels were now well below five inches and her office manner bordered on the ladylike.

My only remaining concern was that she still wore her skirts so short that I worried about the health of our older male clients when she bent down to get a file from the bottom drawer of the cabinet opposite where they sat.

'Ah, I think it cheers people up,' was Gerry's only comment.

'You're the boss.' I retreated behind my computer, comforting myself with the thought that at least she had stopped copying the ludicrous figures she saw on MTV.

Next morning she came to work with an Ivana Trump hairstyle that almost tore the paint off the ceiling and rendered Gerry speechless.

'Ah, I think it cheers people up,' I said and continued filing.

It was coming up to lunchtime and Sandra and I were the only people in the agency, when I had a surprise visitor. Sandra bustled into Gerry's office where I was sweating over the books again, her eyes popping with excitement. 'There's a fella here for you, Annie. A fine thing but very posh.' She wrinkled her nose.

'For me? Are you sure?'

Before she could reply, a head of tousled curls appeared around the door.

'Jamie? How did you get here? I mean, I thought you were in France?'

'I'm home for a couple of days. Family business.' He looked sombre. 'How are you, Annie.' He shook my hand formally, then gave Sandra the dismissive Beecham look.

It was wasted on Sandra. She stood there, hand on hip, her blond beehive swaying gently as she checked him out to her satisfaction.

And Jamie was extremely satisfying to look at. Although he did seem a bit out of place in Gerry's cramped office. Maybe it was because he was wearing a full-length cashmere coat, in royal-blue, with a matching scarf thrown over his shoulders.

'Sandra, will you close the door. On the *outside*, please,' I emphasised as she reached for the handle.

She gave Jamie another curious look before leaving.

He didn't even wait for the door to close. 'How could you just walk out on her, Annie? Without a word of explanation?'

'Is that what she told you? That I walked out?'

'Well, didn't you? After you promised!'

'Now hold on.' I was just about getting my life together again, I didn't have to take this crap from a Beecham. Even if he was dressed in a coat and scarf that probably cost more than the contents of this whole office. 'I didn't promise anything.'

'Yes, you did. That day in the garden? The day we kissed.' He gave me an arch look. 'Have you forgotten?'

I hurried to check that the door was properly closed.

Back at the desk I was the office manager again. I was in charge here. 'You Beechams have extraordinarily selective memories.'

'You promised! If I hadn't been convinced of that I would never have gone to Paris.'

I looked at him in disbelief.

'Well . . . I certainly would have hesitated before going.'

I shook my head at the gall of the man. Where did these Beechams get their egos?

'All right. Maybe I . . . But you did promise.' He threw himself back in the chair like a petulant little boy.

'I didn't make any promises, Jamie. And she's the one you should be talking to. She made it impossible for me to stay. Just like she did to all the others,' I added slyly.

He was staring at the floor. Fortunately, Sandra and I now took turns vacuuming it. I would have

199

hated the Beechams to think I worked in a complete tip.

'I guessed that,' he said. 'But Penelope asked me to come and talk to you.'

'How did you find me? This address wasn't . . .'

'Penelope remembered your friend's name. And you told her he was an ex-Garda. She rang Superintendent Marron. He did the rest.'

I smiled. 'How pleasant it must be for you lot.'

'What do you mean?'

'Having friends in high places. It must make life so easy for you.'

'Not really, Annie.' he looked sad.

'Coffee anyone?' Sandra peeped around the door.

'No coffee.'

'I'll have some.' Jamie turned on the charm. He took the polystyrene cup from her hand as if it were Royal Doulton. I knew he wouldn't normally allow his artist's hands to be contaminated by such a vulgar receptacle, but he thanked Sandra so warmly she practically glowed.

'Sugar?'

She was beginning to annoy me with her sycophantic attitude. 'He doesn't take sugar.'

'Oh, sweet enough, are you.' She gave him a coy look.

'Oh, for God's sake, Sandra!'

She left us alone.

He took a sip of the grey coffee and all but grimaced. Serve him right. He thought he was God's gift. And he didn't even know how to kiss properly.

'Oh, please do finish your coffee.' I smiled when he looked for a place to put it down.

His bluff called, he had to nurse it instead.

'Penelope wants you to come back, Annie. She said to tell you we don't blame you for what happened that night. The night of the break-in.'

'What?'

'Well, you did leave her alone. You were hired as a companion. But we're not blaming you.'

'That's very decent of you.' I almost laughed.

'And we have all agreed that whatever happened between you and mother is in the past. We are willing to forgive and forget. We want you back, Annie. We need you there.' A note of pleading crept into his voice.

'Your mother wants me to come back to Haney Road?' my pulse quickened. Did *she* want me back? Had she reconsidered? Decided that she might have been hasty in her reaction to my confession? A shameful little flicker of hope began to ignite somewhere deep inside me.

'Actually . . . we didn't consult her.'

'You mean she doesn't know you're here?'

'You know what she's like, Annie. But once you come back she'll accept it. She can't be left alone. We are really worried about her,' he insisted.

'Then why the hell doesn't one of you stay with her? If you're so worried. You're her children. She brought you up. Not me.' Now I was really getting cross.

'We employed you. Took you on in good faith. Welcomed you into our home.'

'Oh, get out of here before I say something I'll be sorry for,' I yelled.

'If it's money that's the problem, Annie, we'd be prepared to consider increasing your salary.'

'Get out!' I bellowed.

The door swung open and Declan came in. He stood beside me, his lashless eyes on Jamie's face.

Even I could be a bit frightened of Declan and I knew he wouldn't hurt a fly. I think.

'All right, Annie?' he asked.

'Yes, thank you. This is Jamie. He's just leaving.'

Declan nodded, his eyes still intent on Jamie's face.

Jamie stood up. 'Will you think about what I said, Annie? I'll be in Dublin for the next few days. We could meet for a drink? A meal, if you'd like?'

'I don't think so.' I began sorting some loose papers.

'The door is that way.' Declan spoke without moving his lips.

Jamie left, looking completely intimidated. A new experience for a Beecham, no doubt.

I was so angry I could hardly think. How dare he come here and offer me money to go back and work for them. And then ask me out for a drink? Did he think he was so irresistible? With his big pleading eyes and curly hair and royal-blue scarf? Did he think he could come here and charm me into going back? As if? I wasn't charmed that easily. Well, not by someone who was a lousy kisser anyway.

Declan left without a word.

'Who sent Declan in?' I asked Sandra when I had calmed down.

She giggled. 'Well, you were shouting. Yelling at yer man to get out. I thought you sounded a bit freaked. All I said to Declan was will you see if Annie is all right?'

'Of course I was all right!'

'So how come you looked so relieved when curly bob left? Do you owe him money or something?'

I was pretending to slap her when Gerry came in.

'Who was that in the big Padjero?' he asked curiously.

'A moneylender.' Sandra laughed.

'Everyone's a comedian,' he said wearily and walked on into his office.

21

Almost as good as Sherlock Holmes, or maybe Dr Watson

Working in the agency was restoring my confidence at a rate of knots. The only danger now was overkill as I took to checking every scrap of paper I came across. Especially if there were figures on it. I loved figures. You could always trust figures, that was my creed. They never purported to be something they weren't. Even when they were fractions.

Then I saw Gerry's accounts. How the agency had managed to survive for eight years with such anarchic bookkeeping was a complete mystery. Their accounts followed no rules that I could fathom.

And the petty cash box had a culture all its own. It seemed to be used as some kind of in-office banking system to pay working expenses, overdue phone bills and something even more mind boggling – fifty pounds a week to a prostitute in Baggot Street. I checked Sandra's desk diary to discover that this woman pocketed this weekly sum to keep her eyes peeled for a certain car registration number. According-ing to the slips of paper floating about the petty cash box she had been receiving this spy money for almost seven months, calling in to the front office for it every

Friday at six. But when I checked my newly organised client files I discovered that the case she was *helping* on had been closed for four months. Mainly because the suspect was dead. He had died four months earlier from a pulmonary embolism – a clot in the lungs in layman's language.

The word clot seemed pretty apt here.

I cornered Gerry between clients. 'Do you ever check your account books?' I asked him.

'Oh, Annie, I don't have time for all that.'

'Well, if you had made time you might have discovered that you've been paying someone to keep an eye out for a man who's been dead for four months.'

'What? Let me see. Oh, that's Sandra's writing.' He lost interest.

I hurried out into the small front office. 'Sandra, is this your signature?'

She peered at the page. 'Looks like it.'

'Is it or isn't it?'

'It is.' She went back to her typing.

'All right. Can you give me one good reason why you hand over fifty pounds to a Mary Muldoon every Friday night?'

'Yeah, I can. She watches out for some old geezer around Baggot Street Bridge. For Gerry.'

'That *old geezer*, as you call him, has been *dead* for four months.'

Her Ivana Trump façade collapsed. 'Oh, shit! I don't believe it! He can't be,' she wailed.

'What would it take to convince you? Should we have the body exhumed? Checked for vital signs?'

'Oh, damn him. And damn Mary bloody Muldoon!'

I might have shared this sentiment, except that as things turned out it was dead James Murphy and the very much alive Mary Muldoon who led me to do something that was to benefit everyone in the detective agency, although not immediately.

For such a busy place there appeared to be a bit of a cash flow problem. 'What do you normally do when you come up short at the end of the month?' I asked Sandra.

'Oh, we wouldn't check it every month.'

'All right, every six months? Every year? Every century?'

She turned sulky. 'Gerry tops it up. From the bank.'

'From the agency account?'

'I dunno.'

'It's not his personal account, is it? Please tell me it's not from his personal account.'

'How should I know?' She tossed her head. 'I came from FAS. I'm not a qualified bookkeeper.'

'Where does the money in the bank account come from?'

'From cheques and credit card payments. They're paid directly into the bank.'

'And what percentage of the fees does that cover?'

She looked blank.

'Do you know what your yearly turnover is?'

She looked relieved. 'Oh, that's Gerry's department. But we make enough to cover the wages. And expenses. And the Christmas party.'

The Christmas party? I had seen the desk diary. It was chock-a-block with work. The agency should have been pulling in some serious money.

Was someone on the fiddle here?

I stayed behind late that night with a pot of coffee and an eyeshade. I was going to stay awake until I got to the bottom of this mystery.

It was after midnight when I found my first clue. I got so excited I almost knocked the coffee pot flying as I reached for a magic marker to underline the relevant entries in the ledger. Then, adrenalin pumping like crazy, I marked page after page.

I had discovered something so shocking that it was hard to believe it could have gone unnoticed in a place that boasted three detectives.

Someone was robbing the agency.

In the office diary the names of three corporate clients were repeated over and over again. All three were extremely large firms who used the agency on a regular basis. Had done so for almost two years.

I checked the investigators' reports. Nothing amiss there. There were huge sheaves of paperwork, all confirming jobs completed for the firms.

I checked the dates on the reports against the account books. There was no doubt that the big corporations were worthwhile clients. On every level they appeared to be straightforward. And all three had a satisfactory, ongoing relationship with the agency. They never once queried a report, or threatened to sue, as some private clients did when things didn't turn out as they had hoped. The corporations were also sending the agency more and more investigative work. These people were everyone's dream clients.

Except for one small flaw.

In two years none of them had paid the agency a single penny, despite all the work done on their behalf.

I rang Gerry on his mobile. 'Do you realise that not one of the three big corporations you handle work for has sent you a single payment in the past two years?'

'You mean they don't pay their bills?' He was astonished.

'Well, I can't find a single *recorded* payment.'

'What are you saying, Annie?'

'I can't be positive, but would it be beyond the realms of possibility for someone to intercept their payments?'

'Oh, my Christ!'

Gerry called a staff meeting for the crack of dawn. Well, seven thirty a.m.

I was exhausted from my long night poring over the books. But after a hot shower and enough black coffee to jump-start the most lethargic nervous system I was so wired that I could have raced the bus into town and won.

This was one meeting I was not about to miss. In an office manned by three sharp-eyed detectives I was the one who had uncovered a crime. After the beating my confidence had taken in the past few months this was manna from heaven.

Someone had been getting away with stealing from the agency for two years. It was about the most despicable thing anyone could do to a person as loyal as Gerry. He was fair to everybody, employees and clients alike, never short-changing anyone. And this was how they thanked him? I was so happy to be the one bringing this sly, underhand dealing to his attention. Not that I wanted any thanks for it. It was the least I could do for him.

When I saw the thunderous look on his face as he

came in from an uncomfortable night's surveillance, I knew he took this matter as seriously as I did.

He might be friendly with his staff and always appreciative of all the hard work they did, but he was nobody's fool. He wasn't a man to kick up a fuss over small discrepancies in the petty cash. That could be tolerated. Even overlooked. But having someone deprive the agency of what might be a quarter, or more, of its annual income was another story altogether. That was something he wouldn't take lying down.

If he had I would have lost all respect for him. Being generous with your staff is one thing. Letting them rob you is another. Someone in Gerry's employ was definitely picking up payments on the QT. And we were talking about a lot of money here.

Who needed money badly enough to give in to temptation?

Sandra? She was saving really hard for her wedding. Her father apparently wasn't above rifling her wage packet when he had a few jars on him. And she was the one who spent most time at the books.

Barney didn't appear to be the type. But his girlfriend had expensive tastes. He had complained about that often enough. 'You'd need to rob a bank to keep her happy,' he had once told me. Had he found an easier target?

And Declan? He was the wild card here. You could never be altogether sure what he was thinking. He didn't confide in anyone. But he was ambitious. Deep. Determined to get a law degree and better himself. I sometimes thought he had a chip on his shoulder. Gerry had employed him when no one else would. He had apparently been in trouble with the

Gardai when he was younger. Nothing major. Petty thieving, mostly. Had he reverted to his old ways? Or even moved on to bigger and better things?

Gerry opened the meeting with a speech. It was short, to the point and as diplomatic as only Gerry could make it: 'Right. Listen up. Someone has been robbing this agency blind and none of you is leaving this room until I know who it is.'

There was a stunned silence. Only Barney looked as if he thought it was a joke. The other two were horrified.

I stood up. 'What Gerry means is that we're all here to try to discover what happened to some large amounts of money that . . . that should have been paid to the agency and weren't. Or if they were they . . . they didn't turn up in the books.'

'That's what I said.' Gerry's expression was murderous.

Barney was the first to speak. 'Don't look at me. I'm a detective, not an accountant. I don't go near the books.' He was still grumpy at being called in on his day off. All he cared about now was getting back to his restless girlfriend. He suspected her of becoming overly friendly with the tenant in the upstairs flat, whenever his back was turned.

But it was Declan who worried me now. He sat looking from me to Gerry, his eyes like slits in his narrow unshaven face. Of course he had come directly from eight solid hours of night surveillance outside the corporation house of a man suspected of allowing it to be used as a part-time brothel.

Sandra was the only one who appeared bright-eyed and bushy-tailed. This was the new Sandra I had helped to create. She was wearing a suit that wouldn't have shamed Ivana Trump. That couldn't have come cheap.

'Has anyone got anything to say about this missing money?' Gerry asked.

Nobody said a word.

'Anybody?'

A couple of loose shrugs. But nobody replied.

'Excuse me, Gerry,' I said. 'I'm not sure that the money could be properly described as being missing in the real sense. We have no evidence that it was ever paid out. Do you know what I mean? If the companies never paid it out, then it's not actually missing, if you get my meaning.'

I looked around. Everyone seemed totally confused now.

'Right.' Gerry was as puzzled as they were. 'OK, let's start again,' he said. 'All I know is that we have been doing work for Killara, Bellavon and Greenmore for two years now. And *I* haven't received a penny from any of them. If anyone here got money from any of these corporations and didn't enter it in the books I need to know about it. Now!'

Sandra raised her hand like a kid in school. 'Excuse me, Gerry. Maybe the reason the office doesn't get any payment from those companies is because we have never sent them any bills.'

There was a stunned silence.

Gerry turned lime-green. 'Why not?'

'Because when I started here you said that these people were corporate clients and were to be treated with kid gloves. You said I was to hold off on billing them. They were to be invoiced only once a year.'

'Once a year?'

'Well, they were such big accounts. And ongoing.

That's what you said.'

'So you didn't invoice them at all?' Gerry sounded as if there was a tennis ball stuck in his throat. Maybe a whole rack of them.

'You said you would tell me when to do it. And you never did. I went to you one day and tried to ask about them, but you were on the phone to your wife, shouting and screaming, and you told me to get out. I was straight out of FAS. I didn't know when the invoicing was supposed to start. And they weren't like the other clients. With everyone else I send out the bills as soon as the jobs are done. I thought you had some other arrangement with these big firms.' She began to cry.

Gerry's face was ashen. He looked as if he might throw up.

'Jesus Christ, Gerry! And you practically accused us of stealing from the agency.' Declan shook his head in disbelief. He lit a cigarette, even though the fire regulations strictly forbade it.

'What do you mean practically? He did accuse us.' Barney was livid. 'Got us here to accuse us of thieving.'

Crushed with humiliation, Gerry shrank into the chair. He had called this meeting to flush out whoever was robbing him. And it turned out to be himself. His staff had always respected him. Held him in the highest esteem. There was no one quite like Gerry. He was everyone's hero. Now he had to sit here and be pilloried by his own people.

And it was all my fault. I was the one who had got him all riled up over this missing money, who had phoned him in the middle of the night. Anyone else might have taken their time. Found some other way to check out the discrepancies in the books before going public. Well, before accusing the staff. But I was too busy trying to show off. I had to let everyone see how capable I was. I had made such a mess of everything else in my life that I was determined to show just how clever I was with figures. My one true gift.

What had I done?

I glanced at Gerry as he sat there shamefaced. Looking as if he'd like to kill himself.

Or me.

Sandra and Barney began to bicker. It started out quietly, with sly asides. 'Maybe if you tried thinking for yourself, just once,' he was saying.

'What? Send out bills without the boss's permission? Get a grip.'

'What about the petty cash? You dip into that often enough without asking permission.'

'Are you accusing me of . . . ?'

'If the cap fits.'

'I never take a penny without putting a note in that bleedin' box and you effin' well know it.' Sandra forgot all about her new sophisticated image. She was now the true-blue Dub she had always been and she wasn't letting any culchie from Chapilizod accuse her of being light-fingered.

'Will you put out that bloody cigarette?' Gerry suddenly snarled at Declan.

'Don't take it out on me just because you made a pig's arse of things.'

'It's my agency. I'll make a pig's arse of it if I want to.'

'God, you're a stubborn fucker. No wonder your wife ran off with the pouf.'

Gerry was over the seat at him.

It became a screaming free-for-all.

I grabbed my coat and ran.

The sound of their fighting followed me all the way down the street and into a tiny pub on the corner where I hung my head in shame.

Sandra had called me the kiss of death. Maybe I was. Everything I touched fell apart.

22

A girl should always fight for what she believes in

The atmosphere in the agency was uncomfortably strained for the next few days. People still did their job, but the relaxed camaraderie was missing. And worst of all, Gerry went around with a terrible hang-dog expression on his face.

Every time I looked at him I was crippled with guilt. If only he'd lash out at me. Call me names. Anything. But he didn't say a word.

I had to do something. Find some way to undo the terrible damage I had caused.

I set my alarm for five thirty and was in the office long before anyone else was due to arrive. Then I put together the type of carefully worded business letter I needed. I made three copies, addressing them to the companies who had used the agency's services, with-out the inconvenience of paying for them. Then I filled in three even more carefully worded invoices for the work that had been undertaken on their behalf. At least I could trace all that on the files. This was the most difficult part, as some of the earlier files were practically illegible.

That done, I filled in a little note to the effect that if their payments didn't reach us by the end of the month the agency would be forced to resort to the courts.

Only one small problem remained. How could I get Gerry to sign them? The unbreakable rule was that his name had to be on every letter that left the office.

Sandra came in as I was printing out the final letter. She stood at my elbow, watching. 'Annie! Gerry will go ballistic. He'll lose the head altogether. He said it's dead money!'

'Why should it be? These people could hardly have thought he was running a charitable organisation. Who did they think he was? St Vincent de bloody Paul?'

I ignored her frightened look. 'Sign his name there, please.' I handed her a pen.

'Oh, Jesus, Annie. He'll kill us.'

'Why? You've signed his name before, haven't you?'

'Yeah, but . . . This is different.'

'They owe him the money, don't they?'

'He said we were to write it off.'

'No way!'

'He said we can all learn from this mistake. We'll be wiser next time.'

'Jesus! He's been listening to *Thought for the Day* again. He must be in a bad way.'

Nervous as she was, Sandra giggled.

'I can't believe the man,' I said. 'He grumbles about paying a service charge on a bill. He's tight as tuppence about tipping. And yet he'd let these people get away without paying?'

'They're real big. They give us loads of work.'

'I'm not surprised. You *were* giving them pretty competitive rates.'

Her face fell. 'I know. And it was all my fault. I should have . . .'

216

'Oh, give over, Sandra, you'll have to take a number if you want to join the guilty queue.'

'What do you mean?'

'Don't start snivelling. Just sign the bloody letters before he gets here.'

When Gerry arrived in the office I made Sandra behave as if it was just another 'business as usual' day. Which it was, of course. Nothing was ever allowed to interfere with the work in hand once Gerry was around.

I *was* forced to give her a couple of severe looks when I caught her gazing all teary-eyed at him, once or twice. *Pull yourself together*, I mouthed silently.

Gerry was so polite to me, it hurt. I missed his teasing banter, the razor-sharp insults we used to hurl at each other.

But we were so busy, we wouldn't have had much time for all that fun stuff anyway. Calling him to the phone was about as jocular as it got.

'Can you just have a word with Mr Lennon? He's calling about his wife again.' I handed him the receiver.

Mr Lennon's wife had disappeared without trace over a month before. According to her file she was extremely frail, well into her eighties and suspected of being in the early stages of Alzheimer's. She was last seen walking along the rocky seashore a few hundred yards from her home. Since then, nothing.

The Gardai had done their best, but the search had been wound down, which was why poor Mr Lennon had contacted the agency. Sandra told me that Gerry had been reluctant to take the case. He agreed with the Gardai that the old lady had most likely gone into the sea close to her home. It would be cruel to encourage the man to hope for a positive outcome in this instance. But Mr Lennon wouldn't be put off. He phoned the agency twice a week hoping we'd have some good news for him.

Gerry spoke to him now. 'Sorry. But I'll keep an eye out. I suppose she could be living elsewhere. Moved in with another family, you think? But it's not very likely, is it, Mr Lennon? Well, all right, if you think so. No, it's not completely out of the question. But it is a bit unlikely.'

On a day when he had more than enough real problems to deal with Gerry still had time to listen to the old man's fanciful ideas. 'You too, Mr Lennon. We will, of course.'

I took the phone from him.

'Poor old bastard. He thinks she might have taken on a new identity. Gone underground. He says she once voted for Democratic Left.'

Cruel as it seemed, we both had to laugh. If we hadn't we might have cried.

'OK.' Gerry was on his feet again. 'I'm off to check on the Laurence boy.'

He was gone.

I wasn't as confident about the letters I had sent out as I led Sandra to believe. Whenever the phone rang during the next week I practically jumped out of my skin. And I made sure to intercept the post every day. Before it reached Gerry's desk.

I took the bus in to work a lot. Too cowardly to share long, polite silences with him at every traffic jam. He didn't even seem to notice that I was making my own way into the office more and more. But then he was so busy it probably didn't occur to him.

'Gerry is here,' Sandra hissed dramatically, when she caught sight of his car pulling up as the postman sauntered in the door whistling happily.

I grabbed the bundle of letters from his hand. 'Thank you.'

The whistle died on his lips as he looked from me to Sandra.

'Anything?' Sandra whispered from the side of her mouth like an apprentice Mafioso.

Things were becoming ridiculous. We were both so nervous we were starting to draw attention to ourselves with all the stupid mistakes we were making. The detectives were completely puzzled by all the whispering that was now taking place. And only the previous day Sandra had wiped one third of an important file off her hard drive and it took hours of praying and a humiliating call to Intel before we recovered it.

And the end of the month was looming closer.

And then, just to top things off, I opened my morning paper to see a picture of a fancy fund-raiser emblazoned across the front page and who was looking directly out at me from the dead centre of the fashionably dressed group? None other than Mrs Clare Beecham, her perfect features flatteringly lit by a Waterford crystal chandelier that was fortuitously dangling just above her head. She looked stunning, more relaxed than I had ever seen her. She was clearly less than devastated by my absence. For a split second I imagined the big chandelier dropping from its moorings. But only for a second.

I glanced out through the glass-panelled door, to

see Gerry crossing the street. He was wearing his pugilist's face. Spoiling for a fight. But with who? I stuffed the paper into the bin.

'Nothing today.' I gave Sandra the post. 'But don't look so worried. If they don't pay up I have another plan. Especially if they complain to Gerry. Or withdraw their business.'

Sandra was out of her chair in an instant. 'What is it?'

'We run like hell and take on new identities. If old Mrs Lennon can do it, so can we.'

'Good morning, ladies.' Gerry was behind us.

'Perfect,' Sandra and I said in unison.

He strode into his office, a look of complete puzzlement on his face.

When we finished work that evening, Sandra and I stopped off in the pub to comfort each other.

'I mean, what's the likelihood that they would complain?' I asked. 'All we did was send them their correct bills.'

'Exactly. Two years late.' Sandra was close to tears.

'The worst they can do is refuse to pay.'

'Or withdraw their business.'

'He'll kill us, won't he?'

She nodded. 'I hate pubs.' She looked around.

'Why didn't you say?' I asked. 'We could have gone to the hotel.'

'Gerry was in the office. I didn't want him to start wondering why we were suddenly having a drink together.'

'Why shouldn't we have a drink together?'

'Because I don't drink. At least, I didn't up 'til now.'

'Then why did you order a brandy?'

'Don't ask stupid questions, Annie.' She took a

huge gulp of her Hennessy's. 'I don't know what I'll do if I lose my job, with the wedding coming up.'

'Look, you stop worrying. If there's any trouble I'll take full responsibility.'

'No. We're in this together. Why should you take the blame?'

'Because it was my idea to send out the bills. And you need the job if you're to keep saving for the wedding. I don't have that added worry.'

'I suppose not. You'll probably never get married.' She brightened up.

'Thanks, Sandra. I'm not completely over the hill, you know.'

'I didn't mean that. Just that . . . you don't really like men much. Do you?'

'I like some of them well enough. I just never seem to meet anyone suitable, that's all. Maybe I'm too choosy. I won't settle for just anyone.'

She laughed. 'That's what my mother used to say. Then she ran off with the Arab.'

I wasn't altogether sure if this was a joke. Or if she was being serious. She had such a deadpan way of saying things.

'Have you *got* a fella, Annie?'

'Not at the moment.'

'What about Gerry?' She watched me carefully.

'We're friends,' I snapped.

'All right. All right. Don't get your knickers in a twist. I was just asking.'

'We're friends! All right?'

'That's what my mother said about her and the Arab. Before they ran off. She brought him to tea one Sunday. Made a big salad for him. Huge. Opened a tin of John West salmon and everything. Put little

221

green olives in a dish my Aunt Maura brought back from Majorca. Next thing we know she's in Tripoli.'

'Are you kidding?'

'No. She's in Saudi now. Or one of those queer places where you have to cover your face with a veil, in case you inflame the greengrocer when you squeeze his figs. That's what my Aunt Maura said. Squeeze his figs? You'd have to laugh, wouldn't you?'

But she didn't laugh, for once. She looked desperately sad.

'She met him in the hospital when she went for a mammogram. She was sitting in the canteen having a cup of tea to settle her nerves. You know the way you would? And he sat at her table. Told her she had beautiful eyes and that he was a doctor. She was gone three weeks before my da sobered up. Then we found out that yer man was only a porter. A bloody porter? And she left my da for him? Just because he said she had beautiful eyes. My da is a tradesman. At least he was before he took the disability. Did his back in on the buildings. That's why he drinks. And then she goes off with a porter. A bloody Arab?'

'Sorry.'

'Ah, it's all right. My da and me get on OK when he's sober. It's the drink that changes him. That's why I never drank. I saw enough of it in our house. I swore I'd never touch it.' She raised her glass. 'Here's to us, Annie.'

We clinked glasses.

'Would you divorce a man like Gerry?' she suddenly asked.

'Gerry?'

'Would you divorce him?'

'Only if he was my husband.' I laughed.

222

She watched me with narrowed eyes. 'You can't fool me. You fancy him, don't you?'

'Drink your brandy.'

'You fancy him, I can tell. You get a funny look on your face when he leans over your desk.'

'That's called irritation.'

'Horny, more like.' She giggled.

I threw a napkin at her. But she was only joking. I knew that.

With barely twenty-four hours to go until the end of the month and my nerves coming close to breaking point every time Gerry beat me to the mail, we finally received definitive proof that there was a God.

Three fat corporate cheques arrived. Two of them by courier. The other by the regular post.

I signed the courier's book while he ogled Sandra's legs and she grinned brazenly at him, knowing full well that her hemline practically skimmed her pubic arch when she sat down.

'Sandra, your skirt!'

She ignored me, probably because I reminded her of her mother, who ran off with the Arab.

After scouring all three cheques for any possible inaccuracies, we hugged each other with delight and marched triumphantly into Gerry's office.

'How did this happen?' He was completely flabbergasted.

'Maybe they had a sudden dart of conscience.' I grinned at Sandra.

'Oh, yeah? And this dart of conscience told them exactly how much they owed us? And it struck all of them at exactly the same time?' He frowned.

Sandra suddenly remembered a job that needed

her urgent attention in the outer office.

'Sandra?' I called her back. But she was already on the phone.

'Well?' Gerry was waiting for an explanation.

'Don't be angry, Gerry. Sending them a bill was the . . . the businesslike thing to do.'

'I told Sandra they were to be written off.'

'I'm sorry, but I couldn't let her do that. And . . . you did say I could have free rein with the accounts.'

'I don't remember giving you free rein to hassle my clients.'

'I didn't hassle them. I sent them a very business-like letter. Very politely worded.'

He held the cheques between his thumb and fore-finger, as if they were red-hot. As if any closer contact with them might singe his hands.

'It's your money. They owed you.'

Silence.

'Do you want me to leave?'

'Have you something urgent waiting?'

'I mean the agency?'

He looked up at me, his eyes twinkling, his shoulders shaking with barely suppressed laughter. 'Why would I want someone who recovered all this money to leave? What do you take me for? A complete cretin?'

I giggled with relief. 'Well maybe not a *complete* one.'

Barney came in. 'Is it true? Let me see.'

Gerry handed him the cheques.

'Holy shit. Look at these mothers!' Barney was impressed.

'We have Annie to thank for this. I would have written them off.' Gerry shuffled his feet. 'I'll be able to clear my overdraft now. Pay all those outstanding bills. All those debts I didn't want to face.' He looked at me, his expression uncomfortable.

Had I embarrassed him? In front of his staff? Again?

It was the one thing I didn't want to happen. I had been determined this time. But what was I supposed to do? It was my job to handle the books. And he had worked hard for this money. And he had never pretended to be a bookkeeping genius. He was far more interested in helping people than balancing the books. Not that a bit of both wouldn't have gone amiss. But now was neither the time nor the place to bring this up.

'Don't forget Sandra.' I was determined to keep it light. 'She forged your signature. Without her expertise I couldn't have done it. You owe her a drink.'

'She doesn't drink.'

'I do now.' Sandra joined us, looking more like Ivana Trump than ever, as she had just applied another layer of confidence-building gloss to her already gleaming lips. 'I'll have champagne, please. With a bit of luck I might get a taste for it before the wedding.'

'You can forget that. You're lucky I don't have you busted for forging my signature.'

Her face crumpled.

'He's kidding, Sandra,' I reached out to her. He was kidding, wasn't he?

'I knew that.' Her voice rose thinly.

'Well, just this once, maybe I will treat us all to champagne. We'll nip across to the hotel and toast the growing success of the agency. And its staff.' His eyes were on me.

There was a loud cheer, until he added, 'After work, of course. You get back to the phones, Sandra.

And Barney you go down to that community school and check out the car the head is so worried about. He thinks it's a bit sus, being parked across from the school every lunchtime. If you even get a whiff that the driver is dealing, get on to the Gardai.'

'But the head said he doesn't want to involve them. In case it turns out to be an over-anxious parent.'

'If you're in any way suspicious, get on to the Gardai! I'd rather we all ended up with egg on our face than let that scum get a toe in the schoolyards. Use your mobile.'

Big fat cheques or not, it was back to business for Gerry.

No wonder he hadn't noticed the discrepancy in the books. The man would do the job for nothing. Wasn't he fortunate, then, to have a sharp-eyed office manager watching out for his interests? Then why was I so nervous?

He caught me staring as he collected a pile of notes from the printer.

'Are they all right, Gerry?'

It was a stupid question. Of course they were all right. The printer was practically new, top of the range and the notes had been written up to perfection. By me. And I was standing there like a fool, begging for approval.

He gave me one of those long, enquiring looks I had seen him use so often on new clients. When he was trying to figure out exactly what they wanted from him. And whether they were being honest and not manipulative.

Then he was gone. Off to deal with an adulterous wife this time.

Was he still angry with me? Had he just put on a happy front for his staff, despite still being annoyed with me for putting him through that awful charade about the missing money? But I'd got it back for him, hadn't I? Why didn't he say something? Why didn't he just say what he was thinking, instead of always leaving me guessing?

I wanted to run after him and demand that he tell me. But I had to keep my dignity. I was the office manager, after all. Couldn't let the whole place see me behaving like a neurotic schoolgirl. Or someone who has a crush on the boss.

23

Celebrations and condolences

Gerry was as good as his word about the champagne. Almost. He did pre-order it in the hotel. Three bottles of Dom Perignon, the best they had. But a full hour after we had gathered to drink it he still hadn't arrived. The waiter cracked it open without ceremony, and began filling our glasses.

'Ah. I thought we were waiting for Gerry?' Sandra was disappointed.

'Mr Dunning said for you to go ahead with your celebrations.' The waiter was officious.

'Isn't that just typical! He's caught up with the Stephenson case and everything else is forgotten.' Barney shrugged. 'Oh, well, all the more for the rest of us.' He laughed.

We had nearly finished the third bottle and were keeping our fingers crossed that Gerry would arrive before the bill, when Barney spotted him out in reception. 'Well, if it isn't our revered boss. Get over here, you tight bastard. Trying to get out of paying, were you?' he yelled across the hushed bar.

'God, he looks weird. Or does Dom Perignon affect your eyesight?' Sandra giggled as she stood swaying on her skyscraper heels.

'Just look at him! What some guys won't do to

escape paying.' Even the normally taciturn Declan joined in the slagging. 'Look at him cosying up to the penguin.'

Gerry was indeed in deep conversation with the hotel manager. And showing no signs of wanting to join us.

But thanks to the bubbly we were too happy to care. We were also getting louder and more rumbustious by the second, to the annoyance of several hotel residents who clearly equated downing two halves of best bitter with a hard night on the tiles.

When the laughter in our small group rose to disturbing levels the grim-faced manager approached us, his patent leather shoes squeaking in disapproval.

I thought Barney would choke, he was laughing so hard.

'Ms McHugh? Would you accompany me to reception, please?'

I turned to the others for support. Some hope. They were incapable of doing anything other than falling about in complete hysterics.

Barney finally pulled himself together. 'I knew it! They're going to bar you, Annie. Your reputation precedes you. They think you're going to demand back payments for that job we did checking their security. I told Gerry at the time that he was undercharging them. What did you do when you saw the account, Annie? Doubled it? Trebled it?'

'Shut up, Barney.' Sandra was suddenly serious. She was watching Gerry who was still standing by the reception desk, his back to us. 'I think something is wrong. Will I come with you, Annie?'

'Don't be ridiculous. He probably lost his keys again. That's twice this week. Some detective!'

But Gerry did look a bit odd. Well, even odder than usual.

What had Penelope called him? Primal. That was it. She called him primal. 'He's terribly attractive,' she had said, in her jolly-hockey-sticks voice. 'But there is something almost . . . primal about him.'

'The stuck-up mare!' Gerry laughed when I told him. 'What would she know about primal? She's spent her whole life cocooned by luxury.'

I tried to contain my giggles as I approached him now. *Primal?* You'd have to laugh. Especially when you had just polished off three glasses of Dom Perignon.

The hotel manager showed us into a small, windowless office behind the reception area, then slipped away, closing the door soundlessly behind him.

Gerry was strangely nervous. Unsure. It wasn't at all like him. He could be a lot of things, many of them annoying, but unsure wasn't one of them. He shifted from one foot to the other, obviously building up to saying something to me.

I found this extremely appealing. Sexy, even. Or maybe that was the champagne.

I reached out to touch his face. 'You're so sweet, Gerry. Has anyone ever told you that?'

He caught my hands. 'There's no easy way to break this to you, Annie. She . . . I . . . it might be better if you read this.' He put a folded newspaper in my hand. Folded so that, even tipsy as I was, I couldn't fail to look straight at the paragraph he wanted me to read. It was directly under BIRTHS MARRIAGES AND DEATHS.

And it was the very first name. BEECHAM.

'Oh, I know that name!' I laughed. And then I read on.

BEECHAM, CLARE. Suddenly. Deeply regretted by her heartbroken daughters Penelope and Francesca, her son Jamie, her son-in-law James and loving grandchildren, Simon and Amy. No flowers by request. House private.

And the whole room tilted before the lights went out.

'Take a deep breath, Annie. That's it. You'll be fine.'

I did exactly as I was told, holding my breath for another second, before exhaling carefully through my mouth.

'And again.' Gerry stood over me like an anxious tutor. 'OK?' He began kneading my rock-solid shoulders.

'Thanks. I'm fine. I don't know what came over me.' I straightened up.

'She was your mother, Annie. Of course you went into shock seeing it in the paper like that. I'm really sorry. It was stupid of me to show it to you without any warning. Stupid to let you read it, instead of . . . I should have explained first. I'm sorry, Annie, I wasn't thinking straight.'

'Don't be silly. I had to see it. What else could you do?'

'I'm really sorry.'

'I can't believe I . . . I feel so . . . I feel faint.'

'You wouldn't be human if it didn't affect you.'

'*Suddenly*? That means a heart attack, doesn't it?'

'Usually.'

'All those tablets she was on. They knew. And they

would never say. That's why they were afraid to leave her alone. But nobody told me. If they had I mightn't have said such terrible things to her that last day. Such insulting things. You can't even imagine.'

'I'm sure she said terrible things as well. It was probably a draw.'

I laughed hoarsely. 'It was. I called her a snobby bitch and she called me a cunning little slum dweller. Well, practically. Do they cancel each other out, do you think?' My lips were starting to quiver so much I had to put my hand to them to keep them still.

'Definitely,' Gerry said. 'Because neither of you meant a word of it.'

'I can't believe she's dead. You know Jamie came to see me at the agency? But I wouldn't listen to him. I thought he was trying to manipulate me. Well, he probably was. They knew all along that she was ill. They were always too quick to deny it. Determined to keep it from me. Of course, I was just the paid help. It's not as if I were family. Or anyone remotely important.'

'Will you go to the funeral?'

'Oh, my God. Do I have to?'

'She was your mother, Annie.'

Was this the man who told me not to go near her in the first place? And when I did, to get away as quickly as I could? To have as little as possible to do with her? Who told me she wasn't worth five minutes of my time, because of the way she had treated me?

'Out of respect, Annie. You'll have to go.'

Now that she was no longer alive I was to respect her? When she was she was best avoided. Safely dead, it was another story altogether? I couldn't think straight. I looked up into Gerry's worried face. 'Could I have a drink, please?'

24

Blessed is the fruit of thy womb

No matter how Gerry tried to force the issue, attending Mrs Beecham's funeral was never an option for me. I had already buried my parents. I couldn't go through that again. Not that attending her funeral would be anything like the ordeal burying my beloved parents had been. This was, after all, the woman who rejected me. Twice. Who refused point-blank to acknowledge me no matter how I pleaded. And Gerry thought I should mourn her?

'You might regret it if you don't go,' he said, 'for the rest of your life. I wouldn't wish that on you, Annie. You've been through enough. I advise you to go to the funeral. You need some kind of closure, before you can put it all behind you.'

What was the matter with him? Couldn't he see that I had already done that? Hadn't he noticed how happy I had been? I loved the agency almost as much as he did. Couldn't wait to get there in the morning and get stuck into a job where I was really appreciated. I loved being able to make decisions. In the Beecham house I'd been reduced to hanging around the kitchen and hallway waiting for permission to enter a room. Did Gerry really think I had some lingering regrets about Mrs Beecham?

As if.

I adored my new life. Every day brought some fresh satisfaction. And when a really problematic case was finally sorted the contentment level was immeasurable.

'All life is here, guys!' Barney would exaggerate, in a bad American accent, when we discussed the business. But cheesy as this sounded, it was true. We did see all sides of life in the agency. Good and bad.

The only downside for me was that the others were beginning to accuse me of being as much of a workaholic as Gerry, which was complete and utter rubbish. A workaholic? Just because I loved what I was doing?

And it didn't hurt that the boss happened to be so attractive, but I was fond of all the staff.

When we left the office in the evening I didn't rush to get away from them like I used to in Pussy Grub. Instead, I joined whoever was free to go for a jar and we crossed over to sit in the bar of the hotel discussing the more difficult cases on the books. Or in Barney's case, the ones which made us laugh the most.

Sometimes, only sometimes, we exchanged personal stories.

That's how I discovered how bitterly Gerry regretted not going to *his* mother's funeral.

He didn't tell me this, of course. It came from Barney in an unguarded moment, after he'd consumed five pints of Guinness and a Jameson chaser because Hazel, his girlfriend, had gone away on a girls-only weekend, which he suspected was anything but.

I learned that Gerry had every reason to avoid his mother's funeral. She had neglected him shamefully, in favour of her 'friends', for most of his childhood. In fact, if it hadn't been for a couple of protective aunts, he might never have made it to adulthood.

He hadn't given Barney the actual horrific details, that wasn't Gerry's style, but wasn't Barney a trained detective? He could read between the lines. His normally smiling face turned grim when he spoke about Gerry's mother.

And yet Gerry regretted not attending her funeral?

Was that why he was pushing me to go to Mrs Beecham's?

He seemed to have forgotten that his mother, neglectful as she might have been, had at least kept her child. She hadn't thrown him aside like a soiled rag, before his umbilical cord had fully dried.

I made a decision. I would avoid the funeral but attend the church removal. This would allow me to show my respect without having to go near a graveyard, something I was particularly loath to do.

Inside the packed church the priest solemnly intoned the prayers for the dead. Then lashed the coffin and the first two pews with holy water.

Then the rosary was said: '*Hail Mary full of grace the Lord is with thee, Blessed art thou among women, and blessed is the fruit of thy womb . . . Jesus.*'

Despite a leaden lump trying to block my throat I rattled out the response, with the rest of the congregation: '*Holy Mary mother of God pray for us sinners now and at the hour of our death. Amen.*'

Gerry waited in the porch while I joined the long queue of people duty bound to offer condolences to the immediate family, who were sitting like chalk statues in the front pew.

I saw Penelope first. Well, I couldn't actually see

her but it wasn't difficult to guess who was under the enormous black hat with the cartwheel brim. I gave my condolences to the hat and moved on.

Francesca was next. Her head bare, the church lights glinting off her long, shining hair, turning almost the exact same shade of ash-blond as Mrs Beecham's had been. She looked up at me with pain-glazed eyes.

I shook her trembling hand. 'I'm sorry about your mother,' I whispered.

To my surprise, the words were barely out when I realised I meant them.

'Thank you.' She looked through me.

Then the queue moved forward one place and I was face to face with Jamie.

His eyes were sunken in his tanned face, under-scored with heavy black circles. His clothes were crumpled. He looked as if he had just stepped off a long-haul flight, after travelling in the cargo hold. 'Annie.' He grasped my hand like a drowning man.

And my well-planned little speech disintegrated, leaving me with nothing to say.

We stared at each other, until someone behind me gave an impatient cough.

Jamie suddenly spoke: 'You will be coming back to the house, Annie?'

I froze in disbelief. Then I realised that he meant for the wake. Lots of people would be going to Haney Road for that. It was tradition. I nodded with relief, which he naturally took for acceptance.

'We'll see you later. We can talk then.'

'No, I . . .'

But someone else was already reaching for his hand, nudging me forward.

Outside the church Gerry had to lengthen his stride to keep up with me. 'I need a drink.'

It was Gerry's fault that I had come here. He was the one who had insisted that I acknowledge her passing. Gerry Dunning, armchair psychologist and renowned expert on human relationships. And now Jamie thought I was going back to that house.

'What about the Randy Goat?' Gerry asked.

I stared at him in disbelief.

'The pub near the house. It's usually quiet there.'

'Wherever.'

He was wrong about the Randy Goat. It was anything but quiet. The local soccer team had won a match and the place was overflowing with jubilant fans. I pushed my way into a corner while Gerry battled to get us drinks.

The noise was deafening, making conversation impossible. We had to be satisfied with nodding to each other over our glasses as a sea of club colours swayed backwards and forwards all around us, pushing us up against each other.

Gerry was protective of me, doing his best to secure some free space. But he was no match for a couple of hundred soccer fans. It became so hot and crowded that he had to help me off with my jacket. I tried not to react when his hands brushed against my breasts. And he was uncomfortable, now, I could see that. But it wasn't because of the soccer fans.

We tried avoiding each other's eyes, but this wasn't easy as our faces practically touched whenever the crowd swayed forward, forcing us together.

I told myself I should be ashamed. Having lustful thoughts when I had just stepped out of a church. Then we were thrown against each other again and it was obvious that a church was the last thing on Gerry's mind.

He put his mouth against my ear. 'Another drink?'

We were so close that I could see the tiny dark dots in the hair follicles on his chin. And then his mouth was directly in my eye line. I didn't have to say anything. He knew what I wanted. And it wasn't another whiskey and soda.

I don't know which of us made the first move when we got to the house. We had walked so circumspectly from the pub. But our lips were so tightly glued together that we practically fell into the hallway the minute his key hit the lock. We didn't even notice the cold draught whistling around our legs from the still open door. His mouth was so soft and hard and wonderful, all at once, that nothing else mattered. And his tongue tasted, just slightly, of Southern Comfort. Which I found a complete turn-on.

'Oh, Gerry.' I tore open his shirt and was startled to see a thin line of aggressive-looking dark hairs staring back at me. Then he was kissing me again and I wouldn't have cared if he had had a rainforest under his shirt.

'Annie,' he groaned into my neck and I could feel his teeth against my skin. And his body felt so good against mine, hot and hard and out of control.

He kicked the door closed and we were kissing deeper and deeper, until every part of me was on fire.

He began to unbutton my blouse, his hands trembling with impatience at the intricacies of the narrow openings. It made him clumsy and awkward. And far too slow.

I started to help. And suddenly he wasn't clumsy

any more, but doing all the right things with his hands.

And I knew it was going to be wonderful between us, better than anything I had ever before experienced.

And then he said it. Just a whisper between his wonderful kisses, which had me burning for him. Just the faintest whisper. But there was no mistaking the word. '*Sally*,' he said.

I lashed out with both hands. Punched him away from me with clenched fists.

He staggered back, his expression dazed, his jeans hanging open. 'What? What did I do? What's wrong?'

'What's wrong?' I screeched, covering my breasts, pushing my blouse back into my skirt, deliberately fastening the zip. *All* the way up.

'What's wrong?' he echoed stupidly.

'You called me Sally!' I spat.

'*What?*'

'You called me *Sally*! You bastard.'

'No, I didn't! I said Annie.'

'You said *Sally*! Do you think I wouldn't know my own name? How dare you call me by your wife's name?' Clumsy with fury, I groped around for my fallen bag and grabbed the shoulder strap, dragging it along behind, all the way up the stairs.

'Annie?' he called after me, his voice plaintive as a deserted child's.

Was that what he was? A big, overgrown child, still calling out for his mammy/wife?

'Annie? I'm sorry.'

'Too late, you bastard,' I screamed in temper. *And*, it has to be said, frustration.

'Anyway she's my *ex*-wife,' came the furious yell.

I slammed my bedroom door so hard the house shook to its foundations.

There wasn't sight nor sound of him next morning. Except for a note stuck to the fridge with a magnetic banana.

> Have to be in Wicklow by eight. Some kid has run away to join the eco-warriors down there. His mother wants him back to do his leaving cert. Says she paid a fortune for maths grinds and she's not having them go to waste.
> PS I did *not* call you Sally.

He bloody did.

Serve him right that she had run off with the pouf, if that was the way he carried on in an intimate situation. Calling you by another woman's name? Hardly the most lubricating form of foreplay.

I mean, it wasn't as if I wanted him to swear undying love for me or anything. But I had some pride. And surely expecting a man I was about to give my body to actually to remember my name wasn't asking too much? Imagine being called another woman's name at the peak of passion. Was there anything more degrading? Even Noel had remembered my name, for God's sake. And he was lower than a snake's belly.

I bet even Jamie, the crap kisser, would remember the name of the woman he was in the throes of making love to. And he'd have to remember how to pronounce all those convoluted French vowels.

Surely expecting a man to say Annie wasn't

asking a lot? 'I'm *Annie*! Annie . . . *Somebody*!' I had howled into my pillow, before crying myself to sleep.

Gerry didn't get back to the office until it was gone six that evening. I wasn't looking forward to seeing him. It was bound to be awkward for both of us, coming face to face after the embarrassing scene the previous night. But luck was on my side. There was a bit of a flap on.

Sandra had mislaid an important file that Barney had to have access to if he was to give precise evidence in a case of serious animal neglect. The accused man had a long history of cruelty to animals. And this was all verified in the missing file: dates, times, names of witnesses; even several colour photos of the poor mistreated animals. Without this file there was a very real danger that the accused might get off with nothing more prohibitive than a slap on the wrist: a warning from the bench.

Even Declan, who should have been on his way to set up a hidden camera in a hotel on the coast, stayed back to help us search for this important file.

And in the middle of all this the wannabe eco-warrior's mother was on the phone, demanding to speak to Gerry. For the fifth time that day.

'Oh, you're in luck,' I said to her. 'He's just walked in the door.'

Silently blessing her for her timely distraction, I handed him the phone.

'Mrs Nagle? Yes, I did. Yes, he is. Yes. No. I'd advise patience. *Patience*, Mrs Nagle. Well, it's a difficult age. Yes. Well, short of holding a gun to his head, I . . . No, I *don't* carry a gun. That was a joke. Well, I thought it was mildly funny. I'll talk to him

241

again tomorrow. Yes.' He put down the phone swearing under his breath.

'The eco-warrior isn't keen to return to home and hearth, then?' I was on my knees searching for the file.

'With a mother like that? Do you blame him?'

Barney interrupted us. 'I need the Leeson file, boss. I'm in court first thing in the morning. And the file has gone missing. That whole case is up shit creek if we don't find it.'

'It's not on the database yet?' Gerry turned to me.

I gave him a withering look. I mean, the question wasn't even worthy of a reply. Whenever I began inputting on the still controversial database I was called away to do something else. I had tried to impress on everyone the importance of having such an invaluable work tool. How it should take precedence over all other office work until it was completed. How it would make for a much more efficient workplace for all of us in the end. But it was an uphill battle, trying to convince them just how useful it would be. Nobody was interested.

And now the head Luddite had dared ask me why it wasn't finished yet?

'I found it!' Sandra came rushing in, waving the file.

Barney grabbed it. 'Where was it?'

But Sandra had disappeared back to the front office, where Declan was waiting to give her a lift.

'You'd better get working on that database, Annie,' Barney said.

I held off on hitting him with the date stamper.

'OK, I'm all set,' he added. 'Boss, you're doing that surveillance at the Dalkey apartments tonight, aren't you?'

'I am. Unless Annie has other plans for me?'

'No.' I said it so quickly that they both looked surprised.

'Right, so. I'll grab a takeaway and some coffee. I don't suppose you'd care to keep me company, Annie?' He was throwing things in a holdall, his back turned to me.

'No, I'm going to stay on here and work on inputting the database that everyone is so anxious about,' I said sarcastically. 'Then I'll probably just . . .'

'OK. OK. I didn't ask for your life plan. See you all tomorrow, then.' He was gone.

'Who rattled his cage?' Barney frowned.

'He's tired,' I said.

'We're all fuckin' tired, that's the business we're in. All I do is crash out the minute I get home nowadays. Hazel is threatening to walk, if we don't start doing more things *as a couple*. "*We need to relate more*," she keeps saying. Relate more? How the hell do I do that if I can hardly keep my eyes open after I finish a shift? And what's all this *doing things as a couple*, Annie? How do I get around that? She's into dancing. I hate it. And she loses the head if I as much as ask her to tape *Match of the Day*. Let alone watch it with me. I mean, isn't that something we could do as a couple? Loads of women like football. But not Hazel. Mention it and her eyes glaze over. I'll never understand women. She keeps rabbiting on about some saddo who goes to step aerobics with his girlfriend. I mean, could you picture me doing step aerobics?'

'Not if I had to keep a straight face.'

'See, you understand.' He smiled. 'If only all women were as straightforward as you, Annie.'

25

The Dalkey stalker and whiskey-flavoured jelly

Gerry never once mentioned the night we almost did
it. Maybe he thought I had been so overcome with
grief at the sight of Mrs Beecham's coffin that I was
just looking for comfort that night. If he thought that
he was wrong. I wasn't devastated by her death. I did
find it upsetting, but no more than the death of a
stranger. I absolutely and positively refused to allow
myself to think of her as my mother. She was simply
the vehicle which had brought me into the world.
And then dumped me.

After all, she hadn't even attempted to hide her
repugnance when I told her who I was. She hadn't
shown me a glimmer of kindness. Made no attempt to
recognise me as her daughter. Or answer any of my
questions.

It wasn't grief over Mrs Beecham's death that had
lowered my defences that night in the Randy Goat.
Although I was feeling a bit guilty over wishing a
chandelier would fall on her head when I saw her
picture in the paper. Maybe that's why I drank the
two whiskeys far too fast and lost control. Although
the feel of Gerry's body being pushed against mine
had . . .

Anyway the subject of what had *almost* happened

between Gerry and I never came up. We continued to work well together. He was friendly as ever. I was agreeable. We talked about everything under the sun on our car journeys to and from the agency. No subject was taboo. Except that one.

I began to wonder if it had ever happened. Maybe it was all some kind of weird dream. Wishful thinking. At least the first part. The second bit might be better classed as a nightmare.

Anyway, the Dalkey stalker now consumed Gerry's every waking thought. This case had been a slow starter. Now it was on everyone's lips.

It concerned a middle-aged woman who was being terrified by a shadowy figure who materialised at night, outside her apartment block in a quiet seaside suburb. He only ever appeared after dark. And was slippery as an eel, because he was never seen by anyone else. And yet he got so close to her one night that she could hear his heavy breathing. Felt it on the back of her neck. That's when she called the agency.

The Gardai had been handling the case originally. But after a week of non-appearance by the stalker they had begun to believe that the supposed victim, a fading beauty now hitting sixty, might have imagined the whole thing. Maybe even invented the story to draw a little attention to herself.

She got the agency number from a friend and pleaded with me, on the phone, to send someone to help her. 'Whoever this stalker is, he's cunning,' she said. 'He kept well clear of my apartment all the time the Gardai were watching it. But the minute they left he was back in the gardens below. Ducking behind the lilacs. I saw him several times, but never well enough to identify him. And I'm positive I saw the flash of a knife in his hand.' She sounded terrified.

I managed to convince Gerry that she was genuinely in fear for her life. 'She's not making it up. I can tell.'

'How? How can you tell?' He watched me with narrowed eyes.

'I . . . instinct, I guess.'

'See! Now you're learning how it works.' He took the case.

After a full week of night surveillance, seven long boring nights when he encountered nothing more threatening than marauding tom-cats and was frequently forced to play Country and Western ditties to keep himself awake, Gerry caught the prowler. When he dived into the lilac bushes and immobilised him with a neck hold, the stalker wet himself with fright.

Incandescent with rage at what this monster had put our helpless client through, Gerry dragged him to her doorway, so she could get a good look at the pitiful specimen who had been terrorising her. The woman nearly fainted.

The stalker was her estranged husband. He had been keeping tabs on her to see if she was cohabiting with another man while he was still paying her mortgage. His knife turned out to be a short, steel-tipped umbrella, which he carried everywhere with him.

Nothing in the snooping business, as Barney called it, was ever as simple as it seemed. Instead of being a dangerous psychopath, the Dalkey stalker turned out to be a stockbroker with nervous kidneys, bad sinuses and a bigger overdraft than Charles Haughey.

Next day Gerry had a painful sore throat. He

blamed the long nights spent sitting in his car, with Tammy Wynette *and* the cold air on full blast. He was wrong. The sore throat turned out to be the precursor of mumps, which he got courtesy of his six- and eight-year-olds. Sandra and I both offered to nurse him back to health.

'Nah, you're needed in the office. Both of you.'

His cleaning woman was only too happy to earn a little extra by bringing him home-made soups and raspberry jelly, and taking his sheets to the launderette. He denied that she flavoured the jelly with whiskey. But when I questioned the contents of the soup he refused to answer. 'On the grounds that it might incriminate me.'

He had just about recovered from his mild bout of mumps, which his doctor assured him had in no way impaired his future fertility, when he heard that the pouf was down with them. Only he was so ill the army doctors put him straight into isolation and fed him with an intravenous drip, which started the whole army camp placing bets that there would never be a little junior pouf.

Gerry was on the phone to us within minutes. Promising a party. 'If he croaks I might even consider going to Mass again. Benediction even,' he added cruelly.

The pouf didn't croak. And he wasn't in isolation for long. Within a week three other serving officers had joined him, their cheeks swollen like wintering chipmunks.

Despite Gerry being out of circulation for almost two weeks the agency was busier than ever. Satisfied clients were giving us word-of-mouth recommendations for all types of investigative work.

'You might have to consider taking on another investigator.' I broke the news to Gerry on his first day back. 'And getting bigger premises.'

When he first opened the office in our south Dublin backstreet even calling it an agency must have seemed a bit presumptuous, as he was its sole operator, with one phone line and a battered Remington typewriter at his disposal.

But Dublin had been ripe for the detection business in the early nineties. The Celtic Tiger was about to be born. And blatant affluence brings its own brand of greed, Gerry said. And double-dealing. Within six months he'd been forced to employ a full-time assistant. And shortly after that he had to partition off a small section of his office to interview clients in strict privacy. Big as it was, Dublin still clung to its small-town mentality and nobody was prepared to discuss his or her problems in front of a curious office junior. Or an assistant investigator who looked as if he hadn't yet grown out of his first Holy Communion suit.

The partitioned area became known by the rather grandiose title of the front office. This was where I now worked. With Sandra. But even the front office, which had served the agency well enough for almost seven years, was becoming totally inadequate, given the volume of work the agency now attracted. One of us had to adjourn to the outdoor toilet when there were more than two clients present. That's how short of space we were.

It wasn't that Gerry didn't move with the times. He had already invested in two state-of-the-art computers after I convinced him that the ones we were

using belonged in a museum. Ditto the photocopier.
And shredder.

'Are you trying to bankrupt me?'

'Have I led you astray yet?'

'Chance would be a fine thing.'

Our gazes locked and I found myself blushing to
the roots of my hair that still refused to grow past my
shoulders, no matter how many headstands I
practised before bedtime.

'Annie? Is this what you've been looking for?'
Sandra came in waving a printout of a client's file.
Her hair grew six inches a week. At least. Well, if her
roots were anything to go by.

Glad of the interruption, I turned to her, my face
still scarlet. 'Thanks, Sandra.' I held out my hand for
the file.

'What's happening?' She looked from me to Gerry.

'Annie's trying to bankrupt me,' he said.

'Oh, is that all? I thought there was something sexy
going on, by the look on Annie's face.' She bolted
before either of us could react.

I began to follow her.

'Annie?'

'Yes?' I didn't turn.

'Was there something . . . something else going on?
Between us?'

'That Sandra is daft. It's all that hair bleach she's
using. It seeps through the follicles and down into her
brain, reducing its oxygen supply and blunting her
ability to think.' I raced after her.

I might have given him a different answer if he
would only discard that bloody wedding ring of his.
Why did he insist on wearing it? Was he still harbour-
ing some secret hope of a reconciliation with *Sally*?

Gerry wasn't slow about spending the extra income I had recovered for him. He traded in the old Hiace for a brand-new one and bought a ton of new office equipment. Which only exacerbated our space problems. Mainly because he refused to discard the old filing cabinets. So when two burly surveyors arrived to check out the connecting wall for the proposed extension to the Cyber Café next door, Sandra and I had to vacate the front office.

Sandra grumbled continuously about having to leave her workplace to facilitate a couple of *shifty surveyors*, as she called them. Both men were in their forties and Sandra had an aversion to anyone over thirty-nine. Unless they were distractingly handsome or severely rich, in which case she was sometimes prepared to forgive them their calendar age.

The two surveyors failed miserably on both these counts. 'I hope you won't take all day,' she said, as we tramped into Gerry's office.

'Don't say I never listen to you,' Gerry had boasted before he left. 'You've been moaning for so long about the bathroom facilities here that I'm having them check out the *possibility* of having a whole new toilet built, while they're on the job next door.'

'Are you feeling all right?'

This was the man who not two months ago had dismissed our gripes about the badly leaking toilet roof. 'It's a disgrace, Gerry. Sitting on the loo while the rain bounces off your head is not only undignified, it's got to be breaking some EU law.'

'Give me a break, Annie. If I get that fixed, what'll it be next? A water cooler for the front office?'

'Why didn't I think of that?' I said. 'It would save

us drinking all that poisonous coffee we're supposed to be so grateful for.' Then I dropped the real bombshell. 'What you desperately need, of course, are bigger premises.'

'Bigger premises?' Gerry's yell could be heard three doors down. 'You think I'm going to pay the highway robbery they call fair rents in this town?' he bellowed. 'My lease has ten more years to run. With my blood pressure, I'll be dead before that runs out.'

Gerry was probably the healthiest man in south Dublin. He hadn't an ounce of spare flesh on his trim body. And despite having had a successful career in the Gardai, *and* running his own flourishing investigative agency, he was still only thirty-seven years of age. I reminded him of this.

'Immaterial,' he said. 'Nobody in my family gets to see fifty.'

'You will. You'll live to be a cantankerous old reprobate. I can just picture it.'

'Thanks, Annie.' He grinned delightedly.

Only Gerry would consider being a cantankerous old reprobate something to look forward to.

'How are we going to make more space around here? It's becoming a nightmare,' I called after him.

'Get Barney to carry some of those old filing cabinets out to the jacks.'

'Then we won't be able to sit down out there.'

'You and Sandra can run across the road to the hotel when nature calls. They have great ladies rooms over there. With all sorts of women's essentials. Free talc and all kinds of other doodahs.'

He was gone before I could hit him.

I could see him out on the pavement; stopping to greet two little kids who were notorious street thieves.

251

He was giving them money again. As usual they were tugging at his sleeves asking for more. And of course he reached into his pocket again. The kids danced around as he drove away. I swear they were waving fivers at each other.

That was the infuriating thing about Gerry. Just when you were all prepared really to hate him for saying something disgustingly insensitive, he went and did something so sweet and generous that you began to fantasise about him all over again.

26

Will it all crumble to dust around our ears?

The building surveyors took an age, tapping and tut-tutting their way along every available inch of wall and ceiling, before finally packing up in disgust.

'What is it? What's the problem?' I asked.

'Let me put it this way,' one of them commented. 'If this building were a horse I'd shoot it.'

They laughed their way out the door, making a big deal of closing it extra gently, as if the least tremor might bring the whole edifice crashing down around us.

'Don't mind them,' Sandra said. 'They've been saying that about our flats for years. And they're still standing.'

But the attitude of the surveyors troubled me. Despite their good humour they had seemed to be genuinely concerned about the poor state of the building. Nothing I could do about it anyway. That was Gerry's concern. I consoled myself by working on my fast expanding database, which was beginning to impress even me. I couldn't wait to show off the end product.

I was completely engrossed when the door flew open and two scruffy little figures strutted in. It was the pair of little villains who had been waving the fivers. 'Gerry says we're to help you shift your files.' One of them leaned cheekily against the desk, while the other grabbed a handful of biros and slipped them into his denim pocket.

'You shift yourselves out of here.' Sandra slammed down the phone and marched around the desk. 'And *you* put them biros back, you little knacker.'

'Gerry always lets us take biros.'

'Not to sell them round the corner, he doesn't. I saw you over near Dame Street last Saturday. He said you could have a couple for school. And he's Mr Dunning in your mouth. Anyway, he's not here now, so put them back.'

He threw the biros on her desk, then looked her up and down as if he were a raunchy twenty-year-old and not an undersized ten. 'Legs eleven, ye skinny mare!'

'Get out of here before I call the Gardai.'

I had trouble hiding my grin as they gave both of us a stubby V-sign through the glass door.

'Gerry shouldn't encourage those little scumbags,' Sandra said.

'They're only kids.'

'You wouldn't say that if they smashed your boyfriend's car window and took his new cassette player. And every one of his Oasis tapes. Cost him the best part of a hundred quid, that cassette player did. And that was off the back of a lorry.'

'It couldn't have been those two. They're only babies.'

'Babies? They'd have the eye out of your head and come back for the lashes. You should try living around here. You wouldn't be so charitable.'

I retreated behind the computer.

'Little scumbags,' the normally easygoing Sandra

was muttering to herself. 'Should be in school, anyway. Little knackers.'

She had only just sat down when the two kids were back, hammering on the glass door.

'Jaysus, I'll kill them.' She was on her feet.

'Drunken Danny! Drunken Danny!' the kids chanted, then ran off.

A rough-looking man in his forties staggered up to the door. He was clearly drunk but determined to hold himself upright.

'Come away from the door, Sandra,' I shouted.

'It's OK. It's my da . . .' She was shamefaced. She helped him in and sat him on a chair by the door. He was a big man, who might once have been handsome, but whose features were now bloated by drink.

'Will I get coffee, Sandra?'

'Thanks, Annie. Put three sugars in it. No milk.'

'Drink it, Da,' she insisted when he tried to push it away.

'I need a few quid, Sandie. Just a couple of quid. Tide me over until me disability.'

I kept my head down.

'Drink the coffee, Da.'

'Are you going to give me the few quid?' He became aggressive.

Sandra took her bag from the top drawer of her desk. She put a five-pound note in his hand. 'Go on home, now.'

'A shaggun' fiver? Shure that wouldn't get me a . . .'

'It's all I can spare, Da. Give it here if you don't want it.'

It disappeared into his pocket.

'Go home and get something to eat. There are sausages in the fridge. And some of that curry from last night. And for God's sake turn off the gas when you're finished.'

'Sandra, if you want to take him home, I can finish up here.'

She shook her head. 'It wouldn't make any difference. He'd be out the back door before I left.'

We watched him stagger down the street, making a valiant effort to keep himself upright.

'He gets depressed,' she excused him. 'Since she left.'

'I understand.'

'Can't leave a penny in the house, though. He'd find it no matter what. He found my post office book last Christmas and went through the lot. But he's not a bad man,' she added quickly.

'No.'

'Sometimes I think Jimmy and me should forget about the wedding. It's only one day, after all.'

For the first time I realised why saving for her wedding was such an uphill battle. We watched as her father crossed the road against the lights, dicing with death as he wove his way through lines of tooting cars.

'I don't know how he escapes.' Sandra went back to her desk.

I tried to concentrate on my database. I didn't want Sandra to think I was feeling sorry for her. I knew how she would loathe that.

The letter from the firm of solicitors arrived out of the blue. My first instinct was to torch it unopened. In my experience a letter from a solicitor meant only one thing. Bad news. I took it to work with me and left it on the desk by the computer. At our eleven o'clock break I moved it a little closer to the shredder.

Sandra looked curiously at it, but said nothing.

At lunchtime it was still sitting there, provoking me. Daring me to open it. I tore it open.

It was terse and to the point. Would I ring the office of Williby and Son to arrange an appointment? I would hear something to my advantage.

I doubted it, somehow. But I couldn't resist ringing the number.

Gerry insisted on driving me to the solicitor's office. 'Look at you, Annie, you're trembling. You wouldn't be safe behind the wheel.'

I left him pacing the thickly carpeted reception area while I headed for the inner sanctum. 'I don't suppose you'd have a spare cigarette on you?' I heard him deliberately provoking the snooty faced receptionist.

She didn't reply. Just looked pointedly at the framed *Thank you for not smoking* sign above her desk which was the reason he had asked her for a cigarette in the first place.

Two minutes later I was suffering the agonies of the damned as an old man in a pinstriped suit took an age checking through mounds of legal-looking paperwork on his desk. He cleared his throat before finally turning to me.

He wheezed loudly. 'You are Miss Annie McHugh, formerly of 59 Fernhill Crescent, Dublin 12?'

He bloody knew I was. They'd sent the letter to Fernhill Crescent and the postal service had rerouted it to Gerry's house, because I had given his address to them for that very purpose. 'I am.' You couldn't win with these people.

'You resided there with a Mr and Mrs Frank McHugh?'

'Yes.'

'Both deceased?'

Jesus, Mary and Joseph, what was this? The Inquisition?

'Both deceased?' he repeated, staring at me over his bifocals.

'Yes.' I was bursting to go to the toilet although I had only gone just before we left.

'Good!' He seemed pleased. 'I am requested to inform you that Mrs Clare Beecham, late of 15 Haney Road, Foxrock in the city of Dublin, has willed you those very premises. Freehold and without . . .'

I must have gone into shock because from then on it was like watching a silent movie. I could see his mouth moving, his eyes scanning the page as he read from the typewritten sheet, but no sound reached my ears.

He finished his silent little speech and waited for my reaction.

I was frozen. Incapable of speaking. Or moving.

His lips went into silent motion again, his lower face looking almost comical below the small bifocals, as he indicated where I should sign.

Even while I was writing my name, signing the papers he put in front of me, I couldn't hear a word he was saying. I knew he was speaking, saying quite agreeable things, by the chuffed look on his face. But I still couldn't hear a word.

Trauma-induced deafness, I believe it's called.

I don't even remember leaving the office. But I must have because suddenly Gerry was beside me, tugging at my jacket.

'What?' I turned.

'Are you all right? You look terrible.'

'You . . . you're not going to believe this. She left me the house.'

'Who?'

'Mrs Beecham. *She left me the house.* I own the house on Haney Road. It's mine.' And only then did I believe it. The house on Haney Road was mine. I *owned* it?

'She left it to *you*?' Gerry stared in disbelief.

For some reason this really irritated me. It was as if he was saying that someone like me couldn't possibly own such a house. 'Have you a problem with that?' I snapped.

''Course not. I'm just surprised, that's all. People like the Beechams don't usually will their properties to outsiders.'

I gave him a killer look.

'Sorry, Annie. I'm sorry. I wasn't thinking. It's just all so . . . like . . . ?'

'Justice?'

'Unexpected is what I was going to say.'

Who cared what he was going to say? I now owned the big house on Haney Road. Annie McHugh, who should by rights have been a Beecham anyway, now owned their family home. If that wasn't justice I don't know what was.

I started to laugh.

But I felt like dancing. Mrs Beecham couldn't have despised me as much as she pretended if she willed me the family home. If she hated me, she wouldn't have left me the house she loved more than life, would she? After all, she had three other children. Well, two stepchildren and that snooty bitch Francesca. And she had chosen me to inherit her home? 'She's given me her home, Gerry! Can you believe it? She left me the bloody house!' I practically screamed.

'Are you sure you don't have a cigarette?' Gerry asked the startled receptionist.

She looked ready to dial 999.

Gerry said that even if the family *were* livid there was nothing they could do. Even if they were apoplectic. She had left me her house while she was of sound mind and there was nothing they could do about it. He said Williby and Son would have checked out all the legalities before contacting me.

'Well, I don't know about sound mind.' I was suddenly nervous as we waited to cross the road.

'Of course she was of sound mind. She owed you, big time. Her conscience obviously got to her in the end.'

'Her conscience? You think that's why she did it?'

He gave me a funny little sideways glance. 'Yeah, but also because no matter what, she loved you, Annie. You were her daughter.'

I did a happy little twirl, which could have been my last, because it landed me three feet into the busy road. There was a sudden screech of brakes and a big black cab came to a halt, its front bumper glancing off my skirt. The window wound down. 'You stupid bloody mare! What the hell do you think you're playing at?' The driver was halfway out the window.

'Sorry! Sorry!' But I couldn't stop smiling.

'Are you on something?' he snarled.

'No! My mother just left me her house. In Foxrock!'

He broke into a grin. 'Well, try to live long enough to enjoy it. OK?' He drove on.

'It's a miracle.' Gerry chuckled.

'I know. She did care for me, didn't she? She just couldn't find a way to show it. Until now.'

'I meant that a Dublin cabby smiled at you. After you practically walked under his front wheels. Buy a lottery ticket, Annie. You're obviously steeped in luck.'

27

Home beautiful home!
Or maybe not

Everyone at the agency took time out to congratulate me on my good fortune. In fact, they were almost as excited as I was. Couldn't wait to see the house Gerry kept raving on about.

'Let's all scoot over there now,' Barney enthused. 'Close the office for half an hour and just go. How about it, boss?'

Gerry made it clear that he thought this a pretty lame idea. 'Get back to work.'

'Come on, Gerry, civilisation won't collapse if we take an hour off,' Declan said drily, although he had already seen the place when he collected my major cheque from Mrs Beecham.

'Most votes carry.' Sandra giggled, putting her hand up in the air.

But one look from Gerry was enough to have her lowering her hand and her eyes apologetically.

I said nothing. It wasn't that I had no interest in seeing the house again. It wasn't that at all. The truth was I was practically delirious with joy. Incapable of rational speech. Unable to do anything except stand there, grinning like a fool.

Gerry looked at me and he understood. I could see it in his eyes. 'OK. You've talked me into it. Let's go.'

Sandra and I travelled in the car with him. The two detectives followed behind, in the brand-new Hiace, which Gerry had sworn was only to be used for surveillance duty. But then we were going to survey my property, as I said to Gerry.

The big gates were locked. I had to get out and use the key the old solicitor had given me. My key. I felt like the lady of the manor. As if I should be making a speech, or cutting a ribbon or something. Anything to mark the occasion.

The Hiace pulled up behind me and the two detectives leaped out.

'Oh, my God!' Barney was the most impressed. Or at least the most vocal in his admiration. 'Jaysus! It's a fuckin' mansion.'

Declan walked slowly up the driveway without a word. But then he wasn't a man who ever indulged in loose chat. He had never married. Never come under the civilising influence of women, I suspected. But he was a superb detective and would one day make a great lawyer, Gerry said.

Right now, Gerry wasn't saying anything. He appeared as overawed by the big building as the rest of them, even though he had seen it lots of times before. Of course, it wasn't mine then.

'Hard to believe a single family lived here,' Barney said. 'This place could accommodate a battalion.'

I linked my arm with Gerry's. Army talk could still make him uncomfortable. 'Wait until you see the rest of it,' I said brightly. 'The bedrooms are sensational, aren't they, Gerry?'

He smiled at me and we all trooped into the house. Oops.

Devoid of furniture, the rooms looked even more

263

impressive. Everybody oohed and aahed their way around them.

'But where are the curtains?' I looked questioningly at Gerry.

'Some people take the curtains when they move out. It's just what they do.' He shrugged. 'They take everything they can with them.'

'But she didn't move out. She died.' I was now checking the place more closely and really disappointed to see that even the potted plants from her balcony were gone. It made the place look strangely deserted. Gave it a forlorn, neglected air. Plus I would have liked a little bonsai to remember her by.

'Her family didn't die,' Gerry said. 'They obviously believe in holding on to whatever they can. It doesn't surprise me.' His face was a picture of satisfaction. Sheer delight that once again his view of the upper middle class had been vindicated.

'They took the bloody light bulbs!' Barney was trying the light switches.

Gerry's grin widened.

'They took the light bulbs?' Sandra echoed.

'And half the garden. Come and see this.' Declan was on the balcony looking down, his expression stony.

We all hurried to see the latest dastardly deed perpetrated by the terrible Beechams.

I hardly recognised the garden. Where was the gazebo? Where was the line of little box privets that marked the pathway to the herb garden? They were all gone. Lifted.

There were wide, gaping holes where two tall, slender, golden privets had stood below my window. The beautifully clipped privets had been my particular favourites, reminding me of pictures I had once seen of a villa in Italy where they stood along the sun-drenched terrace in big stone urns with naked men on them. They had been the first things to draw my eye when I walked out on my balcony every morning. 'She thinks they're common,' Rosie had told me when I said how much I admired them. 'The gardener put them in one spring, when she was away.' Common or not, someone had taken them. And they hadn't even bothered to fill in the holes.

'What happened to the gazebo?' Gerry's face was a picture.

'What gazebo?' Barney looked around.

'Exactly.'

'You've been robbed?' Barney asked.

'Ring the police,' Sandra said.

'Now hold on. There's three detectives here, remember?'

'So?' Sandra was disgusted on my behalf.

'We'll look like a right pack of eejits running to the Gardai about a missing gazebo.'

'So now it's just missing? Not stolen?'

'Well, when I think about it, it might not have been your gazebo at all.'

'Of course it was hers. You said it was in her garden. That means it was hers.'

'Not necessarily. It could have been removed before the house was willed to her. Did the solicitor say anything about a gazebo, Annie?'

'No,' I had to admit.

'So let's not get on our high horses here and start reporting something that may not have been stolen after all. OK?' Gerry raised a warning finger.

'I suppose you're right.' I backed down, remembering the missing funds.

'What about the Japanese bonsai, then?' Barney asked. 'You said there was a bonsai, Annie.'

'And the little privets? Didn't you say there was a whole line of little privets over by that pathway?' Declan chipped in.

'I call that really mean. Taking a person's plants.'

They were all talking at once.

'Hold on here! Hold on!' Gerry yelled. 'Annie has been given a house worth a small fortune and you lot are trying to get her all worked up about a few privets?'

'Well, if they're her privets?' Sandra was bursting with indignation.

'Annie, do you want to do battle over a few plants?'

'Er . . . I suppose not. But I did love that gazebo.'

He sighed. 'OK. Do you want to fight for it?'

'No.' I sulked.

'So that's that. Enough about the plants, you lot. Let Annie enjoy her house. Let's go and check out the rest of the place. You haven't even looked at the kitchen yet.'

'Are you sure it's still there? Maybe they took the kitchen sink an' all. It wouldn't surprise me.'

'That's enough, Barney. You're upsetting Annie.'

But he wasn't. What *was* upsetting me was the Beechams' vindictive behaviour. They couldn't stop me getting the house, so they ripped up the garden. They knew how much I loved that garden. How much *she* loved the garden. Were they venting their spite on *her* as much as me by wrecking it? Why else would they have stripped it bare? They were hardly short of a few bob, any of them. I knew how much their father had settled on them. They had more money than the queen of England. And even allowing for Rosie's tendency to exaggerate they were still unlikely to have to dig plants out of the garden to survive. This was an act of pure spite. Sheer vandalism. Done for no other reason but to display their fury at their home being willed to someone outside the family.

If only they knew.

I didn't feel at all guilty about being willed their home. Gerry was right when he said they had been cosseted by wealth and privilege all their lives. My parents had scrimped and saved to give me a halfway decent life. My mother had deprived herself of basic comforts to send me to the best schools.

Mrs Beecham had her cars valeted every week without giving it a second thought.

My father spent every Saturday morning of his adult life washing whichever second-hand car he was the proud owner of at the time. Polishing it for hours, even when there was four inches of snow on the ground. 'It helps it keep its value,' he used to say, his hands turning blue with the cold.

No, I didn't feel guilty about getting the Beecham house. What else had they ever given me? Only trouble.

'Jaysus, you must have been some companion, all the same.' Barney stood back to have a last look at the big house as I locked the door.

'What do you mean?'

'To be left a place like this. What did you do, drug the woman? Hypnotise her? *Leave me your valuables! I want your house!*' he drawled in a deep, sonorous voice.

The others cracked up, as if this were the funniest thing they had ever heard. Nice, kind Annie hypnotising an old woman to get her hands on her property. I didn't laugh. I hated the idea of people even hinting that I might have somehow conned Mrs Beecham out of her home. Even if it was only said in fun.

Gerry opened the car door for me. 'She was Annie's mother,' he said quietly.

The laughter faded. They stood there, transfixed. Gawking like halfwits from me to the big house. And back again.

'Your mother?' Sandra clearly didn't believe it.

'But . . . didn't your parents die in that awful car crash?' Barney was completely flummoxed.

'Yes, they did,' Gerry answered for me.

'But you just said that Mrs Beecham was her mother?' Declan's eyes almost disappeared as he puzzled this out.

'You're the detectives. You figure it out.' Gerry nudged me into the car before walking round to the driver's side, his head stuck in the air.

We drove away leaving them staring after us. Even at a distance their embarrassment was unmistakable.

'You can be a cruel bastard, Gerry Dunning.'

'Life is cruel, Annie. If you don't believe me, go check our files.'

I suppose it was naive of me to expect them to let it go at that. To be satisfied with no further explanation other than that Mrs Beecham was my mother. Of course they weren't. It didn't take them long to figure out that she had been my birth mother. I'd say roughly the duration of their drive back to the office. But knowing that much only fuelled their curiosity.

Now they were dying to know more.

Sandra because she lived in fervent hope of discovering some deeply romantic and moving story under the humdrum existence of people's everyday lives. And the two investigators because they were trained to dislike loose ends.

'Give us all the details, go on,' Sandra urged.

'You know as much as I do. That's the honest truth,' I told her.

'Then how did you find your mother in the first place?'

I gave her a look.

'Gerry?' She grinned.

'Gerry.'

'Then why don't you get him to find out the rest of the story? If anyone can do it, he can. He's the best detective in Ireland. Why don't you ask him to find out how you came to be adopted? There's no better man for sifting through a legal mess.'

'But that's just the problem: there wasn't anything legal about it. I wasn't adopted. She just . . . gave me away.'

'What do you mean, gave you away? Like to St Vincent de Paul or something?'

'Pretty much.'

Sandra was horrified. 'Oh, the old bitc . . . biddy. Gave you away? Just like that?' She gestured.

'Apparently. To be honest I don't really care any more. I had great parents. The best.'

'Didn't they tell you anything about her?'

'No.' Much as I liked Sandra I wasn't about to unburden myself to her. Some things are best kept private.

Fortunately the phones began to ring. And in the

agency that meant that all private conversations had to be abandoned. Business always came first. That was the rule.

When Barney arrived at six we were still writing up files. He was looking unusually clean and smart. So close-shaven that I felt forced to ask him for identification. 'Who are you, sir?'

'Aw, Annie!' He flushed, pulling off his tie.

He had spent the entire afternoon in the district court, waiting to give evidence in a personal assault case. He had been assigned to work with a woman who needed protection against her abusive husband. They were sitting in a café discussing how Barney could best protect her when her husband ran in and hit her over the head with an iron bar. It had taken Barney and two passing brickies to get him under control.

All three detectives hated going to court. They all agreed that, what with the waiting around and the contempt some judges displayed towards private detectives, it could be more dispiriting than an overnight surveillance down by the rat-infested canal. They especially hated what was known as 'domestics', where the victim was sometimes put through the mill a second time by an articulate barrister, intent on winning the case for his client. The abuser. The law called it giving everyone a fair hearing. The detectives called it shite.

Barney poured himself a mug of fresh coffee and sat on the edge of Sandra's desk. When they were busy the investigators moaned about never having any free time. When things eased off, they couldn't wait to be busy again. 'What's happening? Anything exciting coming in?' he asked when the phones went quiet. 'No carnage or corruption in high places? No wild shoot-outs at a bank link? What's happening to this great city of ours? Has all the fun been taken out of life?'

'I told Annie that Gerry can find out about her real mother.' Sandra stopped typing. 'Why she gave her away, I mean.'

'I can tell you that without an investigation. What year was it? Nineteen seventy? And she lived in that massive house? OK. She was young, unmarried, from a conservative Catholic background. Her boyfriend ran off and she was at university or just starting out on a career in one of the professions. Her family refused to support her if she kept the kid. So they arranged a private adoption. Am I right?'

'Wrong on all counts,' I said. 'She wasn't young. *And* she was married. *And* she had dropped out of university years before. *And* she didn't have a career. She was a stay-home wife.'

'Why did she give you away, then?' He was completely astounded.

'Isn't that what we'd all like to know,' Sandra said.

'Not me, not any more,' I contradicted. 'It's all over and done with. In the past.'

'Has Gerry looked into this?'

'He tried, ages ago, but he came to a dead end.'

'Would you like me to try, Annie? Would you like me to have a go?'

'You'd better ask Gerry first,' Sandra warned. 'You know how touchy he can be about his investigations. He doesn't like anyone moving in on his turf.'

Sandra had just got a small part in a local community production of *West Side Story*. Barney had suggested calling it 'Ivana Trump meets the Jets'.

28

Meeting the family. Again

It came as no surprise when the Beechams contacted me. Through their solicitor, of course. I had been expecting it. I knew what they wanted and so did Gerry.

He gave me his considered professional advice. 'Tell them to go to hell.'

I did give his suggestion some thought. Especially when I recalled the spiteful mess they had made of the beautiful garden.

'That's nothing. They would have bulldozed the house if they'd thought they could get away with it.' Gerry was even more unforgiving.

'No, you're wrong, they really love that place. That's what this is all about.'

I did think they had a cheek asking me to meet them in their solicitor's office. Even if it was at my own convenience. Who did they think they were? Did they imagine that I would be so inhibited by a fancy law office that I would end up signing the property over to them?

Even Gerry seemed to doubt my ability to stand up to them. 'I'm coming with you,' he said.

'No. I have to do this on my own.'

'You're going to confront the *three* Beechams *and*

their solicitor? Have you forgotten how long it took you to approach their mother? They'll dance rings around you, Annie. Make mincemeat of you.' I knew he didn't mean to be insulting. He was just being protective.

But I didn't need protecting any more. I could handle the Beechams. Being willed the house had made all the difference. *She* had recognised me at last. Acknowledged me by willing me her home, that great big mansion of a house. I wasn't even sure I wanted it now, but that wasn't the point.

The Beechams were no longer creatures apart, some kind of superior beings with a God-given right to lord it over the rest of us. I was every bit as good as they were. Even if they didn't know it, yet.

I could only imagine the effect it would have when I told them about our close family ties. Not that I was proud to be related to them. But still. I had been sensitive about keeping Mrs Beecham's secret for long enough. For all the good it did me.

I insisted on one small condition to our meeting. I refused, flat out, to meet them in their solicitor's office.

They contacted me again to say I could choose the venue.

I left the letter lying around for a week or so before agreeing to meet them in the hotel just across from the agency. I might not want Gerry to accompany me, but (and I would cut out my tongue before telling him this) I had no objections to him being within shouting distance, in case my meeting with the vultures did go pear-shaped.

Sandra carefully brushed the shoulders of my new, sharply tailored trouser suit. 'You look like a million dollars,' she said. 'I might copy this design for my going-away outfit.'

As if she'd be caught dead in anything that covered her thighs. Just the same, I gave her a grateful hug. 'Thanks, Sandra. I wasn't sure if this was the right thing to wear.'

'It's perfect.'

Gerry watched us, a look of deep incomprehension on his face. 'Why does it matter what you wear to meet these people? You don't even like them.'

'But that's why!' Sandra rolled her eyes heavenwards at the sheer simple-mindedness of men.

'It matters,' I said.

'I'll walk you over.'

'No!'

'She has to go on her own. Can't you see that?' Sandra sighed impatiently again and gave my shoulders a final little brush.

I spotted them the moment I walked in through the big swing doors. It wasn't difficult. All I had to do was look for the most outrageous hat. And there it was in the middle of the lounge, looking like a flying saucer coming into orbit. Beneath it, Penelope's face was pale.

Jamie stood up as I approached them, his hand politely extended.

Penelope also got to her feet. Francesca remained exactly as she was, slouched low on the banquette seat, her expression sour as vinegar. She had clearly dressed for the occasion. She was wearing mud-spattered jodhpurs and riding boots, and her hair looked as if it hadn't seen a comb for a week.

'Hello, Annie. Thank you for coming.' Jamie had

used these exact same words the last time we met. Beside Mrs Beecham's coffin. And his handshake wasn't too different.

'Annie,' Penelope said politely as her cool fingers brushed against mine.

Francesca still had a mouthful of vinegar. She kept her hands firmly at her sides.

'I . . . er . . . what will you have to drink? You will have a drink?' Jamie was edgy and nervous. Not at all like his usual suave self. He didn't seem to know which way to turn as his hands fluttered about like a woman's.

I was just about to feel sorry for him when I remembered that these same fluttering hands had probably held the shovel that had dug up *my* plants. In *my* garden.

'Whiskey, please. Southern Comfort.' I tried to sound like Gerry when he ordered his favourite drink. I paused slightly before sitting down, giving them a chance to get a good look at the power suit I was wearing. This was not the Annie they had known. 'You look like Joan Crawford,' the saleswoman in Debenhams had said when I tried it on. I had been trying to look like Ally McBeal.

'Ice? Soda?' the waiter checked me out.

'Straight up.' That's how Gerry always said it.

Three pairs of Beecham eyes widened at once.

Sharks, I reminded myself. Although, to be honest, Jamie was looking anything but sharkish. In fact, now that I saw him with eyes unclouded by lust, he seemed to have a distinctly effeminate air about him. Of course, that may have been because I was spending most of my time with macho detectives. Well, semi-macho. I had never thought Jamie effeminate before.

He caught me staring and smiled.

Francesca shot him a vicious look. 'Can we get this over with?' she snapped.

'I'm sure you know why we wanted to meet with you, Annie.' Penelope was cool, but well-mannered as always.

Not so well-mannered that she didn't dig up your garden, Annie, I reminded myself.

'We want our house,' Francesca hissed.

Penelope silenced her with a look. 'I'm sure Mummy had her reasons for . . . for giving you . . .'

'Our home.' Francesca leaned forward in case I was hearing impaired.

'Francesca,' Jamie interrupted. 'Shut up!'

'Why should I? Am I to sit here and be polite to this . . . this creature who tricked Mummy into giving away our family home?'

'I don't believe Annie tricked anyone. At least, not deliberately.' He smiled at me.

He was definitely effeminate.

'Oh, what would you know, you live in a dream world. You and your *cher* Paschal.'

The waiter brought my whiskey. I took a large gulp.

'We would like to offer you a fair price for the house, Annie,' Penelope said. 'We know about the rider to the will.'

'Oh, that!' As if I gave a hang about that.

Gerry had pointed it out to me after Williby and Son had sent me a copy of the will. Mr Williby had read it out to me, of course, but from the moment he said 'she left you the house', I had stopped listening. Gerry asked if I realised that the rider meant that while I definitely owned it, I couldn't sell it to anybody outside the family.

In other words if I were a gold-digger, hoping to sell the house on the open market and make a fortune, I would be disappointed. Fortunately I wasn't. Either disappointed, or a gold-digger. So the rider meant nothing to me.

'As you can only sell to a Beecham, it has you in a bit of a bind, I should imagine.' Penelope's eyes never left my face. 'You can't put it on the market and I can't quite see what use you would have for a place that size.'

'Do you mean that anything more than a two up, two down would be beyond me?'

'Of course not. I'm simply saying that a house that size could prove to be a millstone around anybody's neck. You're young and unattached. There must be so many things you want to do with your life without being burdened by the responsibility of such a property. Whereas we, because of our emotional ties to it, are prepared to cope with the downside of owning it. Have you any idea what the upkeep of a place like that can run to? And you may not be aware but there are already quite a few pressing repairs that Mummy neglected to have done. They can't be postponed for ever. It takes a sizeable amount of capital to keep a house like that in good order. You're an intelligent girl, you must have realised that.'

'Oh, for God's sake will you stop buttering her up. You're making me sick. Why are we even talking to her? Look at her. Sitting there all smug and self-satisfied, after tricking Mummy out of her home. You just wait until you come to face us in open court. No judge in the land will allow you to keep a house that has been in the Beecham family for generations.'

'Francesca!' Jamie warned.

'Don't you Francesca me! This creature tricked Mummy. She probably killed her.'

Everybody gasped. Including me.

'Well, Mummy was doing fine until she left her alone, to be assaulted and robbed. That's when her health began to deteriorate. She went downhill from that night on. This . . . this creature should be charged with . . . with something.'

'Francesca, we were all guilty of leaving Mummy alone. At one time or another. You could have stayed with her. But you chose your horses.'

'They can't take care of themselves. Are you saying I should have neglected them?'

'Neglect the horses? God forbid.'

'Don't start your interminable squabbling, you two,' Jamie said angrily. 'We all knew Mother was ailing long before the break-in. And Francesca, you can hardly blame Annie because Mother had a heart attack.'

'I can blame her for stealing our home.' Francesca was practically yelling now.

Aware of the looks we were attracting from other people in the lounge bar, Penelope did her best to calm her. But Francesca wouldn't be controlled. She became increasingly volatile, her voice sounding louder and more strident as she threw insults after insult at me, again practically accusing me of killing her mother and stealing the family home.

I waited until she stopped for breath. Then, keeping my voice as low as possible I said, 'If you could keep her quiet for a second there's something I think you should know.' I cleared my throat. 'Your mother left me the family home because she was my mother as well. I'm her daughter.'

It was as if everything in the hotel suddenly went quiet. As if there was no sound at all. Nothing, except for three pairs of Beecham eyes staring in complete shock.

It was the one time I wished I had one of Gerry's sneaky little cameras on hand. Francesca's reaction alone would have been worth a couple of Polaroids. She turned porridge-coloured under her permatan.

Penelope's jaw practically hit the table.

Only Jamie's expression remained unchanged. But then he tended to have a slightly dazed look about him anyway, that's why I always considered him to be poetic.

It was only long afterwards, when I had time to think back over that afternoon, that I realised not one of them had accused me of lying.

'You have proof of this?' Jamie was the first to speak.

'She left me her house, didn't she? What further proof do you want?' I sipped at my whiskey, hoping they wouldn't notice the way my hands were trembling. I couldn't believe I had said it straight out, just like that. All those times I had tried to say it to Mrs Beecham the words had stuck in my throat. Except for that last time, of course. I had got the words out with a vengeance that day.

And now, five minutes into my conversation with *three* Beechams, I had calmly told them. With no hysteria. No temper. No yelling. At least not on my side. Gerry would be proud of me.

'She could have left you the house for all sorts of reasons.' Penelope recovered her jaw, but she couldn't stop her voice quivering.

'She was my mother,' I said calmly.

'You expect us to take your word?' All the self-righteous fury seemed to have drained out of Francesca.

'I don't care if you do or not. It happens to be true.'

They were looking at each other now. Exchanging long, fearful glances.

'I have my birth certificate with her name on it, if you'd like to check it. But I suspect your solicitors already know about that. Otherwise they would have encouraged you to contest the will. You did want it contested, didn't you? I thought so. Did your legal advisers put you off? Tell you you wouldn't have a leg to stand on? Tell you that you'd be bound to trigger a scandal? And of course you wouldn't want to trigger a scandal, would you? Sully the good Beecham name?'

Francesca lowered her eyes.

I didn't feel anything for them. Sandra meant more to me than these three put together. She believed in fair play, cared about it. All this lot cared about was being a Beecham. And yet they missed the glaringly obvious point: I was possibly as much of a Beecham as any of them.

Penelope turned away, to look fearfully into the distance, the flying saucer quivering visibly on her head.

'I bet you're wishing I would just disappear in a puff of smoke?' I said.

'No. I'm thinking how sad all this is.'

'Sad?' I was really taken aback.

'I . . . we had no idea who you . . . She never once hinted. All we knew was the promise she had extracted from us. That when she was gone we would respect some difficult decisions she'd had to make.

She never said what they were. Didn't mention the house. Never even hinted that she had left it to . . .' She swallowed.

'Her other daughter?'

There was an awkward silence. It dragged on for so long that I began to think no one was ever going to speak again. That I would be left sitting here, like a dummy in my tailored trouser suit that was beginning to chafe at the crotch.

It was Jamie who finally broke the silence. 'What do you want us to do?'

'Why should I care what you do? I'm the one with the house.' The Southern Comfort was beginning to kick in, filling me with Dutch courage. I took another swift mouthful before tugging at the crotch of my suit.

'But it's our family home.'

'You didn't make much use of it while I was there. In fact, you seemed to find visiting your mother a bit of a chore.'

'That's not true,' Penelope said. 'I saw her as often as I could. It's not easy driving up from Wicklow when you have two small children.'

'You seemed to find it easy enough when you wanted me to babysit them.'

'I *was* grateful, Annie.'

'Good. I'd hate to think you weren't. Is there anything else you want to say to me? I have to get back to my office.'

'No matter what you think of us, Annie, that house is our family home. It's my children's inheritance. Our great-grandfather built it. Nobody except Beechams have ever lived there.'

'Isn't it lucky she left it to me, then? Continuing the tradition.' I couldn't resist. I stood up and threw a note on the low table. 'That should cover my drink. Say hello to the children for me, Penelope. Oh, and . . .' They all waited. 'Peppa. Don't forget Peppa.'

'You just walked out? Without saying anything else?' Sandra giggled.

'What more was there to say? Besides, I was terrified that I might burst into tears if I stayed any longer. I wanted to leave while I was ahead. While I still had some dignity.'

'Didn't they call you back? That's what I'd have done if I found out I had a secret sister.'

I shook my head. 'They're not interested in me. The house is all they care about.'

'You should have let me come with you. I'd have told them exactly what I think of them.'

'Oh, I'm sure we'll meet again. I'm just going to let them stew a bit. They really love that house. All of them,' I mused, recalling the befuddled look in Jamie's eyes.

'You're not thinking of giving it to them, are you?' Sandra was horrified.

And until that moment maybe I wasn't. But the more I thought about it the more sense it made. Penelope was right when she said it would be nothing more than a millstone around my neck. How could I afford the upkeep of a property that size? Besides, I didn't even like it. It sort of gave me the creeps. Only my own room, and the garden, had ever held any real appeal for me. And yet, having it willed to me was hugely important.

Funny that not one of them had called me a liar when I said I was her daughter. Even Francesca, who had accused me of everything from trickery to murder, hadn't done so when I said that. Did they know more about their mother's past than they let on?

I wasn't sure that I cared any more. Today I felt more like Annie McHugh than I ever had. But not the old Annie. This was the new, improved Annie. The same, but different. Stronger. More powerful.

I was proud to be Annie McHugh. Someone who had been dearly loved by her parents. I wondered if any of the Beechams could say that. I knew they had been packed off to a boarding school at an indecently early age. My parents worried when I went to the corner shop. OK, they may have tended to be a little over-protective. But better that than lacking in warmth.

I was in no hurry to hear from the Beechams again. Let *them* experience a few sleepless nights for a change. I was too taken up with my work in the agency to waste any more time fretting over them. The detective agency and its staff were my main concerns now. They were the closest thing I had to a family.

The Beechams meant nothing to me. Even when Jamie tried turning his sad, doe-eyed look on me I felt nothing. As for Francesca, the only way you could connect with her would be to eat oats and whinny. Penelope was the nearest to normal, despite her insistence on wearing such peculiar headgear. And speaking like a latter-day Joyce Grenfell.

I decided that the house could wait. It wasn't going anywhere. OK, I might be hit for some tax, but I would worry about that when it happened. I didn't have to make any decisions yet.

29

Worries, worries, worries

The surveyor's report on the state of the office building read like a doomsday scenario. Gerry and the other tenants held a highly pressurised meeting with the landlord and his three legal representatives. He arrived back at the office like an Antichrist. But, being Gerry, he played his cards close to his chest. He was not about to confide in his staff.

'How did it go?' Sandra greeted him anxiously.

'Don't ask!' He stormed into his office and began working furiously at the computer, leaving us wondering if we would all shortly be out of a job.

'It must be truly awful news,' Sandra prophesied. 'He refused coffee. Dug out the single malt instead. That's a really bad sign. And me with the wedding coming up and the cake ordered. And I picked out a gorgeous veil on Saturday. I swear to God I'll throw myself in the Liffey if this place closes.' She went into his office to have him sign a couple of letters. A split-second later she was back out, whey-faced and trembling, the unsigned letters still in her hand. We huddled around the new water cooler, whispering our concerns to each other.

Barney was the only one with the guts to confront him openly: 'You have to tell us what's happening, boss. Are our jobs on the line here?'

Gerry looked puzzled. 'Your jobs?'

'Well, if you have to close the agency.'

'I'm not closing the agency. What the hell made you think that?'

'Well, where will we work from? The guys in the Cyber Café say the whole building has to come down. We'll have no choice but to move out. And even if we did decide to make some kind of a stand, where would that get us? We could find ourselves buried under a heap of rubble the next time a juggernaut rumbles past. Ned in the Cyber Café says the surveyor's report would give you nightmares. He says if we don't get out quickly we'll all be wearing cavity blocks on our heads.'

'The building isn't going to fall on anyone's head. They are going to gut the whole thing. Refurbish it from the ground up. It will be like a new building.'

'But what do we do in the meantime?'

'We're out.'

'How long?'

'They're saying six months. They've offered us temporary premises.'

'Cool! So there's no problem, then?'

'Not if you're happy to work out in Swords.'

'Swords? But that's miles up on the north side? Most of our work is . . .'

'Exactly. That's why I refused.'

'So what happens now?' I spoke from the doorway.

'We get on with our work.' He hit the computer keyboard a thump, bringing the eco-warrior's file on screen, and began adding extra comments with quick-fire typing.

'Gerry?' Barney tried to get his attention.

Gerry ignored him, his fingers tapping away at the speed of light. For a Luddite he had certainly mastered the new computer in double-quick time. But then Gerry allowed very little to get the better of him. I could only hope that the same would apply to this refurbishing business.

Barney and I crept away; practically tiptoeing out the door to where Sandra was waiting, her normally happy face a mask of concern.

'We'll fill you in later,' Barney said to her, putting a finger to his lips.

She turned to me. 'Annie?'

'I don't know what's going to happen,' I said truthfully.

'Sandra?' Gerry yelled. 'Could you get in here and earn your wages?'

'If you want my opinion, I think the boss is losing it,' Barney said glumly.

The four of us were sitting in the hotel bar, trying to decide if we should be doing something about the proposed closure of the building, or if we should just leave everything in Gerry's hands. We all sipped our drinks.

'I blame that wife of his,' Sandra suddenly said.

'Ex-wife,' I reminded her.

'What the hell has she got to do with it?' Barney asked.

'Well, she has him all upset about this moving to Cork business.'

'What moving to Cork business?' Barney and I said, practically in unison.

'Didn't I tell you? His wife is moving to Cork with the pouf. I heard Gerry talking to her on the phone. They were fighting like cats. Imagine anyone going to live in Cork? What normal person would want to live in Cork? And where will that leave Gerry? When will he get to see his kids now?' Sandra spoke as if Cork were on another planet. But then she was a fourth-generation Dubliner who thought the world ended at the Black Lion in Inchicore. Or at least dissolved into wild uncharted territory.

'Sandra, we're here to discuss the possibility of the agency closing, not Gerry's personal life. He's well able to handle his wife,' Barney said.

'Ex-wife,' I muttered.

'Wife, ex-wife, what's the difference?' he said impatiently. 'You're turning into such a bloody pragmatist, Annie.'

'Me?' I was astonished.

'Well, when I suggested we should all lock ourselves in the office and refuse to let the builders in until we were guaranteed proper replacement premises, who vetoed that idea?'

'Because it was stupid. The last thing Gerry needs right now is more hassle.'

'What about us? We could all be out of a job.' He was becoming really annoyed.

'That was my very point. Locking ourselves in the office wouldn't get us anything except some kind of notoriety. The building is unsafe; there is no denying that. You saw the surveyor's report. And he was on Gerry's side. Organising a sit-in like a gang of protesting students won't solve anything.'

'It would get us media attention.'

'Isn't that the problem? I was only in the agency three days when I realised that the whole investigative business is built on trust and discretion. Sorry if that sounds boring. You get your picture in the papers as a radical protester and see how many people will ring our number when they need help to sort out a problem. Surely the whole point of a private agency is its ability to be discreet. As well as having top-class investigators like yourself,' I added diplomatically.

'Annie's right,' Declan growled.

'Oh, the dead arose and appeared to many!' Barney pretended to be shocked by the sudden sound of Declan's gravelly voice.

Declan ignored this. 'If we want to do something positive we should be spending every free second we have out looking for new premises,' he said.

'Good thinking, Declan. I know of at least three great offices going begging. And all within a stone's throw of the city centre. Perfect locations. Only one small drawback. Their monthly rents would get you a villa on Crete. With a maid thrown in. I can't see Gerry paying that kind of rent. He's not that desperate.'

'Maybe he is.' I frowned. 'I saw him looking at a map of the Beara peninsula yesterday. At the time I didn't pay much heed, but with what Sandra's just said?'

Sandra went pale. 'You don't seriously think *he'd* move to Cork, do you?'

My heart plummeted into my new knee-high boots.

Gerry loved his little sons. And we *were* going to have to vacate our building shortly. Gerry had no ties in Dublin other than the agency, which could now work as efficiently from Cork as from some outlying spot in County Dublin, thanks to some fool setting up the new state-of-the-art computers. *And* a comprehensive database, even an Internet link after convincing Gerry that it would take the hard slog out of any search for general information. 'Jesus Christ,

Cork is a desperate long way off,' I said.

We all looked fearfully at each other.

'Cork?' Sandra repeated in the tones you might use for Armageddon.

Barney stood up.

'Where are you going?' Declan snapped.

'To get another round.' Barney headed straight for the bar.

Next day I took the afternoon off and spent hours preparing a special meal for Gerry and me. I had already lashed out a small fortune on a dress that the salesgirl claimed was infallible. 'Knock him dead, this will,' she said, stroking the soft fabric.

But would it keep him from moving to Cork, that was the question?

'In this dress you can't fail.' She smiled.

I wasn't so sure. It might take more than a sexy dress and a great meal to bond Gerry and me so tightly that he would forget all about Cork. And Sally. Besides, the dress was a little too tight. And it showed far too much cleavage. It wasn't me. I didn't feel altogether comfortable in it. But then, as the salesgirl said, you can't have everything. 'Maybe not,' I said. 'But at these prices I had hoped to find something that would cover both my breasts.'

'It's up to you,' she drawled, losing interest. 'But that slashed bodice style is all the rage this season. All the models are wearing it. Naomi, Claudia, Christie. See.' She held up a magazine and right enough there they were, all poured into something not entirely dissimilar. 'At least you have the height,' she said, as she watched me suck in my stomach and hold my breath for as long as I could without blacking out.

'He'll be on his knees.' She winked.

That wasn't quite the position I wanted him in but I was so worried that he might be moving out of my life that I was prepared to take desperate measures to keep him. Even wear this dress, if I had to. I was convinced that if I didn't do something quickly he would be off to Cork without a backward glance. It was up to me to get things sorted between us. For once and for all.

I showered and changed into the slash dress. When I saw myself in my bedroom mirror I almost lost my nerve. But one minor adjustment and it was perfect. Gerry was hardly the type of man to notice that I had pinned the slashed bodice together with a big Celtic brooch. Like the ones the Irish dancers wear on their costumes. It was the only thing available to me and it was either that or face the prospect of having my right breast fall into the lasagne midway through the main course. Naomi Campbell's favourite style, my arse. Only if she had breasts the size of crab apples.

Waiting for Gerry to get home I got through two glasses of wine.

'What's all this?' He went straight to the table when he came in.

I stood there, resplendent in my new dress that all the top models were wearing this year.

'Wow!' He couldn't take his eyes off the melon and ham starter, the bread rolls in the wicker basket, the chequered tablecloth and the bottle of Italian wine, which the man in Tesco had described as fruity but well-balanced. Which was pretty much how I hoped Gerry would view me. 'This is great. I'm starving.' He rubbed his hands together.

'We're dining Italian, as you can see. I know how

fond you are of Italian food.' I tried not to sound too disappointed that he hadn't noticed my new dress. Maybe the brooch *was* a mistake. The sales girl had sworn that any red-blooded male would have to be beaten off me by this stage. 'I thought you needed cheering up,' I said. 'I know you're under a lot of pressure at the moment so tonight I thought I'd try to create a mellow atmosphere.' I waited for his witty reply.

'Thanks, Annie.' He sat down.

All right, so he wasn't feeling particularly witty tonight? No problem. The fruity wine and good food would take care of that. I stood beside him as I filled his glass to the brim, leaning as close as I dared, without actually sitting in his lap.

He didn't react.

I sat down. 'It's all right if you want to talk shop, Gerry. I know how concerned you are about the agency.'

Rule one in the seducer's handbook: listen to his problems. I refilled my glass. 'Or if you're sick of work, the subject will be taboo.'

Rule two: if he doesn't want to talk about work don't force the issue.

'Nothing is taboo with you, Annie,' he said, eating his way through the carefully arranged slices of Parma ham before moving on to the melon balls, without once glancing up.

I sat watching him. Fiddling with my Celtic brooch.

'Great ham, Annie. Where did you find it?'

In the feckin' supermarket, where do you think? I nearly said. But that would have really spoiled the evening. Instead I began to nibble gently at my food, not wanting to smear my new lip gloss.

He continued eating.

Relax, Annie, I told myself, the night is young.

This was one night when everything was going to be perfect. We were going to take it slow and easy tonight. Not rushed and hurried like the last time, after the Randy Goat had raised the temperature between us. But I knew that if he once leaned over to touch my hand, or any other part of me, I would forget about the lasagne verdi in the fan oven and the baked apricots flambé to follow. And the Sambuca, with the little hard beans, that I planned to set alight as a grand finale.

But Gerry continued to eat as if he had been on starvation rations for a month. 'Fantastic ham, Annie.' Again he didn't even glance up.

'Wait until you see the main course,' I said as seductively as I dared.

He looked at me for the first time since he sat down. And I knew the dress was going to work. 'Annie?'

'Yes?' I smiled.

'I don't suppose there's any more of this ham?'

In the chilly kitchen I wrenched open the fridge door. Then kicked it closed after grabbing the remaining slices of the ham that I was beginning to wish I had never set eyes on.

Gerry tucked into the extra slices with almost religious fervour.

Not that I cared any more. I was now drinking the Château Larrivet, a robust red with a lot of backbone. So the wine merchant claimed. I had given up on the fruity.

Then Gerry put down his knife and leaned towards me, raising my hopes again.

I stopped drinking.

'You know, Annie, they're trying to convince me that this refurbishing could be the best thing that ever happened to the agency. They're going on about extending the back office by using up the old yard space. But I don't know.' He frowned. 'And yet that would give us almost five extra square feet. They're going to take out the wall dividing us from the Cyber Café, shift it to the right, which *would* give us an additional three feet. But I'm not so sure. They're talking about chrome hand rails and old Dublin prints on the walls.' He gave a short little laugh. 'Could you picture me with chrome hand rails!'

How about through your head? I thought.

'Are you OK, Annie? Did I forget to tell you how good this ham is?'

'No. You've said. Three times.'

'Best I've ever tasted.'

'Oh, I forgot to light the candles.' I lurched to my feet.

'Ah, don't bother. Save them for a special occasion.'

We were midway through the lasagne verdi and I was feeling no pain when the phone rang.

'That'll be for me.' Gerry looked grim. Well, even grimmer than he had looked all evening. 'I've been expecting this call all day.' He threw down his fork.

'Yes?' His tone was sharp. 'Of course I knew it was you. Don't start! Because they're my kids as well, that's why! What? I see them *most* weekends. If you think I'm going to take this lying down you're crazy. I don't care what he thinks; they're my kids. Yeah, sure. That's why you . . . Well, moving them for the second time in a couple of years is not what I'd call putting them first. No. Why should I? I'm their father, that's why!'

He slammed down the receiver. 'Bloody woman. How did I ever live with her? I must have been out of my head. If it weren't for the kids I'd have . . .'

'More wine?' I was suddenly invigorated. 'Try the Bordeaux this time.'

'No thanks, Annie, I've got to shoot over to Lucan. Somebody has an office there they want me to look at. I know it's too far out and I know I'll probably regret even going to see it. But what can I do? I must have looked at a dozen places already and each one is worse than the next. Or they want a king's ransom in rent. But I've got to keep trying.'

'Got to keep trying.' I waggled an encouraging finger at him.

He smiled and stood up. 'Thanks for the meal, Annie. It was great.'

So great that the cheese sauce I had taken all that time over was now coagulating on his plate? So great that a full portion of pasta verdi was left to dry out, curling up at the edges like stiff green cardboard?

But there was always the microwave later on. I could light the candles then. Take off the brooch. Open more wine. 'What time will you be back? I could always reheat . . .'

'No, don't bother. God knows what time I'll finish with this guy. He's a real oddity. Impossible to tell where you stand with him.'

'You don't say.'

'You know the type, just when you think you're getting somewhere he changes tack completely.' He was halfway out the door when he turned back. 'Oh, Annie? Nice dress.'

I threw the remains of the lasagne into the bin. From three feet away. I really wanted to throw it at the walls but I felt that might be verging on the childish. It might also have tipped Gerry off as to how frustrated I was. I didn't want that. I still had some pride left and I was going to hang on to it. Anyway the night hadn't been a complete waste. I now knew that he didn't really want to go to Cork. It sounded as if it would take very little to keep him in Dublin. I forgot about scraping the plates and sipped at the Bordeaux, letting it slide down my throat like the man in Tesco told me.

Gerry's main problem, apart from being impervious to sexual overtures when he had a problem, wasn't what everyone thought. It wasn't that he had to leave the building. Or that Sally was going to Cork. His problem was a simple lack of funds. He had little or no capital. His house was rented. His original marital home had been sold, with two-thirds of the proceeds going to his wife. On top of that he paid her a generous sum in maintenance. *And* he had a staggering amount of money being drained from his bank account into a college fund for his kids. I had seen the figures for this and it had practically traumatised me. It couldn't have been Gerry who set this up, because he was useless at working out financial details. But he was certainly paying for it. By direct debit. Which meant that despite his thriving business, Gerry was in deep financial shit.

I wasn't. I now owned a property worth more than the building we worked in. And the truth was I really didn't want it. The gesture from Mrs Beecham had been enough. Having her leave it to me was all the recognition I needed. It meant that she had finally acknowledged me. I had no sentimental attachment to the house on Haney Road. In fact, I hated it. My only attachment was to Gerry. Although I'd rather eat my own tongue than say this until I was sure how he felt about me.

The Beechams, on the other hand, loved the house on Haney Road. They had grown up there. To them it was home. Why not let them have their home back? For a price. Nothing too exorbitant, just the going rate. Maybe even a bit less. Always live straight, but plan ahead, my father used to say.

I took another mouthful of the Bordeaux. I had no use for the house on Haney Road. Penelope was right when she described it as a millstone. That's what it would be for me. The upkeep alone would cripple any normal wage earner.

But the Beechams were not normal wage earners. They had plenty of loot. They could give me some of it in exchange for the house. Leaving me with more than enough money to invest in a business I loved. And help Gerry out at the same time. The only stipulation I would make was that they would have to let me have the bulk of the money straight away. That shouldn't be a problem for them.

My problem might be persuading Gerry to part with a half-share of a business he had built up from scratch. But if he was as desperately in need of a cash boost as I suspected it could be done. He would then be able to afford to buy decent office space instead of hanging around in some Nissen hut, waiting six months or longer for use of his old offices, which were pretty inadequate anyway.

No matter which way you looked at it, this could

turn into the sweetest merger since Marks met Spencer. This deal would benefit all concerned. I might have miscalculated with the expensive lip gloss and the three-hundred-pound dress, but when it came to a business deal nobody could outsmart me.

All I had to do now was convince Gerry.

30

A born entrepreneur

Gerry leaned back against the curved banquette seat in the hotel bar and frowned heavily at me. 'Could you repeat all that, Annie?'

'Look, it's simple,' I enthused. 'I have a valuable house that I don't want. In fact, I hate it. I don't ever want to see it again. But the Beechams are desperate to own it. So I'm going to sell it back to them. Surely that makes sense to you?'

'That part of your plan does. It's the next part that I have a problem with. So could you just let me have that again? Please?'

I took a deep breath. 'I want to buy into the agency.'

'My agency?'

'None other.'

'Why?'

'Because I like the business. And I am good at it. Aren't I?'

'At running the office, no question. But there's a lot more to running an investigative agency than balancing the books.'

'But isn't that the beauty of this deal? You can keep complete control of the investigative end and I'll handle all the boring old mundane things, like keeping the books in order, seeing bills are paid on time. Keeping you from going bankrupt and ending your days in a debtor's prison.'

He smiled. 'But you're already doing all that.'

'That's true. But I'll be honest with you, I'm thinking of the future. My future. I don't want to spend the rest of my life working for someone else.'

'Not even me?'

'Especially not you.' I laughed.

The clear blue eyes watched me carefully. 'Jesus, Annie, sometimes you take my breath away.'

'Why, I didn't know you cared, Mr Dunning.'

'Whoa! Don't you try sidetracking me.' He grinned. 'I need to keep a sharp head here.'

'Me too.'

'So we'd keep this strictly on a business level?'

'Agreed.'

'Then tell me why I should take on a partner when I'm doing fine on my own?'

'One, because without my input you can't afford a decent office for the next six months. Or at least you can't without borrowing up to your oxters, which I know you won't do, given your views on banks and how you're convinced they screw their borrowers. And two, because you are working far too hard. You need someone to help shoulder some of the responsibilities of running an expanding business in this new millennium. Someone you can trust to make business decisions. When you're not available.'

'And that's what you'd like to do?'

I smiled. 'I could lighten your burden.'

He was laughing. 'You could set that to music.'

'I think we'd make good partners, Gerry.'

'So do I.'

'Oh, my God! Are you saying yes? Are you?'

'Seems like it. Providing we can come up with an agreement that will benefit both of us.'

'Of course we will. See how quickly we're already agreeing? Oh, this is going to be so exciting, Gerry. For us both.'

'Well, one of us seems pretty excited already,' he said drily, but there was no mistaking the happy gleam in his eyes. He looked really pleased. 'So what's the deal on the house?'

'The house?'

'The deal between you and the Beechams. How much is the house on Haney Road going to change hands for? And even more important, how soon?'

'I . . . I have no idea. I haven't even told them yet.' I was still reeling from the shock of his easy capitulation. I had expected a long drawn-out battle here.

'Oh, Jesus, Annie, what are you playing at? I thought you had it all sown up. You've been talking as if it's a done deal.'

I shook my head. 'I wasn't going to give up the house until I was sure you'd go for the partnership idea. I had to have your answer first. And it's not as if *they're* likely to refuse me, is it?'

'But you thought I might?' He frowned.

'This may come as a bit of a surprise to you, Gerry, but you're not an easy man to deal with. In fact, you're still a complete enigma to me.'

'And yet you want to be my business partner?'

'Maybe I like enigmas. Maybe I find them challenging.'

'Shit. And here I was hoping it was my body that was the real attraction.' He grinned.

I blushed scarlet and turned away, terrified that he might read the wicked thought that had just sprung to my mind. I didn't want that. Yet.

He tilted his head sideways to look closely at me. 'If I had refused, what would you have done?'

This time I looked him straight in the eye. 'If you had said no I would keep the house, turn it into a successful hotel and make a fortune.'

I wasn't going to tell him that I had nightmare visions of myself wandering around, haggard and grey and addled, in the big, empty house, like a latter-day Miss Havisham.

'A hotel?'

'I could run a hotel. No bother.'

'So this *is* purely a business deal? Nothing to do with . . . ?' He shrugged.

'Purely business,' I lied. I wasn't going to risk losing face now, after the fiasco of the other night.

'It has nothing at all to do with . . . you know . . . you and me?'

'Only in a business sense.'

'Well, I guess you've talked me into it.' He sat back again, putting a distance between us.

'I have, haven't I?' I smiled gleefully.

'Before you start clapping yourself on the back, there's something I should tell you. I've been thinking of taking on a partner for months now. It was only a matter of finding the right one.' A big, smug grin almost split his face in two.

'You bastard!'

He laughed. 'I never thought I'd get one as attractive as you.'

'You sly bastard!'

He was laughing so hard that I picked up a newspaper from the coffee table and made a swipe at him with it. 'You let me sweat. You let me grovel!'

'Did I?'

I hit him again.

'Does this mean you want to call it off?' Even with both hands raised in the air for protection, he was still laughing.

'No. But some day I'll make you grovel and sweat.'

'Oh, *yes*. I'll look forward to that. And . . . er . . . wear the dress you had on the other night. The one with the brooch? Only you might drop the brooch this time.' The blue eyes held mine. I raised the paper in fury.

A young porter strode across the room and stood protectively beside Gerry, while glaring daggers at me.

'It's OK, Sean.' Gerry grinned at him. 'She's my new partner. We're having a business meeting.'

'Oh.' The young man began to retreat.

'In fact, I think she's moving in for a complete takeover.' He laughed. 'What do you think, Sean?'

'What would I know, Gerry. I'm still on probation.'

Despite my insistence that the partnership agreement between Gerry and me was strictly business, it did cause a major shift in our relationship. For some reason it heated things up between us. Suddenly everything became more urgent. Not least our unresolved attraction. That had been there for a long time, of course. But it had always been controllable, except for that one time when it shocked both of us by breaking out into sweaty, salivating lust, which had us tearing each other's clothes off in the cold hallway. But then Gerry had mucked that up.

At least our friendship never wavered. Well, it did sometimes, disintegrating a bit into slanging matches and wild outbursts of screaming PMT tempers. But to be fair, that was mostly on my side. Gerry kept a tighter rein on his emotions.

Now that began to change. We were both uncomfortably aware of each other whenever we were within touching distance. And there seemed to be no let-up with this. The two of us began to find it increasingly difficult to pass each other in the tight confines of the office without having severe breathing problems. We sounded like a couple of borderline asthmatics. When he read out a report to me on the instances of increasing break-ins in the Greater Dublin area I had to stop myself fixating on the sexy way his mouth turned up at the corners. When he pointed out startling new crime figures to me, it took every ounce of self-restraint I possessed not to point out his own startling figure in his new Levi's.

When I leaned across him to trace a map reading of a boundary wall involved in a neighbourly dispute, his breath was so hot it all but barbecued my left ear lobe. And it might have been my imagination, but his eyes now seemed to be permanently riveted to the front of my blouse. Even when I had my back to him. Simple office procedures became feats of endurance as we both attempted to exchange files without exchanging glances. Without touching flesh. Even the most benign clerical transaction was fraught with danger. And delicious promise.

Our paths didn't cross at all in the house, now. Declan was coming close to his first-year law exams, and had to study day and night. This meant that Gerry had to stand in for him on the night surveillances he normally handled. So he didn't get home in the morning until long after I had left for the office. But the temperature between us was now coming close to boiling point. Someone would have to give in. I think we both knew that. And although I was fast weakening, it was Gerry who cracked first.

It was early morning, and I was drifting in and out of the twilight world between sleeping and waking when he burst into my room. He was unshaven, unwashed and badly in need of sleep after a long hard night's surveillance. But sometimes a person's other needs can overcome even the basic desire for sleep.

He stood over my bed. 'OK, let's get this straight, Annie. Has this partnership of ours got to remain on a strictly business level?' he panted.

I stretched lazily and peered up at him with sleepy eyes. If anything, being unshaven and unwashed made him even more desirable.

'Has it?' he snarled.

'Don't be ridiculous, Gerry. Come here.' I sat up and pulled off my nightdress.

And it was worth all the waiting. All those times when we had come so tantalisingly close, only to be thwarted by circumstances. It was even better than I had imagined it would be. And I have a pretty fertile imagination. Even chin stubble and male body smells became erotic stimulants instead of the irritants they would have been with anyone else. Nothing in my life had ever matched the intensity of the feelings this man evoked in me as we tumbled and turned and swapped positions to give each other as much pleasure as was physically possible.

It was as if we were the first couple on earth to discover sex. Only with enough innate knowledge of it to make it better and better. We both knew what we liked and neither of us was slow to show it. And the showing aroused us both even more.

Afterwards I lay sated but swearing that I would never, ever leave this bed. 'I'm going to stay in this bed for ever. I want to die like this.'

Gerry held me even tighter. And in one insane moment of wild madness I bit him. Hard. And yet with that unerring instinct that lovers seem sometimes to share he knew better than to bite me.

My only quibble about the whole episode was that it had taken us so damn long to get to this point.

'We should have done this the day we met.' I laughed.

'You were the one who walked away,' Gerry said. 'If it had been up to me I would have had you on the dance floor that night.'

'Oh.'

Before I left for the office he called me back for another long kiss.

But a kiss is never enough. I ended up in the bed again, my clean clothes strewn all over the carpet.

I was convinced that everyone in the office would know what I'd been up to. What had made me nearly an hour late. To my astonishment they hadn't a clue. It wasn't written on my forehead at all.

''Morning, Annie,' was as much as Sandra said, her smile carefree as ever.

'Have you got that file on the kid who went to join the eco-warriors, Annie?' Barney asked. 'He's only done a runner again. His mother got my mobile number and she's been banging on at me all morning.' He looked exhausted.

'Why didn't you put her on to Gerry?' Sandra asked. 'He knows how to deal with her.'

'I tried. He must have his mobile switched off since

early. I wonder what he was doing that was so important he couldn't be interrupted?'

I blushed like a ripe tomato. And still nobody noticed.

'There's a fax here from the Beechams' solicitor, Annie. Want it?'

'Thanks, Sandra.' Gerry and I hadn't yet told the staff about our prospective merger. We had agreed to wait until the deal with the Beechams was further advanced before going public on the big change.

As to our other merger, I had asked Gerry if we could please keep that to ourselves for a while. 'I need time to get used to the idea of being a couple,' I said.

'Right, but you'd better get used to it pretty quickly, because as soon as I get dressed I'm going to move my things in here. OK?'

'That's better than OK. I'd say that's absolutely imperative for my future health and well-being.' I giggled.

'Mine too,' he groaned. And that's when we started our third bout.

Well, we had both been celibate for such a long time.

The Beechams were more than happy with the deal I had offered them. Ecstatic might be the word. 'They have asked me to thank you for your patience and understanding. And your sensitivity to their needs,' Mr Deedy reported back to me.

Patience and understanding? Sensitivity? Well, I suppose compared with the way they had behaved when they first heard I had been left the house. 'Tell them they can now put the gazebo back in the garden.'

Mr Deedy gave a bewildered little smile. 'Is that what's known as alternative humour?'

'No. They stole the gazebo.'

'Oh, dear.'

Penelope rang me to apologise. 'Annie, I give you my word, neither Jamie nor I had any idea that the garden had been . . . rifled.'

'Well, that narrows the list of suspects,' I said. I didn't work in a detective agency for nothing.

'I . . . em . . . all I can say is that she was terribly distressed. At Mummy willing you the house. She was bereft. Close to a breakdown.'

'I see. So she took the only logical step? She took a shovel to the garden?'

'I'm afraid so.'

'I suppose I should consider myself lucky she didn't take a shovel to me?'

She paused. 'Can you forgive us, Annie? For the way we treated you. All of us.'

I out-paused her pause. 'Did you have no idea that there had been another child?'

She paused even longer. 'Actually, Jamie and I often . . . We heard them rowing one night, Mummy and Daddy. She accused him of forcing her to give her baby away. He said it wasn't up to him to raise another man's bastard. He . . . he also said, "I gave you a choice." That's all we heard. We were small children. We talked about it sometimes. But only to each other. And never when we grew up. In retrospect I thought it was one of those grown-up things that children overhear and misinterpret. It was only when she left you the house that I began . . .' Her voice broke. 'I am so sorry, Annie. So sorry.' She hung up.

The phone rang almost instantly.

'Penelope?'

'Mrs Nagle here. Tell Detective Dunning to try north Kerry. Near the Gaeltacht area. I hear there's a gang of those filthy eco-warriors down there. Running around naked, I shouldn't wonder. My husband is desperately upset. My poor Alan, he has never seen a totally naked woman in his whole life.'

'I'm sorry about that, Mrs Nagle, but our concern is your son.'

'Alan *is* my son!'

'Oh, sorry. I wasn't thinking. I'll get on to Detective Dunning straight away.'

It took a whole rake of lawyers to arrange the paperwork for the sale of the house *and* to set me up as a full partner in the detective agency. While I seethed with resentment against their long drawn-out machinations, Gerry took it all in his stride. The man who purported to hate paperwork said this would ensure that our contracts were legally incorruptible.

'What the hell does that mean?' I fumed.

'It means that, two years down the line, we won't have Penelope claiming that because of some squiggle on a piece of paper she actually owns part of the agency, as well as the feckin' house.' He laughed.

He was in top form. Nothing could dent his good humour these days. He even brought his two little boys into the office to meet me. 'This is Annie, she's the new boss,' he said.

'Are you?' The six-year-old looked up at me in wide-eyed wonder.

'No. Your daddy is the real boss. I just pretend.'

'Like playing army games?' He was delighted.

Fortunately Gerry was out of earshot.

They didn't look much like him. And they were extremely well-behaved as well.

'I have a Packard Bell computer,' Brian, the eight-year-old, said shyly.

'Good for you,' Barney said. 'Maybe you can teach your daddy how to use it.'

As Gerry was trapped by Mrs Nagle, who had brought in every existing photograph of her son, including those taken in his baby bath, Sandra and I took Gerry's hungry little boys to lunch.

'McDonald's! McDonald's!' they chanted when we asked for their choice of restaurant.

'Exactly like their father. Big spenders.' I laughed. 'We'll probably have to have the house wine now.'

'But aren't they gorgeous?' Sandra enthused, as we watched them bury their faces in monstrous Big Macs, only coming up for air. And large fries. 'Makes you want to have a couple of your own, doesn't it?'

'Big Macs? No way!'

'Kids, I mean.'

'No.'

'Jimmy and me are going to have three.'

'I see. One of each?'

It took her a second or two before she laughed.

And the two little boys joined in, their mouths smeared with ketchup.

Gerry's boys all right.

But I still fancied the pants off him.

Apart from my problems with solicitors making a fortune out of the sale of the house, it was causing me another worry as well. Penelope was now intent on becoming my *bestest* friend. She took to calling me at the most awkward times imaginable.

'Who the hell is it?' Gerry asked one Sunday at three o'clock in the afternoon.

We were in bed. And at a very crucial moment.

'Let it ring,' he mumbled.

I couldn't. I found it too distracting. Unlike Gerry who wouldn't have found a nuclear attack distracting. I picked it up. 'Hello?'

'Would you meet me for coffee, Annie?' Penelope asked.

'What, right now?' I replied as Gerry ran his tongue along my left breast.

'No.' She laughed. 'Some time tomorrow.'

'Ohhhhh.'

'Well, Tuesday will do. If that suits you better?'

'*Yes.*'

'Oh, good.' She was quite excited by my enthusiasm.

So was Gerry.

'I'll give you a ring in the morning.' She hung up.

Just in time, too, because Gerry's tongue was travelling southwards.

31

Great Victories and
Greater Defeats

Penelope was totally at home in the swish sur-
roundings of the Shelbourne Hotel. I had only been
there once before. With Mrs Beecham. We had
stopped off for afternoon tea after visiting Dr Moran's
consulting rooms in Merrion Square. I had felt
completely ill at ease. Something about the hotel's
old-world ambience made me feel like an impostor.
Which I probably was at the time.

Today's visit was no better. I was as uncomfortable
as ever.

That afternoon with Mrs Beecham I was so nervous I had inadvertently ordered Lapsang Souchong
tea, when what I really wanted was a soothing cup of
Lyons Green Label. Completely intimidated by Mrs
Beecham, and embarrassed by her superior attitude
to the serving staff, I had drunk the whole pot rather
than draw attention to myself by admitting my mistake. I had diarrhoea for two whole days afterwards.

This time I stuck to coffee.

Penelope was wearing one of her seemingly endless
supply of hats. This one was pale lemon and it had a
veil, which practically reached her knees. She looked
like the Queen Mother on Derby Day. 'I wanted to
talk about Mummy.'

I would have preferred another dose of Lapsang Souchong.

'Jamie and I are pretty sure, now, that Daddy was not your father. Would you accept that, Annie?'

'Well, given that you heard him say he wasn't prepared to rear another man's bastard, I think we might safely come to that conclusion.' I was nervous *and* edgy, which always made me retreat into rudeness.

Her face tightened behind the big veil. 'We *are* on your side in this, Annie.'

'Since I gave you back the house, you mean.'

'Are you dissatisfied with the price? We did agree on the figure.' It was her turn to be nervous.

'The money is OK.'

'I don't blame you for feeling bitter about what happened to you as a child.' She looked as if *she* was coming down with a panic attack. 'But Jamie and I are prepared to help you all we can.'

'Help me? How?'

'We want to help you trace your father.'

My father? Where had that come from? I pushed my coffee cup to one side. It had suddenly begun to taste bitter. *Trace my father?*

And then the penny dropped. Of course. They were afraid I might make a claim on the Beecham millions. I had sold them the house for way below the market price and they still saw me as a gold-digger.

Penelope raised the veil so she could drink her coffee. 'We'll do everything we can to help you trace your real father,' she said.

Of course they would. Anything to prove that I wasn't a Beecham and had no claim on their money. I almost laughed. These people had absolutely no idea what I was about. To them everything came down to filthy lucre. Money was the yardstick by which everything had to be measured.

I looked at her, sitting there in her Queen Mother hat, her big Beecham eyes watching from behind the raised veil. Of course they would do their utmost to help me trace my real father. But why pretend she was doing it as a favour to me? Why pretend that any of them gave a damn about me?

'Don't you like the coffee, Annie?'

'The coffee is fine.'

'Would you prefer something else?' She looked around for a waitress. 'You only have to ask.'

That might have been the Beecham family motto. *You only have to ask.*

I thought about Sandra. How she had looked that morning, coming into the office, her eyes red and swollen from crying. That's what had me so on edge. I thought about all the other days when she came in and worked so hard, never mentioning her problems with her father. Never complaining, no matter how bad a time he gave her. She just accepted it. This morning she had been forced to face the fact that her dream wedding was not going to happen. That she was never going to have the big marquee, with the band and crowds of drunken friends wishing her well, throwing coloured confetti in her face and oohing and aahing over her bridal outfit. Sandra expected her life to be peppered with disappointments. It was all part and parcel.

I was the one who had been incensed when I heard that her father had scarpered with most of her savings. Again.

'He's not a bad man, Annie. He can't help his little weakness,' she said.

I would have considered stealing thousands from his own daughter a very big weakness, but Sandra had insisted that the Gardai were not to be called.

I looked at Penelope as she sipped her coffee, at the manicured hands that had never done a proper day's work in their lives. 'There is something you could do for me.'

'You only have to ask.'

'It's not for myself. It's for a friend of mine who was to be married this year. She's had all her savings stolen.'

'Oh, dear.'

'She's always wanted a big wedding.'

'I see.' Penelope was still looking for the waitress.

'The thing is she can still have one if she can get a venue. Cheap. Like for nothing. They have a friend who can get them a marquee. But they need a venue.'

'Where is that girl?'

'Would you agree to let her have the wedding in Haney Road?'

Her face went putty-coloured behind the veil.

'Would you?'

'Oh . . . I . . . er . . . I'd have to ask . . . to think about it.'

'Fine. I'll leave it with you, Penelope. You can get back to me. Thanks for the coffee.'

At the door I turned to give her a big wave. She looked as if she was about to throw up. I hoped she would remember to lift the veil.

Gerry loved the story of Penelope and the marquee. 'You're wicked, Annie. I wish I'd seen her face. Did she think you were serious?'

I gave him a look.

'You're not serious, Annie?'

'Of course I'm serious. Why not?'

'Well, because . . . because they're Beechams.'

'Oh, listen to the great egalitarian. Why do you sound so shocked? Why can't Sandra have her wedding on Haney Road?'

'For one very simple reason. The Beechams won't allow it.'

'We'll see about that.'

'Annie, you can't keep interfering in other people's lives.'

'I beg your pardon, Mr Private Investigator?'

'I'm a detective. I earn my living detecting. Gathering evidence. I don't interfere, I present evidence.'

'What about the Dalkey stalker? You handcuffed him. If that wasn't interfering I'd like to know what is?'

'Stop trying to distract me, Annie. You're always trying to distract me. All I wanted to say is that Sandra wouldn't feel comfortable having her wedding on Haney Road.'

'Wouldn't feel comfortable? She'd love it! Did you ever actually look at the girl?'

'Listen, I don't know why we're rowing over this. It's all immaterial. They'll never give their permission.'

'Want to bet?'

'My God, Annie, what's happening to you? You're becoming machiavellian. You'll be running the bloody country next.' But he was laughing.

'I'm a Beecham, aren't I. Genes will out.'

Penelope and I met in her solicitor's office. I'd just come in the door when he started on me. 'Mrs Beecham Powers has told me of your request. I'm afraid it is out of the question.'

I gave a casual shrug and turned to leave. An exemplary piece of acting if I say so myself. 'Fine,' I said.

'Annie?' Penelope was on her feet blocking my way to the door. 'Where are you going?'

'Home. To rethink my offer about the house.'

'You can't do that,' Mr Williby said.

'Why not, Mr Williby? We haven't signed the final papers yet. I may decide to withdraw from the deal. In retrospect I feel I may have been pressurised into agreeing to let them have the property. I realise now that I was under huge emotional stress at the time, having just discovered that Mrs Beecham was my natural mother.' I put a hand to my forehead. 'And that she gave me away and consequently denied all knowledge of me. If that wouldn't traumatise a person, push them to the edge of a breakdown, I don't know what would.' I watched Penelope out of the corner of my eye.

'You can have the house for the wedding!' she almost shouted.

I smiled. 'We don't need the whole house. Just the garden. And maybe a walkthrough from the front door.' I sat down.

Mr Williby began to bluster: 'It's not as simple as you might imagine. Allowing a crowd of . . . people to take over a private house and garden can be a very complicated business in the legal sense. And there is the matter of insurance. The house insurance will not cover personal injuries.'

'Oh, Mr Williby,' I tut-tutted. 'It's a wedding, not a prizefight. We weren't planning on beating anyone up. Although I do agree with you.' I grinned. 'There's nothing like a good fight to liven up a wedding.'

He turned puce.

'Just joking, Mr Williby! But an experienced legal

representative like yourself should have no trouble arranging comprehensive coverage for a romantic wedding.'

They regarded each other. Penelope nodded her head. She was wearing what I first took to be a small plain Stetson, until I looked closer and saw the little rows of pearls stitched to the brim. It was sort of Tammy Wynette meets the Pearly Queen. 'Nice hat,' I said.

She seemed startled. 'Oh. Thank you.'

'I'll need written confirmation of your permission to use the garden for the wedding. Just in case. You know how sticky some people can be about silly legalities.' I paused. 'In fact, maybe you should include the whole house. Just in case.'

Mr Williby's lip actually curled.

'Oh, and one other thing. The bride dearly loves confetti. You know, the coloured paper kind. You won't object to people throwing confetti in the garden, will you?'

Mr Williby looked as if he was about to explode. But credit where it's due: Penelope raised her hand to shush him into silence. 'Whatever you wish, Annie. The place will be yours for the day.'

We looked at each other. And if Mr Williby hadn't begun to shuffle a load of papers impatiently, I think we might have embraced. Not me and Mr Williby. Me and Penelope. Not that I wanted to or anything. After all, she was one of the dreaded Beechams. Even if she was masquerading as Tammy Wynette.

Gerry called the staff together to give them the news of our exciting new partnership. Not the one we had celebrated, yet again, in a steamy session in the shower that morning, that was still too precious to make public. The one we wanted to share with them was our business partnership. When Gerry broke the news they were surprised. But not unduly so.

'I knew there was something happening between you two. I just couldn't figure out what it was.' Barney grinned.

'And I said there was something in the air as well, didn't I?' Sandra chipped in. 'I said Annie's had a funny look about her for the past few weeks. And she gets really fidgety, now, whenever Gerry is around. Didn't I say that?'

Gerry caught my eye and laughed.

Declan didn't say a word, just nodded his head in agreement, his narrow eyes inscrutable as ever. But then his first-year law exams were looming. He had more things to worry about than who was in partnership with whom.

They were all genuinely pleased with the new arrangement. Delighted to have guessed that something was in the offing between Gerry and me.

'If the agency is going to have this sudden injection of money does that mean we'll all be getting a rise?' Barney asked cheekily.

'Get a grip, Barney,' Gerry said.

'Are you planning on making any changes around here, Annie?' This was Declan.

'I don't see why. I think the business is going incredibly well.'

There was a sigh of relief all round.

'The only real change will be the new premises. We already have our eye on an office space near the docks. Don't worry, it's within walking distance of here. Isn't it, Annie?'

It was if you were into marathons.

'It has a great view of the water. You can see right across the bay. All the foreign ships coming up the mouth of the river. It will be quite an improvement on looking out at exhaust fumes,' he added quickly, as if expecting some dissent about our new location.

There was none.

'Sounds cool to me.' Barney grinned. 'Hazel is always complaining that I work in a dump. Says she's ashamed when she passes by here with her mates. And the actor in the upstairs flat is now letting it be known that he's going to be working in the Abbey for the summer.' He laughed scornfully. 'The Abbey café more like. Can I bring Hazel down to see our new offices?'

'We could throw a party. Invite everyone.' Sandra was suddenly brave.

'But not Gerry's Garda friends,' Barney and Declan chanted in unison. This was a running joke in the agency.

'Maybe we should have a party?' Gerry looked at me.

'I'm on for it,' I said.

'Oh, I can't wait to move into the new offices,' Sandra thrilled. 'Could I have a glass-topped desk, Gerry? And one of those big green plants with holes in the leaves? Or should I be asking you, Annie? Are you my boss now?'

Gerry gave a loud cough.

'Well, not essentially, but I'm sure I'll be called on to take some executive decisions,' I said grandly, sticking my nose in the air.

'Jaysus! The last executive decision taken here was the night Gerry got hammered and decided that a boss shouldn't have to stand his round. Another decision like that and we'll call a strike.'

'Don't worry, Barney, I'll still stand my round.'

'Hear that, Gerry? That's the kind of boss I've always wanted.'

'OK, back to work. There won't *be* any agency if we hang around blabbing all day.'

'He's such a silver-tongued devil, isn't he? Charm oozing from every pore, my partner!' I said.

They all hooted with laughter.

The look Gerry gave me from under his lashes could have given our secret away. Mainly because it made me want to rip his clothes off. I picked up my notepad and hurried into the front office, in case anyone saw how flushed I was. Alone in there I allowed myself a contented little sigh. What a day this was turning out to be. I had a partnership in a business I loved. I had sold the house that held nothing more than bad memories for me. I had a fancy new office on the horizon. I was surrounded by loyal, friendly staff who really liked me. And a couple of minutes ago Gerry had looked as if he couldn't wait for us to be alone together.

In the middle of a working day?

Workaholic Gerry Dunning had given the impression he wanted to brush everything aside and sweep me off my feet. Have his way with me on the big untidy desk, with the all-over coffee stains and the bite marks from the bad-tempered little Jack Russell that we'd had to keep tied up until his elderly owner came to collect him. And OK, Gerry hadn't actually done it. Swept me off my feet, I mean. But the thought was there. I saw it in his eyes.

Life couldn't get any better than this. Could it?

32

Happy reunions

I hadn't heard from Fiona in such a long time. Not even a card, let alone a letter. This meant, of course, that things were going sweetly for her. If Fiona had a problem she wasn't one to keep it to herself. When Fiona suffered, everyone suffered.

We were in the throes of moving to the new offices when the telegram came: 'Arriving Dublin airport Thursday the tenth. Six thirty a.m. Be there. Fiona.' I handed it to Gerry without a word.

He read it at a glance. 'She expects you to drop everything and pick her up. No explanation. Nothing.'

'That's Fiona.' I shrugged. 'She doesn't change. At least she was smart enough to send it to your office. If she had sent it to Haney Road she might have been stepping off the plane before I even got it.'

'So she'd have had to get a taxi? That would hardly put a strain on her resources.'

For some reason he wasn't completely enthusiastic about Fiona's return. Sometimes I got the impression he was jealous of her. Although I didn't talk about her half as much as I used to. I think. Before things had begun to go so well in my life, Fiona's opinion was the barometer against which I measured most things. Nowadays I was my own woman. I made the choices, uninfluenced by anything other people might say. Or think.

Except maybe Gerry, of course. And our times together were getting better and better. Hotter and hotter.

'Not yet, don't go yet,' he mumbled, holding me tightly, the morning her flight was due in.

'I have to if I'm to meet her flight. I've only got thirty minutes to get to the airport.' I pulled away from him, although there was nothing I would have liked better than to stay wrapped around his warm body.

He lay there with one eye open, watching me dress. 'Will you make it back here before heading into the office?'

'You are joking?' I checked my watch.

'I don't care if it makes us late. We can drive in together. The office can wait.'

I laughed. 'All right, own up. What have you done with the real Gerry Dunning? And where's the Pod? Where did you hide it?' I stood over him.

'Annie.' He held out his arms.

'No. We don't have time. I've got to go.'

I almost changed my mind when he kissed me goodbye. Gerry had a mouth made for kissing. And maybe for one or two other things . . .

I couldn't imagine what was bringing Fiona home before Sam's year in Cuba was up. It had to be something important because normally she wouldn't let him out of her sight. Maybe he was with her? No, the wording of the telegram said she was alone. I knew Fiona. If Sam *were* with her she would have put his name to it as well. Circled with a little heart.

Sam was everything Fiona had ever wanted in a man: tall, handsome, attentive, and relatively well-off. That last bit was possibly the most important. When the girls in our class were planning their future careers and prospects, Fiona had only one declared ambition. She wanted to marry a rich man.

We were fifteen and sharing confidences when she confessed this to me. 'I just want a rich husband,' she said, after I declared my ambition to scale the heights of true and everlasting love.

'But what about love?' was my dismayed reaction.

'What about it? My mother and father were in love when they married. And look at the state of them now! He works every hour God sends. All he's short of is bringing his bed into the office. And my mother is haggard as a witch from running after five kids. If that's what love does to you, I'll take money any day.'

'But suppose you fall in love with a poor man?' I asked.

'I won't!' She tossed back her long fair hair, ignoring the school gardener who was making sheep's eyes at her as we passed. But then every man between fourteen and senility made sheep's eyes at Fiona.

'What about a career? You could make lots of money that way. Sister Immaculata says every woman should have a career these days. Not just spend her life taking care of some man's children.' Sister Immaculata was the pin-up of the whole senior school.

'She can talk! She takes care of dozens of children every day. And she doesn't even get a ride at the end of it.'

I couldn't hide my shock at such coarse language.

Of course that was why Fiona used it. No fun in using bad language if you couldn't shock your more prudish classmates. 'I'm going to marry a rich man with a big . . . thing,' she said, her nerve failing her. 'Then I'm going to loll around, all day, eating Black Magic chocolates. And fornicate all night.' Like most convent girls, Fiona tended to lapse into biblical terms, despite considering herself modern beyond belief.

'You're going to loll around all day?' I stuck to the things I knew. 'You'll turn into a load of blubber like Sally Evans.' Sally Evans was the class roly-poly. She wore XX uniforms and suffered constant ridicule. Sally blamed her glands for her outstanding girth.

'No I won't,' Fiona was unperturbed. 'I'll go to a gym twice a week.' Gyms were still exotic places in Dublin then.

Fiona didn't marry a rich husband after all. But he did have prospects. As to the other more personal item on her checklist, I have no idea. But I never heard her complain. When she met Sam she didn't even know he had prospects. He was working part-time with Gerry during his college vacation and he never dressed in anything but frayed jeans and worn-looking sneakers. Fiona was employed in an office along the street and when Gerry ran out of things like copy paper or ink cartridges, he borrowed from her office. In return, Fiona asked him to check out the financial situation of her then boyfriend, who drove a big Mercedes but otherwise showed no evidence of the great wealth he was fond of boasting about.

As Sam was at university doing a Masters, Gerry put him on the case. The relevance of this has always escaped me, for Sam was studying architecture. Sam reported back to Fiona and fell madly in love with her at first sight. He took her to an Italian trattoria and gave her his report over the antipasto. He filled her in on Mercedes man's investments over the chicken tagliatelle. And over the spumoni he told her he loved her.

Despite her resolve to be attracted only to rich men, Fiona felt herself being drawn to Sam in his scuffed trainers and old jeans. She fought hard against it until he swore he would dedicate his whole life to making her happy.

'I'm in love,' she told me.

When he asked her to marry him a few months later, the only proviso was that she had to agree to go to Cuba with him. He had already arranged to spend a year there, working in a voluntary capacity with his old tutor who was a famed Spanish architect. Before you could say Fidel Castro's beard, Fiona was in the chemist's buying bottles of Sun Protection Factor 15 and boxes of condoms that wouldn't melt in the heat. I always suspected that Fiona hoped, deep down, that Sam would never actually go to Cuba. But he did. They did.

Now she was on her way home. Alone.

Fiona was in a right funk because I'd kept her waiting. 'I don't want to hear about the traffic. How do you think I'm feeling after such an exhausting flight?'

'Oh, forgive me, I didn't realise you were actually piloting the plane.'

She gave an impatient snort, before starting to laugh. Then she grabbed me, giving me a warm hug. Then she was complaining again. 'Don't start throwing questions at me, please. I'm in bits. We can talk later when I've had time to catch my breath.'

As I had only said how are you, I thought this was a bit much. But I was too happy to let such a small niggle get me down.

We had only just finished packing her luggage into the boot when she asked, 'Can I stay at your place?'

My horrified look should have given her all the answer she needed, but Fiona had her own way of seeing things. 'Please, Annie, I don't want to meet my folks just yet. You know them, they'll only give me the third degree the minute they open the door. And Mum will have a pregnancy testing kit sitting on the hall table, I shouldn't wonder.'

'You do know I'm staying with . . . I'm staying at Gerry's house,' I corrected myself. I don't know why. Maybe because Fiona sometimes made me feel I needed correcting.

'Oh, that's OK, then. Gerry won't mind me staying. He has plenty of room since the break-up. Sally's not back, is she?'

'No.'

'Thanks be to Jesus. I'm not up to facing anyone at the moment. I mean I look like crap.'

She looked wonderful. She had the most glorious tan and her hair was blonder than ever thanks to all that Cuban sunshine. 'You look like a million dollars.' I smiled.

'Get real, Annie. I look like shit!'

We travelled in silence for a couple of miles. Then she caught me giving her a curious sideways glance. 'I've left him,' she suddenly announced.

The car swerved. I had to pretend to be changing lanes, to escape the wrath of the driver behind me. 'Sam?' I said stupidly, ignoring the furious tooting.

She nodded.

'You've left Sam?'

She burst into tears. 'He has another woman.' She

pulled a wad of paper tissues from a carrier bag that was sitting on her lap. It had a black-and-white picture of Che Guevara on the front, its paper handles rising symmetrically out of his famous black beret.

She blew her nose furiously into the wad of tissues, without even bothering to separate them. 'I wouldn't mind if she were glamorous. Semi-attractive, even.' She gave a loud sob. 'But I swear to you, Annie, she's an ugly cow. A face like the back of a bus. What's wrong with men nowadays? Is all that oestrogen in the water dulling their senses? She's so ugly.'

She seemed more upset by the lack of beauty in Sam's partner in adultery than his actual infidelity. 'She has skin like leather. And an arse like a futon. If I had thighs like hers I'd kill myself. How could he do it to me, Annie? How could he abandon me?'

'I thought you left him?'

'I did, but *after* he abandoned me. *He* did the abandoning. I only left.'

'I see. And this woman he abandoned you for, is she . . . ?'

'A right bitch? I knew you'd understand.'

'I'm truly sorry, Fiona. I thought you and Sam were the ideal couple.'

What was I saying? They were chalk and cheese, Fiona and Sam, everyone knew that. The only surprising thing was that they had lasted this long. *And* that Sam had been the one to have an affair. Sam was quiet, sober and industrious. Fiona was . . . Well, Fiona was Fiona.

Che watched us from the carrier bag, his big brown eyes dark pools of compassion.

'I never thought *he'd* be unfaithful to me, Annie. At

least not with a woman with an arse like a futon.'

We were now nearing the house and I was wondering how I was going to break the news to Gerry that Fiona wanted to stay with us. Then I saw that the Hiace had gone. He had already left.

On the pretext of needing the bathroom I hurried upstairs to lock our bedroom door. If Fiona even glanced in there she'd soon guess what was going on. My tights and Gerry's discarded boxer shorts were entangled on the floor, like eager lovers. And everywhere else you looked there was even more evidence of intimate entanglements. Gerry was not a tidy person.

And this was no time to be explaining romantic liaisons to Fiona.

Not that she appeared to have the least interest in other people's lives, right now. All she wanted to do was give me her list of complaints. Regarding Sam and futon woman. It did sound as if Sam had taken leave of his senses all right.

'See, that's why I wanted to come here. I knew you'd understand. You always listen to me, Annie. My mother would only give me hell. All she cares about is having grandchildren. Jesus Christ I'd like my job. Having a gang of snotty-nosed brats just so she can show their pictures to the other wrinklies at her club. And my father is worse. "When are you going to make me a grandfather?" That's all I ever hear out of him.'

'I'm not being rude, Fiona, but I have to go in to the office. We're moving to our new location this week and the place is in chaos. I can't leave it all to Sandra.'

She gave a sharp laugh. 'I can't believe Gerry is

finally moving out of that dump. Even Sam used to call it a tip. And everyone knows how easily pleased he is.' She howled.

I got her the last pack of tissues from the Che bag. 'Will you be all right on your own?'

'Oh, don't mind me, I have a trillion calls to make. Where's the phone?'

'And how is the fair Fiona?' Gerry asked that afternoon when he rang the new office to check its ascending level of chaos.

I took a deep breath. 'Try ringing your house. If you can get through you can ask her yourself.'

'My house? What the hell is going on, Annie?'

'Got to go, Gerry, I can hear the movers banging the computers against the walls. I swear they're all frustrated demolition workers.' I hung up.

Sandra watched as I sat back and gave a long sigh of relief. She handed me a steaming cup of coffee and we sat together admiring the peaceful harbour scene below. The way the little tugs buzzed around the big tankers like nestlings hungry for comfort. 'He never liked Fiona, didn't you know that?' She dunked a chocolate biscuit in her coffee.

'Of course he likes her. They've been friends for years.'

'No, him and Sam have been friends. He just puts up with Fiona.'

'Oh, God. What am I going to do, Sandra? I said she could stay in the house. I made up a bed for her.'

The removal men arrived. I could hear the computers sliding around inside the boxes. 'Please be careful. Can't you read? See where it says handle with care?'

A muscular man in blue overalls handed me a clipboard. 'Sign here.'

'Where?' I was distracted with worry.

'Where it says, received with thanks.'

I signed.

'Gerry won't be happy.' Sandra was tearing open the boxes.

I joined her. 'You think I am? These monitors will never be the same again.'

'I mean about Fiona being in the house.'

She was right. Gerry wasn't happy. He parked the Hiace outside the new office block and drove me home in the car. 'What do you mean you moved my things out of your room?' This time it was his driving that drew the ire of our fellow Dubliners.

'What else could I do? She's dangerously depressed. I've never seen her so unhappy. What did you expect me to say to her? Well, guess what, Fiona, your life may be down the tubes but me and Gerry are on cloud nine. Our world is perfect. In fact, some days I think I might explode with sheer joy.'

He pulled over on to the hard shoulder and put his arms around me, drawing me close. 'Sheer joy?'

I pushed him away impatiently. 'Exactly! And how could I say that to my best friend when her whole world has just fallen apart? You can't just shove our happiness down her throat when she's so unhappy.'

'So we have to go around pretending to be miserable, because she is?'

'Well, not exactly. But you can't let her see how blissfully happy we are either,' I yelled.

'I've never heard such shite in my whole life. We're not allowed to be happy because Sam wised up and left her?'

'Wised up? What are you talking about?'

'Don't tell me you actually believed that marriage was going to last?'

'You mean you didn't?'

'Come on, Annie, it had disaster written all over it from day one.'

'Oh, well, you'd know, of course, being such an expert on marital harmony.'

'I'm obviously more of an expert on it than you are, if you thought *they* had a chance.'

'You said they were the happiest couple you knew at their wedding.'

'Yeah, at their wedding. What I didn't say was that I thought it wouldn't last beyond the honeymoon. And I wasn't far wrong, was I?'

The row escalated from there. By the time we got to the house we were practically at each other's throats, neither of us capable of exchanging a civil word with the other. There was no need for us to put on a performance for Fiona's benefit after all. We were now fighting each other like unbridled savages.

'Well, all I have to say is thank God I already moved your things out of my room. It saves me having to shag them out the top window.' I slammed into the house.

'Hi, Gerry!' Fiona greeted him with open arms.

Despite her grief, she had taken the time to change into a brief sundress, I noticed. And so did Gerry. Although he tried to pretend that he didn't. Practically all of her deep tan was on show. And the way he looked at her it was hard to believe he didn't like her. But who could blame him? Her nipples were practically hooked over the top of the aquamarine dress. And even from four feet away I could smell the

new body cream I had bought at the weekend and
hadn't yet opened. It certainly suited her. It made her
skin gleam in a way that mine probably never would,
anyway. Even at ten pounds an ounce.

'I hope you don't mind, Annie. I found it in the
bathroom and couldn't resist trying it. It's lovely.
Makes your skin really smooth.' She ran a hand along
her arm, then held it out for Gerry to feel.

He declined. 'I have to make a phone call.'

'Gerry looks great,' she said to his receding back.
'Gorgeous as ever. You're a right eejit never making a
move on him.'

'He's married,' I snapped and began scraping
carrots for dinner.

33

Jealousy is a terrible terrible thing

Over the months Gerry and I had slipped into an easy routine when we were both home at the same time. We either cooked together, giddily experimenting with all sorts of ridiculous recipes, which didn't always turn out as expected, or if we were tired, we simply ordered a takeaway. Whatever we did it always seemed to be punctuated with lots of laughter and gentle – and sometimes not all that gentle – teasing.

Having Fiona in the house changed all this.

This wasn't the old Fiona who could make a cat laugh with her ribald comments about men and life in general. This Fiona sat, soggily watching TV, drinking one vodka and white after another, or crying on Gerry's shoulder while I cooked. 'I can't believe you two are sharing a house,' she said looking extremely sad, but nonetheless sexy.

When I cry I get a swollen nose, bloodshot eyes and my lips start to flake. Fiona somehow managed to cry and look dewy eyed, all at once. Her lips never seemed to lose their glossy shine. And her face paled in an interesting Lady of the Camellias sort of way, when she looked up at Gerry.

He seemed to be immune to her appeal, raising his eyes heavenwards whenever she buried her head in his chest, but you never *can* tell. The little sundresses she was fond of wearing had the most distracting habit of slipping off her narrow shoulders, revealing far too much tanned flesh for my liking. After all, Gerry was only human. And what man wouldn't be enticed by the proximity of firm tanned breasts with a sundress hanging off the nipples?

'Beef Stroganoff, Gerry?' I asked as we sat at the table.

'Any more baby carrots, Annie?' Fiona had to choose the only vegetables I'd have to go back into the kitchen to get more of.

'Try the broccoli.' I smiled.

'Can't. It gives me hives.' She grimaced.

'Really?' I said. 'It gives Gerry wind.'

He looked down at his plate, but there was a little grin breaking out on his face. Or maybe it was just the way his mouth tended to turn up at the corners.

'Great nosh, isn't it, Gerry?' Fiona said when I gave in and brought her an extra helping of baby carrots.

'It's dynamite,' he said, clearly relieved that the atmosphere was finally beginning to lighten.

'No. That's just the effect the broccoli has on you,' I said slyly.

We were both laughing when Fiona suddenly burst into tears.

'What is it, Fiona?'

'Sam loves carrots.' She wept into her Beef Stroganoff.

And Gerry had to let his go cold while he consoled her. Otherwise he would have seemed like a heartless beast.

I ate mine while it was still hot.

*

334

Fiona had now been home for three days, and Gerry and I were still sleeping in separate rooms. And frustration didn't suit me. It wasn't just the sex I missed, it was the physical closeness – we had to keep a respectable distance between us when Fiona was around. I also missed our late-night talks. Those times when we lay in bed, in the dark, chatting about things that concerned us. I missed this almost as much as his teasing banter and his funny, if sometimes infuriating, way of looking at things. And I missed his deep morning kisses. Oh, God how I missed his morning kisses.

'Scrambled eggs anyone?' He had been banging around the kitchen since dawn. Made a huge breakfast for the three of us. Real coffee, the lot.

'I'll have some. *And* some of that French toast.' For a woman who was deeply depressed and incurably broken-hearted, Fiona couldn't half shift her food.

Not that I resented this. Who appreciates the comfort food can bring more than me?

What I did resent was the way she sat around all day, while we were out at work. Painting her nails, making phone calls and watching daytime chat shows. Who did she think she was? The au pair? She made no attempt to cook. Or clean. Just left a trail of wet tissues around the house. If Gerry didn't have a woman who came in for three hours a week to dust and clean the house it would have become a complete tip.

And every day she answered my hopeful 'How are you this morning, Fiona?' with the exact same reply: 'I'm so depressed.'

She was completely unaware of the rift she was causing between Gerry and me. That was partly my fault, of course. I hadn't told her that we were now more than friends. A lot more. She was so shocked when Gerry told her that we were full partners in the detective agency that I was in no rush to give her the rest of the story.

'Partners? When did all this happen? Why didn't you tell me, Annie?'

'I tried. You didn't want to hear it. All you've wanted to do since you got back is talk about Sam and futon arse. And how miserable you are.' My patience was running thin. 'You didn't want to hear anything about our lives. How things have changed here. For all of us.'

'Annie's mother left her a house,' Gerry said. 'The one in Foxrock.'

'In Haney Road? How in God's name did your mother get to own a house in Haney Road?'

'I told you in my letter. I told you Mrs Beecham was my birth mother.'

'Oh, yeah. I forgot. Sorry, Annie.'

'She left me the house and I sold it. Don't ask, it's too complicated to go into right now.'

There was no mistaking the look of relief on her face. She had no interest in anything that didn't directly concern her. Or her *depression*.

Hard to believe this was the same friend I used to run to with my every thought? The one I believed to be a complete tower of strength. I could never have imagined her going to pieces over a man. Although I suppose being abandoned for a futon woman would depress anyone. Especially someone as beautiful as Fiona. Being left for someone four times your size couldn't be easy. Knowing how highly Fiona valued physical beauty, that must have been the cruellest

336

blow of all. I could appreciate how bad she was feeling. If only she wouldn't insist on making a *career* out of her depression.

'How could he be unfaithful to me, Annie? How could he?' She was standing in front of the mirror, checking her reflection, as the tears ran down her smooth cheeks. The cheeks made even smoother by the twice-daily use of my skin cream.

'I don't know, Fiona. Maybe you weren't meant to be together for ever. Sometimes what starts out looking like a suitable marriage has the odds stacked against it. It happens quite a lot, I believe.'

'What do you mean by that? Are you telling me you're not surprised that he left me?'

'No, I'm not saying that. But I did sometimes wonder how well suited you and Sam were. For the long term, I mean.'

'We were bloody better suited than he is with that ugly cow he's with now. She's half Russian, you know. A blatant communist. That's all she ever talks about. Politics. That and the project. *And* the kids. *The kids! The kids!* Nothing else. You'd think with an engineering degree in her pocket she could come up with more interesting subjects to talk about.'

'Like hair or make-up?' Gerry muttered from behind me.

'It's all the project. The pair of them think about nothing else but the bloody international project.'

'Are you sure Sam has been unfaithful? Maybe all they do, when they're together, is discuss their work?'

'In the nude? I don't think so, Annie. I saw them naked. And it was not a pretty sight.'

'Well, it can get pretty hot in Cuba,' Gerry said drily. 'So I'm told.'

'Are you laughing at me?'

'No.'

'Well, you'd better not be, Gerry Dunning. I didn't laugh at you when your wife ran off.'

'Ouch!' Gerry doubled over. But he didn't sound particularly wounded.

I turned to smile at him and he reached over to touch my face.

Then the phone rang and he was Gerry Dunning, detective extraordinaire, again. 'I did check that out, Mr Brady,' he said into the phone. 'Yes. I should have his test results any day now. I'm afraid we need more than twenty-four hours for that. I'll call tomorrow and see if I can hurry things along.' He waved to us as he went out the door.

'Does he ever do anything except work?' Fiona traced the line of her perfectly arched eyebrow as she stared into the mirror.

'Oh, yes,' I said dreamily. 'He does lots of other things. And all of them extremely well.'

Her face suddenly crumpled. 'I thought Sam was only interested in his work. Then he met . . .'

'Futon woman. I know. You've told me. Every single day since you got back.'

'Oh, well, if that's your attitude I'll tell you nothing from now on.'

'Promises, promises,' I whispered as she disappeared up the stairs.

34

Three has always been a crowd

'Why doesn't she go home to her family?'

Sandra had little sympathy for Fiona. Mainly because she saw her as a major bone of contention between myself and Gerry in the office.

And she wasn't far wrong. Things were becoming more and more strained in the small house. Fiona was genuinely heartbroken, no doubt about that. But she would insist on walking around half dressed looking for attention and I kept thinking that if I was frustrated, how must it be for Gerry. He was living in close contact with two women, one of them his lover whom he had to keep at arm's length and the other a weepy, semi-naked woman who threw herself across him every time he sat down.

Fiona was part of the reason we were beginning to arrive in the office like a couple of crabs every morning.

Which was a shame. With all the improvements in our lives this should have been a particularly happy time for us. What with the partnership and moving into the new offices. And our relationship having shifted into such an altogether satisfying stage.

Before Fiona moved in, that is.

We now had to resort to bidding each other

goodnight on the landing, while Fiona cleaned and flossed her teeth, not three feet away. After which she gargled loudly with warm water to ease her aching throat, which was usually raw from her prolonged bouts of crying.

Sandra put her arm around my shoulders. 'Just hang on in there, Annie. Everything passes. As the actress said to the bishop after she swallowed his ring. She can't stay with you for ever. Can she?' She made an inquisitive face.

'Oh, my God. Can you just picture it? Me, Gerry and Fiona living together for the rest of our lives? Me on low-dose HRT, still cooking dinner for her because she never recovered from Sam's betrayal. And Gerry cursing her to hell and back, threatening her with his Zimmer frame? Now that *would* be hell on earth.'

I didn't know it, that day, but there was actually a worse scenario looming just around the corner.

It was one of those wet Monday nights when everyone was in bad form. The three of us had just finished our dinner, which I had cooked, when we had an unexpected visitor.

As Gerry was already on the phone and Fiona wouldn't shift if you put Semtex in her drawers I went to open the door.

There was a small, pretty woman standing there, holding Gerry's two sons by the hands. 'Hello. I'm Sally. All right if I come in?' She walked up the hall and straight into the living room where Gerry was on the phone.

'Why don't you come in?' I said to the empty doorway.

There was a little Fiat parked, very badly, by the gate. It was chock-a-block with suitcases and cardboard boxes with clothes hanging out of them. And children's toys. It looked as if someone was moving house.

'This is Annie,' Gerry introduced us, when I put my head around the living-room door. 'Annie this is Sally.'

We shook hands, trying not to scrutinise each other too openly.

Not that she had anything to worry about. She was like a fragile little doll. A little porcelain doll with blue eyes and immaculate fair hair held tidily in place with a black velvet band that wouldn't have been out of place on a twelve-year-old. She had on a pale-blue shift dress that skimmed her slim knees and toned perfectly with her little blue pumps.

I'd had a particularly trying day. Plus I was so fed up about dealing with Fiona and her depression that the moment I came in from work I had changed out of my neat suit and thrown on a big bathrobe, with the full intention of soaking in a long, hot bath.

I can't remember what brought me downstairs. Maybe it was to collect my precious skin cream that Fiona had left on the mantelpiece. But then I went into the kitchen to get an elastic band to hold my hair back and somehow I ended up preparing dinner. Postponing the bath. I had never before cooked dinner wearing a big bulky bathrobe, so that's probably how I ended up with grease stains, blobs of tomato purée and dribbles of red wine all over the front of it. Too tired to care, I sat down to dinner looking like Waynetta Slob.

And naturally Sally arrived.

She pumped my hand now. 'You're Gerry's new partner?' She seemed fascinated by the bathrobe.

'I . . . er . . . I cooked dinner.' I brushed at the stains.

'Yes.' She tried to pretend she hadn't noticed them. It didn't work.

I had always visualised Gerry's ex as a big woman. The only other Sally I had ever known was Sally Evans, the terror of the school hockey team. Somehow, every time Gerry mentioned his ex I got a picture of Sally Evans in my head. I imagined her scouring the shops in vain attempts at finding clothes to fit her outsize person. And here was this perfectly proportioned little creature who probably had extra room in a size eight. Plus she looked as if she had just been dry-cleaned from head to toe.

As for the supposed pregnancy that had put Gerry in such a funk the night we were in the dance club, that was clearly nothing more than malicious gossip. If this little body was pregnant, it was with an ant.

The boys were now leaping all over Gerry, trying to wrestle him to the ground.

'Sally?' There was a delighted scream from behind us. Fiona appeared in a cloud of perfume, having changed into yet another stunning sundress. Her hair was caught up in a shining French pleat.

'Hello, Fiona.'

'What are you doing here?'

'I could ask you the same thing.' Sally might be gentle and doll-like, but she didn't miss a trick. Despite the fact that she made me feel like a big awkward slut, I liked her.

After a respectable interval, during which Fiona succeeded in regaling Sally with the full and unabridged story of her betrayal by Sam and futon woman, I managed to drag her out of the living room. 'Give them a chance to talk to each other, for God's sake,' I whispered when she protested that she hadn't finished speaking to Sally. I pushed her into the kitchen.

The rain had stopped and the two boys disappeared into the back garden. They were chasing frogs that up until now had lived untroubled lives in the knee-high grass that Gerry was loath to cut. Not because of any strong ecological leanings, but because he always had 'better things to do'. I watched the boys from the window, while Fiona sat with her ear practically glued to the half-open door that led back to the dining room.

It appeared that Sally had left the pouf. Their main disagreement, as far as Fiona could make out, was over where they should live for the next five years. And where the boys would attend school. The pouf, being a career officer, thought the army knew best.

However, Sally apparently thought she did. At least where her children were concerned. 'I don't *want* to take them to Cork,' she was telling Gerry.

To Fiona's annoyance that was when I closed the door. 'What did you do that for?' she asked.

I didn't reply, just poured her a generous vodka to dilute her sulk. It worked. An even more generous one had her chattering away again. 'Isn't she gorgeous? Did you ever see anything so dainty? Wouldn't you kill to look like that?'

I wasn't sure if she meant me or women in general. I strongly suspected she meant me. 'She is lovely,' I had to agree.

'He's still mad about her, that's obvious. He was

devastated when she left. I bet you they'll get back together. See the way she came straight back here, when she left yer man.'

I looked out at the boys. They were still chasing frogs. But weren't we all?

Fiona droned on, telling me all about the great marriage Gerry and Sally used to have. How terrific they were together. How Gerry couldn't keep his hands off her. How everyone *knew* they would end up back together again.

Then why have you been flaunting yourself in front of him since you got back, I wanted to ask. But I knew the answer to that. Flirting was second nature to Fiona; she hardly knew she was doing it. She had to keep proving how attractive she was. Competing with a trio of beautiful sisters hadn't been easy for her. They used to upstage each other every chance they got. No wonder she hung around with me. I could be guaranteed not to upstage anybody. And now that Sam had left her for futon woman she had to prove that her currency, which was beauty, wasn't really devalued. It was just going through a slump. I opened my mouth to say that, to tell her that she was so much more than a pretty face. And a beautiful body.

But that's not how it came out. 'Gerry's divorce is almost final,' I heard myself saying.

'Ah, that doesn't mean anything. How could any man resist Sally? She's like a perfect little doll.'

Fiona had no idea of the effect all this was having on me. My chest felt as if someone was piling cavity blocks on to it, one on top of the other.

There was a loud burst of laughter from the hallway.

Another cavity block slipped into place.

Now the laughter was coming from the garden. They were all out there together. Like a proper family.

The eldest boy, the one who looked a bit like Gerry, was suddenly walking the high wall that divided the garden from the one next door. 'Daddy, look at me!' he shouted. 'See how I can balance.' He had just got the words out when he fell, crashing a full six feet to the ground.

Gerry and Sally were beside him in a flash. Wiping away his tears, checking him for breakages. Making soothing parental noises. Looking like a family in a Kodak ad. And I knew that my whole future had crashed to the ground with him.

'Bloody little brats.' Fiona came up behind me. 'I hate kids.'

'We know that, Fiona.'

'What's wrong, Annie? Why are you on such bad form? Come on, I'll make you a cup of tea.' She gave me a quick hug. 'Coffee?' she peered into my face.

'Tea would be fine. Thanks, Fiona.'

She surpassed herself by making tea for everyone. Even offering some to the *little brats*.

I considered hiding away upstairs so I wouldn't have to look at Gerry smiling at Sally. And Sally smiling back at him. And the kids smiling at them both. Then I castigated myself for being such a coward. After all, you can't spend your life hiding when things don't go the way you want them to.

Besides, Sally was a nice woman. A good mother. Here she was, walking away from a strong relationship because she chose to put her children first. That was really grown-up stuff in my book, putting your children before a relationship with a man. If she could do that surely I could drink tea and smile, even though my heart was breaking every time I looked at her and Gerry.

'Are you all right, Brian?' I asked the boy who had taken the tumble.

'He fell on a frog.' David grinned.

'I did not. I did not.' Brian's tears were not far away.

'You said he did, that's why he wasn't hurt,' David accused his father.

Sally came to stand beside me as Gerry tried to keep the peace. 'I know you took them to McDonald's when Gerry was busy that Saturday. Thanks, Annie. They can be a bit of a handful.' She waited for me to protest.

I obliged. 'Oh, they were no trouble.'

Her smile widened. 'I'm glad about the agency. It's the best thing Gerry could have done, taking on a partner. He'll kill himself with work if someone doesn't step in and prevent it.'

So not only was she taking him from me, she was asking me to save his life? I wanted to hate her, but how could I? She even thanked Fiona for making the tea.

Behind her back Fiona caught my eye and began making signals to indicate two lovebirds kissing.

Gerry got to his feet. 'Come on, guys. We'd better get a move on. We have things to do before we get you settled. And it's getting late.' He looked at me. 'OK, Annie?'

What was he looking at me for? He had his wife back, hadn't he? His whole family. He didn't have to clock in and out with me, just because I was his business partner.

''Bye, Annie. See you later.' Sally hurried out to the car.

346

The little boys offered their cheeks for a kiss. Fiona disappeared as soon as she saw this.

''Bye Annie,' the boys chanted in unison from the car. I knew they were waving but I could hardly see them because my eyes were filling up with big tears of self-pity.

Still I stood at the door waving back blindly, fully resigned to my future as a dried-up old maid, while Gerry, Sally and their two adorable little boys drove off into a golden future together. A future full of everlasting love and tenderness.

And hot sex.

I finally got to run my steaming, relaxing bath. Then ruined the effect by lying in it until the water turned cold and my skin crinkled up like an octogenarian's. Not that this mattered any more because the only man I wanted had gone back to his perfect doll-like wife who had skin like a peach. I dried my eyes, wrapped my crinkly self in a warm bath towel and lay on the bed, too depressed even to blow-dry my hair.

'Annie?'

I opened my eyes to see Gerry sitting on the edge of the bed, his hand smoothing my still damp hair back from my face.

'What time is it?' I asked sleepily.

'Nearly eleven.'

'I must have fallen asleep. Where are the boys? Sally?'

'At her mother's. They're staying there until she decides what to do about a house.'

'But I thought they were . . . ?'

'Coming back here? No. Sally is far too smart to take such a backward step. Her mother has a rooming house over on the Terenure Road. It's handy for me to visit the boys there.'

'Then you're not getting back together, you and Sally?'

He frowned. 'Where did you get that crazy idea? How could I get back with Sally when you and I are . . . What do you take me for, Annie?'

And in the time-honoured tradition of Annie McHugh, who never does the right thing when the wrong choice is readily available, I turned my back to him and burst into tears all over again.

But he understood. Somehow he understood. He was the first man in my life who knew that I was crying because of the intensity of my feelings. And not just because I was a total and utter eejit.

So things moved on nicely, and Gerry was just unwrapping the big towel and kissing me in soft, warm, freshly bathed, places, when Fiona's head appeared round the door. 'Annie? I heard Gerry come back but I can't find him. Jesus, what are you doing?' she screeched.

Gerry jumped back, like a scalded cat.

'What the hell is going on here? What are you doing to her?'

'Get out, Fiona,' he said sullenly.

She ignored him, coming towards the bed to stare at me. 'Annie McHugh, you cover yourself up!' She was scandalised: a Victorian maiden aunt, her eyes popping out of her head.

I pulled the towel up around me. 'It's OK, Fiona.'

'It's bloody well not! What the hell do you think you're doing?'

Gerry had had enough. 'Mind your own business, Fiona. This is nothing to do with you.'

'Jesus Christ, Annie McHugh, I can't turn my back

on you for a minute.' She gestured at the bed. 'What were you thinking of?'

'I . . .'

Gerry exploded. 'What the fuck has it got to do with you? Get out of here, Fiona, before I throw you out.'

'Don't speak to her like that, Gerry.'

He actually laughed. 'I don't believe this. We are two fully fledged adults and we have to have Fiona's permission?'

'He's right, Fiona.' I reached for his hand. 'We've been . . .'

'Oh, no, I don't want to hear this.' She put her hands over her ears in horror.

As Gerry said later, she was behaving as if she had caught her parents indulging in cunnilingus on the hearthrug. 'I can't believe it.' She shook her head in disbelief. 'You two?'

Gerry and I smiled at each other.

'All the time you two have been . . . ?'

'Well, not all the time, your arrival took care of that,' I accused.

'Jesus Christ, I can't leave you alone for ten minutes, Annie McHugh!' She stamped out.

Gerry locked the door and came back to the bed. 'Now where were we?'

'Just a minute,' I said. 'Give me your hand. No, your left one.'

He held out his hand.

It took a bit of tugging but the slim ring was soon off his finger. I put it on the bedside table.

'Annie?' He looked amused.

I took off the towel. '*Now* where were we?'

35

A wedding is arranged and Noel gets his come-uppance

Mr Williby of Williby and Son finally drew up a legal document declaring that Sandra and Jimmy had the Beechams' permission to hold their wedding reception in Haney Road. It was full of 'whereas' and 'the party of the first part', and took up two full A4 pages. I filed it and wrote my own version, one paragraph long.

I couldn't wait to show it to Sandra. This would be the first hint she had that her wedding reception could go ahead after all. A proper reception, not just a party in the back room of her local pub, an idea that she was becoming resigned to. Gerry called her into his office. Without saying a word I handed her the sheet of paper.

'What does it mean?' Her eyes widened as she read the simplified version.

'It means you can have a marquee the size of Fosset's circus tent in the back garden of the house, if you want. It means you won't have to pay for a venue. It means that if your Jimmy can hire a tent as cheaply as he says, you'll be laughing. You've seen that house. The guests can walk in the front door, along the big hallway, then out through the glass conservatory and straight into a flower-filled marquee. He *can* get the flowers at cost, your Jimmy? And somebody in catering owes Gerry a favour. You remember our eco-warrior? His father has a catering business in Sandyford. If we can persuade the eco-warrior to go home and talk to his parents without cursing them from a height, you'll be guaranteed a full buffet at rock-bottom rates. As long as you don't start to invite the whole of Dublin city, if you know what I mean? How does that sound?'

'Oh, God!'

'Well, all right, you can invite Him. But that's it, mind. No other late invitees.'

'Oh, Annie.' The tears started.

'No tears.' Gerry began to panic. 'You can be as grateful as you like. You can even send Annie one of those stupid thank you cards with a smiley face on it. But for Christ's sake don't start crying. I've seen enough tears in the past few weeks to last me a lifetime.'

Sandra dabbed at her eyes. 'Thank you, Annie,' she said with quiet dignity.

'Perfect. Now can we get back to work?'

'Not so fast. There's one other thing we forgot to tell her. Sandra, Gerry has agreed to shell out for the booze that day. No matter how many guests there are,' I added slyly.

'Ah, now hold on, I never said . . .'

But Sandra had already thrown her arms around him. She showered him with kisses.

'Jesus. I should do this more often,' he said, coming up for air.

'Over my dead body.' I stood, hands on hips.

'I'm going, I'm going.' Sandra was laughing and crying all at once. 'I've left the notes from Mr Noel Reid's interview on your desk, Gerry.'

'Could I see those notes?' I asked when she left.

There couldn't possibly be two Mr Noel Reids in Dublin, could there? Well, it was possible, I suppose. I checked the notes. Mr Noel Reid, they said, managing director of Pussy Grub, Ireland.

'Are you OK, Annie?' Gerry glanced over at me as I flicked through the pages.

'I'm fine. Glad to have been able to help Sandra.'

'Me too.' He continued signing letters.

It appeared that Gerry had come highly recommended to Mr Noel Reid. By a junior politician, who still dabbled in business. And it seemed that only Gerry would do. Only the boss was good enough for Noel Reid.

'And what exactly is Mr Noel Reid's problem?' I asked as Gerry held out his hand for the file.

'He wants his wife shadowed. He needs evidence of her adultery.'

'The pig!'

'Why? By the sound of it she is being unfaithful.'

'So has he been for most of their married life. And now he wants evidence against her? He's a pig.'

'We're not here to make moral judgements, Annie. We just collect evidence.'

'Is that all? Then why give all that time to old Mr Lennon? There's no further evidence to be collected there. Everyone knows his wife is dead. So why don't you tell him that's what the evidence says? Tell him it's pretty unlikely that she's living in a commune, under an assumed name, at eighty-two years of age.'

'Hey! Calm down, Annie. Mr Lennon is a special

case. He's an old man. And he's ailing. She was all he had in the world. If we take his last hope away it might kill him. What's all this interest in Noel Reid anyway?'

'You don't remember? He's the MD of Pussy Grub.'

'Your old firm.'

'Yes.'

'Your old boss?'

'Yes.'

Gerry went to check the door. This was a long-ingrained habit from his old office where the sound of every creak could be heard outside if the door wasn't firmly closed. He came back and sat on the edge of his desk.

I stood looking out the window at the ships. 'We had an affair. Of sorts. It was a disaster.'

Gerry read through the notes, his expression impossible to decipher. 'Do you want me to turn down the case?'

'No. It's business, after all. I would like you to keep in mind that this man is probably looking for more than a divorce. My guess is that he's trying to find some way of getting rid of his wife, while keeping control of the business. I don't know how the shares were allocated when they amalgamated with the American company. She used to be the major share-holder. It was her late father who owned Pussy Grub originally. It was called Cat Food Ltd then.'

'That pretty much says it all.'

'The man is a serial adulterer. He's had more affairs than you've had hot dinners. Well, since Fiona moved in.' I threw him a sly look. 'I wouldn't be surprised if he set up this whole adultery thing just to get rid of his wife. She never played around, as far as I knew. Last I heard of him he was involved with the MD of the American company. I'd say they're two of a kind. His wife would be better off without him but I can guarantee he's up to no good. She'll be the loser somehow. The man would sell his own mother for Pussy Grub.'

'I'll talk to him.' He picked up the phone.

I went to my own office.

There was a fax waiting for me: 'For the attention of Ms Annie McHugh. I'll never forget what you're doing for me. Yours truly. Sandra Murphy.'

I had occasion to ring Penelope a couple of times over the next few weeks. When I first rang and said that I needed a favour, a note of terror crept into her voice. But when I explained what I wanted she entered into the spirit of the thing with great enthusiasm. Being on semi-friendly terms with her was proving to be quite pleasant. It was certainly preferable to us being deadly enemies, which was pretty much the state of play between myself and Francesca. And being deadly enemies was a bit inconvenient right now, as I needed someone in their social circle to help me out. It wasn't as if I had a large selection of A-list acquaintances to choose from.

The developing relationship with Penelope also made things go a lot smoother when I had to drive Sandra and Paddy, who was in charge of the marquee, over to the big house. Paddy said it was essential that he check out the ground, for the big day. Take all sorts of crucial measurements. 'Or case the joint, as we say in the trade.' He laughed heartily.

'Do you trust him?' I whispered to Sandra as we stepped out of the car.

'Paddy? He's sound as a bell.' She hurried to catch up with him.

Rosie opened the door to us. 'Annie.' She was clearly delighted to see me.

'Hi, Rosie. Long time no see. We're here to check out the garden for the wedding.'

Penelope was on the phone in the library. 'Don't leave them standing there, Rosie,' she called out. 'Come on in, Annie.'

'We don't have to come through the house, we can use the side entrance and begin measuring from there.'

'You'll do no such thing. Come on through. I'll be finished here in a second.'

Rosie was escorting us through the conservatory, behaving as if I were the bride to be, when Pepper burst in and launched herself at me.

'Sit, Peppa.' The sharp voice behind me made the hair stand up on the back of my neck. But it was only Penelope. Sounding enough like Mrs Beecham to make me shiver. This place was full of ghosts. Through the open library door I had already spotted the picture of the judge, back in its rightful position above the mantel. He still looked as if he ate babies for breakfast. No wonder the burglars hadn't touched this portrait.

Paddy gave a loud cough and indicated Pepper who was sniffing at his crotch.

I pushed her away. 'This is Paddy, he'll be erecting the marquee. And this is Sandra. The bride.'

Sandra practically genuflected at the sight of Penelope and her hat. And Penelope seemed almost as overawed to discover that it was Ivana Trump who would be celebrating her wedding in the back garden. 'Would you like a drink?' Penelope was mesmerised by Sandra, obviously trying to recall where she had seen her before.

Trump Towers, I almost said.

To Paddy's disgust I declined the drink offer on everyone's behalf.

'Could I have a word with you, Annie.' Penelope drew me aside while Paddy explained his master plan for the marquee to Sandra and the ever curious Rosie. 'Jamie said to tell you we haven't forgotten. He's been speaking to as many of her old friends as possible. Discreetly, mind. But so far, nothing.'

'I've told you, Penelope, I'm not interested. The past is the past as far as I'm concerned.'

She wasn't listening. 'We promised to help you and we will.'

I followed the others into the garden and Sandra came hurrying over, her cheeks flushed, her eyes sparkling with happiness. 'Oh, Annie, it's going to be perfect. The little gazebo is massive.'

The gazebo? It was back, then?

'It'll be magic for the photos. And the marquee on that huge lawn! Paddy said a white one, but I said no way. I'm having a big striped marquee. With flowers and balloons everywhere. And ribbons. Pink ribbons all along the side. Like I saw in a film once.' She ran back to join Paddy who was still measuring everything in sight.

'Annie?' Penelope was at my elbow again, looking extremely serious this time.

I shook my arm free. 'Now listen, Penelope, if Sandra wants a striped marquee she can have one.

That's the deal. Whatever Sandra wants she gets. I don't care how common you think it is.' She looked puzzled. 'I never . . . This is not about the wedding. It's about that other little favour you asked for.'

She glanced over her shoulder, checking that we couldn't be overheard. 'About Darina Reid and the young French trainer? You were right, Francesca knows both of them. Well, that lot all know each other, always in and out of each other's breeches. Darina's chap is twenty-six and from the Deauville area. Came to Ireland a year ago. His family are well-known in bloodstock circles, but came on hard times. Had to sell most of their breeding stock. That's what brought him to Ireland. He travelled with two mares. Apparently he and Darina *are* close. Besotted is the word Francesca used. They ride out together every day. Francesca thinks it's too amusing, because it was Darina's husband who brought the chap here in the first place. Apparently the husband is a dreadful pleb. The very worst kind. But she can't leave him because their money is all tied up. Besides, he could get to keep the children. He has friends in Government.'

'Thanks, Penelope. I knew you'd be able to help me with this.'

'You're welcome. I quite enjoyed playing detective. Found it terribly exciting. My heart actually went thumpety-thump a couple of times. What a stimulating life you must be leading, Annie, involved in all these undercover investigations.'

I didn't bother to explain that I just ran the office. And that the only time my heart went thumpety-thump was when I heard Gerry coming to bed.

For the next half-hour, while Paddy was busy jotting down notes and Sandra walked around dreamy

357

eyed, Penelope continued to give me conspiratorial little winks and nudges. She was convinced that I was now a sort of female Dirty Harry, up to my armpits in murder and mayhem.

Then again, I *was* living with Fiona.

Fiona was sitting in my office when I got back. Swinging around on my new leather chair like a seven-year-old. 'I had to come and see the place. After hearing all the talk,' she said by way of explanation. 'Very impressive.'

'Isn't it?' I was glad to see her looking a bit lively.

'You and Gerry, that's pretty impressive as well.'

'Is it?' I said coolly.

'I'm sorry for the way I reacted, Annie. It was just such a shock. You and Gerry?' Her voice rose. 'I mean I think of you as my little sister. Someone I have to watch out for.'

'It's not as if he took my virginity, Fiona.'

She threw her head back to laugh. 'Hardly!'

'Ah, now let's not get too carried away.' I waved a threatening finger.

'God, you've changed, Annie,' She stopped laughing but she didn't look displeased.

'Oh, I hope so. I used to be such a fool.'

'No, you weren't. You were just . . .'

'Everyone's fool.'

'Is it serious with you and Gerry?'

'Doesn't this look serious to you?' I indicated the big, airy office with its wall-to-wall technology, the sweeping view of the harbour.

'See, you have changed, I'm asking about your love life and you point out your business successes.'

'Maybe they're all part of the same thing.'

'Is he any good, then?' She grinned. 'And I don't mean his computer skills.'

'He's the best.'

'Jaysus?' Her eyes widened. 'You and Gerry, I still can't believe it. It gives me palpitations!'

'Me too.' I gave a wicked smile.

'But I mean . . . Gerry? Nice going, Annie.'

He came in right on cue. 'Did someone call?'

Fiona almost went into flirt mode, but caught herself in time. 'Annie's been telling me how randy you are,' she said cheekily.

'Fiona! Pay no heed to her, Gerry. She's just being silly.'

'Don't knock it. It beats crying,' he said.

'That's what I say.' She clapped her hands. 'Let's go for a drink. The three of us.'

'A drink?'

'It's after six. Surely the agency closes at six?'

'We never close.' He grinned. 'We're like the Samaritans, aren't we, Annie? On call twenty-four hours a day.'

'Maybe the answering machines are.' I switched them on. 'But I'm not. I could murder a drink.'

'OK, let's hit our friendly local, then.'

'Oh, you mean the hotel with the doodahs in the ladies room? In that case we'd better take the car.'

He laughed. 'I suppose it was stretching it a bit calling it a short walk.'

Fiona looked from me to Gerry. 'Do you two speak in some kind of code now, or what?' she asked.

It wasn't intentional, but I suppose the conversation in the hotel bar was bound to turn to business. I was anxious to know how things were going with shadowing Noel's wife. Only I knew better than to use his real name. 'What's happening with Mrs Pig?' I asked Gerry.

'She has a male friend all right. They go horse riding.'

'No harm in that.'

'They also spend most afternoons at his place. With the blinds pulled.'

'Maybe they watch daytime TV?'

'Yeah, right.'

'Does she neglect her children?'

'I'd say not. She gets home before they do.'

'And he has no children, of course?'

He shrugged. 'He's twenty-six.'

'And she's forty-three? What does that prove?'

'Who are these people?' Fiona was burning with curiosity.

I shot Gerry a warning look. 'Clients. People with serious problems.'

'But having a great time by the sound of it. How come your forty-three-year-old client has a twenty-six-year-old lover and here I am with nobody? What's wrong with me? I'm back on the shelf at thirty-one, playing gooseberry with you two. I couldn't even hold on to my own husband. And she has two men? How does she do it at forty-three?'

'She's a very nice woman.'

'Meaning I'm not?'

'Meaning nothing of the sort. This is just a special case.'

'At least tell me he's ugly. Please tell me the lover is ugly. Facially deformed.'

'He's very handsome,' Gerry said.

'Jesus wept!'

'Well, I'm glad she has someone to love. She deserves it.'

'I told you, Annie, no moralising. That's not our job.'

'But she's in love with him. I imagine,' I said quickly.

'She's in love?' Fiona said. 'Jesus, I'd settle for a decent fuc . . .'

'Fiona!'

'Well, it's so bloody unfair. Some scraggy forty-three-year-old, probably with a rich husband, has a handsome twenty-six-year-old drooling over her. Riding with her every day while I sit at home alone, watching TV.'

'You know nothing about her situation. If you did, you wouldn't envy her.'

'Wanna bet?'

'I got the pictures he wanted.' Gerry looked glum.

'Not clear enough?'

'Too clear.' He sighed. 'They radiate happiness.'

'Now, Gerry, no moralising. That's not our job.'

He made a mock swipe at my head.

'Who's for another drink?' Fiona asked glumly.

'Me,' Gerry and I answered as one.

'At least tell me he's poor. With the arse out of his trousers,' Fiona pleaded as we made short work of our fresh drinks.

'He is.'

'Not.'

'Annie?' Gerry frowned at me. 'What do you know about him?

'Who's for a Chinese?' Fiona interrupted us. 'Or an Italian. Or a Spaniard. Any nationality as long as he's a man.'

That night Gerry and I looked through the photos together. Gerry was right, Darina Reid and her lover were radiant. I couldn't remember when I last saw two people who appeared so perfect together. This couple just looked right. Clearly in love and reluctant to part as they kissed goodbye at her car.

'She's a good mother, always makes sure to get home before the kids get there, and she still accompanies her husband to all his charity bashes. Gives dinner parties for his business connections. Dances politely with all his boring political buddies.'

'You sound as if you like her.'

He nodded. 'When you shadow someone you get to know a lot about them. The real person. They don't know they're being watched so they don't bother to put on a public face. She's a nice woman. Straightforward. Attractive.'

I got a sudden dart of jealousy. 'She's two-timing her husband.'

'There is that,' he said calmly.

'What are you going to do?'

'What I always do. I'm going to write my report and hand it over to the client. That's what I'm paid for.' He looked at me.

'Do you have to give him the photos?'

He was already putting them away, closing the envelope.

'It seems a shame not to give her and what's-his-name, a chance?' I said.

'Noel.'

'No, that's her husband. What's the lover's name?'

'His name is Noel as well.' He laughed.

'Oh. At least she won't have to worry about calling

out the wrong name in a moment of high passion.'

'We're not going to open up that old argument again, are we?'

'What? Oh, I didn't mean. I promise I had forgotten about that.'

I couldn't get Noel's wife out of my mind. I lay in the bath thinking of the unfairness of it all. Noel could whore around for years without suffering any consequences. His wife finds some happiness with a young lover and she has to pay for it by losing her children. Maybe even the business that was her father's brainchild. I had no doubt that Noel would somehow con her out of Pussy Grub.

I didn't turn on the light when I went into the bedroom where Gerry was already in bed. I slipped in behind him and put my arms around him.

'Who's that?' he asked.

'Name your fantasy.'

'A World Cup Final at Wembley and a bottle of Southern Comfort in my hip pocket.'

'Would you settle for a quickie and a good night's sleep?'

'All right, then.'

Afterwards, in the dark, I asked him to do something truly shameful: 'Could you say in your report to Noel that you found no evidence of his wife's adultery?'

'What?' He snapped on the light. 'Are you asking me to . . .'

'Give the woman a chance. Maybe she'll divorce him. That way she'll get to hold on to her children and her rights to Pussy Grub. You said young Noel has nothing except for his job with the horses. And that can't pay much. Noel the Pig will have them out in the street if he can. I know him. He can be vicious. Tell him you couldn't find any evidence against her.'

'You're asking me to lie? Ruin my reputation as a straight player?'

'Don't worry about your reputation. You're already well up there with Sam Spade, Dashiell Hammett, Inspector Clouseau.'

He laughed and nuzzled my neck. 'Noel might hire another investigator.'

'Well, there's nothing you can do about that. But don't help him to destroy her, Gerry. You said yourself she's a very nice woman.'

'Yeah. But then I used to think you were as well.' His eyes crinkled up at the edges. 'And look at the slut you turned out to be.'

'Yes. Great, isn't it?'

We collapsed in uncontrollable giggles.

'I can hear you two!' There was a yell from Fiona's room across the hall.

'Oh, my God,' I whispered. 'I keep forgetting about Fiona.'

'She's messing. Anyway we're not doing anything. Just laughing.'

'That's what you think.' I climbed on top of him.

36

Everyone needs someone!

Sally arrived at the house, eager to share some exciting news with Gerry. 'No, don't go, Annie,' she said as I made to leave the room. 'I'd like you to hear this. You are Gerry's partner, after all.' She gave me one of her pretty little-girl smiles. 'Simon and I are getting back together,' she announced triumphantly.

'Simon?' I said stupidly. 'Oh, Simon.' Simon was the pouf's real name. 'I'm pleased for you.' I gave her a warm hug. It seemed the appropriate thing to do.

Obviously not to Gerry. He just stood there, his arms by his sides.

'How did this big reconciliation come about?' I asked, determinedly upbeat.

Apparently they had met for a civilised lunch to discuss dividing up the furniture. Then found themselves lingering over their coffee and brandies. Ordering more. And more. They ended up spending the remainder of the afternoon discussing their future instead of their past.

'You see, Simon had already decided that I should have the hi-fi system. And I had decided that he should have the La-zee-boy recliner, with the vibrating cushions.' She giggled happily.

'Vibrating cushions?' I looked at Gerry.

He made a comical face.

'And then we both decided that we can't live without each other.' She giggled again.

'Well, that's always a good reason to get back together,' I said, as Gerry disappeared into the kitchen to make coffee.

'Vibrating cushions?' I could hear him muttering.

Sally was in no hurry to leave. Like all people in love she was determined to share the pouf's many virtues with us. It appeared that he had offered to remain in the Curragh army camp for the foreseeable future, even though this decision was bound to weigh heavily against him when he was next in line for a serious promotion.

'Like a generalship?' I was determined to keep things light.

Sally ignored this. 'He's the most understanding man I have ever known.' She beamed at Gerry as he handed us our coffee.

My powers of deduction told me that this might indicate that Gerry had not been, during their time together. But that was the old Gerry. We had all grown up since then. Learned our lessons well. I would have liked to tell her that Gerry now spent quite an amount of time off duty. That these days he considered his personal life to be just as important as his career. Well, almost. Hadn't he shredded every single shot he had taken of Noel's wife, with young Noel, after I pleaded their case? The old Gerry would have shredded his own flesh before doing that.

When Sally finally left, he looked at me, aghast. 'Vibrating cushions?'

*

What with Sally and Simon happily reconciled, and the ecstatic Sandra and Jimmy's wedding date drawing closer, and myself and Gerry hardly able to keep our hands off each other, the world seemed to be full of happy satisfied couples. But then there was Fiona. Although, as the days passed, she was beginning to appear less maudlin than she had been. In fact, if I wasn't mistaken she was coming back to her old cheeky self. At my instigation she wrote to Sam asking him exactly where she stood and nobody was more pleased than Gerry when the letter from Sam arrived early one morning. 'Another happy ending.' He smiled waving it about. 'Fiona?' he called up the stairs. 'You've got a love letter. Get down here on the double.'

She tore open the flimsy envelope, then threw herself down at the table. 'He wants a divorce,' she wailed.

Gerry panicked. 'I'm already late. Are you ready, Annie?' He abandoned his breakfast.

'No, you go ahead. I'll stay with Fiona for a while. Go on, I'll get the bus,' I said, when he hesitated.

'No need. I'll take the Hiace. You can have the car.' He hated driving the big van around town when it wasn't absolutely essential. The fact that he was prepared to take it this morning showed how upset he was for Fiona. Even if he did want to run a mile. He put a hand on her shoulder. 'Sorry about Sam, Fiona. But maybe it's all for the best.'

'Don't be so bloody stupid. How can it be for the best? I want Sam,' she wailed into my chest.

'I'll see you later.' Gerry gave me a quick kiss.

I turned back to Fiona. 'Are you sure he didn't just write this letter on impulse? People sometimes do things like that and then regret it.'

'She's four months pregnant. How impulsive is that?'

I picked up the letter as if it might inspire me to say the right thing. But all I could say was: 'Four months? That's sixteen weeks.'

'I didn't even know they were doing it for that long.'

'Don't cry.' I patted her back.

'She's such an ugly cow, Annie. What does he see in her?'

'I don't know, honey.'

'Bitch!'

'Now, Fiona,' I chided her gently. 'It takes two to tango.'

'Tango? What the fuck are you talking about? They're in Cuba. Not Buenos Aires.'

I finally made it into the office. Sandra ran to the door when she saw me arriving. 'Look what came for us this morning. Interflora, no less.' She was holding a huge display of flowers. Big, waxy lilies, lacy baby's breath, yellow-veined tulips. And the whole arrangement dotted through with tiny red rosebuds.

'For us?'

'For the agency. It's from the eco-warrior. Well, his mother. He's home safe and sound. Arrived back with a girlfriend he met in the camp. His mother sent us these. Isn't love great, Annie?' She danced across the office holding the flowers like a bridal bouquet, sending the sweet scent of lilies wafting around the room.

'So everything is sorted with the eco-warrior. He's staying put now?'

'Better than that. He's signing up for college. The

girl he met is a second-year environmental science student. Posh. She's convinced him to get a degree. His mother loves her. She was on the phone first thing this morning to thank us and then these came. Look at them. They must have cost a fortune.'

'Has Gerry seen them?'

'Gerry? He'd hardly be interested in flowers.'

'You'd be surprised.'

'Annie, tell me the truth.' She frowned, putting the flowers on my desk. 'Is there something going on between you and Gerry?'

I blushed.

'There is, isn't there? You're red as a beetroot.'

'I didn't want to say anything yet. It's difficult with the lads here and everything. And his divorce doesn't become final until September so . . .'

'I knew it.' She grabbed me. 'You're getting married?'

'No. Not that. But we are living together.' I grinned. 'I mean really living together.'

'Oh, that's so romantic.'

'It is?'

'Well, you'll be marrying your boss! Isn't that every girl's dream?'

'Not mine. And we're not getting married.'

'Tell me that in six months' time!' She laughed.

She was still going on about weddings, and romance, and everlasting love, when the phone rang. 'The Dunning Investigative Agency,' she practically cooed into the receiver. 'Sandra speaking. May I help you?' She listened for a second, then indicated for me to pick up the connecting phone, her face tightening.

The man on the line was a Garda from the local station. They wanted Gerry to know that old Mrs

Lennon's body had been washed ashore during the night. A man walking his dog had found it wedged between rocks on a narrow headland, nearly a hundred miles from where they suspected she had gone into the sea. 'It's to do with tidal flows. We *were* watching this particular part of the coast.' Of course we all knew this was going to happen some day. Sometimes we even wished for it to happen quickly so that it would be all over with and poor old Mr Lennon could get on with his life. But it was still heart-breaking news.

'I'll tell Gerry,' Sandra said. 'He'll want to go see the old man.'

She caught Gerry on his mobile. 'Yeah. Sorry, Gerry, I know how much you like him. But that's the way it goes, I suppose. 1 mean they had nearly sixty years together. Imagine. Sixty years. No, I don't think they've told him yet. They want you to ring them at the station. Yeah she's here. I'll tell her. 'Bye.' She put down the phone and turned to me. 'He's gone to see Mr Lennon. He said he won't get back until late tonight.' She picked up the big bunch of flowers and buried her face in the fragrant blooms. 'If anything happened to my Jimmy I'd top myself.'

In fact, Mr Lennon took the tragic news with exceptional calm. Even though he had still been hoping, to the very end, he said, that she was living elsewhere under an assumed name. He asked Gerry to take him to the spot where they had found her body, but there were no histrionics. Just a few quiet, resigned tears, which Gerry said were even more upsetting than full-blown sobbing.

It was full-blown sobbing back at the house when

Fiona discovered that she couldn't get a flight to Cuba for nearly a week.

'It's high season there at the moment,' I tried to reason with her. 'That's why every seat is taken.'

'I'm not going on a fuckin' holiday! This is not a pleasure trip, you know. This is a marital emergency.'

'I know that, Fiona. But a booking is a booking. They don't have special seats reserved for women whose husbands have dumped them for fat Russians. Or even half Russians,' I corrected myself. I knew I was being harsh and insensitive, and that she had been a great friend to me when I was in need. It was just that her problems seemed so minor when measured against poor old Mr Lennon's, who had insisted on viewing the sea-ravaged body of his partner of sixty years.

'Oh, I see, Annie. You're happy with Gerry so the rest of us can get stuffed. Is that it? Never mind that my heart is broken. You have Gerry and that's all that matters.' She threw herself down on the sofa in floods of tears.

When I tried to explain she blanked me out completely. 'You've become so selfish, Annie.'

Gerry arrived home looking ghastly but even so, he did his best to console her. We both did, to no avail. So the three of us drifted into an uncomfortable silence.

'What about something to eat, Fiona?' I ventured. 'We could go out if you wanted. That new Italian place is supposed to be excellent.'

Gerry looked at me as if I had lost my marbles.

'I wouldn't mind going out.' Fiona sniffed. 'It might make me feel better.'

We went to the new Italian. Fiona cried all through the antipasto.

The waiter brought her a special serving of calamari. Compliments of the owner, who was keeping an eye on her from a nearby table, probably terrified that she'd frighten away the rest of his customers. She stopped crying long enough to eat the calamari.

Then she was offered a special spumoni for dessert. On the house. The restaurant owner smiled encouragingly as she bravely ate her way through it, without once breaking down. Next thing we know he's sitting at the table with us, patting her tanned knee.

As he was relatively young and extremely handsome in a slightly overweight fashion, she didn't rebuff him. In fact, she cheered up quite considerably, as he patted her tanned thigh, while telling her all about his two other restaurants, which apparently did a roaring trade. By the time we reached the coffee stage, Pino was showing us photos of his elderly parents, standing outside their sumptuous villa near Rimini, and Fiona was practically smiling.

When he offered to drive her home in his Porsche, she was out of her seat like greased lightning.

'No rush,' Pino said, smouldering and running a finger along her tanned forearm.

She sat down and said, 'Of course, you're a night-owl, Pino. Me too. This pair like to be in bed before twelve.'

This was true, except that it wasn't usually sleep that was the attraction. Anyway we took the hint and said goodnight.

Gerry fell into the car, laughing. 'Do you believe it?' He was convulsed. 'Three hours ago she said her life had come to an end. That's the only reason I agreed to go out to eat. I would have preferred a ham sandwich and a couple of beers at home. There are reruns of *Morse* on RTE.'

'He is pretty dishy.'

'He has three restaurants,' Gerry said cynically. 'Please God let him have a big house with lots of rooms.'

A week later we got the opportunity to check out the size of Pino's house. He invited us to dinner. A formal invitation, as if he were a hopeful suitor and we were the prospective in-laws. The house wasn't big but it wasn't exactly a cottage either. It stood on the brow of Killiney Hill, overlooking the sea, within spitting distance of a spot called millionaires' row.

It had a sauna and a Jacuzzi. And a smouldering-eyed Pino, standing at the door to welcome us.

We ate in a candlelit dining room. The food was to die for, And Pino was an attentive and generous host. Especially to Fiona, whom he insisted on calling Feena. 'This time next year I open my fourth restaurant. I will call it Casa Feena in honour of my beautiful Feena.' He kissed her hand and she positively glowed.

'I think I'm in love,' she whispered excitedly when we went to the bathroom together. 'Did you cop the size of his Jacuzzi?' There wasn't a hint of a smile on her face.

'Don't rush into anything, Fiona,' I cautioned. 'You'll be going to Cuba in a few days.'

She looked at me as if I were simple. 'I'm not going to Cuba. I finally got through to Sam yesterday and *she* answered. She's welcome to him. Him and his project.'

'But you . . . ?'

'Oh, Annie, I never thought I'd feel like this again. I thought my whole life was over. Pino says I'm the most beautiful woman he has ever seen. He can't wait to bring me to Italy.' Her eyes shining, she caught my hand and pulled me back to the dining room where Pino was in deep conversation with Gerry.

'I want many children,' he was saying.

'Oh, yes.' Fiona gazed around the beautifully furnished room like a woman crazed.

At least that's how Gerry described her to me on the way home. Fiona wasn't with us, having felt an urgent need for a hot sauna round about midnight. Not that I blamed her. She had been through a shitty time and life was for living.

She phoned me next day. 'Guess where I'm sitting?'

'On Pino's lap?'

'At the cash desk in the restaurant near Sutton. I'm going to do for Pino what you did for Gerry.'

'Pardon?'

She didn't even titter.

I sighed. 'He already has three restaurants, Fiona. And *his* books are in perfect order by the sound of things. I don't want to be a party pooper but I doubt he needs much input from you.'

'Maybe not. But I'm going to put my own stamp on this place, anyway.'

'She'll ruin him,' Gerry commented. 'He'll be bankrupt within the year.'

'Ah, she's happy,' I said. 'And I suspect Signor Pino is too shrewd to allow anyone to mess around with his hard-earned spondulicks.'

'I didn't notice him objecting last night.'

'Don't be such an old cynic. Don't you want her to move in with him?'

'It's all I live for.'

Pino sent a scowling Sicilian to collect Fiona's things. He also sent us a crate of Asti Spumante with love from him and Feena.

As soon as the Porsche squealed away as if it were taking the final bend at Le Mans, Gerry opened a bottle of Asti. 'I always said Fiona was well worth knowing.'

'Liar!'

Between us we drained the bottle, toasting Fiona with every glass. And Pino. We were two very happy people and nearly halfway up to bed when the doorbell rang.

'Don't answer it,' I pleaded.

'You never know, it might be Pino. With more wine.' Gerry nearly fell down the stairs.

I went into the bathroom. When I came out he was standing at the bottom of the stairs looking ten years older. 'What is it?' My heart gave a terrified lurch.

'Mr Lennon.' He paused. 'They want me to identify him.'

'Oh, God. I'm so sorry, Gerry.' I was instantly sober and hurrying down to him.

'I should have gone over there tonight. I haven't been to see him for days. How could I have been so stupid? I should have seen this coming. He was too calm, far too composed when he saw her body. It wasn't natural. And I left him alone.'

'You can't be everywhere.'

'His body has been lying in the house, the Gardai say. I should have made time for him. I'm getting lazy.'

'He wasn't your responsibility. You have enough to think about without worrying . . .'

375

'I should have made time,' he repeated, which was a very bad sign. Gerry only ever repeated himself when he was deeply upset.

'I'll come with you. I'll just throw on my coat.'

'No. You stay here. No need for both of us to . . . I'll see you later.' He squeezed my hand and was gone. He didn't even kiss me.

I ran to the window to watch him go. He was limping slightly as he walked to the Garda car. I wanted to run after him and throw my arms around him. Tell him I loved him. Tell him it wasn't his fault. He hadn't limped in such a long time.

I should have known something would happen. All this happiness should have alerted me. I was too happy. Fiona was happy. Gerry was happy. Even the Beechams were happy, having their house back. And Sandra was ecstatic. I should have known it was all too good to be true. Jesus, even Sally and the pouf were happy with their vibrating cushions.

And now poor Mr Lennon was dead. And Gerry was distraught. I should have gone with him. What kind of partner was I, letting him face that on his own? He protected me all the time. What did I do for him? Well.

I called Barney's mobile. 'Barney, I know you're not working but the Gardai have just told us that Mr Lennon . . . died. Tablets, I think. Gerry has gone over to identify . . . oh, would you, Barney? You're a saint.'

I went into the kitchen and made myself a hot whiskey, then carried it into the living room turning on all the lights as I passed. I couldn't go to bed now. I wanted Gerry to find the lights on and someone waiting when he got home.

37

Magical days

Sandra's wedding went like a dream. Everyone agreed that the bridal couple were the handsomest pair imaginable. And the most relaxed. They seemed to float around on a cloud of love and happiness, touching everyone with their special brand of magic.

The garden in Haney Road had never looked more beautiful. The gazebo was garlanded with late summer roses. The inside of the marquee looked like an alternative Chelsea Flower Show.

If Sandra was missing her father you couldn't tell. Gerry had traced him to a hostel in Liverpool but he hadn't even bothered to return our phone calls. Instead, Gerry gave the bride away, walking her up the aisle of her local church with such a look of pride on his face, you'd swear she was his daughter and not just his FAS-trained assistant.

The woman in the seat beside me sniffled when they passed. 'Jaysus, they're like a couple of film stars. He's the picture of yer man on the telly,' she said, without specifying who.

Even the weather was on its best behaviour. The sun shone all day, with hardly a cloud to remind us not to get too complacent. Rosie took full credit for the good weather. 'I put the child of Prague out in the garden last night. It never rains on the child of Prague,' she told anyone who would listen.

I was surprised to see the Beechams mingling with the wedding guests. Right up to the last minute I had been convinced they would take to the hills once the marquee was erected. But they were all here. And they seemed to be enjoying themselves.

Penelope swanned around the lawn with her husband Jim, giving people a regal wave as she passed. She was wearing an ivory tulle creation that rivalled the marquee for sheer girth and one or two of the guests seemed unsure whether to smile or curtsy when she came into view.

Even Francesca was there, wearing a cream trouser suit in place of her usual muddy jodhpurs and sweater. I saw her early in the afternoon, talking to Declan, their heads almost touching, as they carried on an animated conversation in the corner of the marquee. At first I thought I was seeing things but later I spotted them strolling side by side around the garden, Francesca pointing out the more exotic grasses that grew here in such abundance. It was quite a shock to see Declan looking enthusiastic. The only grass he had previously shown any interest in was the kind he sometimes used in his roll-ups when Gerry wasn't around. And who could have guessed that snobby Francesca would have so much to say to someone who, despite his legal studies, still had the look of a man who belonged on the wrong side of the law.

It was a day for strange couplings.

I spotted Jamie flirting shamelessly with Jimmy's attractive first cousin. The groomsman.

'What's wrong? You look as if you've seen a ghost.' Gerry came up behind me, catching me in his arms.

'No, not a ghost. Just someone I thought I knew.'

'And did you know them?'

'Obviously not as well as I thought,' I said, watching Jamie toss his curly locks teasingly at the shaven-headed cousin, who boasted a long white scar under his chin.

Then Penelope joined them and it soon became obvious that I was the only one surprised by Jamie's interest in the young man. I had assumed that the lascivious looks he had been throwing at the wedding party all afternoon were directed at the pretty young bridesmaids.

Despite these surprises there wasn't a single unpleasant moment in the whole day. Even Pepper behaved impeccably, only stealing the hors-d'oeuvres after they fell on the lawn. And Pino and Fiona stopped gazing into each other's eyes long enough to present Sandra and Jimmy with an expensive stainless-steel pasta-maker tied up with a satin ribbon.

'A woman who don't make pasta don't make children,' Pino smouldered, causing every matron in the vicinity to break out in a hot flush.

Children? I mouthed silently at Fiona.

She gave me a brazen wink. The girl was shameless. Shameless but happy. It was that kind of day.

'A girl can change her mind, can't she,' she said when I questioned her about this. 'And I wouldn't begrudge him a couple of little Pinos.'

Sandra called for all the unmarried women to gather while she threw the bridal bouquet. The moment we did she deliberately fired it in my direction. I stood there, mortified, allowing it to sail past my head. When it hit Jamie in the face and he grabbed it, there was consternation. The oestrogen brigade went ballistic. But Gerry called for calm and insisted that in these times of equal opportunities Jamie was entitled to keep the bouquet.

Jamie was about to kiss him when he caught my warning look. He shook his hand instead, then moved back quickly.

'You should have caught the bouquet, *cara*.' Pino pouted, kissing Fiona's neck.

'Isn't this the most romantic wedding?' one of Sandra's old neighbours asked me as we got befuddled on champagne.

'It certainly is. Don't even look at him, Jamie.' I waved a warning finger as he passed.

'Do you mind me asking, love, whose side are you on?' the neighbour was curious.

'Oh, Annie is on everyone's side.' Gerry came up behind me and ran his hand shamelessly along my bare back. Even a gentle kick to the ankle couldn't wipe the smile off his face. And I was still trying to get him to behave when I saw Declan and Francesca slipping into her Land Rover.

Barney and his girlfriend spent most of the day entwined. They didn't appear to have a single spat. My mother used to say that one wedding leads to another, and looking at Barney and Hazel I would have bet on it. Even if it was Jamie who caught the bouquet.

With the marquee cleared for dancing, we were treated to the sounds of an emerging local band, Rave O'Rama. And rave we did, the noise reaching litigation levels within the first hour. But there were no complaints from the neighbours.

'Where we live they'd be flinging rocks over the wall by now,' I heard the groomsman tell Jamie as he lit his cheroot.

I couldn't help wondering what Mrs Beecham would have made of it all. Then again, if she were still here there wouldn't be a wedding in this garden. But I have to say that the rest of the Beechams shot up in my estimation as the night wore on. They didn't renege on a single thing, not even complaining when the celebrations continued until four in the morning, way past the agreed time.

A coach arrived to take everyone home, including the bride and groom who weren't going on honeymoon until the next day.

Everyone said it was a day to remember, but it was the following day that I'll recall for ever. That was the day I finally got the answers to the questions Mr Deedy had triggered, that horrible afternoon, in his stuffy office.

38

Two's company

The day started with an early morning phone call. Far too early for someone who hadn't gone to bed until five a.m. I did my best to sound lucid. 'Penelope? What are you doing ringing at this hour of the morning?'

'Can you come over, Annie?'

'What? What time is it?'

'Eight thirty.'

Jesus, was the woman insane? I must have had three hours' sleep. 'Could you call me later, Penelope? I'm wrecked.'

'No, don't hang up. We have something here I'm sure you'll be anxious to see.'

'Please, all I'm seeing at the moment is double.'

'It's a diary.' She sounded funny.

'A diary?'

'They found it among the books we gave to the charity shop when we cleared out Mummy's room. They thought we would like to have it. They dropped it off this morning.'

This morning? Did these people never sleep?

'It's an old diary of Mummy's. I never knew her to keep a diary. Not a proper one. Although this one is not very comprehensive. Some of the entries are no more than quick scribbles and lots of the pages are completely blank. It wouldn't be of any interest if it weren't for the fact that it's for nineteen seventy.'

I was suddenly wide awake. 'I'll be there as quick as I can.'

'Let me come with you?' Gerry sat up in bed as I got dressed.

'I need to go alone.'

'What did she say, exactly?' He looked as if he'd been in an accident.

'Nothing much. Just that they found a diary. There may be nothing of importance in it. She said most of the pages are blank.'

'Let me at least drive you there. I'll wait in the car. Whatever you want.'

'I want to go on my own.'

'Annie?'

'I want to go alone.' I was adamant.

'Ring me as soon as you . . . as soon as you know anything.' He slid under the covers.

Rosie opened the door, her little face tight as a snare drum. 'They're in the library. Can I get you some tea, Annie?'

I shook my head.

Penelope and Jim, who was practically a stranger to me, were sitting close together on the compact sofa. They straightened up, moving slightly apart when Rosie showed me in.

'Good morning, Annie.'

'Where is it?'

'It's difficult to read,' Jim warned.

'Can I see it, please?' The words came out sharper than I intended.

Jim handed it over.

It didn't look like much. Just a little diary covered in cheap leatherette. Scuffed.

Smelling a bit of mould. And damp.

I flicked through it nervously. The first page that fell open was stained with what might have been coffee. Or maybe strong tea. Whatever it was it stuck several pages together, making them feel like fine cardboard. Impossible to pry apart. Elsewhere it was equally impossible to make out any words, they were so badly scribbled.

Some of the writing was fashioned in circles, sentences going round and round each other until they stopped abruptly in the centre of the page. It was like something a teenager might do to prevent anyone reading her private musings.

'I . . . I couldn't read it.' Penelope shifted uncomfortably.

'Neither can I. Well, just the odd word here and there.'

'Oh, it wasn't the writing that I had difficulty with.' Penelope was defensive. 'I couldn't read it because it made me feel like a voyeur. As if I were eavesdropping on her innermost thoughts.'

These silly scribbles?

Mossy. Michela. Matty. Munchies. One of the lines read.

'Some of the relevant passages are clear enough,' Jim said quietly.

'Relevant?' My heart gave a skip.

'About her pregnancy.'

'Oh, God.' My hands began to shake so much I had to put the book down.

'That was my first reaction, Annie. I couldn't read it. I had to leave it to Jim.'

Jim was even more embarrassed than she was. But his expression was kind as he turned to me. 'Do you want to take it with you, Annie? Read it in private?'

I didn't reply.

'Do you want me to tell you what's in it?'

'I . . .'

'Don't worry, she doesn't go into any intimate detail. It's in no way comprehensive.'

I swallowed hard. 'Tell me.'

'Well, as you can see, a lot of the pages are completely blank.'

Get on with it, I wanted to scream, as he ran his finger along a scribbled line.

'Some of this is nothing more than cryptic messages. Silly hippie stuff.' He dismissed it with a shake of the head.

Hippie? Mrs Beecham? Where had I heard that before?

'What . . . what about the pregnancy?'

He looked at Penelope. She caught his hand and held fast. 'Tell her in your own words, Jim. It's simpler that way.'

He nodded, his kind eyes on my face. 'Clare and Penny's father were engaged to be married. He was deeply in love, no doubt about that. And she cared for him.' He paused. 'But I have to tell you that in here she comes across as being more impressed with him being a Beecham and a leading barrister than anything else. She also comes across as being thoroughly spoiled. Her family appears to have refused her nothing. And Lewis, Penny's father, fell into the same trap.'

'It's true,' Penelope interrupted.

'A few months before the wedding she discovered

that a group of her friends were planning an overland trip to Marrakesh, so she threw a tantrum. How dare they go without her! They wouldn't have been roughing it. One of them had a large camper van with all mod cons and it was to be the fun trip of a lifetime. Her words. She was determined not to be left out.' He looked up at me. 'But she was shortly to be married, to the catch of the year. That's how she described Lewis. They were to honeymoon in the South of France. Move into this beautiful house on their return. And she threw a tantrum because she couldn't go on a trip to Marrekesh?' He didn't try to disguise the impatience in his voice.

'She didn't want to miss out on the fun,' Penelope said. 'Everybody was into overland treks, then.'

'It was the era of *dropping out*. Being pseudo radical.' Jim gave a little shrug of distaste. 'And Clare couldn't bear to miss out. On anything.'

'She *was* spoiled,' Penelope agreed.

'She somehow convinced her friends to drop one of the original group *and* leave earlier than planned. That way she could go with them. And *still* be home in time for her wedding.'

He sounded as if he didn't like Mrs Beecham. But it wasn't her popularity that concerned me. 'The pregnancy? What about the pregnancy?'

'Ah, the pregnancy.' He sighed, flipping through the diary. 'Well, all this is about the excitement of preparing for the trip. Not a single word to do with how Lewis felt about her plan to disappear off to North Africa for six weeks.'

Disappointment hit me like a thick, choking cloud. 'Is that it?'

'Oh, no! The next entry is written in Calais. She's

386

in the camper van. It's too scrappy to make sense. But she seems to be having a good time. The entries after that are hit and miss. Lots of exclamation marks. Words like love and peace feature a lot,' he said cynically. 'The next *legible* sets of entries are around the time of her wedding. How beautiful everyone says she looks. How she's the envy of all her friends. The next entry is six weeks after the wedding. She notes that she is pregnant. There are scribbled dates. Lots of dates. Lewis is delighted. But she knows it's not his child.'

'Whose . . . ?'

'One of the young men on the trip. She doesn't even appear to have had any particular feelings for him. Not her class, apparently. *He* only got to Trinity on a scholarship. A bit of a whizz-kid at mathematics, it seems. Are you all right, Annie?'

'I'm fine. Go on.'

'She never mentions him again. It's all Lewis after that.'

'She told him it wasn't his child!' Penelope began to rage. 'Knowing Daddy, knowing how proud he was, she told him it wasn't his child. If she had kept quiet, nobody would have been any the wiser. Who would have counted the weeks? Babies have been known to arrive early. Why didn't she just keep her mouth shut?'

I had never seen Penelope so angry. Was all this rage on my behalf? 'It's OK.' I caught her hand.

'It just makes me so angry to think about it.' She was close to tears.

'Are you all right, Annie?' Jim was uneasy.

'Is that it?'

'There's no great detail after that. Just scribbled

entries. Bits and pieces. Nothing of any real importance.'

'Can I see?' There appeared to be a couple of pages he was intent on flicking past.

The writing here was perfectly clear. It said: 'Brat finally born. Can't stand it. Hate it! Hate it!' I gasped.

'Oh, no, Annie, that doesn't have to mean you. She was most likely referring to the atmosphere between herself and Daddy at that time. It would have been pretty bad. Wouldn't it, Jim?' She looked to him for reassurance.

'Undoubtedly.' He took the diary from my hand.

'What about my parents? The McHughs? Is there nothing at all about them?'

'Sorry, Annie. There is one . . . nothing more than a scribble. It might mean something. Or nothing.'

'Show me.'

He thumbed through the pages. 'Here we are.'

'"Lewis finds couple,"' I read out. 'Is that it?'

'There is one other entry. But it's too silly. There can't be a connection.'

'What does it say?'

He looked sheepish. 'Hooray for tennis! Underlined.'

'Tennis?'

He nodded. 'I don't understand it either. She was hardly playing tennis three days after giving birth, which is when it was written.'

The tennis club. That was the connection to my father. They must have known he wanted a child. Maybe they knew his wife couldn't have them?

'It means something to you, Annie? Tennis?' Jim asked.

I nodded. 'What about my . . . my natural father? Is there nothing more about him?'

'No. She never mentions him again. I rang some-one who would have been at Trinity about then. Got him out of bed this morning. He knew Matty all right. They graduated the same year. Then Matty went to the States. He's somewhere in California, I believe. Brian faxed me an old press photo of him. A graduation shot, not very clear, I'm afraid.'

I took the thin sheet of paper. Blurred as it was, I recognised the young smiling face instantly. This was the young man in the photo Gerry had shown me. Looking at him now, I wondered how we had missed seeing the likeness. I might have been looking into my own eyes. It was an eerie feeling. This young man, whose surname I didn't even know, was my father. He looked like a kid. 'What about his family?'

Jim shook his head. 'His parents were elderly, even then.'

'But he was good at maths.' I smiled. 'A whizz-kid? Is that what they called him? That's what he looks like, a kid. Hardly old enough to take responsibility for himself, let alone a child.'

Jim seemed relieved that I wasn't tearing my hair out with grief. He rubbed his hands together. 'I think we all deserve a drink.'

'It's nine thirty in the morning.' Penelope went into head girl mode.

'Enjoyed working with figures, did he? Had an orderly mind?' I was still looking at the photo. I felt as if I knew this young man and I couldn't stop myself smiling. He didn't look as if he would have flown into a panic at the first sign of illness. Or sat by a child's bed all night, worrying that her temperature might take a turn for the worse even though she was suffering from nothing more threatening than the mildest bout of chickenpox. Satisfied, I put the flimsy picture down on the table. The last piece of the jigsaw had just slotted neatly into place. I turned to Jim. 'I'll have a glass of champagne, if there's any left over from the wedding.'

Penelope and Jim invited me to stay for lunch but I declined. I needed time to think. To reflect on what had happened in this house thirty years ago. Clare Beecham would have been roughly my age, then. When she discovered that she was pregnant with the wrong man's child she must have flown into an absolute panic. Thought her whole life was about to crumble around her ears.

The decision she had ultimately made *was* selfish but then she was a self-centred woman and I had a feeling that she had been paying for what she did ever since. The cold, icy woman I knew was a far cry from the happy laughing girl in the photo Gerry had shown me. Anyway, who was I to judge her? I had once made a hard decision regarding an unwanted pregnancy. I didn't hate her any more. What I had yelled at her that day in the library was the truth. She had done me a favour by giving me to the McHughs.

'Annie?' Penelope came walking down the garden holding out a tall glass of champagne. 'Your drink. You didn't finish it.'

We walked across the lawn together. There was confetti everywhere and coloured balloons doing their best to become airborne. And all around us was the scent of roses.

'Would it be all right if I picked some flowers?' I asked.

'You can have anything you want from this house, Annie.' Penelope became emotional again.

The diary had upset her more than it did me. It had made me feel sorry for Mrs Beecham, a woman who had built her own prison and didn't dare break out of it. She had to spend her life here pretending to be better than God.

'We owe you, Annie.'

'You were a child, Penelope. You're not responsible for what people did thirty-odd years ago.'

'But they gave you away, like a piece of unwanted furniture. A little baby? I can't bear to think that my father could have been party to such a wicked deed. He was always such an unbending moralist.'

Maybe that was part of the problem, I thought.

She sniffed. 'Take all the flowers you want, Annie. And don't you dare disappear from our lives again. Whatever mistakes our respective parents made, the fact remains, we are family.'

'Try telling that to Francesca,' I quipped.

She laughed for the first time that morning. 'Francesca? She's a law unto herself.'

The little graveyard lay at the foot of the Dublin Mountains. In a place called Boharnabreena above the sprawling suburb of Tallagh. Not a million miles from where I had grown up. I hadn't been back to it since the funeral.

The inscription on the headstone was simple. It said: Francis and Bernadette McHugh. Beloved parents.

I spread the huge armful of flowers across the grave until it was carpeted with colour. 'I'm sorry it took me so long. It hurt too much to come back after the funeral. And I'm not angry any more. Just grateful. Thank you for loving me so much. Thank you for being my parents.' I blew my nose like a trumpet.

Walking back along the narrow pathway I was so busy sniffling that I almost collided with the tall figure hurrying towards me. 'Gerry? How did you know where to find me?'

'Penelope rang. She guessed where you might be heading when you raided her garden. She's worried about you. She told me what was in the diary. Are you all right?'

I smiled. 'Never better.'

'I let you down, didn't I, Annie? I should have traced the story for you.'

'Don't be daft! Nobody traced it. If it weren't for that old diary turning up nobody would have known what happened. It had nothing to do with skill. It was just sheer luck.' I smiled happily, stuffing my wet hankie back into my pocket.

'And you're OK with it? You don't feel cheated any more?'

'Cheated? I had the best parents on the whole planet.'

'And you don't feel bitter about Mrs Beecham?'

'Well, I wouldn't be her number one fan, proposing her for mother of the year or anything. But I think she was punished enough. People just didn't see it because of all that wealth. And if she hadn't given me away, you and I mightn't be together. How about that for a thought?'

'My God, you are in top form.'

'Why shouldn't I be? I'm young, free and singl . . .' I caught his outraged look. 'Well, maybe not *altogether* single. But I am part owner of a booming investigative agency. I have you. And tomorrow we interview another investigator to lighten your load.'

'I thought I vetoed that idea. We have enough staff.'

'I took an executive decision when you weren't available.'

'Where was I?'

'In the jacks. Anyway, you're working far too hard. And I can't take any more of this all-night surveillance.'

'*You* can't?'

I raised my eyebrows.

He laughed.

'Gerry.'

He was all soppy eyed. 'You're standing on a grave,' I said.

'Argh!' He jumped as if his feet were on fire.

I doubled over with giggles.

He held out his arms. 'I love you, Annie.'

'I should bloody well hope so, all I do for you.'

'What about all I do for you?' He pretended to be offended.

'Ah, that's only for your own selfish pleasure.'

He laughed again and held me even tighter.

I loosened his grip. 'There's something I've been meaning to ask you.'

'Will you marry me, Annie?'

I gasped. 'I said *I* want to ask *you* something.'

'OK. But I think we should get married. Oh, God, I'm starting to feel a bit queasy.'

'Now there's a proposal you don't hear every day.'

'It's that bloody scampi we had yesterday. Shellfish does it to me every time.'

'Shellfish? Oh, thank God. For a minute I thought it might have been the six glasses of champagne and the seven – or was it eight? – double whiskeys?'

That set him laughing again and I grabbed *him* this time. Any excuse.

The only other early-morning visitor to the grave-yard, an old man placing red carnations in a moss-covered urn, smiled over at us, not at all offended that we were so obviously happy among the sad grave-stones.

'Annie?'

'Yes, I'll marry you.'

And the sun came out and I didn't need Rosie to tell me that this was a good omen for our future. *And* for something I wanted to ask Gerry.

I waited until we were walking along the pathway again, then cleared my throat. 'The name of the agency, Gerry. I think it's time we changed it. I was thinking about McHugh Dunning.'

He didn't bat an eyelid. Or break step. 'Dunning McHugh,' he said firmly.

'McHugh Dunning!'

'Dunning McHugh! That's my final offer.'

It didn't worry me. 'Gerry?' I stopped walking.

He turned to smile at me, his eyes crinkling up at the corners in that sexy way I had loved from the very first time I spotted him at Fiona's party.

I kissed him. Hard. Gave him time to come up for air, then kissed him again. Deeper this time.

'McHugh Dunning it is,' he said breathlessly.

'You see, that's what I love about you, Gerry. A clear, well-reasoned argument can always win you over.'

The old man passed us on his way out. 'Beautiful day, isn't it?' He raised his cap.

'Perfect,' we said in unison and walked out the gate together.